The
Seven Seals

THE TRIBULATION SERIES

The
Agenda
Book One

The
Lights of God
Book Two

The
Seven Seals
Book Three

The
Seven Trumpets
Book Four

THE TRIBULATION SERIES
Book Three

The
Seven Seals

Ralph D. Curtin

RESOURCE *Publications* · Eugene, Oregon

Resource Publications
A division of Wipf and Stock Publishers
199 W 8th Ave, Suite 3
Eugene, OR 97401

The Seven Seals
The Tribulation Series Book Three
By Curtin, Ralph D.
Copyright©2008 by Curtin, Ralph D.
ISBN 13: 978-1-5326-8771-6
Publication date 4/6/2019
Previously published by Oaktara, 2008

The Seven Seals is a work of fiction. References to real people, events, establishments, organizations, or locales are intended only to provide a sense of authenticity and are used fictitiously. All other characters, incidents, and dialogue are drawn from the author's imagination.

To Winifred Keahon,
my godly mother-in-law,
who is an ongoing source of inspiration in Christian virtue.
Her sincere determination to honor the Lord through her life
has set the example for her children and grandchildren.
Her steadfast faith and joyful spirit continues to abound
as she ministers to her family and friends.

To the student of prophecy,
I, along with Paul, salute you.
For your longing and study of Christ's soon coming,
an imperishable crown of rejoicing awaits you:
"For what is our hope, or joy, or crown of rejoicing?
Are not even you in the presence
of our Lord Jesus Christ at his coming?"
(1 Thess. 2:19)

Acknowledgments

This work of prophetic fiction would not be possible if it were not for the Word of God and the many scholars who have labored over the years to produce an accurate rendering of the events depicted therein that will soon come upon the earth. The bibliography lists some of those worthy contributors.

ONE

Port Everglades, Florida

The 40,000-ton dry bulk carrier ship, *Sanatana Dharma,* out of Cuttack, India, arrived at pier 26 just after midnight to begin offloading its cargo before the blazing August sun would rise. The ship's captain, Balwinder Sachedina, a seasoned mariner, was thankful to his gods that they saw fit to grant his ship and crew a safe journey and reprieve from any hurricane, what he believed Florida was best known for in his country.

Once the tie lines were secure and the offloading began, the barrel-chested captain with a handlebar mustache (who looked younger than his 55 years) began to relax. He slowly walked the main deck from the bow to the fantail, wiping the perspiration from his neck with his handkerchief while enjoying a Turkish cigarette. Moments of pleasure filled his mind as the cranes lifted the cargo out of the freighter's hold while he mentally calculated his bonus for bringing the ship to port on the appointed time. After 30 minutes of self back-patting bravado, he was approached by a deckhand holding a large plastic food bag.

"Captain," the deckhand said in his native tongue as he stood before him, looking worried, "there is much problem."

"Problem?" Captain Sachedina asked coolly, controlling his voice. "What do you mean?"

The deckhand reached into the bag and pulled out three dead black rats by their tails as he walked toward the light on the nearby bulkhead.

Sachedina froze in place as the color drained from his face. "Where did you find them?!" He gulped, with eyes darting back and forth.

"In the number two hold—the grain hold," the deckhand replied with heightening alarm. "There are many."

Captain Sachedina stomped out his cigarette and ran to the ship railing to look at the forward and aft tie lines before turning to the deckhand and snarling through his teeth, "Where are the rat guards?!"

The deckhand swallowed hard, then sliced his hand in the air and said in contrition, "Deck officer no put rat cones on. Maybe he forget."

There would be time to assess blame later, Sachedina thought, but for now, he had to take action.

"Tell him to meet me at the number two hold immediately!" Sachedina barked as he grabbed the bag from the deckhand, firmly sealing in its contents. *Don't panic,* he scolded himself. *Wait until you have proof.*

"Open the hatch and lift the grill," Captain Sachedina commanded the deck officer who breathed nervously as he loosened the locking levers on the hatch on the top of the number two hold, then quickly lifted the heavy grill.

The deck officer gagged, then covered his mouth with his hand as he backed off from the hatch. "There are many dead ones, captain," he gabbled.

Sachedina pushed him aside to peer into the giant hold that carried two thousand tons of grain. Within seconds, his worst fear was realized. More than 75 rats were lying on the surface of the grain.

He shook his head in disgust, then held up the bag in his hand to the light to see hundreds of brown specs flitting around, jumping off the dead rats. He scratched his leg and grit his teeth while muttering a Hindu expletive. Pivoting swiftly, he grabbed the deck officer by the throat. "You fool! Do you realize what you have done?!"

Sunriseville, Florida

Luke Morrison casually walked behind his five-year-old Irish setter as he ran along the embankment of the C-14 canal that ran behind their house. After a hectic day as a postal carrier in the hot Florida sun, he slowly meandered along and sipped his beer as Blarney bolted ahead, then abruptly slowed to sniff his way toward the end of their property line.

Suddenly Blarney stopped short and started to bark violently when he smelled something in the tall saw grass lining the canal. Within 30 seconds, Luke was pulling Blarney away from the dead black rat.

But by that time, it was too late.

After two hours had passed: "Honey, would you get me four Bufferin caplets," Luke pleaded with his wife, Darlene, as he lay on the sofa. "I have a killer headache."

Luke propped his feet up on the sofa, then clicked off the TV with the remote control. He had to get rid of the headache before his Harley-Davidson bike meeting that night. He had to be on top of his game in order to ride.

"Was it the beer?" Darlene asked as she walked up to him with a glass of water and the caplets in her hand.

"Don't think so, babe," he replied.

"Go look at your face in the mirror," Darlene cried out. "It's turning black!"

Luke's face was erupting with black blotches, along with bite-like bumps on the skin that had a white center. The blackening was worsening with every passing moment.

Luke slowly rose off the sofa and started projectile coughing, spitting up blood mixed with mucus. He walked several feet, stumbled, and collapsed on the floor.

Darlene dropped to his side, looked at his blank stare, then rushed to the phone and called 911.

When the paramedics arrived, Luke and Darlene were both dead.

Emergency Room, Holy Cross Hospital
Fort Lauderdale, Florida

Dr. Leon Singh donned his rubber gloves before lifting the white sheet off Luke Morrison's face. He proceeded to examine the bite-like bumps that covered his body, then walked to the gurney next to him to see Luke's wife, Darlene, lifting the white sheet off her face to compare the two. The character of the bumps, blotches, and skin pallor was similar, but not identical.

"What do you think, Dr. Singh?" Ann, the duty head nurse, asked as she looked on with bewilderment.

Dr. Singh looked up but remained silent. He nibbled on his lower lip as his hands began to tightly ball at his sides. He seemed to be distant, impervious to the duty nurse's inquiry. *I've seen this before,* he realized, *and it just can't be! Not with our modern medicines!* As a boy, his father had told him stories of how his grandfather's village was nearly destroyed by a plague that killed more than 12 million people in India and China alone. It had become known as the Third Pandemic.

"Get me the Center for Disease Control immediately," he said trenchantly, fighting back the urge to panic.

The duty nurse must have read the fear in his eyes, for she put her palm to her forehead. "Yes, Doctor!" she exclaimed as she rushed from the room.

Before the day was half over, 47 persons from Broward County alone were declared dead, all diagnosed with similar symptoms.

Centers for Disease Control and Prevention
Dekalb County, Georgia

Joshua Rheems, the middle-aged head of the Special Pathogens Branch at CDC, slowly lowered the phone onto its cradle. He turned in his swivel chair and looked out the window into the garden area at the end of the CDC parking lot. *This is unreal. A terrible nightmare.* Moments passed before he picked up the phone once again.

"Nancy, call in all our team leaders. We have an outbreak."

Nancy would follow protocol and systematically page all six team leaders for an emergency meeting that would take place within 90 minutes of their notification.

Without hesitation, Dr. Rheems ordered samples from the Bio-Safety Level 4 laboratory to compare with the samples received from dead crewmembers of the *Sanatana Dharma* and the victims at Holy Cross Hospital. By the time his team leaders arrived, his findings were conclusive. America was being hit with the bubonic plague.

Researchers at the CDC were familiar with outbreaks. When the rapidly mutating SARS virus hit Hong Kong in 2003, killing 81 and adding to the 185 already dead, the CDC was on high alert, waiting for the next shoe to drop in the States. Then there was the bird flu that threatened but never really got off the ground. God was merciful.

When the rapid advancing, mosquito-borne disease, the West Nile Virus, hit America, infecting hundreds and killing 284 in 2002 and 164 in 2003, the CDC braced itself for another pandemic. The deadly virus potentially led to encephalitis or meningitis, affecting mostly the elderly in America. But again, God was merciful and the outbreak was limited in scope.

But this outbreak would be different; God was going to let it happen to advance His prophetic timetable.

"We've isolated the infectious agent," Rheems announced at the outset of the emergency meeting. "It's the dreaded *Yersinia pestis.*"

Several heads bobbed as they looked up at the PowerPoint images on the display screen Rheems set up in the conference room.

"Origin? Pathogenicity (disease-producing capacity of the micro-organism)?" his younger colleague, Dr. Eugene Morris, asked.

"Our preliminary findings in the short time we've had since notification seem to indicate that, two days ago, a freighter out of India offloaded in Port Everglades with both a cargo of grain and infected rats. The ship originated in Patna, northern India, south of Nepal, by southern China. It traveled south down the Ganges River to Calcutta, eastward to the Bay of Bengal, where the black rats probably boarded. From there the ship entered the Indian Ocean to Florida.

"At Port Everglades, as destiny would have it, the ship's captain discovered almost 100 dead rats, triggering the suspicion of some form of contamination. When he inspected some of the dead rats more closely, he saw the fleas. When he found out that the crew neglected to install the rat cones, he concluded that many of the live rats carrying infected fleas walked to freedom down the tie lines."

"Ah, the fleas!" Morris exclaimed. "Those voracious little parasites that hitchhike on their bloody hosts and cause the horrible death of hundreds of millions."

Morris had studied about the bubonic plague during his internship and the whole history thing had turned his stomach. Back in 1347, a fleet of Genovese trading ships fleeing Caffa reached the port of Messina, Italy, where all the crewmembers were found to be either infected or dead from diseased rats and fleas. Some ships were found grounded along shorelines, with no one aboard remaining alive. The looting of these ships helped spread the disease. From there the plague spread to Genoa and Venice and on to Europe.

The plague continued to haunt Europe throughout the fourteenth to seventeenth centuries, making the Black Death the largest death toll from any known nonviral epidemic. While accurate statistical data does not exist, it is estimated that 1/4 of England's population, totally 4.2 million, died from 1347 to 1351. Records, although scant for the period of the Middle Ages indicate that over 75 million died of the disease. The plague continued intermittently until the Great Fire of London in 1666, when most of the plague-bearing rats and fleas were killed off.

"Yeah, the fleas," Rheems echoed. "For the benefit of some of you newer members on the team, I'm reviewing some of the known facts about the little buggers." Rheems clicked the computer mouse to bring a split image on PowerPoint: a black rat and a swamp-laden river. "The Ganges River has become the perfect environment for the black rat and the *Yersinia pestis* flea to multiply since the waterway has been slowed to a swampland near the Haridwar dam that diverts much of the Himalayan snowmelt into the upper Ganges Canal. Originally built by the British in 1854 to irrigate the surrounding land, this dam caused severe deterioration to the waterflow in the Ganga, and is a major cause for the decay of Ganga as an inland waterway. Now with inadequate cremation procedures contributing to the large number of partially burned or unburned human and livestock corpses floating down the Ganga, the rats, a very dangerous plague reservoir, have found an abundant food supply. The infected fleas that ride the rats have multiplied exponentially.

"The bubonic plague is primarily a disease in rodents and fleas," Rheems continued, "where infection in a human occurs when a person is bitten by a flea that has been infected by biting a rodent, and in this case, the black rat (*Rattus rattus*) that has been infected by the bite of another infected flea. The bacteria multiply inside the flea, sticking together to form a plug that blocks its stomach and causes it to begin to starve..." He paused to glance at their faces: grimacing and glaring eyes.

"The flea then voraciously bites a host and continues to feed, even though it cannot fulfill its hunger, and consequently the flea vomits blood tainted with the bacteria back into the bite wound. The bubonic plague bacterium then infects a new host, and the flea eventually dies from starvation. When the rodent population begins to die off from the disease, the fleas seek other sources of blood. Namely, humans. So whenever there is a large number of rats found dead, it is a clear sign of a plague outbreak."

A hand went up. "What about Streptomycin, Chloramphenicol, and Tetracycline for treatment?"

Rheems nodded. "They have been found to be effective in the past, although not entirely because of rising resistance due to genetic selection. But more recently, research on plague samples has shown Gentamicin and Doxycycline to be more potent." He turned and looked at the team and added, "But remember, if this strain proves to be some form of a mutation—and these do mutate—then it's possible that none of these drugs will work."

"Sort of like the AIDS epidemic," a young woman researcher said, nodding support. "The virus continues to mutate so no vaccine or cure can be found."

Rheems scratched his head in frustration. "Yes, a good point. However, the social, economic, and depopulation factors are quite different. AIDS victims can linger for years, often infecting countless others before they die. The cost for hospitalization and drugs is incalculable. But with the bubonic plague, most of the victims that come down with it die on the same day symptoms appear. A nation can be depopulated within six months to one year."

"Mortality rate?" Dr. Morris asked, his face showing signs of emotional stress.

"Without diagnosis and treatment, the infection can be fatal in one to six days; mortality in untreated cases is 50-90 percent," Rheems explained. "This is based on old data, not this current strain. At this stage of the plague, anything can happen. When you're dealing with the short incubation period and the mobile rat-flea vector that drives the disease, the transmission of the plague is going to be very fast."

Another hand went up, a veteran doctor at CDC. "Yes, Jerry?" Rheems said.

"Back in 2006, I remember getting an E-mail from one of my buddies who works at the Public Health Research Institute at the University of Medicine and Dentistry of New Jersey, which conducts anti-bioterrorism for the government. He said that three mice infected with *Yersinia pestis* mysteriously disappeared from the laboratory. Could there be any connection?"

Another hand went up. "And what about the incident in 2007 where an eight-year-old hooded capuchin monkey in the Denver Zoo, along with five squirrels and a rabbit, died of the bubonic plague?" He turned to the rest of the team and added, "Not to mention the case in 2007 where a woman in Torrance County, New Mexico, developed bubonic."

Rheems' shoulders rose and fell. "Hey, I'm not in the place of God, guys," he reminded them laconically. "I don't have all the answers—that's what they pay us to do—discover the answers. But I can tell you this: we need to keep this from the public as long as possible to avoid a panic or until God intervenes. If He doesn't—"

Rheems had no way of knowing how true his prophetic statement would be.

Heralded as the original pioneer of the most effective AIDS vaccine to date, Lane Drugs, under the direction of Matthew Lane, was the first drug company to receive the call for help from Rheems. Lane not only had the label of a conservative Christian but also ran his life and his company as a sterling testimony to that title. Integrity, truth, and compassion for the sick was the outworking of his relationship with Christ, and it was this witness that made his company the most reliable in the nation.

But it was not always so. Three years had passed since Lane did battle with Kavidas and his apologist Stein—his archenemies who, through the medium of Kavidas' Rainbow Pharmaceuticals, prematurely announced the development of an AIDS vaccine called TOI-VAX, which proved to be innocuous. Lane later discovered that Kavidas' conspiracy to use the insipid vaccine to gain public recognition was only part of a devilish master plan to gain control of the whole world. Kavidas in turn used every political and economic weapon at his disposal to silence and ruin Lane's credibility and destroy his company...a feat that God would not allow.

Recovery from Kavidas' onslaught was slow, but deliberate. God allowed Lane to develop a serum called ZOE, which indeed helped the AIDS epidemic tremendously but would not totally eradicate it. Lane later realized that God would not lift the plague completely until humanity dealt with the sin of homosexuality.

"Bring me up to speed on its advance," Matthew Lane instructed Rheems. The call from Rheems came hours after Lane had secretly learned of the outbreak from one of his fellow church members who worked as a stevedore at Port Everglades. A source he would not disclose to anyone else.

"The plague has branched out from South Florida to other parts of the nation," Rheems advised. "We believe the high level of transients and tourists in Florida accelerated the outbreak. We have climbing numbers throughout the Eastern seaboard. And this is only the third day."

Aggravation was beginning to knot in his chest when he realized the enormity of the problem. "Have you contacted the Indian government?" Lane inquired.

"I've spoken to the Indian ambassador," Rheems replied somberly, "who admitted that his government has been keeping a low profile on the problem, applying pesticides in the acute areas, but, and this is the part that hurts, because of trade agreements with the United States that includes the service systems many of your telecommunication firms have out-sourced to them, they have kept it under wraps."

"So in other words, notifying us of a potential epidemic was bad for business, right?" Lane replied with a tinge of sarcasm. Raising his voice an octave he added: "Doesn't that smack of America's debacle with China with them producing lead-laced toys for Mattel and then shipping them to us so that our children can ingest the lead and suffer brain seizures?"

"Matthew," Rheems begged, "I'm not the enemy here. I need your help, so can you set aside the rhetoric?"

"Yes, you're right," Lane admitted. "These things just boil my blood when lives are sacrificed so people can make more money."

"For my own sanity and for the sanity of my team here at CDC, I need to concentrate on the solution, so let's talk about treatment," Rheems said in a reasonably controlled voice. "Do you have enough antibiotics on hand for the outbreak?"

In the unforgiving calculus of life, Lane knew that drugs alone would never be enough to stop the advance of a plague of this magnitude. It was going to take a miracle. "Setting aside the traditional first line of treatment and trying the fluroquinolones, with a backup of Doxycycline and Gentamicin, we can handle the first fourteen days, but my fear is that these drugs may be impotent when dealing with bubonic in this environment."

"What do you mean, 'this environment,'?"

"Well, with AIDS already at epidemic proportions, the selective pressures induced by the plague might have changed how the pathogen manifests in humans, selecting against the individuals or population which are the most susceptible," Lane instructed. "Furthermore, we must exercise caution since any formalin-inactivated vaccine carries with it a high risk of contracting the plague."

Rheems had already thought of that; Lane brought confirmation. "We can't stop the selection process from happening, but we can work to develop a vaccine that will halt the spread elsewhere."

"Agreed," Lane replied. "We must try to save as much of the population as possible. I will personally instruct and oversee our team of genetic engineers to work on a new antigen. I will work together with some of my former army buddies over at Fort Detrick in their biomedical and infectious disease research unit. Meanwhile, you need to contact the other major drug companies and alert them while at the same time, keeping the media from getting hold of this until we can sort this mess out."

"As soon as I get off the phone with you I'm calling Pfizer and Merck and our PR man here at CDC," Rheems concluded.

Lane ended the call, then walked to the large window in his office that gave a clear view of the Miami seaport, especially Bayside, one of his favorite places to stroll and shop. *I'm going to need a lot of help on this one, Lord. I'm going to have to call in Brandon and all his friends to rise to the challenge.*

Petra, Southwestern Jordan

Famous for having many stone structures carved into the rose-colored sandstone rock that surrounds the city, Petra lies on the slope of Mount Hor in a basin among the mountains that form the eastern flank of Arabah, the large valley running from the Dead Sea to the Gulf of Aqaba. Considered an impregnable fortress over the centuries, no method has been found to determine the origin of the city that dates back to unknown antiquity—certainly before 587 B.C. when the Old Testament prophet Obadiah referred to it then as *Sela*.

The architecture and buildings with its temples, tombs, and 3000-seat theater being hewn with great skill from the living rock, have defied the erosive hands of time to an astonishing degree, many of the carvings looking as they were cut yesterday. The Nabataeans took possession about the end of the fourth century B.C., and continued their sway until overcome by Hadrian, who gave his own name to the city-Hadriana. This name, however, soon disappeared. Under the Romans, Petra saw the days of her greatest splendor. According to an old tradition Paul visited Petra when he went into Arabia, noted in Galatians 1:17. Of this there is no certainty; but Christianity was early introduced, and the city became the seat of an early Christian church. Petra shared in the declining fortunes of Rome; and her deathblow was dealt by the conquering Moslems, who desolated Arabia Petraea in 629-632 AD.

But God had plans for Petra and would not leave it desolate forever. In time the city would become the Christian *Masada*, the stronghold where Christians would flee from the rise of evil incarnate, Kavidas and Stein, and his forces that determined to take over the world. But for now it was a place of archeological importance that fascinated the curious and adventurous. A place where Matthew Lane would track down and summon his son, Brandon.

David Douglas' cell phone vibrated and beeped as he sat with his wife, Kathy, in the outdoor Monastery, Petra's largest monument.

Douglas pulled the cell phone out of his pant pocket, looked at the caller-ID, then up at Kathy, and said exuberantly, "It's Matthew Lane!"

"Where are you, David?" Matthew asked, almost cryptically. "Is this line secure?"

"I'm here at Petra, and yes, Matthew, the line is secure," David replied. Lane knew Douglas was in Israel teaching Old Testament Biblical Studies at the Jerusalem University under the assumed name of Joshua Rogers, to avoid detection from Kavidas and Stein, who sought to destroy his ministry.

"What are you doing in Petra? I thought you would be in Jerusalem," Lane asked.

"I am living in Jerusalem now, but we're setting up somewhat of a bastion in Petra for Christians when things get rough over here," David noted. "Most of the work is being carried out by my friend, Nathan Cohen, and his wife, Leah," he added.

"The way things are happening to fulfill Bible prophecy, it's a great idea," Lane affirmed. "Kathy and the family okay?"

"Yes, the Lord is good, a stronghold in the day of trouble. He's keeping us safe, out of harm's way," David answered as he smiled at Kathy.

"David, I hate to burden you with this," Lane began to explain, "but America is undergoing a terrible trial, apparently orchestrated by the Lord to humble our wayward nation in preparation for his return. It's serious enough to warrant my asking for help."

"What kind of trial?" Douglas asked, puzzled.

"It's the bubonic plague," Lane replied. "The government and the CDC is keeping it quiet to avoid a panic so you won't hear about it over there for a while, but the Black Death has killed off hundreds already and it's only three or four days old."

Douglas was aghast. "I just can't believe it! It's—oh, the human suffering! Oh, the children!"

"What is it?" Kathy jumped to her feet and stood in front of him.

"America has been hit with the bubonic plague!" he said.

Kathy dropped back onto the rock ledge behind her and squeezed her eyes shut in grief.

"What can I do, Matthew?" David asked.

"Locate Brandon and tell him I need him back here as soon as possible," Lane pleaded. "Do you know where he is?"

"I have a general idea where he's working. In the vicinity around the Sea of Galilee near Capernaum. Dr. Barrett has him working with one of his crews at the first-century synagogue and Canaanite ruins. He comes here once a week during his field expeditions now that there's a natural bridge across the Dead Sea from Israel to Jordan. As you know, he's become quite the explorer while taking courses in archeology in Jerusalem."

"Yes, and I'm very proud of him. Now we have a different expedition to embark on and it's not in the field of archeology; it's in the field of microbiology. Lane Drugs has been given a grant by the CDC to come up with a viable vaccine to combat the plague and I'm going to need Brandon here to help me bring that about."

"I'll call his field office and find out where he's supposed to be and get this message to him right away," David said, his voice vibrating with intensity.

"Tell him it's an emergency."

TWO

Miami

The excessive lines of traffic at Miami International airport were beginning to reflect the upcoming Jewish New Year, Rosh Hashana. Apparently thousands of Jewish people were starting their holiday travels a week early to avoid the inevitable long lines and inspection delays. With heightened security permanently in place, exiting Florida for a vacation or religious holiday was a major event at the airports.

El Al flight 283 out of Tel Aviv arrived on time with Brandon aboard. The drive home to Miami Shores estates was both a celebration and a news brief.

"It's so good to see you again," Matthew said, his eyes raking his son's face with admiration. "You're looking wonderful!"

Brandon was, in Matthew's language, "mean and lean" even in his mid-thirties.

"The dry heat of the Negev agrees with me, Dad." Brandon rolled up his sleeves to show off his suntanned arms.

Matthew looked at him, his expression enigmatic. "We have much work to do. The plague is spreading exponentially as we speak. I'm hoping some of your studies in Jerusalem may help up unravel this mysterious plague."

"What do you mean by mysterious?" Brandon asked as he kneaded his temples. The whole thing about being called home because of the bubonic plague was very overwhelming.

"Well, if I'm right, this appears to be some form of a prophetic plague that borders on biblical proportions. It's called *pestilence.*" Matthew motioned with one hand to form quotation marks in the air.

"Wow," Brandon replied with a whistle. "Where I just came from—Israel—that word is a whopper."

At last they arrived at home. As they entered the house, Matthew carried Brandon's suitcase to his room as Brandon walked to the kitchen and opened the refrigerator. He pulled out the box marked *Tiramisu* and proceeded to make a pot of coffee. *Haven't had a decent cup of coffee since leaving the States. Coffee and tiramisu—sweet.*

"What did you mean by *pestilence?*" he asked his dad as he walked into the kitchen and sat down at the table.

Matthew signaled he also wanted a cup of coffee and a slab of the tiramisu. "There's this Bible verse in Ezekiel 7:15 where *pestilence*, rendered *plague* in the King James version, is defined as a form of divine judgment connected with signs of the end. In ancient times the prophets of Israel usually connected sword, pestilence, and famine together, as in Second Samuel 24:15.

"*Pestilence* is the derivation of a Hebrew word, *deber*, referring to a contagious disease of devastating proportions and is never portrayed in the Bible as an aimless, naturally occurring phenomenon. It is always regarded as a judgment or punishment sent by God. Because pestilence is a punishment for sin, it is not applied indiscriminately upon all."

Matthew paused to bite off a piece of tiramisu and slug down a gulp of coffee. "Since I received the call from the CDC about the outbreak, I've been studying some Bible passages both in Jeremiah and Ezekiel. The one in Ezekiel 7, when coupled with New Testament prophecies, carries with it the admonition that this kind of thing is compared to the plagues of Egypt!"

Brandon set his cup of coffee down. "Does it affect everybody?"

"We don't know yet, but the preliminary reports seem to indicate that some family members are stricken and others are not, even though they were exposed to the same infectious agent," Matthew said dolefully. Then he broke out in a smile. "But I'm persuaded that God will protect His own."

A muscle jerked in Brandon's left cheek. "Meaning?"

Matthew reached over and grasped Brandon's hand. "Meaning, if we belong to Christ, we will be protected from pestilence. That's God's promise in Psalm 91."

Brandon fell silent and nodded as his eyes wandered off his father's face to the nearby window.

The deafening silence sent a deluge of memories into Matthew's mind. The pain of discovering that Brandon had been involved in a homosexual relationship still disturbed him. He wondered if Brandon had ever settled the issue with God.

That question will wait for another time. But for now, rejoice that he's home.

Several moments passed, then finally Matthew said, "Brandon, suppose you wash up. Then we can go down to the lab and get to work. Sound good?"

Brandon expelled a sigh of fatigue but rose to the occasion. "Sure, Dad."

Matthew smiled. "I'm sure glad you're home."

Lane Drugs, Miami

Maryjane Larsen looked up from her console at the information desk to see Matthew and Brandon walk through the revolving door into the lobby. She stood up and yelled out, "Brandon, you're home!"

Maryjane has been Lane Drugs' switchboard operator and greeter for the past 22 years, claiming Brandon as her "second son."

"It's wonderful to see you," Brandon said as he wrapped his arms around the largish matron who may not have been in an executive position, but she really knew what was going on at Lane.

"Let's see, how long has it been?" she asked as she pushed him away at arm's length to scan him up and down.

"Probably five years," Brandon replied warmly.

"Staying for a while, I hope?"

Brandon looked at his father. "As long as Dad needs me."

Maryjane smiled, then shot Matthew a look. "We've got problems." With that she walked back to her desk and held up a handful of telephone messages. "People are frightened. Here's at least 40 calls about this crazy plague from people here in Miami." Then she held up another batch. "There's at least 26 more from outside of Florida. Things are getting nuts, Mr. Lane."

"Bring in more help and call each one of them, Maryjane," Matthew said in a soothing, calming voice, "and tell them we're working with the CDC to find a suitable vaccine, but for now they'll have to trust their family physician to inoculate them with some antibiotic. Further, a public announcement will be made shortly."

Overcome by the enormity of the crisis, Maryjane inhaled a deep breath and nodded in agreement. "We'll do lunch next week," she told Brandon.

"She hasn't changed. Maryjane is a class act," Brandon said to Matthew as he gave Maryjane a thumbs-up.

Once inside his office, Matthew handed Brandon a report from the CDC that came via E-mail. Brandon walked to a stuffed chair and began to read the report. After several minutes he observed, "This says they ruled out the bubonic as a biological weapon…bioterrorism if you will. You mean there are countries that actually inflicted the plague on people intentionally?" Brandon couldn't help but be shocked.

Matthew nodded. "In our research library at Lane we have documented historical accounts from medieval Europe, detailing the use of infected animal carcasses, such as cows or horses, and even human carcasses used by the Mongols and Turks to contaminate enemy water supplies. What's more, plague victims were often tossed by catapult into cities under siege.

"During World War II, the Japanese Army developed a plague based on the breeding and release of large numbers of fleas. During the Japanese occupation of Manchuria, Unit 731 deliberately infected Chinese, Korean, and Manchurian civilians and prisoners of war with the plague bacterium. The victims were then studied by dissection, others by vivisection while still conscious. After World War II, both the United States and the Soviet Union developed means of weaponizing pneumonic plague. Experiments included various delivery methods, vacuum drying, sizing the bacterium, developing strains resistant to antibiotics through genetic engineering, combining the bacterium with other diseases such as diphtheria. In fact, aerosolized pneumonic plague remains the most significant threat, especially in this age with Islamic terrorists gaining access to communicable disease depositories.

"In 1995 a laboratory technician in Ohio, a Larry Harris, ordered the bubonic plague bacterium from a Maryland biomedical supply firm, the American Type Culture Collection in Rockville, who in turn mailed him three vials of the *Yersinia pestis*, the very germ we're fighting. He was later found to be a member of a white supremacist organization. So you see, there are a lot of unfriendly people out there who want to bring harm on their fellow human beings."

Brandon shook his head in amazement. He scanned through two more pages then stopped, astonished. "It says here, 'The great Plague of Justinian in A.D. 541-542, the first known pandemic of the bubonic on record, claimed 10,000 people every day in Constantinople, ultimately destroying 40 percent of the city's inhabitants.' " Tears welled in his eyes. "You don't think that could happen here, in America, do you?"

Lane's phone beeped. He glanced down at his desk phone and read the caller-ID. "It's David from Israel," he said and picked up the phone.

Speaking with controlled urgency, Matthew explained the situation in Florida for several minutes, then listened intently, his voice routed via America's standard landlines to a Starlink satellite gateway in Maine, transmitted to a low-earth-orbit communications satellite, electronically amplified, retransmitted to a tracking antenna operated by an Israeli cellular service, and sent to David's cell phone—all virtually instantaneously.

"You heard my side," Matthew said to Brandon after ending the call. "David asked for you and prays for our success. He went on to say that he was informed there is an outbreak in the Mideast, and that Israel, like America, is keeping this under wraps as long as possible."

Lane rose from his chair and walked to his bookcase. "Strangely, he observed that, in Israel, there were no Christians who came down with the plague. He has a friend—a research doctor at Bikur Holim Hospital in Jerusalem—who told him that in their initial discoveries, some unique gene that affects T-cell function could possibly be providing protection against the plague. Of course, not everyone has it."

"This is very mysterious, Dad. This whole thing is getting really hairy, even apocalyptic," Brandon observed bleakly. He flicked the CDC E-mail report. "Some of this stuff is hard to believe. Listen to this. Quoting from Black Death literature, the report states:

Father abandoned child, wife husband, one brother after another, for this illness seemed to strike through the breath and sight. And so they died. And none could be found to bury the dead for money or friendship. Members of a household brought their dead to a ditch as best they could, without priest, without divine offices...great pits were dug and piled deep with the multitude of dead. And they died by the hundreds both day and night...as soon as the ditches were filled, more were dug. There were also those who were so sparsely covered with earth that the dogs dragged them forth and devoured many bodies throughout the city. There was no one who wept for any death, for all awaited death. And so many died that all believed it was the end of the world.

"Do you think this could happen here in America?" Brandon asked. "Could this be the 'end of the world'?"

"God hasn't given me the wisdom or understanding to know the answer to those questions," Matthew said softly, "but I can tell you this much. America, as well as the rest of the world, has abandoned the God of the Bible for other gods that provide fulfillment to the senses and our carnal nature. Namely, all the 'isms' gods—the god of hedonism, narcissism, materialism, secularism, existentialism, post-modernism, and on and on. So for God to bring an end to the world is certainly understandable since we live as though He doesn't exist.

"Honestly, in my view of the Scriptures, since all prophecies necessary for the return of Christ at the Rapture have been fulfilled, God is preparing our planet for the Tribulation period by giving the Christian a small taste of what it will be like after they are removed from the earth."

"Hmm, well, I know that's your view, Dad," Brandon countered as

20

he raised his eyebrows somewhat defensively, "but I'm not convinced a loving God would inflict this kind of calamity on his creation just to make a point."

"Well, son—" Matthew's eyes pleaded for understanding—"one could make the argument that God allowed the AIDS epidemic as a judgment on homosexuality and aberrant sexual behavior to demonstrate his holiness and disdain for disobeying both Mosaic and Pauline Law. In other words, is AIDS a blessing or a curse? And naturally, we can extrapolate and apply this reasoning to all catastrophes of biblical proportions throughout the ages. The point is, if we disobey God's laws, there are consequences, just as if we disobey scientific laws we can expect repercussions."

Brandon flinched at his father's reasoning, then nodded tentatively. Not in agreement, but to move the agenda along. He stood up and walked to the window that gave a sweeping view of downtown Miami. "Are we able to find a vaccine to stop the plague?"

"My greatest fear, as it was with the AIDS vaccine and serum," Matthew explained, "is that the strain continues to mutate, making it extremely difficult to isolate. By the time we can develop a viable vaccine, millions will probably die."

"I guess we better get to work then," Brandon concluded glumly.

"Remember," Matthew said, "nothing happens in the sight of the sovereign God without his knowledge and purpose. There's a reason for everything, even this plague."

A blending of eerie thoughts of spiritual compromises in times past, a lack of biblical knowledge and unbelief filled Brandon's mind. When he did an internal assessment as to where he was with God, he wasn't sure. But now wasn't the time to sort this all out. "I don't understand any of this, Dad, but reason dictates we should do everything we can to help people."

"Then let's get to work," Matthew concluded as he clapped his hands.

"By the way," Brandon said as they walked out of Matthew's office, "whatever happened to those friends of David and Kathy—Eddie and Sydelle, the couple who helped them during that battle with Rainbow Pharmaceuticals? Are they still around? Maybe we can enlist them in our cause."

"Brandon, we're going to need as much help as we can muster up to win this war, from both God and man. Track them down and get them in here."

Brandon agreed that the battle could not be won unless more help arrived, but he wasn't sure if God was going to show up this time.

Coral Springs, Florida

The Swain home was an imposing brick colonial that sprawled on a two-acre plot with a backyard that featured a wide canal with bulkhead and davits to hoist their boat during inclement weather. Complete with barrel tile roof, circular driveway, and manicured lawn, the Swain home looked like a plantation from Margaret Mitchell's novel. Brandon surmised that Eddie Swain's insurance adjusting business had done well with all the hurricanes Florida had been hit with over the past ten years.

But as he drove up to the mansion in midday, he was surprised there was not even one neighbor outside. No children playing or riding their bikes in the fair weather, no adults or teens washing their cars. No, the neighborhood looked deserted.

While walking on the cobblestone pathway to the house, he stopped dead in his tracks and turned his head to sniff the air. *What in the world is that smell!?*

An alien stench wafted through the palm trees and filled his nostrils. He covered his nose with his handkerchief and continued to the front door when he suddenly noticed a cute little girl pressing her face to the outside window, carefully watching his every move. She turned and mouthed something he couldn't hear to an unseen person.

The front door flew open, and a man holding a pistol pointed it right at Brandon. "Hold it right there, buddy! Don't take another step toward this house!" the man shouted.

"Eddie, it's Brandon Lane!" Brandon cried out as he threw his arms in the air.

Eddie holstered his gun and shook his head. "I'm really sorry, Brandon, we didn't recognize you. You should have called first." He motioned for Brandon to follow him into the house.

"I didn't think an old friend had to call, so I thought I'd surprise you. But instead, you're the one who surprised me!" Brandon blurted out. He paused inside the doorway and pointed outside. "Eddie, what is that smell?"

Eddie swallowed hard. "That," he exclaimed as he securely closed the door, "is the smell of death. We are surrounded by death!"

"Well, hello, stranger!" Eddie's wife, Sydelle, announced as she walked into the foyer. She pointed to Eddie's gun and shook her head. "We're not taking any chances around here. Eleven of our neighbors have died from the 'B' as I call it, and no person, creature, or thing, passes our doorway unless we know they're *clean*. By the looks of your handkerchief, I take it you smelled the death in the air."

Brandon nodded with a grimace, then blew his nose. "It's unbearable."

Eddie pointed to the ceiling vent. "It's not too bad in here with the A/C on max, but to go outside, we have to wear a dust mask." He reached toward a basket by the doorway containing a batch of surgical masks. "This is the ultimate air pollution, the odor of rotting human flesh."

"Hi, I'm Julie," a child's voice interrupted.

Brandon turned to see the little girl from the window peeking around the corner. He smiled as he bent down to greet the precocious child. "So you're the family's lookout, are you?"

Julie did a curtsy, then ran off out of sight.

"My, my, she sure has grown up since I've last seen her."

"That's our little gift from heaven, and she's a handful. Running on nitro most of the time," Sydelle remarked with a grin, then escorted Brandon into the kitchen. "How about some coffee? I just made a new pot."

"Sounds great," Brandon replied as he scanned the perimeter. "Nice home."

"Thanks," Eddie said as he pulled up a chair. "With what's going on all around us, I wonder where we'll be living next week. If we'll even be alive."

"That's sort of why I stopped by." Brandon fumbled for words. "You see, I'm forming a task force here in Florida to help out my dad at Lane Drugs, and I thought of you two guys because we have battled together in another war when we were fighting Kavidas and Stein at Rainbow. So I thought you'd be perfect to join in with us to fight this war against—" he turned to Sydelle—"the 'B,' as you put it."

Eddie hesitated, catching Sydelle's eye. "We've never run from a challenge, but this 'B' is monstrous." He scratched his ear. "I wouldn't know where to start; it's really out of our field."

"Granted," Brandon agreed. "But what my dad and I are looking for is a group that can stay holed up at our lab—we have sleeping quarters and an adequate food supply in an underground bunker for national emergencies as dictated by the CDC—so you'll be separated from the plague. Then when we've isolated the vaccine and inoculated the public, you can return to your lives."

What Brandon didn't say was, *That's if we can accomplish this miracle within a short period of time.*

"This sounds like you're attempting to preserve a remnant from extermination," Eddie discerned, "as if we were to go into a fallout shelter deep in the earth until the radiation from a nuclear bomb dissipates so we can repopulate the earth."

Brandon looked up at the ceiling, as if giving an invocation. "May it never come to that."

"Staying here is too risky, Eddie," Sydelle put in definitively as she served the coffee. "We have to consider Julie."

Brandon's eyes scanned the kitchen counter, then settled on a box of chocolate-covered Oreos sitting on top of the refrigerator.

Sydelle took the hint. "You're hungry, right? Some cookies?"

Brandon smiled as Sydelle served the dessert.

Then he grew thoughtful. "You know, Eddie," Brandon ventured anew, "when we were warring against Rainbow, you developed the support group, *Koinonos*, the 'partakers' or 'partners,' to help us. What's happened to them?"

With his arms crossed across his chest, Eddie hesitated, assessed, then responded. "After the whole debacle with Rainbow, *Koinonos* sort of disbanded. There hasn't been a real need since Kavidas and Stein moved to the Mideast."

Brandon smiled mirthlessly. "There's a great need now, Eddie. We need to—" he paused to make quotation marks in the air—" 'resurrect' *Koinonos.* I believe we're going to need them more now than ever."

Hebrew University, Mt. Scopus
Jerusalem

Douglas sat on a masonry bench outside the auditorium waiting for the key speaker to exit the Solomonic symposium, a series of studies on the reign of King Solomon, when his cell phone rang. He reflexively tensed until he read the caller-ID.

"Matthew, is everything okay?" he asked.

"I'm all right, but are you able to talk right now?" Matthew replied cryptically.

"Well, yes, I can talk," David replied, hesitantly. "I'm at Mount Scopus attending a symposium for my continuing education. What about you? And did Brandon arrive safely?"

"I'm fine, praise the Lord, and yes, Brandon is here helping in our time of crisis." Matthew cleared his throat. "Tell me about the plague over there. What's going on?"

Douglas stood up and walked to a secluded area. "The Israeli government has announced that we are now in a state of emergency with the death toll from the plague in the hundreds, and ordered the population to remain indoors, allowing only vital workers a day pass to travel, and then only with a surgical mask. Most of the smaller restaurants are closed out of fear that rats may be attracted to the foodstuffs and thereby increase the chance of spreading the disease.

"But strangely enough, like I mentioned in our last conversation, there are no reports of Christians coming down with this plague. It's very eerie. In fact, the Christian church of the Nazarene, where I attend under my alias, Joshua Rogers, has not reported a single fatality. So we believe we are experiencing divine protection."

"Any reprisals from the population?" Matthew asked intuitively.

David closed his eyes and put his palm to his forehead. "Well, now that you mention it, there have been rumors that the Christians may have had something to do with this—some kind of conspiracy theory— since only the born-again Christians seem to be immune over here."

"We're going through the same thing here in the States. The CDC has narrowed it down to only the 'born-again' folk who are being spared. Frankly, I'm not really sure where that leaves us in terms of explaining it. Maybe it's like the tenth plague of Egypt recorded in Exodus, where only the Egyptians were struck. The Hebrews were untouched as long as they had the blood over the doorway of their houses."

"A good spiritual analogy."

"Well, David, I wanted you to know that Brandon has contacted Eddie and Sydelle Swain to assist him over here in fighting this plague with us, and in turn he has reassembled the *Koinonos* group to aid in the battle So, I thought you might do the same thing over there, because—" Matthew stopped abruptly.

"Because...?" David asked curiously. "Because?"

"Well," Matthew said haltingly, "because this could be the beginning of something extraordinary, if you know what I mean." There was a pause. Then, " 'as it was in the days of Noah, so it will be at the coming of the Son of Man, for in the days before the flood, people were eating and drinking, marrying and giving in marriage up to the day Noah entered the ark, and they knew nothing about what would happen until the flood came and took them all away. That is how it will be at the coming of the Son of Man,' " he quoted.

David's spiritual antenna went up. "Meaning?"

"Well, if we extend my application of the plague of Exodus one might come to the conclusion that the Lord might very well be planning an 'exodus' for His Church. Remember the outcome after the tenth plague? God's people were 'ejected' out of Egypt—they were 'released'…free to go! The way I see it, our society is decadent, rivaling the time of Noah."

Douglas let out a long sigh and leaned back on a nearby wall in triumph. "Well, if I read you right and you're talking about the Rapture, then let it rip because this guy is ready!"

"May it go from your lips to God's ears," Matthew replied in praise. "But until then, we have plenty of things to keep us busy. So I need you to put together the remnant of the *Koinonos* group over there to prepare for just that eventuality. They need to stir up the complacent and 'lukewarm' Christians to get the word out."

Douglas agreed, then flipped the phone closed. He squinted into the entranceway for the key speaker to come out, then shook his head and hurried to his car.

He had work to do.

Mount Zion Hotel, Jerusalem

The overcast sky above the Mount Zion Hotel extended clear to the horizon. It was an omen that Gregory Kavidas interpreted to mean that it would be a bad day, being confirmed by a restless night's sleep over the past three days.

"You look tired," Mortimer Stein said as they ate their breakfast in the Orchid room of the hotel. "Have you been sleeping okay?"

Kavidas stared blankly. "My spirit is very troubled. Keeping me up at night. This whole thing with the plague is like a two-edged sword, and I fear our entire program is going to be ratcheted up very soon."

"But if the Christians take some heat—are being blamed for bringing it on—so be it. That's good for us, right?" Stein replied, his eyes looking for understanding.

"That part is good," Kavidas said as he nibbled on his dry toast, "but my spirit tells me there's a downside, and I need divine illumination on how to respond if the other edge works against our purposes."

Stein pushed the rest of his omelet away. He suddenly lost his appetite. "That sounds very ominous," he said with escalating alarm. "Is it something we should be worried about? Take some precautions?"

Kavidas' response was disarming. "Let's just say the time is right for...perhaps it even has come—" he mockingly pointed upward—"for His program to move along. Meaning we will be facing a completely new set of players on the field."

Stein, discerning Kavidas' anxiety, determined in his heart not to push things any further than Kavidas would allow. Whatever the turn of events would be, Kavidas would ensure they would be prepared.

Pensive, Stein stood and walked to the large window that offered a panoramic view of the Valley of Hinnom, that infamous valley dating back to antiquity. The valley formed the southern border of ancient Jerusalem and stretched from the foot of Mount Zion, eastward, to the Kidron Valley. It was first mentioned in the Old Testament book of Joshua as a deep, narrow ravine at the foot of the walls of Jerusalem where refuse was burned. It was here that the bodies of executed criminals or others deemed unworthy of a proper burial were dumped to be eaten by wild dogs. It was here that pagans once sacrificed their children to the god Moloch in defiance to the God of Israel. It was here that attendants kept the fires burning to consume the rubbish of the city, sending up a stench that could be smelled for miles.

In time, the Valley of Hinnom had become metaphorically identified with the entrance to the underworld of punishment in the afterlife. The prophet Joel had referred to it as the Valley of Jehoshaphat, the abode of the dead who would experience perpetual punishment. Such associations led to the name, Ge-Hinnom, or in the New Testament, *Gehenna*, a type of hell, the destination of the wicked in fiery torment. Christ referred to it in Matthew as the place where both soul and body will be destroyed, and in Mark as the place of unquenchable fire.

The whole concept of eternal punishment for the wicked upset Stein as his eyes panned the valley that presently was covered with acacia and palma trees. The trees, along with the prickly plant scolymus or thistles seemed to blanket the valley in an attempt to cover its horrible past while the narcissus tazetta, the rose of Sharon, gave off an aroma that tried to overpower the foul odor that emerged from primordial times. Despite the window dressing, the stench of death from the bubonic plague seemed to be everywhere.

Stein walked back to the table.

Kavidas eyed him. "Are you all right? You look like *you* had the terrible night's sleep."

More like a nightmare, Stein thought, but he didn't say it. He forcefully pushed the thoughts of Gehenna, the destination of the wicked, from his mind. He sat down and replied, "Yes, I'll be fine...as long as I don't dwell on the distant future or other negative thoughts."

Kavidas clearly knew the mind of his comrade, Stein. "Don't worry about the future, Mort," Kavidas assured. "Our confidence is not in man nor events—" he held his right hand to his heart—"but in him who controls our destiny."

Kavidas smiled. "In him we will trust. He will bring us through triumphantly whatever—" he motioned with a dismissive wave of the hand, then pointed skyward—"whatever the other side throws at us."

He lied.

David Douglas' Apartment
Hativt Yerushalayim Street

Douglas sat waiting at his desk, gazing at the wall calendar, recognizing that Rosh Hashanah was only two days away.

I wonder what the Lord has in mind.

A knock sounded at the door.

David rushed to the front door and peered through the peephole. He saw five men talking; two were his teenage sons, Alan and Paul.

As David opened the door, Alan stepped in and pointed to two of the men. "Dad, this is Jonathan and Simon Landau." Then Alan put his hand on the shoulder of the fifth man. "And this is Shlomo Rubin, a friend of Jonathan's. They're here to help us."

"Welcome, welcome, men," Douglas said gregariously. He ushered them into his small living room and motioned for his son Paul to get refreshments for them. "Shlomo, your name sounds familiar," Douglas said curiously. "Who are your people?"

"My uncle was the former prime minister," Shlomo replied guardedly. "But he and I didn't see eye-to-eye. Politically, that is. And," he added with eyes sparkling, "for a time Leah Krasnoff and I dated."

A silent alarm went off in Douglas' head. *Sure, now I remember. You dated my friend Nathan's wife before they were married and your uncle formed an alliance with Kavidas and Stein that lasted until he left office.*

"Interesting," Douglas replied, then turned to the other two newcomers. "And these young men?"

Alan smiled. "Sons of Yasur and Estelle Landau of Jerusalem. My fellow classmates who are always looking for a cause to follow."

"With people dying all over the world from an ancient plague that God has seen fit to resurrect," Douglas said impulsively, "and with Christians being pointed to as the possible cause, yes, I would say we have a *cause!*"

The cause to raise up the *Koinonos* group, the K-group, who would defend against false accusations, and take every measure to protect its Christian members from adversaries was indeed a cause that Douglas wholeheartedly believed God would pronounce his blessing upon.

"Mr. Douglas," Jonathan, the eldest member to be added to the K-group asked as he nodded to Alan for affirmation, "what's the next move?"

Douglas strode back to his desk and sat down. "Our role, until God shows us otherwise, is to maintain a defensive posture against the plague, and then against Kavidas and Stein, whom I believe to be operating surreptitiously here in Israel." He turned his attention on his sons. "By defensively I mean we split into two teams. Team one is responsible for gathering data from any and all sources on potential attacks to our K-group."

Then he nodded to Jonathan, Simon, and Shlomo. "Team two is assigned to be more tactical…in other words, prepare our defenses at Petra in the event the plague worsens, as well as planning insertion and exiting procedures for the K-group if we have to evacuate out of Israel in an emergency."

"Do you really think it could come to that, Mr. Douglas?" Shlomo asked, looking tense.

Douglas fell silent. After a minute of contemplation, he wrapped his arms around himself. "Yes, I really do believe it will come to that."

David Douglas had no way of knowing he had uttered a divine oracle.

Lane Drugs, Miami

The revolving door in the lobby seemed to turn unusually fast as Maryjane looked up from her desk to see a man dressed in a black suit rapidly approaching her welcome center.

"I'm Joshua Rheems, the director head of the Special Pathogens Branch at CDC outside Atlanta, and I'm here to see Mr. Lane," he said gruffly.

"Do you have an appointment, Mr. Rheems?" Maryjane asked.

He leaned over the counter. "This is an emergency; I don't need an appointment. Buzz Mr. Lane and tell him I'm here!"

Maryjane stiffened. "Yes, sir." She stood up with the wireless phone and walked to the back of her station, then turned away from Rheems' view. "Mr. Lane, there's a man here from the CDC to see you, and he looks bristling mad."

"Show him to my office right away," Lane intoned.

"Follow me, Mr. Rheems," Maryjane said as she replaced the phone.

When Maryjane opened Lane's door, Brandon stood up from his chair and folded the manila envelope he was holding.

Matthew smiled at their surprise guest. "Mr. Rheems, nice to meet you. We've spoken on the phone but never actually met." He quickly turned to Brandon and added, "This is my son, Brandon Lane."

Rheems discourteously nodded in both of their directions, then waited until Maryjane closed the door behind her as she departed. "Matthew," he began stoically, "we've got a colossal problem on our hands." He opened up his attaché case and pulled out several documents. "Reports from all over the country are coming in that there are thousands of people dying from the plague, but none—I repeat, none—of them are what is being called the 'Cs' or Christians who have a so-called 'born-again experience' with God. Now as a 'Christian' myself, it's nice to know we can receive special treatment, but charges are being made that Lane Drugs has indeed developed the vaccine to stop the plague but that you're keeping it to yourself—to be used to rid the planet of non-Christians."

Matthew and Brandon exchanged glances as the accusation sunk in. Matthew blinked several times to gain time to think. *Could Kavidas and Stein have gotten to this guy? This is outrageous! Why would he think that of us?*

"You're not serious," Matthew barked as he rose from his chair. "Do you honestly think we would withhold from the public a vaccine that could save thousands of lives?" He approached Rheems with an open hand. "Come on, now, Joshua. Our longstanding integrity and reputation doesn't permit us to tamper with vaccines or restrict their distributions."

Brandon's eyes began to blaze. "Mr. Rheems," he said with a lethal gaze, "we haven't developed *any* vaccine yet. We're still two to three weeks away! This virus is not like any past or conventional bubonic plague. All of the standard vaccines are innocuous."

Rheems threw his hands up in the air. "Then explain to me why certain people are not being infected? I've been an M.D. for over 22 years and in all my research, I've never heard of 'selective diseases.' Sure, there are exceptions when a plague is running rampant. Individuals within the same household or town will be spared because of certain inherent traits or DNA attributes that render the virus harmless. But not when you're dealing with this monster. This is the 'mother germ' of the ages." He exhaled deeply. "Few escape its tenacious grip."

Rheems had spent his fury. Now it was time to rationalize.

"Joshua," Matthew said as he shot a look at Brandon, who nodded approvingly, "I can't answer your question when I haven't a clue. We've done comparative DNA explorations on Christian and non-Christian alike. From what we gather, there's no distinguishable difference. Even in our T-cell studies, there's nothing definitive we can point to."

Rheems' brow furrowed. "What then?"

"Maybe it's a supernatural thing?" Brandon ventured.

Rheems spun and glared at him. "You're kidding, right? You're telling me that God has orchestrated this plague and that only Christians are immune?" He paced the room, then stopped abruptly. "Maybe you could sell that one in your church or to those who have the IQ of a gnat, but that is ridiculous!" He rotated in place to smirk at Matthew. "Don't tell me you believe that one too, Mr. Lane. As a professional medical researcher who has developed drugs for decades, you could never believe that, could you?"

Matthew steepled his fingers. "From a professional perspective, no, I don't believe that." He paused to catch Rheems' eyes. "But from a spiritual perspective as a God-fearing man, recognizing where we are in God's timetable, yes. With God, anything is possible."

Rheems closed his attaché case while shaking his head. "I expected more from you, Matthew. We're in the throes of a national disaster and all you can tell me is that you think God is 'pushing the button' on this and that if we're not a Christian according to your definition, then we get the plague. If that's what you really believe, then we're done here, and you can trust me that our endowment for your continued research has been terminated as of this moment."

He stormed out the door and never even said good-bye.

San Francisco

Mort directed his chauffeur to drive by the Fisherman's Wharf district of San Francisco to survey the extent of the plague in an area perpetually exposed to vermin. As he expected, the population was experiencing severe trauma. There was no one milling around or shopping. There were no visitors taking tours to Alcatraz island or boating under the Golden Gate Bridge. There were no private sailing boats or commercial fishing vessels in the harbor. There were no panhandlers or mimes performing for donations.

The area was deserted except for the National Guardsmen crews who wore surgical masks, rubber gloves, and special insect-resistant uniforms that picked up the dead bodies, slid them into body bags, and loaded them into tarpaulin-covered trucks. One truck appeared to be full while another stood idle in the distance, waiting for the signal to move into the wharf and begin loading up the remaining carcasses.

"I've seen enough, Jeffrey," Mort said to his driver through the intercom. "Bring me to the Transamerica Pyramid professional building in the financial district. I have an important meeting to attend."

Fifteen minutes later Mort was on the 36th floor of the Transamerica Pyramid building, looking out the spacious office window at the San Francisco skyline.

"They're ready, Mr. Stein," his shapely stateside secretary, Janet, said. "They're assembled in the Palisades conference room."

Masterlink's West Coast corporate office boasted two conference rooms, six guest rooms, and the corporate office rotunda.

"Very good," Mort said with a wink.

Representatives from the ACLU, LAMDA, and two newly formed neo-Christian groups, the Community Christian Coalition and the American Unified Church, greeted Stein with back-patting bluster and enthusiasm as he walked into the conference room. The promise of remuneration from *Masterlink* for services rendered appeared to provide an environment of comradery.

In Stein's mind, the goal of the confederation was to form an axis power to combat any legitimate Christian group, and in particular, *Koinonos*. Knowing the times were right for a supernatural conflict to start up again hastened his urgency to develop a strategy.

Once Mort called the meeting to order he held up a PowerPoint presentation remote control and pointed it to a wall screen, then pressed a button. A chart appeared on the screen showing three different laboratory locations of the Public Health Research Institute.

"We have developed information that technicians, two of them being medical professionals, have deliberately produced the bubonic plague virus, *Yersinia pestis*, and infected both chipmunks and rats to spread the plague for the purpose of terrorizing the world's population in an effort to bring about what I call a 'Christian nation.'"

The group all traded looks. Several gulped in air in ragged gasps and one slammed his fist down on the conference table. "This is outrageous. This is blasphemous!" he cried out.

Mort motioned for them to calm down. "I know you're all as upset as I am, but the point I want to make is that we have secured confirmation that these medical people are all 'born-again Christians' who have developed a vaccine that renders them immune to the plague." He pressed the remote button again to display another graphic on the screen. "Here are the numbers that show the states and countries that have been afflicted so far. We have documentation that states that there hasn't been one report of a 'born-again' coming down with the plague. So, what are we to assume? Naturally our logic for cause points us in their direction, and with the resurgence of their *Koinonos* 'vigilante' group, we can see where this thing is going.

"And if that were not bad enough," he added with heightening alarm, "we have narrowed down our search through our *Masterlink* supercomputers to the firm that is producing the vaccine. It is a drug company out of Miami: Lane Drugs."

The LAMDA rep covered her mouth in disbelief. Two of the others in the group simply shook their heads as Stein stood before them with his brow furrowed.

The leader from the American Unified Church gestured angrily. "So what are the authorities doing about this?"

"Good question," Mort replied. "Doctors with their research grants funded by *Masterlink* are forming a consensus with their findings and will present them to the CDC as early as next week. Once the Surgeon General has all the facts, there should be a senate investigation and hearing to decide what punishment should be meted out."

"But that could take weeks," one member objected. "What about all those who will die in the meantime?"

"Our hearts go out to their families," Stein lamented, "but our hands are tied due to CDC rulings and protocol procedures. The wheels of justice turn very slowly...."He turned off the PowerPoint projector. He had made his statement.

Within 30 minutes, the infuriated group had determined what they would do. If it meant the expunging of those "born-again" people to save the human race, then using the sword of violence would be justified. After all, they reasoned collectively, didn't God say in the Bible about the Christians who claimed to be "born again,": "you will be handed over to be persecuted and put to death, and you will be hated by all nations because of me..."? Since God had written this in advance, who were they to argue against God?

Mort Stein, knowing their thoughts and resolve, believed that if you told a lie often enough, people believed it as truth.

Mount Zion Hotel, Jerusalem

Despite the splendor of the refulgent sunset over the Temple Mount that ordinarily brought awe and wonderment, Kavidas drew restless. His spirit testified of the disquietude in his soul. Something was about to happen, that he felt sure of, but his mind refused to accept any notion of any supernatural intervention. *Take control!* he commanded himself. *Push the negative thoughts from your mind!*

Stein walked up to him while he stood on the veranda overlooking the City of God. Immediately his mind and heart obeyed his instruction, bringing a persona of calmness over his appearance.

"The trip to the States was a rousing success!" Stein opened with gusto as he embraced Kavidas. "I believe the Christians and, in particular, that blasted *Koinonos* group will begin to feel the heat and disband very soon."

Kavidas hesitated fractionally before nodding approvingly. He patted Stein on the back and said with conviction, "Well done. I'm confident that this tactic will silence them before they get out of hand."

Stein turned and scanned the horizon, settled his gaze on the Temple Mount. "The landscape here is going to be radically different very soon, isn't it?" he said optimistically.

Kavidas searched his mind for an appropriate reply. Momentary silence, then, "Who knows the mind of the Lord?"

Stein shivered involuntarily, as if taken back by his answer.

David Douglas' Apartment
Hativt Yerushalayim Street

It was not David's alarm clock that awakened him, but the tap-tap-tapping of a mourning dove on his bedroom windowsill. *Strange*, he thought as he sat up in his bed and looked over at Kathy, his wife, curled up in a semi-fetal position—her favorite sleeping posture to gain a good night's rest.

The dove continued tapping as David went to the window. He raised the window and shooed the bird away. Then, all of a sudden, he realized there was no traffic sounds coming from the street below, only an eerie silence.

He looked back at his alarm clock. *Seven ten. People must be on their way to work, right?* he reasoned. *Where is everybody?*

Then he realized it was a holiday. It was Rosh Hashanah, the feast of Trumpets—the beginning of the days of penitence and awe. The days when the sound of the shofar, the ram's horn, calls man to self-judgment and summons him to prayer and solemn repentance. Faithful Jews were home, preparing their hearts for the special day. There would be no business transactions today. No, today was a day of silence and meditation.

It was on this special day he remembered, according to a Talmudic statement, that three books are opened: the righteous are inscribed for life, the wicked for death, while the intermediate remain in suspense until the Day of Atonement—by means of good works and repentance they can make the swaying balance incline in their favor, that they may live.

Well, he thought, *I don't believe in all of that tradition, but it's strange that I was awakened by a dove. Hmmm, yes, today is going to be a special day.*

He walked back to his bed and kneeled down to pray as apocalyptic thoughts filtered into his mind. Thoughts of supernatural silences, and even pauses and divine interludes orchestrated by God in the past to emphasize meaning.

A suspension of normalcy. An intervening episode of silence between parts. Yes, that's it. An intervening silence between parts, he concluded.

With that mystery settled in his heart, he was able to pray.

THREE

Heaven
The Dwelling Place of God

F ar above the immediate heaven, where birds and man-made machines fly, where atmospheric conditions influence mankind, and far above the celestial heaven or expanse where the sun, planets, stars, and innumerable heavenly bodies reside is a place called the Third Heaven. The *shamayi h'shamayim*—the Heaven of Heavens—the dwelling place of God.

Astronomers cannot see, nor can cosmologists imagine where the lofty abode of God is located, but the eye of faith knows it's there. It is in this lustrous and magnificent place, the Third Heaven, where is found the original patterns from which all things created on earth were fashioned. Here in the Third Heaven, where no mortal is permitted, is the original Garden of Eden, the Tree of Life, Noah's Ark, the Wilderness Tabernacle, Solomon's Temple, and the Ark of the Covenant.

In this celestial paradise there are chambers of thunder and lightning. There are great rivers and mountains that have been set in place to garnish the view of the inhabitants of many mansions. Where the four winds that turn the earth and cause the sun and the stars to rise and set are harnessed and released by divine decree.

Where multitudes of angelic armies are arrayed for the Day of Judgment. Where vast assemblies of archangels pray for the righteous. Where angels of lower estates are dispatched to earthly domains to protect and assist the redeemed. It is in this eternal place of joy that the saints, clothed in glorified bodies, perpetually remain in the presence of God, where they see Him face-to-face, where they fellowship with and worship the resurrected One unceasingly. It is in this place that the apostle Paul heard inexpressible things; things that man is not permitted to tell. The place where the human eye has not seen, nor ear heard; neither has it entered into the hearts of man the great things God has prepared for those who love Him.

There is a conspicuous absence of sin in heaven. There is no want, sorrow, pain, or death. There is rest from earthly labors and cares with unending praise and service to God Most High. There will be an innumerable community of saints to share in the beauty of God's universe. Heaven will be the fulfillment of God's plan for the ages.

By the authority of the Holy One, there is unhindered access to God's throne, where the three Members of the Godhead sit and the saints and angels of God give audience and obeisance. Where the Lamb of God who took away the sins of the world has waited for the predetermined Day in which would be the realization of the prophesied proclamation that God would call His own to be with Him.

The long-awaited day has come. The order from the Father has been issued.

The Son will now carry it out.

Holy Sepulcher Cemetery
Roanoke, Virginia

Steven Dolci maneuvered the John Deere backhoe into position over the plot of ground owned by the Renquist family in preparation for digging the grave for the newest member of that family. Marie Renquist, who went to be with her Lord five days earlier, would be added to the family plot and buried later that day next to her late husband, George Renquist, who died ten years ago.

Dolci knew very little about each of the interred of Holy Sepulcher Cemetery, being restricted to what he read on the tombstones as he meticulously cared for the cemetery property. In addition to the name of the deceased and their life span, many of the marble grave markers were etched with either an epigram or a Bible verse. Dolci was not a man of faith but paid particular attention to the Bible verses because this was the only exposure he had to passages that spoke of death and eternal life...subjects he often pondered but was afraid to explore.

The sky was overcast and threatened to rain. It was a dreary-looking day, a day seemingly fit for death, funerals, and burials; a day of sadness. But for days like today, Dolci's cheery nature and optimistic attitude worked overtime to combat the doldrums that frequented his line of work. He whistled happy tunes and thought about his wife and children to brighten his day.

As he pulled the lever on the scoop to begin digging the trench for Marie's casket, he paused to read her husband's headstone. Engraved in the stone was a caption that arrested his attention. *"I am the resurrection and the life. He who believes in me will live, even though he dies...,"* he mouthed to himself.

Hmmm. Interesting words. But what do they mean? he wondered. *I really need to search out a church or something that will answer some of my questions...*

Suddenly the earth above George Renquist's grave began to vibrate! Jolted by disbelief, Dolci froze, his eyes fastened on the gravesite. Particles of earth started springing up and down from the ground like falling raindrops in what looked like anticipation of something. *Yes, something is about to happen!* Dolci thought.

He raised his eyes to scan the rest of the cemetery and realized other sites were undergoing the same phenomenon. Several of the mausoleums and vaults seemed to be shaking; they were taking on some sort of glow in a refulgent color he'd never seen before, but it had the brilliance of a very precious jewel.

He quickly removed his protective goggles and rubbed his eyes. *Is this real? Am I imagining this?*

Without warning, there was a dynamic parting of the clouds in the sky above, followed by the shooting out of multiple rays of sunlight that spread out over the entire horizon and to the earth beyond his view. His mind raced back to several science-fiction films where alien spacecraft fired ultra-white light rays in their tractor beams to seize earthlings or to neutralize their weapons.

But this isn't a science fiction film, he feared. *This is really happening.* He was trembling.

He jumped up from his seat on the backhoe, then fell to the ground and covered his head as his body began to shudder.

A loud noise came from the clouds. No, not a noise...more like a rumbling. No, it wasn't thunder; it was more melodic. Like an angelic command from an unseen force or deity.

Dolci raised his head, rubbed his eyes once again, then peered into the opening of the clouds as the rays began to fade.

But his heart seemed to break because he couldn't see anything.

When he looked back at George's tombstone, the engraved words *He who believes in me will live, even though he dies* seemed to radiate in the lingering light beams...

Then, almost simultaneously—during this twinkling of an eye— the least conceivable duration of time...

Pediatric surgeon Jacob Marks, M. D., examined the X-ray films of four-year-old Emily Ferris as she lay on the operating table. Turning to his assistant, intern George McKay, he said, "Her ileum is extended way too far; we need to fix it."

George McKay nodded and signaled the head nurse, who in turn administered the anesthesia to the child.

Emily had been born with Hirschprung's disease, rendering the large intestine incapable of safely processing intestinal waste. At age two, the little warrior had undergone radical surgery to remove 90 percent of her colon, requiring a manual irrigation cleaning several times daily to remove any fecal matter from her intestinal tract. As the next two years passed, however, the initial operation proved to be ineffective, and frequent blockages that required emergency surgery to correct twisted intestines had brought her parents to agree with the head surgeon that the remedy required an ileostomy. An ileostomy is a stoma (an orifice or aperture) that has been constructed by bringing the end of the small intestine, the ileum, out onto the surface of the skin. Intestinal waste passes out of the ileostomy and is collected in an external pouching system stuck to the skin, above the groin on the right side of the abdomen.

But Emily Ferris was not doing well with her ileostomy. Apart from severe limitations that resulted in curtailing or refraining from many activities a little girl would enjoy, the collection bag frequently burst, day or night; a doctor dictated her diet, and her normal growth pattern was greatly interrupted. From one year to the next, her body didn't grow since her digestive system was unable to receive the necessary nourishment from food ingested. Her shoe size remained the same; her clothes size remained the same, while her two-year younger brother grew at a normal rate. Now, six months after the ileostomy, the stoma extended three inches out from the stomach wall. Corrective surgery was vitally needed.

As Emily lay on the operating table, rapidly falling into a drug-induced unconsciousness, her mother and father sat patiently in the surgery waiting room, praying, an act of worship they were all too familiar with since the discovery of the disease. But today was different from all the other surgeries Emily underwent, because her parents had received assurance from God and Christ their Savior that Emily was going to be healed....

Dr. Marks made the initial incision into the scar tissue of the last operation on little Emily's abdomen, then realized something was wrong. Very wrong. Emily's heart rate began to soar. "Her body's under tremendous strain from her past surgeries; I'm afraid her heart won't make it. Call the duty pediatric cardiologist stat!" he yelled to McKay. Resident McKay blinked, then reflexively turned and leaped to the intercom and gave the order.

Emily's chest began to heave. "Bring the paddles!" Dr. Marks barked to the head nurse. "She's going into cardiac arrest!"

Dr. Marks stood over Emily as the paddles were applied. "Clear!" the head nurse shouted as the button releasing the electric current into Emily's heart was pressed.

Emily's eyes flashed open to the distant sound of a trumpet. Then she suddenly disappeared.

Simultaneously...

Kennedy International Airport, New York

AmeriEast flight 637 from New York to Los Angeles with 210 passengers aboard climbed out into the air from the tarmac at John F. Kennedy International Airport and within six minutes reached its cruising altitude of 37,000 feet. The skies were clear except for pillowy alto-cumulus clouds that glowed with a golden lining that extended to the horizon. The passengers were enthralled with the spectacular display as the captain announced his forecast for a smooth flight.

Twenty-two minutes into the flight is when it happened. The horror of horrors to the unsuspecting traveler.

Ibn Wahhab, seated in 29 F, signaled his compatriot, Abdul Azzam, seated in 27 C. Both were Saudi nationals in their early thirties. Azzam reached into his carry-on and pulled out his holy book, the Koran, in its leatherbound case. Turning aside to conceal his actions, he placed the Koran on his lap. Opening the front cover, he separated the Velcro strip that fastened the binding together to reveal a hollowed-out compartment that held a small sandwich-size container. He removed the container, then threw the small toggle switch to the Initiator circuit connected to five ounces of the explosive Semtex. With one flick of his index finger Azzam switched the Initiator from its *Off* position to

Standby. A miniature icon on the LCD attached to the container went from black to yellow. Only the green indicator remained.

By that time Wahhab already had secured the 24 inches of Dacron cofilament fishing line from the hidden compartment of his holy book that he needed to complete his part of the blasphemous mission.

As the flight attendants dispensed the drink orders, Azzam shot a look of confirmation to Wahhab, then stood up and shouted to the flight attendant, "*Allah Akbar! Allah Akbar!*"

The stewardess screamed as Wahhab grabbed her from behind and wrapped the cofilament around her neck. He pulled it tight, then yanked it as the drinks dropped to the floor. Azzam held up the explosive device in the air and yelled, "Nobody move! I have a bomb!" His thumb hovered menacingly over the Initiator button.

From the rear galley a male flight attendant accurately assessed the emergency and pressed the concealed switch that signaled the flight deck of a hijacking in progress.

Without warning a stocky woman in her early forties sitting seven rows away jumped up and pointed her service weapon at Wahhab and shouted, "U.S. Marshal! On the floor!"

Wahhab grimaced and blinked several times in confusion, unwittingly relaxing his grip. The stewardess gulped in air, collapsing into a nearby seat.

"I will blow up this aircraft!" Azzam cried out to the marshal, "unless you do as I command!"

Suddenly the aircraft slowed, then rapidly descended in a near free-fall.

"They're going to land!" Wahhab yelled in panic.

"Put down your gun!" Azzam screamed as his face contorted with rage. He raised up the explosive device in the air once again and warned, "Do as I say!"

The marshal dropped to the floor of the aircraft to a sniper's stance, took aim at Azzam's head, and—

In the twinkling of an eye, a millisecond of time, seven passengers who heard the distant sound of a trumpet, including the stewardess who collapsed on the floor, vanished!

Simultaneously...

Temple Mount, Jerusalem

Avi Ganor stood in front of the Western Wailing Wall. He carefully folded then placed his family's prayer request paper into one of the many cracks between the giant stones that make up the wall...a tradition known to Sabras, native-born Israelis, and visiting Jews and Gentiles alike. Many of the prayer requests wedged between the stones were faxed over from American Jews unable to visit Israel, for it is believed that the Wall, the last remaining vestige of the first century Herodian temple and a direct link to Solomon's Temple, has special powers to entreat the God of Israel.

As Avi turned and looked to his side, he saw hundreds of Orthodox Jews in their bola hats and long coats dovening and chanting their prayers as they stood only inches from the Wall. Others laid Tefillin with those who wanted to share in a blessing.

After wedging the request into the crack, Avi lifted his hand above his head and placed it on the wall and prayed for several minutes as his wife and daughter looked on from the side of the women, just 20 yards away.

Avi Ganor and his family, all completed Jews who had come to a saving knowledge of the Messiah Yeshua after hearing a gospel message at a Passover Seder conducted at a Baptist church in Maryland by Jews for Jesus, had longed to visit the land of his forefathers once he was born-again. This trip was a dream come true for him and his family.

He turned and walked out of the Wailing Wall compound and joined his wife, Sadie, and daughter, Rachel, in the common square. "I believe the Lord is going to answer my prayer for my boss's salvation," Avi said optimistically to them as they headed for their tour of the Rabbi's Tunnel, part of the ancient subterranean labyrinth that runs under the Temple Mount.

"Do you think God reads those prayers stuffed in the cracks, Dad?" his precocious ten-year-old, Rachel, asked.

Avi smiled at his daughter. "Yes, I believe He does, honey."

Rachel returned the smile and snuggled under her dad's arm.

"There's something special about being here," Sadie began. "To think we're actually here in the land of the Bible, where Abraham, David, and the prophets lived...together with Paul and Timothy, where the New Testament began...it's so exciting!"

Avi agreed wholeheartedly. "Just putting my hand on the Wall sent chills through my body."

"Just think," Sadie added brightly as an afterthought, "it won't be long before the Tribulation Temple is completed right here on this sight."

Avi paused and looked back at the Wall, then at the remains of the Muslim Dome of the Rock that had been nearly totally destroyed by a terrorist attack three years earlier and was currently undergoing demolition as the new Temple was being built. "Well, the way I see events unfolding here in the Mideast, it won't be too long before God looks at His divine timepiece, Israel, and says, 'time to wrap things up.'"

Rachel perked up. "Daddy, when do you think that will happen?"

In an infinitesimal period of time, the Avi Ganor family—and 229 other believing worshipers at the Temple Mount—heard the distant sound of a trumpet, and they were no more. They disappeared from the earth!

Simultaneously...

Raiford State Prison
Starke, Florida

The calling of God to be a prison chaplain was something Bernie Sloan never doubted. Throughout the 22 years of his marriage to Helen, it was common knowledge to all the family members that she supported his ministry. Helen, who by most standards was considered a boring domestic housewife since she liked to stay at home and take care of her household, sew their children's clothes, iron Bernie's shirts, and make wholesome dinners, prayed for her husband every day that he would touch lives for Christ. Granted, his ministry was a grim one that offered little accolades and few praises from his captive audience, but in his heart he achieved great satisfaction and spiritual fulfillment because he believed he was accomplishing God's will to preach the gospel and minister to those few cared about—the condemned on death row.

Bernie believed in the providence of God, and that by divine appointment he became the chaplain to this maximum-security facility housing Florida's most dangerous criminals. With over 1,400 inmates, Raiford was one of the largest prisons in the state with one of the state's three death-row cell blocks along with the state's execution chamber.

So to Bernie, it was all part of God's plan and no accident that the warden, Jack Mertz, called his home and instructed him to come and counsel the death-row convict, Jessie Payne, scheduled to be executed at 4:00 P.M. For some inexplicable reason, Jessie asked for him by name.

Arriving after the noon hour, Bernie went directly to Warden Mertz's office to advise him of his presence and get his authorization, then walked to cell block D, where Jessie was being held, pending the governor's approval of the execution. There remained only three hours left in Jessie Payne's life.

Bernie concealed his dismay when the guard brought him to Jessie's cell. Jessie was in leg shackles and handcuffs. The guard noticed Bernie's consternation and said in defense, "This is our standard operating procedure for short-time death-row inmates."

Bernie simply nodded as the cell door rolled back into the wall pocket and greeted Jessie with a wave. "Jessie, I'm Chaplain Bernie. Warden Mertz said you asked for me."

The guard turned and walked outside the cell to stand sentry as Jessie took a deep breath. "Thanks for coming," Jessie said roughly.

Bernie placed his hand on Jessie's shoulder as he sat on the edge of the bed and asked as he pulled a small Bible out of his pocket, "Would you like me to read you some comforting Psalms?"

Jessie, a large, muscular man in his early forties, sighed deeply and said in a hoarse whisper, "I asked to see you because I want to get right with God."

Chaplain Bernie studied the man before him. That this guy would ever have asked to see a chaplain was nothing short of miraculous. Warden Mertz had filled Bernie in on his case history, and Bernie couldn't imagine this convicted felon ever saying, "I want to get right with God."

Over a fifteen-month period he had raped three Florida college girls, then brutally beat them to death, and in two cases, cut off some of the body parts and buried them in shallow graves in a swamp near Lake Okeechobee. Following in the footsteps of the notorious rapist, Ted Bundy, Jessie was apprehended by the Florida State Police in a routine traffic stop outside the Florida State University in Tallahassee when they pulled him over for inoperative brake lights on his van. When they ran his license number, they realized who he was and arrested him on the spot before another female student could be tortured and murdered. Now, after nine years in Raiford with his appeal process exhausted, his final day had come.

Bernie acknowledged God's leading and rose to the challenge. He opened his Bible to the Gospel of John. "Jessie, I would like to share some verses out of the Bible with you, then ask you some questions before I pray with you to get right with God. Is that all right with you?"

"I'm not going anywhere, Bernie," Jessie managed with a wink.

Bernie slowly took Jessie through the steps in chapter three where Christ deals with the doctrine of rebirth, then asked Jessie if he were sorry and repentant over his sins.

"Their faces are before me day and night," he began. "For years I pushed these thoughts out of my mind with booze and drugs, but now, in my last days, their faces and cries for mercy haunt me." He began to sob. "I'm asking God to forgive me. If only I could live my life over again, I would make it up to God and the girls I killed."

Bernie was familiar with so-called deathbed confessions and how criminals attempt to salve their consciences moments before they die in a vain attempt to make things right. But this was different. Jessie wanted to make things right with God, the One who really mattered in the realm of forgiveness. If Jessie would make things right with God and his sins were forgiven, then he would have settled that part of his debt to God. The debt to the girls, their families, and society, he would pay with his life, which was soon to be taken from him by the State.

"Jessie," Bernie explained consolingly, "God is willing to forgive you of your sins, provided you trust Christ as your Savior and believe that He died on the cross for you. It's that simple." Bernie then touched Jessie once again. "As far as living your life over—that's not going to happen, and you and I know that. God's Word says, 'It is committed unto men once to die, afterward the judgment.' There are no second chances in life. You are right in asking to make things right with God now, before you die."

Bernie patted Jessie on the shoulder, then lifted the Bible in his hand. "You have God's promise here in His Word, that if you receive Christ as your personal Savior, your sins will be forgiven and you will go to be with Jesus in glory."

A wave of disbelief washed over Jessie. He couldn't believe it was that easy for a condemned man who admitted taking three lives to ever be forgiven by God. But he was willing to take Chaplain Bernie's word for it because as he looked into the chaplain's eyes, he didn't necessarily believe what Bernie had to say, but he *did* believe Bernie. "Tell me what to do," Jessie said through muffled sobs.

Bernie shot a look up at the guard outside the cell who was avidly listening and said, "Let's pray." Bernie then spoke a sinner's prayer and asked Jessie to silently confess his known sins to God and ask Christ to come into his heart.

When Jessie finished praying, his tears stopped flowing. "I feel a thousand pounds lighter," he said in contrition.

"All the angels in heaven are rejoicing for you, Jessie," Bernie said in a soothing voice, "because today you are a child of God."

Jessie smiled, then said to the guard outside the cell, "Hey Andy, how about that? I'm a child of God!"

Andy said with a derisive snort, "That'll be the day." Then he mouthed a string of curses.

"It's true," Bernie confirmed to Andy. "And you can be too, if you just trust Christ as your Savior."

Andy ignored Bernie's remark. He jerked his head to shake off the religious chatter and took a giant step backward to get out of hearing range, then took a stance of indifference.

"I'm going to stay with you until the end," Bernie said as he turned his focus on Jessie. "I'll pray you through this until Jesus comes for you."

"You mean Jesus will come for me?" Jessie replied in disbelief. "Really?"

"That's His promise," Bernie assured.

Jessie grew silent. Moments later Chaplain Bernie stood up and said to the guard, "I would like to use the rest room."

Andy nodded, then led him out of the cell, locking the bars behind him. When Bernie returned, Jessie was resting—almost sleeping— quietly, as if he were at peace. Bernie smiled at him, raised his eyes heavenward to thank the Lord for another soul being saved, then sat in the corner and prayed.

The next two and one-quarter hours were relatively quiet. Then two new, higher-ranking guards came and stood in front of the cell. "Jessie," the taller guard commanded, "it's time to go."

"I'm ready," Jessie replied as he and Bernie rose to their feet. Jessie waddled to the doorway as the guards waited, then walked between them to the room where Jessie would be executed for his capital offenses.

In the preparation room, a male nurse shaved Jessie's head and legs, then he was escorted to the electric chair. After an official read Jessie's death warrant, the taller guard placed a moist sponge to aid conductivity on Jessie's head, then a metal plate with an electrode attached to it above the sponge. A second electrode was attached to his leg to provide a closed circuit.

The electrocution system, in place in the Unites States since 1889, typically sends a lethal 2,000-volt AC, 10 amperes current for up to fifteen seconds to the victim to induce unconsciousness and to stop the heart. The voltage is then lowered to reduce current flow to approximately eight amperes. The body of the person may heat up to approximately 138 degrees F., and the electric current will generally cause severe damage to internal organs that often spill out, requiring a major cleanup. To mitigate this, alterations to modern electric chairs include padding and an inertia style retractable seat belt.

Chaplain Bernie looked at the clock on the wall behind the electric chair. It was 3:55 P.M. He momentarily closed his eyes in prayer, then looked at Jessie's face, somewhat contorted by the strap around his jaw that held the metal plate in place, and saw his smile. *Yes,* he thought as he looked up and mouthed a good-bye. *Today you will be with Jesus.*

When Bernie looked at the clock, it was 3:57.

That is when it happened!

It was the time interval like the wing flapping from a honeybee. Maybe five milliseconds or less...

Chaplain Bernie and Jessie just vanished into thin air.

Simultaneously...

Alliance Christian Church, Baltimore

Four teenage girls with banners and signs marked *ACC Youth Car Wash* performed various gymnastics outside the Alliance Christian Church to attract cars passing by to their fund raiser while the 35-year-old youth pastor, Vic Henry, and his wife, stood nearby to oversee them and to direct the traffic to the waiting all-boy crew who performed the washing. He was very pleased with the youth of his church. Not because of their good deeds, nor their ability to raise money for the youth ministry, but for their uncompromising stand with Jesus. Many of their parents , who had questionable relationships with God, were being provoked to attend ACC because of the noticeable change in their children's lives. *Changed lives is an important tool to win people to Christ,* he knew, *but their parents needed to hear the Word of God and respond to it before he could expect them to come to salvation.*

Yes, his aim and mission was to reach the youths for Christ, but another target was their parents. In his previous church, much to his embarrassment, the unchurched parents of the youth showed little or no interest in Bible doctrine or living a separated life. When he studied the problem, he came to realize that the majority of the membership, too, had little or no interest in doctrine or living a separated life. Their fulfillment seemed to come with an increasing identity with the things of the world, not the things of God.

He soon came to recognize that the church was in spiritual decline because the pastor constantly preached "feel-good" sermons and promoted a post-modern philosophy of ministry that questioned the Bible, both in its authenticity and effectiveness to change lives. To that pastor, the Bible was merely an historical and poetic book that carried with it important principles to use as reference when addressing social, marital, or individual challenges of the day. Sermons on how to get along with your employer, or how to manage friendships, or how to raise your children were common themes. Spending thousands of dollars from the church budget on advertising in the community to promote seminars on how to have a healthy sex relationship with your wife seemed to eclipse topics that would address a sinner's ultimate accountability to God.

Pastor Vic remembered an event where that pastor was followed for two weeks by a videographer into nearly every area of his private life so that pastor could preach on the subject, "My Personal Life," purportedly designed to show his sanctified life. But the teaching or preaching of biblical concepts that taught on divine inspiration, conviction of sin by the Holy Spirit, and living a consecrated, holy life for Christ was something he simply couldn't agree to propagate when the church was full every Sunday.

It had become obvious to Pastor Vic that his former pastor didn't want to offend his congregation with truth but was more interested in the numbers game. After two years of strained mentoring under that pastor's leadership, Pastor Vic had to leave before he looked in the mirror and called himself an apostate.

Janine, one of the teens from the car wash group, a pretty girl with long legs and a blond ponytail, ran to Ellie, Pastor Vic's wife. "The girls want to know how much money we've made so far."

Ellie smiled at the girl's enthusiasm. "We're at 265 dollars so far!"

Janine jumped into the air. "Yes!" she shouted with a gesture of triumph, then ran off to rejoin her girlfriends at the street.

In the next instant, a strange sensation overpowered Pastor Vic. His skin began to tingle and his heart started racing. He felt light-headed and thought he was about to faint. "Do *you* feel okay?" he asked his wife as he turned and looked into her eyes.

She clutched his arm with eyes narrowing on his. "Something's happening."

Pastor Vic's eyes widened as he looked up at the girls in the street to see them standing still, silently staring up at the sky with outstretched arms. When he glanced at the boys washing the cars, they were all motionless, staring up into space.

That's when they heard it. It was a loud blast from a horn coming from heaven!

It was unmistakably the blast from a horn, probably a trumpet or an ancient shofar taken from a ram's horn. The kind used by the Hebrews to warn of an approaching enemy or to announce the celebration of the New Year.

"LOOK!" Pastor Vic screamed to his wife as he pointed to the sky. "It's—"

His voice halted abruptly when his eyes focused on the clouds that had just parted to reveal myriads—thousands upon ten thousands—of glorified saints dressed in radiant white robes and sparkling crowns who had come not to judge but to greet the living Church. They were arranged in staircase-like tiers that appeared to climb up to the stars. The glorified ones, all with outstretched arms, were singing "Holy, Holy, Holy, is the Lamb who takes away the sins of the world."

In what seemed like only a millisecond they moved aside to allow a procession of the angelic host, who marched down a transparent pure gold flight of stairs. Innumerable celestial beings with six wings led the procession, followed by those angelic beings with four wings. They were the cherubim and the seraphim, followed by those with two wings, the messengers of God. Then they stepped aside to allow other members of the heavenly hierarchy, the archangels, to march forward until they stood in place. Then all at once the entire assembly bowed in obeisance as a corridor in the sky opened that seemed to extend clear to the Third Heaven, the Throne Room...the very dwelling place of God.

"This is it, Ellie!" Pastor Vic cried out. "This is the moment we've been promised!" He grabbed and held her to himself as they fastened their eyes on the unfolding of God's timetable as the sky appeared to catch fire. It turned blazing red with yellow and blue flames as if the entire atmosphere were engulfed in a cosmic nuclear inferno. But there was no heat—only the refulgent colors that spoke of God's omnipotent ownership over his creation.

"Here He comes!" Ellie exclaimed as Jesus Christ, the Holy One, stood up from His majestic seat and walked down the golden staircase.

Time stood still for God's people.

The King's face emitted radiant beams and His white regal robe seemed to flow far behind Him as He walked down the staircase and came to a stop in mid-air. He raised His diamond-studded scepter that sparkled from the beams shining through and shouted, "COME UP HERE!"

The command was heard by those who believed around the world.

In reality it was only in the blink of the eye—perhaps a hundred milliseconds or so, but Pastor Vic and his wife, along with countless millions who heard the command, knew in their hearts they couldn't refuse.

Then they all disappeared ...

David Douglas' Apartment
Hativt Yerushalayim Street

Public realization of the events to the human mind of the yet unlabeled day would take months to settle, but for Paul Douglas and those left behind who heard and knew of the Rapture, it would be instantaneous. The Scripture, the warnings, the signs, the preaching, and finally, the fulfilled prophecies were all undeniable truths that were mocked and ignored over the ages. Seconds after the disappearance, those who had heard that the promise of the Rapture was real, knew it throughout the world and that the terrible judgments to befall the earth would soon follow. The centuries of theological and eschatological debate over the timing of the Rapture were now over. The opportunities for mankind to make things right with God before the terrible Tribulation period would take place were now only a lingering memory.

Paul walked into his parents' bedroom to see their unmade bed, his mother's vacant nightgown sticking out from underneath the blanket and his father's robe and pajamas in a heap on the floor next to his night table. He sat down on the end of the bed and stared out the window as tears stung his eyes.

Alan? Hillary? Where are you? he thought. *I must find them.* He reached into his pant pocket and pulled out his cell phone.

Just then there was a heavy knock at the door!

Paul bolted upright and sped to the door. When he looked through the peephole he saw a man in a suit with a holstered weapon on his belt. A wave of foreboding swept over him.

As he opened the door, the middle-aged man sporting a moustache peered beyond him into the apartment and announced, "I'm Gabi Klifi with the Israeli Intelligence and Special Operations." He flashed a badge. "And you are?" He gave Paul the impression that he was surprised at his youthful appearance.

"Paul Douglas," he replied, somewhat numb with shock.

Mustering up additional courage to face the challenge, Paul invited him in. *Israeli Intelligence?* Paul remembered vaguely. From his father's discussions he recalled that Israeli Intelligence and Special Operations was known as Mossad, the equivalent to the CIA in America, and that the Mossad is one of the main intelligence community entities in Israel along with Aman, military intelligence, and Shin Bet, internal security, and is responsible for intelligence collection, counter-terrorism, covert operations, and paramilitary activities. It was an organization to be feared.

"I'm here to investigate—" Klifi waved his hand in the air—"the strange phenomenon that's happened. We have orders to question all non-Israelis and Christians who may have been evangelizing or might know something about—"

Paul rubbed his eyes to clear the tears and finished his sentence. "It's called the Rapture," he said, sounding amazed, "and I'm still here."

"What does *that* mean?" Klifi asked scoffingly.

Paul took a deep breath, then jerked his thumb over his shoulder toward the bedroom, "My parents disappeared because of their beliefs."

"Oh," Klifi said, "they were M'shummad, who believed that Jesus would come for them, right?"

Living in Israel, Paul was familiar with contemptible Jewish epithets. *M'shummad* meant "apostates."

"*M'shummad,* no. True believers in the Messiah, yes," Paul replied discordantly. "Didn't you ever hear of the Rapture, where Christians who received Jesus as their Messiah would be 'taken up' to heaven?"

Klifi shrugged, then waved a hand to stop the flow of information. "Heaven, phew! Don't give me that *bob'bbe ma'ase* story (fairy tale)." He reached over and put his hand on Paul's shoulder, then patted it several times while saying, "Now if you know where they really went and whether or not they had anything to do with the plague, you should tell me. Otherwise, I may have to arrest you.

"Remember," Klifi added gruffly, "under Israeli law, any proselytizing to Christianity is punishable by imprisonment or deportation."

"Mr. Klifi," Paul began with respect, "my family is gone, and from what I gathered on the way over here, there are thousands of Christians here in Israel who have disappeared, and probably millions around the world, and you're asking me to tell you where they went?"

Klifi scratched his head. "It does sound a little crazy, doesn't it?" Then he squinted at Paul. "Say, if your family all disappeared like you say, how come you're still here?"

"I'm still here because I *didn't* believe," Paul said dolefully. Then he shook his head and continued, "At my age, I thought I had plenty of time to decide on Christ. I didn't want Christianity to cramp my lifestyle."

"Whatever," Klifi said sarcastically.

Paul realized Klifi was only acting on orders, not really forming a calculated position of the dilemma on his own. "Just out of curiosity, what do they say about the disappearance down at your director's office?" he asked.

Klifi studied Paul for several seconds. "Officially," Klifi said, "there is no strategy for handling this freakish thing since we're still working to solve the cursed plague. But I can tell you this: everyone I've talked to in my field believes one thing, and that is God removed all those troublemakers who were obviously responsible for starting this whole plague business in the first place."

Paul had enough common sense to keep his mouth shut from incriminating himself further. In his mind, using comparative analysis, the entire population of the earth was suffering like Sodom and Gomorrah suffered for allowing wickedness to flourish and grow. "Well, Mr. Klifi, if there isn't anything else, I have a lot to take care of."

Klifi nodded and began to retreat to the door when he stopped and pointed his finger at him. "You be a good boy, ya' hear?"

"I'll try to remember," Paul said solemnly.

Paul bolted the door behind Klifi, then stepped out the sliding glass doors to the outside deck and stood at the rail to look at the city below. To a great degree, it was difficult for the human mind to absorb the cataclysm. Off in the distance he saw what looked like a corporate twin engine jet with half of its fuselage jutting out of an apartment building wall with a plume of smoke ascending to the heavens. Hundreds of automobiles were askew on the roads; many were crashed into storefronts. Other cars were up in flames or had radiator steam rising aimlessly into the air. Horns blaring from disgruntled and angry motorists stranded on the blocked arteries seemed to form a dirge that echoed off the pavements into the surrounding city. Israeli military were seen directing traffic while attempting to calm down the population with their presence.

Civilians were meandering around like lost children, calling names of their loved ones, apparently wondering where their family members were hiding. Several skirmishes broke out as Paul looked on; he imagined blame was being accessed to account for the missing people.

Shaking his head in disgust, Paul headed back into the apartment. Pangs of regret and sorrow filled his heart as he surveyed the empty home where his family once lived.

I have to go on, he demanded of himself. *I have to carry on where my parents and siblings left off. I have to go on with the mission. Dear God,* he prayed, *I don't understand all this, but one thing I've come to know: I'm going to need help, and I must start with you.*

Kneeling down in the very place where his father prayed, Paul invited Christ to come into his heart.

Strengthened in his resolve to go on, he stood up and reached for the phone. He had some calls to make.

FOUR

Paul Douglas' Apartment
Hativt Yerushalayim Street

Paul attempted to rebound from his melancholy and somber mood in the presence of his friends, but the haunting memories of his family suddenly departing into thin air was taking its toll.

"I'm sick of the whole—" he was about to use a vile word, but something from within checked him—"mess." He pointed to Jonathan Landau and added, "You don't know how it feels to lose your whole family in one second. Your family is still here!" Then he turned to Simon Landau, his brother, and said as he pointed to the evidence of his parents' disappearance, "Can you imagine finding the very clothes they were wearing seconds before they were taken in a rumpled pile? And then you come to realize that this is their last remains?"

Simon shrugged, then shook his head as he shot a look at Jonathan. "No, I can't imagine it. It's all too scary for me."

A knock at the door!

Paul and Jonathan exchanged glances. "I'll get it," Simon offered.

"No!" Paul insisted as the specter of another Klifi entered his mind.

"It's probably Shlomo," Jonathan announced. "I called him on my way over here."

Paul nodded then looked through the peephole. It was a young man and woman in their twenties.

"This is Shira Keinon," Shlomo said as he walked in with Shira trailing behind. "She's a Sabra in the IDF (Israeli Defense Force). She can only stay for an hour because her unit is on alert since this—" He stopped short for lack of words.

"It's called the 'Rapture,' " Paul announced to the group,

remembering the very words said to Klifi earlier. Paul escorted his friends into the living room where they plopped into the sofa. Seconds later he continued as they sat there pensively in anticipation. "It's the fulfillment of a Bible prophecy where those Christians who trusted Christ as their Messiah were taken up to heaven." He waved his hand in the air, then held it up, palm forward as he sensed their curiosity. "No need to ask me any questions because I don't have any answers. What I've seen here today makes it very clear to me that we're going into the period that my parents called the 'Tribulation' and things are going to get rough around the world. So I have made my peace with God and have prayed to ask Jesus to come into my life. If you guys are smart, you'll do the same thing."

"The word on the street is that God removed those *Christians* who started the plague," Shlomo said trenchantly. His tone conveyed disbelief.

"I don't believe that at all," Paul argued. "From what I understand in the Bible—and it isn't as much as I would like to know—is that Satan would have people believe that lie so as to keep those who are left behind from seeking after Christ. This way he can go about his plan of deception unhindered."

Shira listened to Paul's explanation then shook her head in amazement. "My, my," she said in wonder. "You certainly sound very matured—way beyond your years. You seem to really know about what's going on around the world."

Embarrassed, Paul gazed at the attractive brunette. "I don't mean to come across as a know-it-all; it's just that with the loss of my family, I realize I have to survive to carry on my parents' mission. I guess that motivation is making me really think things out. So, together with God's help, we can make it."

Shira was curious. "Tell me more about this deal you made with God."

For the next 25 minutes, Paul shared his faith as Shira, Jonathan, Simon, and Shlomo listened in, but their hearts were not ready to receive truth just yet.

The phone rang and everyone automatically tensed.

Paul jumped to the phone and read the caller-ID. Caution dictated that he confirm the call's origin before answering it. "It's from the States," he announced as he picked it up. "From Florida. Lane Drugs."

"This is Brandon Lane," the caller declared with a degree of hesitation. "Who am I speaking to?"

"This is Paul Douglas, Brandon. Remember, the youngest male member of the family?"

"Of course I remember, Paul," Brandon replied. "Is your family around?" he ventured.

"I'm the only one left," Paul lamented. "My parents, brother, sister—all gone."

A deep sigh. "My dad was taken," Brandon said as his breath caught in his throat. "I'm trying to put together some of the pieces of this whole thing, so I thought I'd call your dad for help." A pause, then: "I guess I wasn't really thinking clearly. It stands to reason, now that we know that all the true Christians have been removed, that of course your parents would be included, along with Nathan and Leah Cohen out at Petra. But—"

"I know what you're thinking, Brandon," Paul said solemnly, "how come I'm still here, right?"

"I just thought with *your* family, that everybody would go together," Brandon replied. "But I guess you could say the same thing about me."

"I could, but won't," Paul said. "I believe you thought you protected yourself by denial just like the rest of us who are here. But that's behind us now. I can only tell you that I've made my peace with God over this and asked the Lord to guide me."

"I'm not sure where all this leaves me," Brandon said wearily, "but I'm determined to find out what my dad believed in."

"Then let's leave it there for now," Paul suggested. "Tell me the condition of things there in Florida."

"As I look out the window of my dad's office," Brandon began, "the sight is very frightening, even nightmarish. Several Dade County Sheriff's Office helicopters are circling over the Bayside seaport and from what I can see an oil tanker has collided with a cruise ship out of the Port of Miami. I gather one of the captains and key crewmembers were whisked away and caused the catastrophe.

"It's pandemonium out on the streets. On the local news they are showing tow trucks hauling away thousands of what they call 'abandoned' vehicles to some federally designated depot. There are military jeeps and personnel all over the place. They are stopping people and checking IDs. From what I understand, the entire military is on the highest alert. The National Guard, along with the border patrol, is policing the airports and streets along with all seaports and every border. It's like the nation is in lockdown while they look for the enemy. Martial law will probably be next.

"The hospitals are jammed with those injured victims who were traveling or working with Christians who suddenly disappeared. Those Christians who vanished while driving school buses, cabs, even boats—for that matter, every conceivable mode of transportation—left only a pile of clothes as a grim reminder of their departure. If there wasn't a copilot or some person to take the controls, the vehicle either came to a stop or crashed. I'm sure the death toll will be in the hundreds of thousands, not to mention the millions that just disappeared."

"It's the same here. Probably worldwide."

"What about the plague? Any sign of a change?" Brandon asked.

"As far as I know things are the same. If there is any difference, I don't know about it yet."

"I'm sure you know that we here at Lane have been blamed for withholding the vaccine to halt the plague. Of course it's a huge lie, and unfortunately, with the disappearance and us losing all our legal heavyweights, I'm not sure we're going to be able to solve it. Our funding has been withdrawn and all of our research scientists disappeared, so we will have to hire those from the secular world. This makes things terribly difficult especially since the wave of public sentiment against Lane has become a tsunami. My dad believed there are supernatural forces at work and that unless God did something to protect us, we would lose the war. Now I know he was right. God has to do something or we are paralyzed."

Paul reached into his memory. "What about that group *Koinonos* my parents always talked about? Can you call upon them for help?"

A light bulb switched on in Brandon's mind. "Truthfully, with everything unwinding all around us, I totally forgot about Eddie and

Sydelle. They're the ones who agreed to resurrect *Koinonos*. So, yes, I will contact them to help me—" He stopped short. "That's if—"

"What's the *if?*"

"...that's *if* they haven't disappeared. Nowadays, one has to check the 'who's here' and 'who's not here' book before calling anyone," Brandon said blandly.

Paul pondered Brandon's words. A whole new set of rules for living had been thrust upon the world. "Yes, I know what you mean. We have the same situation here. Let me know how things work out."

Paul ended the call then explained it to the group. Moments later Shira signaled it was time to go.

"We meet tomorrow, right here," Paul, the newly appointed young leader announced. Seconds later, something Brandon said came back to him. He located his father's cell phone then ran down the directory until he spotted the number he hoped to find.

"Good work, Dad," he whispered as he looked heavenward. He pressed the speed dial and prayed.

"Who is this?" the person answering the phone asked.

"This is Paul Douglas. Is this Nathan Cohen?" In his heart, he knew it couldn't be.

"This is Yair Kaplinsky, a dear friend and co-laborer of Nathan and Leah here at Petra. You're David and Kathy's son, right?"

Paul remembered this Yair from a day trip to Petra some time earlier. He was an engineer working on the water system for the Petra fortress. "Well, yes," Paul said, "but help me out here—"

"Sorry to keep you in the dark, Paul," Yair replied. "Obviously you know what's going on, so it's no surprise when I tell you that Nathan and Leah have disappeared. Why their son, Levi, remained is a mystery, but I'm sure we'll find out in time." The voice paused, then: "The Cohens appointed me guardian over the lad."

Paul decided not to ask why Yair was left behind; common sense dictated the answer. Until he knew more about Yair, he'd have to keep a low profile. "As soon as time permits and I can find transportation, Yair, I will make a visit to Petra and we can talk further."

"I look forward to it, Paul."

Paul ended the call.

David Citadel Hotel
King David Street, Jerusalem

Stein and Kavidas reveled in the moment as they sat comfortably in the Regency Room restaurant waiting for their waiter to finish pouring their champaign. Then Stein gracefully hoisted his glass into the air to make a toast. "To Operation Recovery!"

Operation Recovery was Stein's label for the enactment of his plan to brighten the lives of those left behind by gifting every *Masterlink* subscriber a one-time 500 dollar credit for each family member lost. In his mind, their loss would be mitigated by the gift and would hasten the recovery of the population. His experience in corporate administration dictated that *Masterlink* use would in turn double, thus returning a huge profit while the gift would be heralded as a worldwide benevolent act. *Besides*, Stein thought, *the sooner we get their minds off this Rapture thing, the better our chances of success will be.*

Kavidas nodded approvingly. "Being rid of those Christians will be a great blessing!"

They clinked their glasses together.

"My preliminary observations and findings," Kavidas explained almost conspiratorially, "is that our claim that those reborn Christians who disappeared were the cause of the plague seems to be working. Promoting the notion that God removed them to spare humanity the plague was a stroke of genius. There is a foul taste in every soul's mouth from them constantly presenting their sanctimonious and self-righteous 'only-one-way-to-God' path. So, together with the blame of the plague, we are in a good position to move our agenda along. This is a good thing."

"Then there's the removal of the—" The words seem to stall in Stein's mouth. "You know—"

"You can say it, Mort," Kavidas replied, "there's nothing to fear."

"Well, what *do* we call *it*? Do we call *it*—." he pointed upward contemptuously—"His Spirit? The Holy Spirit? The Restrainer? What is *its* name?"

"Let's refer to *it* in the sense of the modern vernacular, the 'Force.' It is the innocuous representation of a god that is not only detached but unconcerned with humanity. I can liken it unto gravity. It is a mindless law that must be observed, but can be overtaken, like when an aircraft employs the law of lift. We can overcome it by employing our own laws.

"We are here on this planet to be deeply involved in the lives of mankind, not to be far off in the outer rim of the universe supposedly caring for humanity. Just review all the tragedies, catastrophes, disasters, and of course, plagues that have come upon this planet. Does the God of the Christian really care? Hardly! The fact that we can deliver on man's needs, cravings, and wants is what makes us real and appealing."

Kavidas was slightly edgy as he gave the explanation, biting his lip, staring off into a void, avoiding Stein's eyes. He held up his hand and ticked the points off to make sure he had his argument right. "Here's the way I see it, Mort. The Church totally lost its credibility when they concocted several different views of—" he sneered and pointed upward—"this Rapture thing. Now we know what position was correct, but it's a moot point. To our benefit, their theology and mission was weakened throughout the ages because of that division."

Stein nodded. "The strategy in the corporate church to relax its stand on biblical doctrine and sin and place the emphasis on felt-needs in one fell-swoop was a move few realized would benefit our cause."

"Here, here," Kavidas consented with a grin. "The capitulation of the sleeping church has unwittingly paved the way for our acceptance, Mort, and that will make it easier for us in this period to have our own way and thwart the purposes of God."

Stein turned and gazed momentarily out the window into the street to see a sample of the ocean of human beings going about the business of recovery then looked back at his mentor and leader, Gregory A. Kavidas sitting across from him. He marveled that the masses would soon come to understand and appreciate the divine decree that they would both rise to world dominance through the suffering of those human beings.

Paul Douglas' Apartment
Hativt Yerushalayim Street
The Night Hours

It was a mysterious sensation, bordering on an apparition. Yet it was not an apparition, nor was it astral projection or dissociation. No, it was not an hallucination or an illusion. It was a vision. At first Paul thought he was dreaming, but no, this was not a dream. Dreams occur while asleep, but he was sitting on the sofa, wide-awake, reading his father's Bible just before midnight. Yes, it was a special consciousness of God to give him purpose and direction. To give him a glimpse into the future.

The furnishings and material walls of the apartment seemed to fade into oblivion as the vision began to form and come into view. There were images and creatures floating into his consciousness that were totally alien to him. Unfamiliar entities of celestial origin that seemed to beckon him out of his earthly body to a spiritual domain where untold secrets would be revealed.

He suddenly saw himself standing on a lofty cliff overlooking a vast body of water. *Yes, it is the great sea, the Mediterranean,* he realized. A beast emerged out of the sea that had a blasphemous name. It was a mutated beast that resembled a leopard, but had feet like those of a bear and a mouth like that of a lion. Then another beast, a dragon, gave the beast his power and his throne and great authority. Then the beast out of the water suffered a fatal head wound, but the fatal wound was later healed.

The whole world was astonished and followed the beast. Then he saw a hideous dragon and men worshiping the dragon because he had given authority to the beast, and they also worshiped the beast who exercised his authority for 42 months. He was given power to make war against the saints and to conquer them.

A divine messenger tapped Paul on the shoulder and pointed him in the direction of a platform suspended in mid-air, where many books were set on pedestals. The messenger then silently escorted him to a special book covered with blood and wiped away the blood so Paul could read the title: *The Lamb's Book.* The messenger spoke to his heart: *All those whose names have not been written in the Book of Life belonging to the Lamb will worship the beast.*

Paul clutched his arms. *Yes, I'm still alive and awake.*

Another heavenly messenger walked him away toward the earth, where another beast emerged. He spoke like the dragon and exercised all authority on behalf of the beast from the sea and made all the inhabitants of the earth worship the first beast who had the fatal head wound that was healed. He performed great and miraculous signs, even causing fire to come down from heaven to earth in full view of men. And with this power he deceived the inhabitants of the earth when he ordered an image of the beast who was wounded to have breath and speak. All those who refused to worship the beast were killed.

Paul began to cringe as the vision deepened. He saw the beast from earth force everyone to receive a mark on his right hand or on his forehead so no one could buy or sell unless he had the mark—the number of the beast.

The messenger cried out in a heavenly voice, "Let everyone be warned: the number of the beast is 666."

Paul stood up from the sofa and fell, unconscious, on the floor....

Paul looked up at the ceiling, then blinked rapidly and looked at his wristwatch. Nearly two hours had passed. *Get up, Paul,* he commanded himself. He took stock of his body, feeling his breathing, his heart, his deep fatigue. He gulped in some fresh air before walked to the wall phone and punching in Brandon's number.

"Good timing, Paul," Brandon said into his cell phone. "I'm sitting down at a pizza joint having dinner with one of my lab technicians. What's the latest?"

Paul realized the six-hour time differential between Israel and the States. "Can you get to a private location for a few minutes? I need to talk to you before I leave Jerusalem for Petra."

"Hold on a minute, pal," Brandon replied, then excused himself and walked outside the restaurant onto the sidewalk. "Leaving for Petra? What's up?"

"Brandon, I know this may sound crazy, but I had a vision from God today and I have to get to Petra to see Levi."

"Yeah, right," Brandon mocked.

"No, seriously. I wouldn't fool around with something like this in these times."

Brandon moved into a secluded spot. "What was it about?"

"Well, I think it was about the future, but I'm not sure. There were many images, symbols, and characters, but from reading my dad's Bible, I can figure some of it out."

"Uh-oh." Brandon's heart jumped as he located a chair and plopped into it. "I'm listening."

"Part of it was about Kavidas and Stein, I'm sure of it. They were represented in the form of beasts who rise to world power. Then there was the part about the 'saints.' I think that's referring to people like myself and the *Koinonos* group who have become Believers since the Rapture."

Brandon was on a fishing trip to find faith, but wasn't about to jump in the water if it was getting too hot. "What did it say about *those* people?"

Paul cleared his throat. It wasn't his job to scare Brandon with full revelation. That was up to God. "Well, the saints will have a tough time for a while as they war against Kavidas, Stein, and their system."

Brandon's response was surprising. "Well, that's not too bad. We already are at war with them. Was anything said about the plague?"

"Curiously, there wasn't," Paul said, almost in wonder. "So I take it to mean that in the absence of it, the plague will subside and give way to other calamities."

Brandon wasn't up on Bible prophecy. "Other calamities? Like what?"

"Like the Seven Seals judgments."

Traveling through the Dead Sea region to get to Petra in Jordan ordinarily brought on the spirit of adventure and excitement for Paul as he passed by the archeological monuments of Masada and Qumram, but the heightened level of anxiety from the disappearance cast a dark pall over the trip that eclipsed any enjoyment. Fortunately, he had others to accompany him to help attenuate his concerns.

"Paul, we're taking the bridge across to Petra," Shira announced as they neared the middle of the Dead Sea area. Due to recent geological developments, the travel time was shortened by the formation of a natural bridge across the Dead Sea that led to Petra in southwestern Jordan. The formation of the natural bridge came about through extraordinary means: the evaporation of the seawater to dangerous levels. While the Jordan River continued to supply the water to the ancient body of water located in the lowest point on earth, the rate of evaporation, together with the absence of rainfall, brought the Israeli government to form study groups to explore the possibility of digging a canal to the Red Sea at its northern border to replenish and supply the Dead Sea with the much-needed water. Until then, the drastic drop in the water level of the Dead Sea allowed a natural bridge to form. Many Bible scholars viewed the phenomenon as a fulfillment of prophecy.

"Fine with me," Paul agreed. "You're driving."

Shlomo, Jonathan, and Simon simply gestured they too were in agreement.

Shira had offered to chauffeur the group to break in her new four-wheel drive vehicle. To her it was new, but in fact it was a two-year-old Mercedes Benz that she'd acquired at a good price from a now-defunct taxi service. The taxi companies use the German cars because of their durability and because Germany sold them to Israel without any sales or excise tax. Many believed it was a form of restitution.

After another hour, they arrived at the entrance to the fortress.

Popular as a tourist attraction and archeological site, the city of Petra warranted police protection to keep treasure hunters from defiling the monument. It was here in 312 B.C. that the Nabateans successfully defended themselves against the Greeks, and again in 63 B.C. against the Roman General Pompey. It would not be until A.D. 106 that Trajan would finally defeat the Nabatean armies elsewhere, leading to the abandonment of the city.

The Jordanian Antiquities Bureau allowed public access, provided adequate security measures were in place to protect the ancient memorial. The Hebrew-Christians, under permit from the Jordanian government to act as custodians of the site under a *pro bono publico* agreement, were now conspicuously absent. Paul immediately recognized the vacuum caused by the Rapture. There were numerous Bedouins scurrying about and several Jordanian officials, but the Hebrew-Christian custodians that were responsible for maintaining the sites were now missing, allowing the site to decline into ruin.

Within moments of their arrival a Bedouin led Paul and the group to a primordial underground water shaft where Yair Kaplinsky was working. The entire city's drinking and irrigation water supply came from several subterranean cisterns and water conduits fed by flash floods common to the area.

"Yair! Friends to visit with you!" the Bedouin guide yelled to Kaplinsky over the noise of the water pump being used to bring drinking water from the shaft to a series of newly fitted PVC pipes that ran to the housing complexes.

Yair quickly shut down the pump, wiped his hands clean, and embraced Paul. He was a tall, wiry Israeli in his fifties with muscular features to match the extreme physical demands of the fortress. His black bushy mustache, when set against his penetrating blue eyes, seemed to become one of his trademarks over the years.

"It is so good to see you, Paul," he said as he smiled luminously. He nodded to the others, then escorted Paul aside and added consolingly, "I'm very sorry about your family. They were very good to me, and I especially was very fond of your sister, Hillary. Your brother, Alan, was quite the adventurer, and I enjoyed exploring the caves in the Dead Sea area with him."

"Thank you, Yair," Paul replied in appreciation as a tear welled up in his eye. "Come meet my friends," he said, regaining his smile. Paul introduced the group to Yair, then asked, "What is the condition of the fortress ,and how did the remaining people fare from the plague?"

As they walked out of the underground passage Yair explained, "Firstly, the fortress is a mighty stronghold that will serve the inhabitants well. Secondly, the remaining people here are either Bedouins or curiosity-seeking Jordanian Arabs who are looking for work, so we've been using them as day laborers. As far as fellow Israelites is concerned, there is only a handful. There are, however, some Jewish and Gentile stragglers from the families that disappeared that didn't go with them."

Move evidence of selective salvation, Paul thought. *What did my father call it? Oh yes, election.* "Hmm, they may come in handy as time goes on," Paul replied. Immediately his spiritual antenna shot up. *Potential Koinonos members*, he envisioned.

Yair put his arm around Paul's shoulder. "As I said on the phone, Levi is fine. He is adjusting slowly to the loss of his parents by mingling with the other children in the compound. Of course, I don't understand why he was left behind, but that question is for another day. As far as that dirty plague business is concerned, we haven't been affected here. Strangely, this compound seems to have some kind of divine shield because these Bedouins and Arabs come and go and mingle with other tribesmen outside of the compound here at Petra, yet we haven't experienced even a single case of the plague. I guess we have some kind of strange immunity. Besides, I hear from Jerusalem that the plague has subsided."

Paul had heard several reports via the car radio en route to Petra that the plague was ending as mysteriously as it started. "God is good," he replied.

In time the inhabitants of earth would come to understand that God sent the judgment of the plague as a precursor to the Tribulation period.

The walk from the water shaft to the amphitheater, where the children played, was only about 400 meters. Once there, Paul scanned the playground area and pointed to a small group of children, "I see him. The boy with the baseball cap."

"That's him," Yair agreed. He then placed his two index fingers in his mouth, took a deep breath, and let out with a whistle that echoed off the city walls. Levi stopped short at the sound of the whistle, turned toward Yair and ran over to him. "The children here have no cell phones so we communicate by whistle," Yair quipped.

"Hello, Levi," Paul said gently. "Do you remember me? I'm Paul Douglas."

Levi nodded ruefully. "Yes, I remember you. You're Hillary's brother."

"He used to play with Hillary often," Yair advised just above a whisper. "He told me he really misses her."

Paul gazed at Levi momentarily and wondered why God didn't take him in the Rapture. He knew it wasn't a question of appearances or his family background, nor was it a matter of salvation, because he knew from his father that all the members of the Cohen family professed Christ. The fact that his parents were regenerated Christians who would have a sanctified child assured of salvation and that he was still left behind was very perplexing. *It must be something we haven't seen yet*, he reasoned.

Paul extended his hand to Levi. "Let's have a little talk."

He gestured to the others that he wanted to be alone with the child. Levi grabbed his hand and walked alongside for several meters until they reached a stone bench outside the amphitheater entrance.

Levi sat on the stone bench and folded his hands into his lap as he gazed into Paul's eyes. "God told me to be a good boy because he loves me."

At such a comment, Paul had to explore further. "Of course God loves you and wants all little boys to be good. But did God say anything else to you?"

"Yes. I had a dream two nights ago, and he talked with me," Levi replied as he looked up into the sky. "It was about things here on the earth," he added, turning his face toward Paul and pointing downward.

Paul quickly connected the dots. Now he knew why he had such an urgency to see Levi. "What kind of things?"

Levi kicked the dirt under his feet as he gathered his thoughts. "Things like what is going to happen here." He turned to point at the stone monuments. "We're going to be living in this place until Jesus comes back, but it won't be until after the big war."

Paul stared blankly as his heart jumped. "Oh? The big war?"

"Yes, he told me that it's coming and that we should prepare this place for his people."

Paul took a deep breath and gulped in some fresh air as the portend of things to come assaulted his senses. He suddenly realized that Bible prophecy cannot be altered and that the "war" would most certainly occur. "How long before it happens?"

Levi shrugged with a youthful expression. "He didn't tell me when, but I know it's soon." He shot a look over at Yair. "Can I go now?"

"Go on your way," Paul said as he patted his baseball cap, "I'll return as soon as I can to see you and help things along here."

As Levi ran off, he yelled out, "Bye, Uncle Paul."

After another hour of discussion, preparations, and refreshments with Yair and his people, Paul collected his group and departed for Jerusalem.

A great amount of work had to be done.

FIVE

Office of the Israeli Prime Minister
Jerusalem

Prime Minister Benjamin Zeman sat at his desk and re-read the official letter from the newly elected President of the European Parliament, Gregory A. Kavidas, who asked for an audience to present what the letter called "an exceptional opportunity for Israel." Zeman readily agreed to the audience on the basis of Kavidas' continuous political and financial support to his party over the past five years.

Zeman flicked the side of the letter as it triggered several memories of his earlier encounters with Kavidas. While acting as Israel's ambassador to the United States, he had met Kavidas at a summit conference in Athens. Zeman had been overwhelmed by the European Union director's strong stand in regard to Israel's sovereignty and his utter disdain for the Palestinian Liberation Organization's claim to Jerusalem.

I knew I liked him from that moment on.

Soon after that experience Zeman had discovered this same Kavidas was the former owner of the American-based Rainbow Pharmaceuticals that developed the first trial of an AIDS vaccine that was brought to fruition by his competitor, Lane Drugs of Miami. *Kavidas, a man with the public interest at heart,* Zeman thought.

Other fragments of his path crossing with Kavidas came to mind. Zeman recalled when a fellow constituent explained that Kavidas was also the former co-owner of the Athens-based *Masterlink* financial system that simultaneously gobbled up all the European credit cards with the advent of the Euro-dollar. This *Masterlink* system utilized a micro-processor chip, similar to the RFID, that was implanted just below the surface of the skin in the right hand by an emollient absorption method and did away with driver's licenses, Social Security cards, and other forms of ID at a time when Americans were frantic over identification problems emerging from foreign terrorist threats. Fingerprinting, hand-shaped ID systems, along with iris pattern, voice- and face-print identification processes were extremely effective but proved to be very costly, while the *Masterlink* system simply required placing the hand under a scanner wand, similar to the procedure already in place at supermarket checkouts.

Naturally, the *Masterlink* system received a warm welcome when it eliminated all possible forms of theft and mislaid cards since the chip was now a part of the human body, going everywhere the host took it. All medical history was encoded in the chip to provide instant information in the event of a medical emergency. Once the *Masterlink* system went global, Kavidas and his partner, Mortimer Stein, promised all missing children, adults suffering from Alzheimer's disease, fugitives from the law, military MIAs, etc., could be located within minutes since the chip is linked to a GPS network with ready-access to law enforcement. Another benefit that brought accolades from police officials was the plummeting crime rates, since most *Masterlink* patrons no longer needed to carry cash; their *ML* chip did it all.

Sometime down the line, Zeman thought, *Masterlink* would be good for the people of Israel as well. The slightly rotund prime minister, who was the successor to Rubin, walked to his bathroom mirror to trim his full beard. As he took a deep look at his reflection, he said to himself, *The weight of this administration is aging you fast. Too many "encounters."*

The most significant encounter he'd had in the past three years was with Kavidas. It was shortly after that Kavidas had predicted the 433 Eros asteroid would threaten the Earth. Some newspapers applauded Kavidas as the Gentile answer to Uri Geller, the famed Israeli psychic-prognosticator. Zeman had been at the Athens Consulate when Kavidas made the forecast and immediately sought him out for an explanation. Looking to grant diplomats special attention, Kavidas welcomed the discussion. At his *Masterlink* financial headquarters in Athens, directly across from the famed Acropolis, Kavidas confided in Zeman and detailed his foreboding dream and how it led to the prediction that became public the following day when his partner announced it to a Miami newspaper.

The astounding prediction foretold that this massive asteroid would skip out of its orbit and put Earth in its cross hairs, threatening it with extinction. Despite astrophysical evidence to the contrary, Eros' trajectory was interrupted by planetary perturbations and did in fact skip orbit precisely as Kavidas prophesied. 433 Eros, an S-type asteroid, was expected to maintain an elliptical orbit and stay at least 13-14 million miles from Earth, considered a "near miss" by astronomer's standards. Every human on planet Earth held their breath until the Russians unexpectedly fired a high-yield, multiple warhead nuclear missile at the asteroid, realigning its trajectory and miraculously deflecting the huge rock from outer space, saving humankind from annihilation. Scientists later announced that 433 Eros was scheduled to return years later, hopefully in a non-threatening orbit.

Kavidas was hailed as some kind of Savior and that title in turn catapulted his political career tremendously. Six months later he was unanimously elected to the prestigious office of President of the European Parliament. Publicly, he quickly divested himself of all ownership in *Masterlink* to devote himself strictly to the needs of the EU.

Zeman walked now to the panoramic window that overlooked the ancient Temple Mount. He gazed off in the distance at the cranes hoisting the massive stone blocks being used as capstones for the new Temple, arising out of the ruins of the Dome of the Rock. The structure had been severely damaged by Arab terrorists three years earlier in a foiled attempt to blow up the Rabbi's Tunnel that runs underneath the ancient ruins of Solomon's Temple Mount, where the Dome was situated. The terrorist attack, aimed at thwarting Israel's attempt to establish Mount ownership, had backfired, seriously damaging the Dome's foundation. Both Israeli and Muslim geologists, archeologists, and clerics had no choice but to condemn the Muslim holy place due to structural damage. The Arab authorities conceded that their Hamas terrorists were responsible and thereby capitulated on the issue of

Mount ownership, allowing Israel to rebuild their temple.

But the ongoing instability among the Arab states troubled Zeman. His cabinet also agreed that the star of the Islamic crescent was presently at its zenith with oil wealth lubricating the skids that could bring the Arab-bloc nations against his people at any time. In fact, it probably would be soon, since many acclaimed geologists predicted that the subterranean oil reserves under the sand of Arab deserts would be exhausted within the next 40 years. This meant the Arab world would have to make their move soon if their plan for Muslim domination was to become a reality.

The idea of saber rattling unnerves me. I need some classical music to soothe my spirit, Zeman thought. Turning to his sound theater, he selected an audio CD that featured violinist Itzhak Perlman, playing his rendition of Saint-Sáens Violin Concerto No. 3. He smiled as he pushed the CD into the player, increased the volume, then walked to his recliner to wait for Mr. Kavidas to show up. Seconds later he closed his eyes to rest.

Zeman's power nap was interrupted ten minutes later when his secretary announced Gregory Kavidas' arrival. He was precisely on time.

Two years had passed since their last meeting, and at Zeman's first glance he was surprised that the political affairs of the President of the EU, unlike himself, had no adverse effect on Kavidas' appearance. In his late fifties, Kavidas had a full head of jet-black hair. His European features—his father being Greek, his mother Italian—accentuated his natural comeliness, no doubt greatly adding to his political persona. Carrying only an attaché case that matched his three-piece suit, Kavidas projected an image of control. He was extremely articulate and capable of drawing on his photographic memory wherever he traveled.

I wonder why he never married? Zeman thought. *Too busy developing his entrepreneurship and concentrating on his political career?*

"It was very good of you to see me, Mr. Prime Minister," Kavidas began cordially as he shook the prime minister's hand.

"Tell me, Mr. Kavidas, how do you like living in Luxembourg?" Zeman asked as he escorted him over to a small coffee table set between a pair of stuffed chairs nestled in a far corner of the office.

"I prefer living in Athens," Kavidas explained energetically, "but I am enjoying my tour there as President of the EU, especially since they have me located in a beautiful refurbished castle in the old medieval city located on Bock Peninsula that lies between two rivers. Actually, Luxembourg is built on the ruins of a Roman settlement and developed in the tenth century as a fortress community. The refreshing breezes off the rivers eliminate the need for air conditioning—just like in times of the knights of old—and by keeping the windows open I'm afforded a grand view of the fast-growing residential and modern industrial suburbs surrounding the castle while still experiencing some of the ancient heritage of the city."

Nodding with sincere interest so as not to dispense with the amenities, Zeman moved the agenda along. "I'm delighted to meet with you, Mr. Kavidas; what brings you to Jerusalem?"

Kavidas crossed his legs and steepled his fingers before he spoke, conveying the image that his voice needed to be heard. "Mr. Prime Minister, I have been watching your administration very carefully, and I believe you are doing an exemplary job of keeping the peace here in Israel. Your hard line to squash the Hamas/PLO terrorism with force greater than they exert, especially with their suicide bombings, is setting an example for the rest of the world to follow. As you know, many national leaders in the free world are now emulating your policies to rid their country of this barbaric form of blackmail. Unfortunately, however, the West, and I'm sure their attitude is influenced by the Arab states that supply them with oil, feel that your military responses to the PLO's terrorists activities border on brutality and only give you marginal support, and that is only after the PLO commits some abominable act such as blowing up a bus filled with innocent civilians. Otherwise, public sentiment, fueled by the biased media, is in favor of the Palestinians, the so-called 'little people,' because anti-Semitism toward your Jewish people never has, nor never will, go away." Kavidas then paused to reach for a glass of water.

This man really understands my people, Zeman thought. *It would be good for our nation to have his support among the European community.* "We are very concerned with our image to the world," Zeman said humbly and solicitously. "Every time we are attacked by the Hamas, we respond proportionately so as not to come down to their level of genocide. In fact, our response is always directed at military targets or terrorist bases in occupied territories so as to minimize the loss of innocent lives, while they deliberately set out to kill our civilians and destroy our property for a cause that can be solved through peaceful negotiations—provided, of course, those negotiations conform to their demands. But you, as a political leader, know as well as we do, that the Arab states want to keep the PLO stirred up so as to give rise to a cause to attack us like they have in the past." He paused to recall a quote and added, "I'll remind you of Anton Chekhov's remark, 'Love, friendship, and respect do not unite people as much as common hatred for something.' You see, Mr. Kavidas, the PLO hatred for us Jews has galvanized the Islamic community against us and, I might add, any nation that favors us."

Kavidas nodded in assent. "I have come to visit you for this very reason, Mr. Prime Minister, to present a plan to you that I, and my fellow Europeans, believe will bring some relief from the constant barrage of negativity generated by the West, and settle once and for all the *problem* with the Palestinians here in Israel. You're not the only one who thinks that if the PLO really want a homeland, then why don't their fellow neighboring Muslim brothers open up their borders and let them in to *their* countries where they can all worship Allah together instead of blowing up Jews for land that doesn't belong to them?"

Zeman gently slapped Kavidas' knee. "That's *exactly* the way our people think, Mr. Kavidas! And they wonder why the Americans don't see it that way." He looked upward for a second and wondered if God had sent Kavidas to him to provide some solution to the never-ending conflict between Israel and the Arab world.

"The European community knows the West is bound by their agreements with the petrol-rich Arab states," Kavidas continued, raising his level of animation to meet Zeman's rising interest. "If push came to shove, the West will avoid offending the Arabs, even though they have a stake here in Israel. Yes, they will offer support, but only if it fits their agenda. When squeezed by spiraling oil prices that threaten the driving habits of their gas-guzzling SUVs, ATVs, CRVs, Cadillacs, and Lexuses back in the States, they will hold off on helping you in hopes that you can pull yourself out of any war without engaging them, just like you have in the past—"

A sudden flash of lightning followed by a violent thunderclap that shook the windows broke Kavidas' momentum. He squinted out the window to see the approaching storm while Zeman jumped up and walked to the window. Off in the distance, huge black altocumulus clouds engulfed the Mount of Olives with lightning strikes dancing in erratic patterns that seemed to signal the strength of the turbulent weather.

"Quite a storm brewing," Zeman remarked. *Is this some kind of portend?*

"I see another storm approaching on the horizon, Mr. Prime Minister," Kavidas warned, as he join Zeman at the window. "But not from nature. The storm I'm referring to will rise out of the nations you have been fighting all along. Only this time, they're going to fight to the death." He turned and walked to the bookshelves that lined the south wall of Zeman's office and continued his discussion. "I shall also quote, but my quote is from the Koran, specifically, the Sura: 'Fight against such of those to whom the Scriptures were given as believe not in Allah. They must be utterly subdued, for they worship their rabbis and their monks as gods.' " He shook his head in dismay. "This declaration of war is directed right at you and your people! Believe me, I'm afraid the cry of the Hamas, *Itbakh al Yahud*—slaughter the Jews— will be shouted from the Temple Mount very soon."

Kavidas' last words echoed off Zeman like an oracle forecasting an unwelcome event. They caught Zeman by surprise. He found himself captivated by the driving force of persuasion that appeared to be gaining in strength. Ultimately it could only culminate in some kind of impasse since, in his mind, there would be no solution to the Arab problem until the Messiah came to make Israel the head of all the nations. "That sounded like a prophecy, Mr. Kavidas," Zeman finally replied as his palms began to sweat, "and knowing your background is hallmarked by such prognostications, what are you suggesting? That we prepare for war?"

The light seemed to change all around them. The rapidly moving storm had passed, allowing the setting sun to cast long shadows outside the building, while allowing an eerie form of light to creep into the room and paint a dark mask over Kavidas' face. Zeman walked to the doorway and turned on the ceiling lights as Kavidas motioned for him to join him in the stuffed chairs once again. "What I'm about to say, Mr. Prime Minister, must be kept between you and me as prominent leaders who control the destiny of millions of people. Are you in agreement?"

The tension in the room soared to a near palpable level. Zeman could feel his heart rate beginning to climb. "Yes, I suppose I'm in agreement, Mr. Kavidas."

His consensus gave rise to Kavidas' success. "Then we're in agreement. What I am proposing might possibly be called a deterrent to war. The proposal involves the present alliance of the fifteen-member nations of the EU, and you know who they are—from Ireland, to the UK, to Portugal and Greece, to Germany, Denmark, and the nine other members to help you in your dilemma with the Arabs. The plan involves the initial relocation of between 950,000 to 1,000,000 of their Jewish population to a newly created homeland here in Israel. Then after the initial relocation, so as not to overcrowd your nation and give you time to accommodate them, we would assign 30,000 immigrants per year for the next ten years. We have taken a random poll and many disenfranchised Jews would welcome the offer, just like they did after World War II. We propose to pay these 'homesteaders' a flat 'relocation fee,' and we simply ask you to provide them with the land to settle in."

Kavidas looked over at Zeman's desk and spotted a pad. He quickly fetched it and wrote down several figures and notes, then turned to Zeman once again. "With an influx of one million Jews on the outset, a disproportionate population figure will begin to take control here in your nation. You remember, Mr. Prime Minister, that the Arabs have a demographic plan to outnumber the Jewish population here in Israel. Well, once this repatriation program becomes a reality, the Arab leadership will think twice before rising up against you because *you are displacing them.*" He made a fist and slowly brought it to the coffee table and said with fervor, "Believe me, this is your deterrent to war!"

Zeman's eyes were locked on Kavidas' face as he laid out this plan. It was an odd plan, one that had never been thought of before, *to displace the Arabs.* It had a spin on it that conjured up curiosity. Obviously a plan coming from a man like Kavidas could not be taken lightly, no matter how farfetched it sounded. In a way, he thought, Israel was slowly deporting suicide bombers and their families— together with Hamas radicals—so this program would merely be an extension of this plan, on a much greater scale. "Tell me more."

Kavidas took off his outer suit jacket and placed in on the back of the chair as he brought new ideas to Zeman. "With this fifteen-member European nation endorsement of your administration, it will be very difficult for the Arab nations to censure you in the future. In the past, if there was to be any approval of Israel taking measures to protect itself, all the countries except the U.S. and England were as silent as church mice—never speaking up for the injustices you have endured at the hands of the Arabs. Well, this will all change from now on. If you have support from the EU, both financially and militarily, the rest of the Gentile nations will have to take notice and fall in line to save face. Our military, the RRF, may not be massive, but it is a wholesome deterrent. And, believe me, a string of financial sanctions against the Arab world will send a clear message to their oil sheiks!"

He shot a look at Zeman, who kept nodding as he carefully weighed the plan. "An expansion of this magnitude into the Mideast by the EU," Kavidas continued with heightening volume, "will ultimately rid your land of Muslim interference, while honoring the prayers of your forefathers who believe the Jews have an inviolate right to this land!"

Several pangs of guilt stabbed Zeman in the heart when he thought of how the patriarchs of old, be it Abraham, Jacob, Moses or David, would feel about the recent statement made by Abdul Aziz Ibn Saud regarding Israel's right to the land. *"We shall never call for or accept a negotiated peace. We shall only accept war—Ji'had—the holy war. We have resolved to drench the lands of Palestine and Arabia with the blood of the infidels or to accept martyrdom for the glory of Allah."* No doubt they would fight the Arabs to the death or make any alliance they could with a nation or nations friendly to Israel in order for her to keep her sovereignty and self-respect intact. "Don't get me wrong, Mr. Kavidas, I'm very interested in what you have to offer, but don't sell the U.S. and the Brits short just yet. I'm trusting that they would come to help us if we needed them."

Kavidas smiled, as if hoping Zeman would say just that. "It is very important to our discussion, Mr. Prime Minister, that you bring them up." With that he paused to pull from his attaché case several photographs and copies of front-page headlines from leading American newspapers, along with a complete work-up of the history of America and England toward Israel. He placed them on the table and said nothing for nearly a minute.

Zeman's eyebrows shot up. Kavidas obviously had done his homework before their meeting.

Kavidas then held up an old black-and-white photograph of a partially destroyed naval vessel. "This is a photo of the ship *Exodus* after it was intercepted and rammed by British warships on July 18, 1947, when it attempted to dock in Palestine after setting sail from war-torn France. The ships, carrying 4,550 fragile, Jewish death-camp survivors, hoping to find peace and a homeland after enduring unspeakable horrors under the Nazi war machine, were turned away by British forces only to be herded onto a prison ship in Haifa Harbor and sent back to France. They were later taken to Germany and dumped in what was called 'misplaced person's' camps." He pursed his lips, then nodded twice. "Yes, this is what you can expect from the British! Believe me, they will not be there for you in your time of need."

Zeman could not respond immediately, for the memory was too painful. He had instantly recognized the photograph of the *Exodus* that was permanently engraved on his mind, just as Americans have the picture of planes flying into the World Trade Center in New York engraved on their minds. "I see your point," he conceded.

Next, Kavidas exhibited several photographs from 1973 of Americans waiting in their cars in long lines at gas stations during the oil shortage. "Now we all know that the 1973 oil shortage was nothing

84

more than a colossal scam by both the oil companies and the oil-rich Arab countries to drive up the price of gas. Agreed?"

Zeman gave him a silent nod as he thought on that remark. *If the oil crisis was indeed legitimate, where did all the oil mysteriously come from once the price went over one dollar per gallon? The shortage suddenly vanished.*

"And do you remember the sentiments coming from the Americans during that crisis? In short, their collective attitude was expressed on the bumper stickers of many of their cars, 'We need oil, not Jews.' " Kavidas put up his hand in a halting motion. "I know what you're thinking, Mr. Prime Minister: America is a godly nation that won't turn their backs on the only vestige of democracy here in the Mideast. But if you think about that position for a moment, you can't help but realize that America is no longer the spiritual nation it once was. This is the real reason public sentiment toward your people has changed. While at one time they would stick their necks out to protect Israel because of their Christian view of the Bible and its promises to those who care for Israel, you can no longer depend on that because a vast number of Americans and their churches have turned their backs on the Bible. Not to mention the influx of Arabs and Arab lovers into American political parties who persuade the media against Israel."

Zeman flinched. Kavidas was getting through.

"Let's face the facts, Mr. Prime Minister," Kavidas continued, "Israel is the world's scapegoat and you as a nation are dispensable." His presentation increased in intensity as he pulled out a map of the Middle East and pointed his finger at Israel saying, "Israel occupies just a small sliver of land, some 8,019 square miles in area." He waved his hand over the entire Mideast. "But look at the extent of your hostile neighbors— some 2.2 million square miles…270 times more land than you have!"

Finally, Kavidas pulled out a chart and held it up to prove another point. "Your country has a population of 5.8 million, while your neighbors, the Arabs, total some 203 million—outnumbering you 35 to 1! Believe me, if you don't take steps to form an alliance with me, or rather the EU, who *will not* 'knuckle under' to the demands of the Arabs, I personally do not foresee a favorable future for your people."

Zeman took it for granted that Kavidas had much more proof to support his position if he were so inclined to challenge him further. But in his heart, he knew everything Kavidas said was true. "One question that comes to mind, Mr. Kavidas," he asked with just a slight rise of one eyebrow. "How would this arrangement benefit the EU?"

While slowly replacing his exhibits back into his attaché case, Kavidas explained, "The purpose of the EU is, first, to broaden the scale of citizenship through monetary and economic union between member nations. I believe we would mutually improve our financial condition through enhanced trade agreements and ease of travel for our citizens between the EU and Israel. This, in turn, would improve our commercial standing in the markets of the free world." He broke out with a smile. "Secondly, this being one of my initiatives, is to work toward installing a serious defense mechanism with you as our Mideast ally in the event that a Muslim nation decides to turn on one of *our* member states. Frankly, with your recent military history of successfully repelling the Arab terrorist campaigns, we would want you on our side. I mean, after all, any non-Islamic country is at risk as long as the flag displaying the Arab crescent flies in so many parts of the world."

The statement of a notable American journalist flew into Zeman's mind. He remembered the columnist writing that he could not point to a single Islamic state where tolerance and understanding is extended to non-Muslims. "I can think of another," Zeman postulated after several seconds of meditation. "That you would want the God of Israel to be on your side, to bless you and the EU."

Kavidas gave him a puzzled look. "Uh, yes, I would want that blessing, too," he replied dryly.

Slowly rising from his chair, Zeman stretched his arms as he yawned. "I'm getting old, and there seems to be no rest for the weary." Then, while gazing at Kavidas, he said in a somber tone with arms crossed over his chest, "Mr. Kavidas, you have persuaded me. My intellect agrees with your arguments, while my heart yearns for the added protection you and the EU promise. In my spirit I believe this kind of agreement would be good for Israel. But needless to say, I must confer with my cabinet and seek counsel from them. If they are in agreement, we can move your agenda along."

Kavidas watched Zeman with piercing eyes. He extended his arms to Zeman to embrace him. Kavidas' spirit attested that the prime minister's body, soul, and spirit believed in him and would do everything possible to convince the hearts of his cabinet members that this was the right thing to do. There was a meeting of the minds today, and in his mind, that was all that was needed. Actually getting the approval from the cabinet would simply be an academic and political exercise.

"Mr. Prime Minister, I hope to hear from you soon."

They hugged, then shook hands.

SIX

Bushehr, Southwest Iran

The four-hour tour of Bushehr's major fishing and commercial port offered Anis Hatem and other specialized personnel a refreshing break from the scientific and technological bombardment to their minds that had occurred over the past two weeks. The much-needed excursion to various seafood canneries and food-processing plants that lined the Persian Gulf at Bushehr was diversionary and mildly entertaining but did nothing to erase the images of the cooling towers, gas centrifuges, or the diagram of the thousands of thin stainless steel tubes containing mixed uranium and plutonium oxide fuel that made up the core of the nuclear reactor he was sent to examine. No, the images continued to fade in and out of his mind with no sign of abating. Terms like the "moderator" and the "breeder blanket" that were alien to him at one time were now swimming around in his head along with haunting images of sodium loops, coolant pumps, and heat exchangers used for heat removal in liquid-metal fast breeder reactors.

In a way, Hatem felt honored that a 29-year-old Palestinian from Jerusalem with only an undergraduate degree in electrical engineering was asked to participate in the important assignment, but then again he felt inadequate and intimidated by the enormous amount of information and instruction he was expected to absorb in just three weeks of training. Because of his background, learning came hard to Hatem. His parents were refugees from war-torn Lebanon who worked in a clothing factory owned by Israelis outside Tel Aviv and their meager salaries kept them just above poverty wages, certainly ill-prepared to send their only son to college. But Hatem had steeled himself early in life to rise above his parents' humble lifestyle, even if it meant trafficking in illegal arms to provide for his education and entertainment. Recruited at age fifteen, Hatem and three other Palestinian youths braved the Syrian-Israeli border twice a week after school to smuggle in arms for Hamas. In his mind and in the mind of Hamas, it was not illegal, except maybe to the Israelis, but then, Israel's occupation, in the mind of Hamas, was an illegal act that needed to be corrected. This part-time job severely hindered his academic study time, requiring summer school and repeat courses throughout high school and college.

The only thing that matters now is this mission, he thought. *I have deliberately pushed every other thought out of my head so I may focus on every detail of this operation. Once this operation is complete, I can choose my place in Mujahideen, the warriors of Jihad! Then all of this sacrificing will pay off!*

"Anis, look over there!" Ali Akbar Said yelled out in Arabic as he pointed to a small fishing village on the shore of the Gulf. "Check out all the fish stacked up on the backs of the boats." Seconds later the touring bus came to a slow stop to allow the passengers a closer view of the harbor. "At one time that village was the location of the first Iranian naval base when Nadir Shah was in power back in 1734," Said added in commentary form, attempting once again to build a bridge of friendship to Hatem.

Hatem simply nodded in indifference to his newly acquired Iranian comrade and makeshift guide. He was not really interested in this city or making new friends at this juncture of his life, especially when he would be leaving for home in seven days. *When I'm not at work*, he argued with himself, *I want to be left alone.*

Looking at the harbor and the surrounding environment disinterested him. In reflection, Bushehr really did nothing for him except provide a training ground for his appointment with destiny. Iranian history, ornamental buildings, business enterprises and landscapes left him empty and longing for his home in Gaza, where all the action was continuing to unfold. For the present, the excitement of learning how to sabotage a nuclear power plant was all he could handle.

The bus climbed one of the many hills that encircled the nuclear power plant, and upon reaching the plateau on the top, it slowed to afford a panoramic view of the reactor compound. The 440-megawatt breeder reactor, together with a heavy water treatment plant, consumed over 50 percent of the sprawling 80-acre plot of land in what appeared to be a naturally formed location to house such a potentially dangerous facility. Armament research and technician housing buildings made up for another 25 percent, leaving the commissary, lounge, and parking lot for the remainder.

One of the few interesting items he learned from Said was that Iranian geologists confirmed that the hill surrounding the facility formed a natural barrier that formed a crater-like wall and contained an usually high concentration of lead deposits that would shield the outlying communities of any radiation leak. That barrier, together with massive concrete fences, added secondary protection from radiological hazards as well as providing security for the facility. The "community," officially and publically declared as a commercially run electricity-generating station, was in fact a secret military installation.

As the bus descended the hill and neared the heavily guarded security gate, Hatem noticed off to the extreme northwest corner of the compound a special section that housed the skeletal remains of the old German-built reactor that had been bombed by Saddam Hussein's air force during the Iran-Iraq war in 1992. The director of the Bushehr center referred to the remains as a monument that should serve as a perpetual reminder to Muslims that Arab brothers should not wage war on each other, for in his words, the real enemy was Israel and their harlot benefactor, America.

Once Hatem and Said were inside the security zone they donned their radiation detection badges and walked toward their respective quarters located in the personnel building adjacent to the laboratory complex. Hatem stopped for a sandwich at the commissary, then went to his apartment, where he found his compatriot and roommate, Ahmed Saideh, fast asleep on the sofa. He walked over to him and kicked his foot sticking out from under the blankets. "What's this, Ahmed," he chided in his native tongue. "Only half a day today?"

Saideh was being trained during the day, while Hatem trained at night so that together, regardless of what time of day the mission would be called, at least one of them would be able to operate the reactor's controls. Saideh roused from sleep, then walked to a window as Hatem walked into the kitchen to make some Turkish coffee. "What did you do today, Ahmed?" Hatem asked curiously.

The brash 30-year old, Saideh, ran his fingers through his black bushy hair and yawned. "Abduhl Ruhollah, the chief technician in charge of the reactor control room, brought me over to the uranium mine and processing plant at Sighand. The whole set-up here is really fascinating." He sat down on the chair next to the window and gazed off into the distance at the cooling towers, the huge concrete funnels that discharged great volumes of harmless heated water into the atmosphere.

"Did he tell you about their 'civilian research institute' at Isfahan?" Hatem asked with a smirk.

Saideh returned the smirk with a smile. "You mean the uranium enrichment plant in disguise, right?"

"That's it." Hatem nodded. "Quite an elaborate network over here, wouldn't you say?" Hatem was overwhelmed with the extent to which the Iranian government spent their petrol-dollars on nuclear equipment that had the potential to harness the atom to make bombs.

"The entire 'organization' is really impressive," he said with an expansive grin. "Everything necessary for Hamas to learn how to bring down Israel is right here." He walked to the table to drink his coffee and added with intensity, "Just think, once our mission is complete, our people will have their own homeland."

Hatem meditated momentarily on Saideh's remarks. *I wonder what the price will be? Will it be worth it?* But he didn't say that. "Yes, may Allah be praised!"

The following morning, both Hatem and Saideh were summoned to the reactor control room to learn the final steps on how to bring about a nuclear explosion. From there the Iranian technician, Ruhollah, brought them to the confinement chamber of the Russian-built breeder reactor that uses uranium-238 as fertile material. He explained to them in layman's terms that when uranium-238 absorbs neutrons in the reactor, it is transmuted to a new fissionable material, plutonium, through a nuclear process called beta decay. Ruhollah made a point of adding to his commentary that when the spent uranium-238 was reprocessed at a diffusion plant, plutonium-239 was produced. What he didn't add (probably due to his conscience being salved so as to reject the truth) was that the weapons-grade plutonium-239 would indeed be used in the manufacture of offensive weapons.

Hatem stared at the reactor and shook his head. *What are the essentials here that I need to know?* he asked himself. He walked around the reactor and put his hand on the breeder blanket that surrounded the core. He was told that it contained rods filled with uranium oxide and that it measured about 10 feet high by about 5 feet in diameter, being supported in a large vessel containing molten sodium that leaves the reactor at about 930 Degrees F.. From there steam is produced in a second sodium loop, separated from the radioactive reactor coolant loop by the intermediate heat exchangers in the reactor vessel. The steam in turn is directed to turbines to produce electricity. The entire nuclear reactor system is contained in a large steel and concrete containment building. This is what the public saw; but at Bushehr, the electricity-generating plant was nothing more than a cover.

"Now that we know how it works," Hatem said impatiently while pointing to the reactor, "show us how to turn this monster into a bomb." *Military might is the only way to achieve our goals,* he reminded himself.

Ruhollah, a middle-aged man of Islamic principle, grimaced upon the realization of the real reason the two Palestinians were at Bushehr.

They were there as terrorists authorized by certain "higher-up" Iranian fundamentalists determined to aid and abet any other Muslim cause to bring about the demise of the Jewish nation. They were not the slightest bit concerned about the scientific, energy-producing aspect of the reactor that would benefit mankind. No, their only purpose was to learn how to bring about the release of volatile fissionable material into the atmosphere to kill as many Jews as possible.

"Once you're inside the control room," Ruhollah began as he walked them over to the station that housed the coolant controls, "look for this instrument panel." He pointed to the computer monitor on the panel that displayed various oscillating graphs. "You'll notice here that this shows the core temperature and, as you can see, it is in the normal operating range." Then he swiped his ID card on a security module, lifted the protective covers on two red buttons on the console and simultaneously pressed them.

"Whoa! What's that?" Hatem asked as the graphs began to flash red.

Ruhollah squinted as he watched the graph and then checked a series of gauges before answering. "When I pressed these two buttons, I restricted the coolant that surrounds the core, causing the core temperature to rise dramatically." He shook his head. "Of course this demonstration only lasted two seconds, but had the restriction been sustained, the emergency coolant system would have kicked in."

"And if the emergency coolant system does not 'kick in'?" Saideh asked with a tight smile.

"If the coolant system is breached, then severe core damage occurs and the release of volatile fission products from the reactor vessel will escape. The radioactive gasses that will vent from the containment building will pose an enormous threat to all human life for many miles and if the winds are contrary and carry the cloud—" he closed his eyes with a pang of guilt—"then perhaps an entire nation will be affected."

Hatem clenched his fists and grinned at Ruhollah, who returned the gesture with a dirty look. *Do I really want to train these men to kill innocent people?*

"Abduhl, isn't that what sort of happened at Chernobyl back in 1986?" Saideh asked while trading a look with Hatem.

"Not exactly," Ruhollah explained, reeling from an attack of his conscience. "At Chernobyl, the reactor went out of control and there were two explosions. The top of the reactor blew off, and the core was ignited. Core ignition at 2800 Degrees F. generated radiation more than 50 times that of the American Three Mile Island disaster and the radioactive fallout cloud spread into Scandinavia and northern Europe. About 135,000 people needed to be evacuated and more than 30 died." He wiped the mounting perspiration off his brow. "Nuclear disasters are dirty business."

Hatem reminded himself that, once back in Israel, their goal was to bring about a "situation" where his people would be able to realign the political members of the Middle East using a weapon much greater than oil. His people would issue the ultimatum that unless the Israelis met their demands, the horror of nuclear contamination would be the consequence. "Show us how to bring about a 'situation,' " Hatem said trenchantly as he opened up his notebook to record the procedure.

Pursing his lips in a moment of contemplation, while his conscience provoked him to question his moral and ethical values, Ruhollah nodded and retraced the steps necessary to disable the primary cooling system while simultaneously sabotaging the backup system. He explained that once the core coolant complex failed and the fuel began to melt, allowing fission products to enter the reactor building, a catastrophic nuclear accident allowing radioactive fuel to burn through the floor of its container and go straight down into the earth could occur. It was known as the China syndrome.

Saideh's eyebrows shot up. "The radiological effect on human life?"

Ruhollah leaned against the console and held up three fingers sequentially as he replied, "First and foremost is the loss of life. Radioactive materials emit penetrating, ionizing radiation that will injure or even kill human tissue. A release from the reactor you're being sent to will most assuredly result in many fatalities. Secondly, there is the psychological aspect. Nuclear accidents cause severe stress on society, especially when there is a high kill rate. And then, finally, there is the financial damage that will occur. In all probability this figure will climb into the billions, perhaps even the hundreds of billions when the extent of the contamination finally comes to rest."

Saideh closed his eyes to recount other financial disaster figures. "That's good," he exclaimed luminously. "That should eclipse the September 11, 2001 property damage on America."

The rest of the week was spent by Hatem and Saideh totally familiarizing themselves with the instrumentation and reviewing their diagrams and notes. Any concerns they had about gaining access to Israel's plant at Yeroham would be handled by another cell group, and at the right time, they would simply dovetail their two operations to form one formidable attack force. They agreed they were not going to worry about any more details. Now was the time to just relax and allow Allah to sort it all out.

SEVEN

Northern Yeroham, Israel

S hortly after Nahman Arav received his master's degree in nuclear engineering from the Hebrew University in Jerusalem, he was appointed as a nuclear reactor operator at the Northern Yeroham generating station located on the outskirts of the Negev desert. Being quick to connect his education with practical application, he advanced rapidly in his field so that within five years, he was promoted to power station supervisor. The supervisor of the power station was responsible for the visual inspection of power systems operations that included grid and pneumatic controlled switchboard monitoring as well as constant surveillance on related equipment leading to the distribution of electrical power to the transmission networks and substations. He regulated the operation of the reactor, the turbines, the boilers, the condensers, the generators, and the coolant systems.

The fifteen-year old American-built 85 megawatt Pressurized Water Reactor at Yeroham provided 85 million watts of electrical power to over 75,000 consumers that ranged from the northern Negev to southern Hebron. Seven other conventional power stations strategically scattered throughout the nation supplied the remainder of central and northern Israel with their power needs.

Over the years Arav managed to isolate himself from the continuous and oftentimes overwhelming demands of the facility by carving out his own niche in the control room in what became known as his cubicle. At his cubicle he visually inspected the station instruments, meters, and alarms to ensure transmission voltages and line loadings were within prescribed limits. Detecting equipment failure, line disturbances, and outages was within the scope of his job description. With a top-secret clearance, his access and work was only scrutinized by his superiors who were quite satisfied with his performance. However, many of his subordinates rumored that Arav took his job too seriously and, at age 46, was regarded as being too persnickety and too bossy, and therefore very unpopular.

Now, adding to his dismay, was the murder of his son, Asher.

Arav examined his son's photo that was prominently displayed on his monitor console with a wistful expression. He expelled a sigh as his shoulders slumped, desperately trying to lift himself from his maudlin frame of mind that inevitably led to a secret night of escape with his bottle of bourbon.

A tap on his shoulder interrupted his fixation on the photograph.

"Nahman," one of the NPP [Nuclear Power Plant] generator technicians ventured softly, "a few of us are going to stop off at Sarnoff's restaurant on the way home tonight. Will you join us for dinner?" Despite Arav's austere personality, his fellow workers admired him and with compassion attempted to lift his spirits out of the bottomless pit of despair.

Arav was in no hurry to go home anymore. His wife, Haleh, an Egyptian-born research analyst, could not bring herself to absolve Nahman of the guilt of their son's death. He knew, she accused, that Asher was an Arab sympathizer and surreptitiously working with Hamas and that she absolutely forbid it. *Why wouldn't he take up her dream and join the General Security Service and look to defend Israel instead of putting in with PLO terrorists?* she constantly asked. She did not want the family involved in Israel's ongoing struggle with the PLO or any other self-proclaimed group that allegedly stood for peace while in fact masterminding continuous waves of violence.

But Nahman had said nothing, nor did he intervene in his son's involvement with a movement that sought to breed suicide bombers who fanatically strapped sticks of dynamite to their bodies and indiscriminately killed and maimed innocent civilian targets for their own political gains.

In her mind they were nothing but cold-blooded murderers. Despite her incessant laments, nothing changed. She reasoned, sadly, that one day her son would be nothing more than a statistic. So when

Mossad, the Israeli intelligence service, raided a makeshift bomb factory in Gaza and summarily executed her son, along with seven other explosive specialists caught in the act, she had held Arav gravely responsible. Arav in turn held Israel's government responsible for what he deemed an *execution*, and from that day forward determined in his heart to get back at them in the only way he knew how.

After a moment of contemplation, he spun around in his swivel chair and with a dismissive wave said, "Not tonight. I'm tired, and I have a meeting to attend later this afternoon. Perhaps tomorrow."

The fellow technician nodded in disappointment, noting that Arav did look particularly haggard today, and resolved to ask him again before the weekend.

In an apartment above a pottery shop in Khan Yunis, Gaza, Arav was introduced to Hatem and Saideh for the first time. Principals in the Hamas network that solely organized the cell groups to protect its sovereignty as well as the identity of the individuals had arranged the appointment. Arav was simply told where to meet.

The dismal setting of the apartment along with the waning sunlight of the day only added to his melancholy and gloomy outlook on life. Apart from the squalid conditions that represented the hapless history of Gaza, Arav disdained the look of the decrepit Palestinian refugee camps surrounding the town that served as a constant reminder of the perpetual conflict in his nation. In a way, they had brought this condition on themselves, he thought, because from Gaza, the Fedayeen, the *commandos*, constantly launched hit-and-run attacks against Israel to protest their refusal to negotiate for recognition for statehood. In retaliation, the IDF, the Israeli Defense Force, maintained border restrictions to safeguard against breaches in security agreements. This relentless friction created a war-like environment that just would not go away. *Maybe my contribution to the age-old conflict will change that.*

He wasn't particularly fond of the idea of meeting in a hostile strip of land that was once a part of the seafaring Philistine federation that in time would host the Crusaders, the Turks, and the British, who in later times maintained a military presence among the longstanding Muslim population. From this group of Muslims in Gaza, Egyptian President Nasser assembled the first Fedayeen and encouraged their terrorism against Israel. Even though the Palestinians displaced the British after 1948 and were now autonomous, it seemed that hostility with Israel would always prevail. Whenever peace efforts appeared on the horizon, action by some faction would inevitably bring a dark cloud over the process and thereby destroy the initiative. Peace appeared as elusive as the proverbial butterfly in search of delicious nectar amidst a vast array of beautiful flowers in a garden.

As Hatem opened up his briefcase and proceeded to spread two diagrams of the Yeroham nuclear plant on the table, Arav walked pensively to the only window that offered a view of the village square contiguous with the street below. He felt severely intimidated by these unknown Palestinians and self-conscious that he was betraying his people. But then again, his life had spiraled downward since Asher's death to the place where duplicity had become second nature with him. He paused in his brief meditation to allow his eyes to scan the people in the street, never thinking of looking into the open window of the opposite building. He noticed Arab women in long black robes with plastic baskets balanced atop their heads walking busily through the marketplace where merchants displayed their wares of cotton clothing, trinkets, and framed pictures of revolutionary heroes. *Man adjusts...life goes on.*

"What am I expected to do?" Arav asked the two Arab men as he spun around and walked toward the table before him. With a renewed spirit of resolve, he willfully set all suspicion of intrigue aside, knowing that these men were chosen, screened, and cleared by Hamas security before he was even contacted.

Hatem motioned toward a chair to invite Arav to sit down, then went on to explain, "First, we need to discuss the plant's security system, including the number of guards per shift. Then we need to know the exact location of the reactor's coolant apparatus control station."

Arav nodded in assent, wrote out the shift information, then marked the location of the control station on one of the diagrams with a highlighter.

"Pinpointing where the video cameras are situated will help," Saideh said while tapping the second diagram. "And if you know the electrical layout of the instrument panels that control the auxiliary generators, that would be a bonus."

Arav mechanically complied while his jaw tightened at the *bonus* word. *This is just a game to these people,* he thought, *a colossal game for Allah ,who promised each of his soldiers an eternity of hedonism for their sacrifices here on earth for the advancement of Islam.* The notion that death and destruction would be the cause of celebration revolted him.

Removing his pen from his shirt pocket, Arav bit his lip as he drew three circles on the first diagram. "Here are your *bonuses,*" he replied perfunctorily with a slight tinge of sarcasm. "The location of the static excitation system, the voltage regulator system, and the generator auto-synchronizing and multifunction monitor."

"We will concentrate on sabotaging the coolant system, my friend," Saideh replied tersely.

Hatem snorted in victory as the deluge of information needed to complete their mission came to them at the hands of a Jew. "Ahh," he said with a luminous smile, "we shall be the very vessels Mohammed uses to bring about his kingdom."

A wave of both fear and guilt washed over Arav at the realization that he undoubtedly would die in the upcoming melee and that he had just sold his soul to Satan out of revenge. He stiffened and said in somber tones, "What is the mission control launch code?"

"Harakat," Hatem replied solemnly as if it were a prelude to a doxology.

"Harakat?" Arav asked in return. He knew Arabic but had never heard the word before.

"*Harakat* is an Arabic word that is not used today," Saideh explained while making a fist. "It is the first word of the acronym for Hamas: *Harakat al-Muqawama al-Islamiyya*, the Islamic Resistance Movement."

Arav nodded as he imbedded the operation launch code in his mind. "When?" he asked numbly.

Hatem pointed upward. "It is not for us to decide, but we have it on the highest authority that it probably will be within the next 24 hours so that all of our information and arrangements stay fresh."

Saideh clasped Arav's hand and said in a conciliatory tone, "Nor do we want to give Israeli security a chance to stop us." His brow furrowed. "We don't have to worry about you, do we? I mean, you're in with us...right...?" Saideh shot a look at Hatem before giving Arav a thumbs-up and then a thumbs-down, waiting for a response.

Arav gave each one of them a long stare, as if to say that the pact had been made. But he refused to shake hands or to engage in a Muslim brotherhood embrace. He only turned to give them a thumbs-up, then walked out.

Apocalyptic thoughts of great magnitude began to fill his mind on the way to his car. *How far could this thing go? All the way?* The specter of a nuclear crisis was something Israel had never experienced, and he wasn't really sure he wanted to be a part of the first one. *Now I am become death, the destroyer of worlds*, he said to himself, quoting the physicist Oppenheimer, who in 1945 quoted the Hindu poet's words after he witnessed the first test explosion of an atomic bomb that he helped build. His thoughts quickly progressed to another nuclear bomb-maker, Edward Teller. He remembered the recent remarks from the famous physicist after he experienced the testing of the hydrogen bomb he helped develop back in the 1950s.

I was at the New Mexico test on 16 July. I was 2 miles away, lying down in the sand with my face turned illegally toward the bomb. I put some suntan lotion on my face and very dark glasses. A spot lit up in the distance. The luminous region spread, more sideways than upwards, then began to rise, and within a minute it reached the atmosphere—with some imagination you could claim that it looked like a question mark—and then the bang arrived half a minute after the explosion. That was when the first atomic bombs were equivalent to about 30,000 tons of TNT, but the bombs now stockpiled are ten times bigger and can blow away the atmosphere into outer space.

The melding of eerie thoughts continued to tumble into Arav's conscience all the way home.

Ze've Ben-Yehuda came out of the shadows and walked toward the open window to remove the flash drive from the digital surveillance camera. He then placed the flash drive into a portable remote facial recognition scanner and pressed the *Search* button. Lighting up an American cigarette, he pulled up a chair to wait for the results. "This should be interesting," he said with a nod to his partner, Nachman Meshel.

Ben-Yehuda, a middle-aged member of the Likud, the right wing political party, had spent fifteen years working for the Israeli General Security Services, the Shin Bet, in their counter-terrorism division, then moved into the Mossad in order to feed his passion of gathering intelligence on those dedicated to the destruction of his homeland.

Meshel, an aspiring 27-year old Mossad agent with a ferocious temperament, had lost both parents in a PLO terrorist bombing while visiting relatives in Ramallah, and had a propensity for violence when it came to Arabs. He'd had to be restrained from using brute force on several occasions when interrogating suspected Hamas collaborators. His V-shaped physique with bulging biceps and a punk hairstyle engendered fear in his adversaries. That made him feel good. "Here it comes now," he said, pointing to the scanner.

"Uh, oh," Ben-Yehuda said as his heart jumped. He leaned over Meshel's shoulder for a closer look at Arav's picture and ID data as it downloaded to the scanner. "We have a real problem. This new player works down at the nuke plant."

For the past three months, their intelligence-gathering network had Hatem and Saideh on their priority list, not knowing where or when they would make their next strike. Then they disappeared for a few weeks, so their standing on the terrorist hot list slipped a little. For Mossad, this meant they were either out of the country or dead since they knew the whereabouts of every insurgent in Gaza. But the inclusion of this man, Arav—a nuclear engineer—raised the stakes considerably, if not exponentially.

Almost one mile west of the Old City of Jerusalem is Zion Square. Always crowded, always frenzied. Zion Square, so named as a rallying place for young Zionists in the 1930s, now hosted the recently relocated Mossad, who sought to be as inconspicuous as possible while integrating into the busy commercial neighborhood it was situated in.

"This is a unwelcome development," Moshe Ravitzky, the director of Mossad, said with rising concern as he pored over Ben-Yehuda's report that included Arav's face print. "Not only does he work at a place that can really hurt us, but he's one of ours."

Ravitzky, at age 57, was a seasoned veteran who had seen it all. After 30 years of hard battle with the leading terrorist groups—the Hezbollah, the Fatah, the Intifada, the Hamas and the al-Qaeda—nothing could surprise him.

"Not really," Meschel noted with a tinge of sarcasm. "He's half-Israeli, half-Arab. His mother is Egyptian, and so is his wife, for that matter." His resentment for the Arabs always seemed to permeate his thinking. He flicked the end of one of the pages of the report in contempt and added, "I guess his worst half won."

Ravitzky refused to engage Meschel in a discussion about the Muslim threat at this time since the political aspect of the Jerusalem End Game, as the Bible scholars called it, was strictly in the hands of God. He remembered the backlash in Jerusalem that had occurred when PLO chairman Yasser Arafat announced at a World Summit in Switzerland his intent to declare a Palestinian state with or without Israel's approval. This brash move only proved that war was inevitable. Ravitzky's only hope was that the war would not involve other Arab states, since that could easily escalate into a major conflict. At this time of his life, he wanted to live long enough to enjoy his grandchildren. For now, he had more important things to worry about. "I will have to inform the prime minister of this before we take any further action," he announced.

"How much time will that take?" Ben-Yehuda said.

Ravitzky knew what Ben-Yehuda feared—that bureaucratic procedure would get in the way of their response.

Ravitzky felt a muscle jerk in his left cheek. With a shrug he said, "With our priority-one clearance, we should get approval to move within twenty-four hours."

Their eyes met as they turned to Meschel.

They were all thinking the same thing: *We pray it's not too late.*

It was 2 A.M. when the phone next to Arav's bed rang. From a restless sleep he wearily picked up the handset to hear an electronic voice say, "Operation Harakat begins in four and one-half hours." Then the line went dead. He looked over at Haleh's bed and observed that she was fast asleep. He shook his head as he stared at her. *Sleep on, my darling. When you awake, the world will be different. Forgive me.*

Despite the early morning light, it was overcast and dismally gray when Arav arrived at the Yeroham NPP parking lot to start his shift. *The day mirrors my mood*, he thought as he stepped out of his car and locked the door. Even at dawn, the lot was one-third filled from the night personnel and security teams.

Headlights blinked twice. *The signal*, he thought as he peered at an old pickup truck parked several rows behind him. *They are in place.*

Once inside and at his station, Arav marked the time. It was 6:15 A.M. "Right on schedule. Fifteen minutes to game time," he whispered to himself. With that he reached into his attaché case, pulled out a flash drive, and inserted it into the mainframe computer access port. He quickly uploaded a virus he'd created that would corrupt the program that controlled the auxiliary electric generator power station. This auxiliary diesel generator and battery reserve system provided emergency backup power to the reactor coolant system pumps in the event of a main electrical failure. If the electrical power to the main reactor core heat removal system was disabled, the auxiliary system that powers the coolant pumps had to be operational to prevent core damage and the release of fissionable material into the atmosphere.

At 6:17 A.M., a red warning light under the Auxiliary Generator indicator flashed on Arav's control board. He knew the Auxiliary Generator was now off-line. He started to perspire profusely. For the next 13 minutes Arav carefully monitored the grid voltage coming from the offsite electrical source, since any drop or disturbance would automatically trip an alarm that would in turn require the auxiliary power station to immediately begin supplying the needed power to the coolant system to maintain safe core temperatures.

When 6:30 A.M. arrived, Arav looked at the surveillance TVs above his head. *All is quiet,* he thought. He scanned his console monitors. *We're okay.*

Suddenly a huge explosion came from the main entrance...then the faint sounds of blast debris striking the roof and cars in the parking lot. Within seconds a siren blared an intermittent signal, then a prerecorded strident voice came over the PA system, repeating every two seconds, "SECURITY BREACH."

A fellow technician watching a security monitor yelled over to Arav, "Nahman, two men with RPGs (Rocket Propelled Grenades), just blasted a hole through the outside wall, killing our security guards!"

"See what's going on!" Arav shouted back.

The technician nodded to Arav and ran out of the control room door toward the main entrance. Arav heard several shots from a semiautomatic gun. "Good-bye my friend," he muttered.

Several more shots sounded in the hallway directly outside the control room before two men, wearing jeans, polo shirts, and baseball caps rounded a doorway corner. He acted totally shocked.

One of the attackers looked up at the ceiling line and fired four rounds from his AK-47 at the security cameras, destroying both of them. He then walked up to Arav and embraced him.

Once Arav knew the security videos were demolished, he returned the embrace with a curt nod. "Good work, Saideh."

"The power plant at Yeroham has been hit!" was all that Ravitzky heard when he picked up the phone at 6:55 A.M.

"Calm down, Meshel!" Ravitzky growled into the handset. "Explain," he soothed. Meshel was not one for details, just action.

Meshel rattled off all known facts. "Two rat-dog Arabs—probably Hamas—fired RPGs into the security wall at Yeroham, killing the guards, then proceeded to execute everyone else in their path. Then they seized the control room!"

"Where are you now, and how were you notified?" Ravitzky asked reflexively.

"I'm at central in Zion Square. We received a desperate phone call on our secure line from one of the guards at the wall seconds before they breached it and shot him dead," Meshel replied with heightening alarm.

"Hostages?" Ravitzky asked, his voice vibrating with intensity.

"I'm not sure."

"Demands?" Ravitzky shot back.

"None, yet."

"Where's our boy, Arav, in all of this?" Ravitzky probed methodically.

"The guard croaked out that he was inside with them—" Meshel stopped to catch his breath then gabbled—"just before they killed him."

"Get Ben-Yehuda and our Response Team down to the plant immediately. I'll notify the prime minister and meet you there as soon as possible," Ravitzky ordered.

As soon as he clicked off he called Prime Minister Zeman, who alerted the Commanding Officer of the Israeli Defense Forces. Then the prime minister notified the director of General Security Forces and gave him an update on the crisis. Zeman ordered both of them to mobilize their forces and converge at Yeroham without delay.

Inside the power plant, Arav pointed Hatem in the direction of the control panel that read *Reactor Coolant Pressure* while Saideh, with his Kalashnikov AK-47, stood watch at the control room entranceway. "We want to send a signal to the authorities to authenticate our threat," Arav instructed Hatem calmly yet resolutely, "so reduce the voltage from the grid to the reactor coolant pumps by 15 percent. This will cause the heat removal motors to slow down and activate the central alarm."

Hatem swallowed hard at the intensity of the moment. "Won't the auxiliary system kick in?"

"I disabled it!" Arav shouted. "Now do it!"

Fifteen minutes later the temperature in the containment vessel reached the boundary limits. That's when the phone inside the control room rang.

Hatem picked up the phone.

"This is Moshe Ravitzky, director of Mossad, speaking. Who is this?"

Hatem smiled in triumph at Saideh. His smile broadened, then he clenched his teeth before yelling into the phone, "This is the voice of Hamas—Palestine's freedom-fighting machine!"

"We purpose to settle this peaceably," Ravitzky said calmly. "We can negotiate your demands."

"Our demands are non-negotiable!" Hatem screamed into the phone, then slammed it down on the cradle.

Ravitzky shook his head as he stood looking into the mouthpiece of his mobile phone once the line went dead. He walked from the mangled guard gate to the field command trailer being set up at the far end of the parking lot. Seeing Ben-Yehuda and Meshel, he motioned for them to get him a cup of coffee and meet him immediately. "This problem is not going to go away too soon," he mumbled to himself.

"What did they say?" Ben-Yehuda asked as he passed Ravitzky a donut to accompany his coffee.

"That their demands are *non*-negotiable," he informed them.

In all of Ravitzky's years of service, he had never heard a terrorist say that before with such finality. This worried him.

Meshel handed Ravitzky a sheet of paper with a hand-written note. "This just came in from Central. The core temperature of the reactor is rising fast. They must have done something to the cooling system to activate the alarm system."

"Oh, great God in heaven!" he exclaimed. "Do we have any nuclear engineers here yet?"

Ben-Yehuda nodded. "They're on their way. They should be here, probably, within 15 minutes." He snorted then added, "We had to pull them from the IDF."

Several moments later Ravitzky's mobile phone rang, and he automatically tensed when he looked at the flashing number. The caller-ID indicated the call came from inside the power plant.

He pressed the *Talk* button. "This is Moshe Ravitzky."

"The time has come for Israel to pay for their crimes," the voice said. "You now know that we control the reactor and can bring the generator to a critical temperature that will bring about fuel rod damage and ultimately release fissionable materials into the air. This will greatly endanger the population."

Ravitzky was not an engineer nor was he a negotiator. His expertise was in terrorist prevention and hostage rescue. But then again, he thought, Israel *is* being held hostage by terrorists. "We will do whatever is necessary to protect our civilians," he placated. "What are your demands?"

"First," the voice stated, "let us set some ground rules. We want to remind you and Zeman that we are prepared to die as martyrs for what we believe, so make no mistake by attempting to rush us or send in any military to abort our mission. It will only end in a bloodbath."

Ravitzky recoiled from the phone at the mere mention by these terrorists of the word *martyr*. His definition of a martyr was one who is willing to die for their religious convictions *without* taking innocent civilians with them. In his mind these terrorists were just murderers, bloodthirsty murderers who cry out, "You must die for what I believe." No, they must pay for their crimes against humanity. "Go on."

Hatem began the demands. "Your government must partition Israel to allow for a Palestinian state that is autonomous—not just in Gaza or the West Bank—allowing us to maintain our own defense force. Jerusalem will be our capital, and your Temple rebuilding project on the Mount must cease. *We* will rebuild our mosque to Allah once we have dominion over the Mount. In addition, we want all Hamas and Fatah prisoners released with a promise of immunity from reprisals..."

Hearing the pause, Ravitzky asked sarcastically, "Is that all?"

"You have 24 hours," the voice replied coldly before the call ended.

Ravitzky walked to the status boards in the command center to survey their present and incoming data. He located a clipboard and wrote out the IDF's nuclear engineer's report for future reference. He lowered his head and murmured, "This is getting serious."

In his mind, the Israeli government would never agree to partition Jerusalem nor allow for a separate Palestinian state alongside them since that would be suicide for Israel. To have an armed enemy living right next door who could easily acquire nuclear weapons despite treaties, and in turn use them without hesitation, would mean certain death for the nation of Israel.

Then there was the Temple. When the Dome of the Rock was destroyed three years ago by Hamas terrorists who bombed the Rabbi's Tunnel under the Mount, the sacred piece of land was reacquired by Israel, who in turn seized the opportunity to rebuild their Temple. To relinquish the Mount at this time to allow Islam to desecrate it with one of their mosques would be nothing short of a traitorous act and downright apostasy in the mind of the biblical patriarchs and every modern Jew on the planet.

There was a tap on Ravitzky's shoulder.

A uniformed soldier from the IDF stood next to him and handed him a portable phone. "It's the prime minister. He wants a threat assessment."

To minimize the potential for escalating concern in the command center, Ravitzky nodded to Ben-Yehuda and Meshel, who were tracking his every movement. They read his body language and realized he needed to be alone.

Walking into a corner of the trailer, Ravitzky gave Zemen his qualified evaluation. "This is no bluff, Mr. Prime Minister," he began. "They do have control of the station, along with the backup generating system needed to power the reactor coolant apparatus. I believe they have sufficient technical ability to cause severe core damage and the release of radioactive materials from the reactor vessel into the air." He cleared his throat before giving his summary statement. "Our entire population is in danger."

"What are their demands, and how much time do we have?"

"They want *everything* they've been butchering our people over!" Ravitzky said in disgust. "And they want it within the next 24 hours." He turned in anger and kicked over a table before repeating the demands to Zeman.

"Just hold your position while I convene an emergency session with the Knesset and confer with America's President Reynolds," Zeman replied with controlled alarm. "I will contact you in four hours."

Terrorism was part of Ravitzky's business as a public servant, but he also knew about politics, especially when it involved his beloved land. He knew very clearly that militant Islam does not hate Americans because of Israel; they hate Israel because of the Americans. They believe that Israel is a representative slice of Western democratic values in the Middle East and their hatred for Western virtues and freedoms causes them to want to destroy Israel. In Ravitzky's mind, he saw Israel strictly as a diversionary tactic to get to the real target, America.

"Mr. Prime Minister," Ravitzky warned, "bringing the U.S. into this will only antagonize the situation and potentially inflame it."

"I agree, Moshe," Zeman replied. "I am only consulting with them at this point. I will talk to you later."

Benjamin Zeman hung up the phone, then reached into his pocket for his antacid pills. He popped two into his mouth and chewed them before swallowing to ensure proper results. His reflux esophagitis condition was worsening by the minute as the drama at Yeroham unfolded.

Ravitzky sank down into the nearest chair to have a conversation with God as Ben-Yehuda and Meshel looked on solicitously.

God, what are we going to do with these Arab terrorists who put a gun to our heads and demand what is not theirs to begin with? You gave this land to our fathers Abraham, Isaac, and Jacob, who handed it down to us for our inheritance. Why do they insist on taking it from us? Why do they insist on destroying Israel with the thinking that we are nothing more than a Western intrusion into the Pan-Arab world? God, we're going to need your help.

His conversational prayer with God was cut short. "Moshe," Ben-Yehuda interrupted, "we are receiving flash traffic from Central that Syria, Iran, and Egypt are at full mobilization!"

Ravitzky jumped up from his chair. *God, didn't you hear my prayer?*

EIGHT

At Tanf, Southeastern Syrian Desert

The great plateau of At Tanf in southeastern Syria is delineated by a mountain range that extends in a northwest and southeast direction, creating a corridor that provides shelter for the petroleum pipelines that crisscross the land to connect the oil fields of Saudi Arabia and Iraq with Mediterranean ports. The At Tanf plateau is broken in the southeast by a series of uplifts that give character to the barren desert and several wadis or watercourses that traverse the plateau, which are dry except in the rainy season. Extreme heat and aridity, ranging in winter from 47-68 degrees F. to the summer with temperatures over 120 degrees F., make up the climate in At Tanf. Although it is not a hospitable location to live, strategically it is one of the ideal locations in the Mideast to establish a staging area to launch an invasion. With minimal satellite surveillance over this desert region and high mountains to shield the buildup of armed forces from the penetrating eyes of radar, At Tanf had been picked by Egyptian, Iranian, and Syrian military advisors to be the place where they would converge and wait for the signal to attack Israel.

Secretly transporting vital military supplies into At Tanf was only part of the problem the Arab commanders had faced over the past three-month period. Keeping over 2,000 tanks and 1,500 heavy guns camouflaged from the snooping eyes of orbiting satellites was a formidable task as well. What represented a significant improvement in warfare that the combined Arab forces prized was the acquisition of their laser weaponry from Russia. Over several years the technology had been procured by Russian scientists from American military interests and in short order made available to their terrorist states.

The American-based Raytheon Company had developed the non-metallic solid-state laser gun as part of their E-System defense program, giving U.S. forces the Patriot missiles used in the Persian Gulf War. The continuous/pulse light beam gun was extremely lightweight and versatile, made of durable carbon and fiberglass, housed in heat resistant plastic. Producing the highest output of all lasers in the laser field, the solid-state laser gun generated a devastating xenon flash tube beam that had been enhanced by multiplying the original laser frequency with crystal-like potassium dihydrogen phosphate. This placed the weapon in the X-ray frequency range, developing sufficient energy to serve as a remarkably effective strategic and tactical piece of military armament. Designed for both offensive and defensive warfare, the weapon was fashioned into side arms, rifles, and broad-beam bazooka-type cannons that could penetrate armor up to three inches thick.

Two divisions of fast-moving mechanized units along with the mobile commandos stationed at At Tanf would be airlifted first to Israel by military transport based in Dumayr, Syria. Using the petroleum pipeline access road at At Tanf as a makeshift airstrip, the Syrian Air Force was set to provide the air cover with their Soviet-built MIG-26s necessary for the invasion. Then two thousand Egyptian light infantry and armored cavalry soldiers would be airlifted on CH-53 class twin rotor transport helicopters. The armaments, together with the 15 divisions from the combined forces of the three Arab-bloc nations would form the massive army needed to annihilate Israel while they were busy marshaling their forces to defend themselves from an impending nuclear disaster.

The coordinated surprise attack on Israel during a nuclear crisis had been developed and masterfully planned one year earlier by Syrian President Abdul Assam and his defense minister, Gamal Hassad, who in turn had recruited the Palestinian Hamas soldiers Anis Hatem and Ahmed Saideh. It was their duty to recruit an Arab-Israeli who would cooperate. Once the defense secretaries of Iran and the Egyptian government secretly approved the plan and the troops and equipment were in place, it was just a matter of waiting for the signal to launch operation *Harakat*.

One hour before the takeover of the Yeroham NPP, the encrypted call to initiate operation *Harakat* was received at the operations headquarters at At Tanf.

Operators at the Golan Heights early warning station using scanner search and tracking radar confirmed the satellite imaging photos that Syrian war planes were launched from At Tanf and heading toward Israel's northern border. Defense Minister Zeev Drori, acting on the authority of Prime Minister Zeman, immediately ordered the 12th fighter wing made up of 24 American-built F-117 interceptors with laser-guided smart bombs located at the heavily guarded Palmachim airbase south of Tel Aviv to scramble and hold defensive positions just outside Syrian airspace. Also from Palmachim, seven Israeli B-4 bombers were dispatched and directed to head toward Damascus and prepare for a counterstrike, while at the same time, the intermediate range ballistic missile [IRBM] base at Zefat, northern Israel, was directed to arm 17 conventional warheads and remain on standby.

Anticipating a major attack by Muslim Arab states that could conceivably be waged on three fronts, Defense Minister Drori ordered the call up of all reservists, both men and women up to age 49, to broaden the base of armed personnel, fearing that this multinational attack could bring devastating casualties. The heavily fortified artillery positions along the Lebanese border were directed to defend the nation against any infantry offensive, should Lebanon decide to join in the invasion. Israel's American-built Apache class attack helicopters not needed at the Yeroham NPP were sent to Jerusalem in order to defend the nation's holy sites. Simultaneously, Israel's armored divisions were divided and sent to protect their southern and western borders against any incursion from Jordan.

Despite Drori's assurance to the prime minister that their vulnerable areas were secured, he recognized that Israel's defenses were very thin and the nation was in great peril.

Inside the NPP, Hatem and Saideh jubilantly celebrated the news that the invasion of Israel had begun. They rejoiced while Arav continued to watch the monitor recording the core temperatures, never letting on that he felt betrayed. He was never told that the attack on the power plant was really a diversionary tactic of a much greater master plan by conspiring Arab nations to invade his country. Being used by Hamas to force Israel to settle on the Palestinian claim for statehood was one thing; being used as a patsy to bring about the destruction of his homeland was quite another.

When Ravitzky heard fighter aircraft overhead, he immediately dropped his network cell phone and ran outside the command center. He was relieved to see a squadron of Israeli jets circling in a wide pattern high above the Yeroham NPP complex. He felt safe, for the moment.

"Moshe! The prime minister is on the phone." Ravitzky turned and ran inside the command center, retrieving his phone from Ben-Yehuda.

"Moshe," Zeman began, "Drori sent a flock of fighter birds to watch over you until you bring this crisis under control. This is the best we can do at this time with our resources being stretched to the max..."

Zeman paused to cough, allowing Ravitzky to interject, "Mr. Prime Minister, what is our present military status and options?"

"Moshe, we're in trouble. I have to admit it," Zeman continued with a slight quiver in his voice. "This scenario is much more ominous than the invasion we faced back in '67 or '73 with the Yom Kippur War because of this nuclear terrorism threat. In addition to what you have there at Yeroham, the Syrians have moved their tank division over our border into the Palestinian-controlled West Bank, heading toward Jerusalem. Their heavy guns are being trucked, as we speak, into Israel through the Jordanian border over to Bet Shan, severely threatening our eastern frontier. We are tracking several military transports out of Dumayr that appear to be heading toward Haifa and Tel-Aviv. Our radar is also tracking what looks like a squadron of fighter jets—probably Syrian—shielding the transports. If they purpose to bring in bombers, we haven't seen them yet. As far as the Iranians and the Egyptian armies are concerned, they are only supplying the infantry at this point. As far as our options go, we can hold our own for a while, but if there are any others that join in, we'll need help."

"What is your estimate of their army?"

"Drori calculates about 15 divisions, and that's without their paratroopers," Zeman replied.

Drawing on his military service, Ravitzky made some quick mental calculations. That would be a minimum of 250,000 troops, including support command, combat battalions, combat engineers and the like. "This is very serious," he said with a gulp.

"What's more, Moshe," Zeman added wearily, "our intel advises us that this is just the beginning. I believe this is going to be a big one that may bring in other major players."

When Zeman sighed, Ravitzky knew the prime minister was calling upon his internal strength and faith that had contributed to his landslide election.

"We are going to need God's help with this," Zeman said, "so let's be strong and call upon Him to remember His people."

Prime Minister Zeman ended the call and walked to the nearest chair. His mind raced to think on his wife and son. *Where are they now?* he wondered. *They must be kept safe.*

He picked up the phone again and ordered the Mossad to

immediately pick up his family and take them to the remote underground shelter/military command center deep in the Yattir mountains northeast of Beer Sheva.

Ravitzky motioned for Meshel and Ben-Yehuda to bring him another cup of coffee.

"What's the situation?" Ben-Yehuda asked Ravitzky while he dunked a donut in his coffee.

After he wiped his mouth, Ravitzky shook his head. "Things don't look good. You'll remember how in the Six Day War of 1967, despite incalculable odds, we beat back the Egyptians to our south, the Jordanians on our eastern border, and the Syrians in the north, all with our army, paratroopers, and air force.

"Then in the Yom Kippur War of '73, when both Egypt and Syria launched coordinated surprise attacks into the Sinai Peninsula and the Golan Heights, thinking they would destroy us if they ambushed us during our holiday, we again defeated them miserably."

He stood up and rubbed his neck as he summed up his thinking with the lament, "I distinctly remember, however, as the war began to turn in our favor, the international community felt the need to embrace our oil-rich Arab neighbors, having no concern for them starting the war. Then the Russians declared a red alert and prepared to send in troops to assist their allies in annihilating us. The Americans then planned to support us until the Russians backed down after the United Nations Security Council pressured us to a cease-fire and to yield to Arab demands. Then the crisis blew over. But this time things are different. Zeman is a hawk and will never give in to Arab demands; he will never agree to give them Jerusalem, but will in fact fight to the last Jew as if this were another Masada. He wholeheartedly agrees with my old friend, Sharon, who made it very clear to the United Nations that they should not try to appease the Arabs at Israel's expense. "

Meshel brightened the discussion with his optimism. "Five times since our statehood in 1948, the Arabs have chosen the military option in attempting to destroy us. But each time they tried to finish us off, they failed."

Tapping his finger on the table Ravitzky replied somberly, "This battle may give them the opportunity to avenge their disgraces."

Zeman stood at his second-floor office window of the Knesset and swallowed down his tea seconds before Defense Minister Drori burst into his room. As soon as Zeman saw his face, he knew the crisis had worsened.

The 50-year old widower never could conceal his fears. "Mr. Prime Minister, the Russians are attacking," he spluttered. "Their attack fighters and heavy personnel transport aircraft have cleared the southern Urals, heading for the Caspian Sea!" He took a breath and exclaimed, "Based on the trajectory and course imaging from our DSP, Defense Support Program, and MEO (Medium Earth Orbit satellites), they will be over Jerusalem in 50 minutes!"

Zeman dropped into the nearest seat and held his hand on his brow. *Lord, is this the invasion your prophets foretold? Is this the time?* "God of Abraham, Isaac and Jacob," he prayed, "save us!" He pointed to his wall map and walked toward it as Drori pulled a wax pencil from his suit jacket pocket. "Show me."

Drori quickly drew arrows on the map indicating the three fronts they were already engaged in, then drew a semi-circle showing the new threat of the Russian invasion force. "I just spoke with Michael Weinstein, the Chief of Staff in charge of the IDF, and his intelligence network just advised him that there was a massive military call-up of Sunni Muslims at Tatarstan (Republic in east central European Russia located in the Volga River valley)—you know, the same Sunnis that make up the majority of the Muslims in the Golan Heights. So, together with their regular army, this looks like a major offensive coming at us."

"Sure, the Russkies call upon Islam to do their dirty work here in Israel," Zeman said in disgust, "just like the Saudis use the PLO to do theirs." He walked to his phone console and pressed the intercom button. Ilana, get President Reynolds on the phone for me." As a hawk, Zeman had an excellent rapport with the America's President Reynolds, considered by most to be both politically and religiously liberal.

"Tell me where you're going with this," Drori entreated.

"We are America's best friend here in the Mideast," Zeman explained. "We are like a 'little America' over here. We have the only democratic nation with a Western civilization and culture, and we can provide the U.S. with the necessary real estate to maintain a military presence in a hostile Arab world—that is not contingent on the purchase of oil. This is the big reason Islam hates us so, and why they hate America more. When you factor in the element that they support us to the tune of $840 million annually in economic aid and $3 billion in military aid, it's almost as if we're their 51st state."

Drori nodded in assent. "But do you think they'll help us now that they're cozy with the Saudis and are trying to kiss up to the Syrians, Jordanians, and the Egyptians? Then add in the Russians, and there's a big question mark." He scratched his head in bewilderment. "I mean, after all, we learned after the notorious September 11, 2001 that any attack by the U.S. on a Muslim nation will bring isolation by Islam. Don't you remember back in '73 that Americans cried out that they need oil, not Jews? And I'm afraid things haven't changed much." Shaking his head, he added ruefully, "In the end, we'll be all alone."

"Yes, yes, I remember America's sentiments," Zeman agreed. "In fact, someone just quoted that slogan to me recently."

Triggered by Drori's comment, Kavidas' face flashed in his mind. *I'm beginning to remember many thoughts of my meeting with Kavidas, as a matter of fact.*

"I also remember Yasser Arafat's *kind* words when speaking for the Arab world: 'Peace for us means the destruction of Israel.' But I believe we can count on the Americans." Zeman put his arm around his defense minister and smiled. "Remember this as well: we have God on *our* side, and with Him, that's a majority."

His aide stuck her head into his office. "Mr. Prime Minister, President Reynolds is on the phone."

After 20 minutes of watching and listening to Zeman detail Israel's emergency status with President Reynolds, Drori began to get the impression that the help the prime minister was asking for would not be forthcoming too soon. It seemed like the only concern the President had was whether Israel would unleash their nuclear arsenal, thereby causing a nuclear exchange nobody wanted. Several minutes later Zeman ended the call with a promise to call Reynolds every hour.

"That sounded to me like we're being let out on the line to dry," Drori observed as his jaw tightened.

After several moments of contemplation, Zeman replied in an apocalyptic tone, "I remember the words of American patriot, John Quincy Adams: 'I studied politics and war that my sons might study mathematics and philosophy, so that their children will study art.' " He rose from his seat and slowly walked to the window as he murmured, "History began here in the Middle East, and it will surely end here."

Seconds later Drori rushed to the window to join Zeman when he heard the rumbling of bomber aircraft overhead.

NINE

Office of the Prime Minister, Jerusalem

Zeman's worst nightmare was rapidly becoming a reality. The sight of four Russian bombers, escorted by six fighter MIG-25s, followed by heavy personnel transports high above the ancient Wailing Wall was an atrocity of unprecedented proportions—a sight his mind refused to accept. He shot a prayer to God in hopes he would intervene and save his nation from the invaders as well as give him the presence of mind to act prudently in the face of disaster when the bombs started to fall.

"Drori, come in here!" he shouted at his door.

Drori bolted into the PM's office with Michael Weinstein following in his wake. "Yes, sir?" Drori asked with eyes blazing and a handful of charts.

"We need to get to our secure location at once!" Zeman directed with finality. "But before we go, give the order for all the F-117s at Yeroham to relocate to the skies here in Jerusalem and do what they can with the Russians, then dispatch the Israeli elite commando units to replace them at Yeroham. We need to breach that stranglehold ASAP so we can concentrate on our other concerns."

"Sir, did you sign the orders?" Weinstein blurted out. Weinstein was one for orders. With the 49-year old having two sons as officers in the IDF, orders were a part of the family life.

Zeman shook his head, then grabbed several official documents off his desk as he hastily departed out of his office with both Drori and Weinstein in tow. It was Weinstein and Drori's responsibility to direct the troop movements, but Israeli protocol required the PM's final signature.

"Done," he said as he signed the order while walking to the elevator that would take them down into the emergency command center chamber well beneath the surface of the Knesset building. Zeman's signature simply validated the war act powers already enacted to immediately mobilize the full 177,000 member military as well as the 433,000 reservists into combat. In his heart, he knew these numbers were not going to be enough this time.

After examining the Arrow anti-missile status boards for several moments, Zeman turned to Drori. "Where have you relocated our mobile SAM (Surface-To-Air Missile) launchers to?"

Both the permanent and mobile SAM launchers would be needed to take out the Syrian and Russian aircraft, but the Arrows would take out any missile threat. In one split-second Drori pinpointed their placements, then turned to Zeman for the command.

"Give the order to launch Arrow missiles when any scud missile is fired upon us," Zeman directed. "When a hard target (aircraft) is in view, use the SAM's!"

Drori and Weinstein nodded, then turned to their subordinates to act on the directives. Once the orders were in place for Israel to take every measure to defend itself, Zeman put his arm on Drori's shoulder, blinked several times, then whispered, "Zeev, how did the Russkies get past our perimeter defenses?" His intention was not to assess blame but to correct the failure.

Drori spun around to answer his superior. Tears glimmered in his eyes as he said, "We are spread too thin, and they know it. They seized upon this opportunity to devour us like a vicious rattlesnake would a wounded bird. For my money, they've been in concert with the Arabs from the beginning, calculating and planning this whole attack. Once our forces were diverted to Yeroham and then to defend our borders from the Arabs, they engaged their heaviest armament to destroy us."

Zeman refused to admit defeat when the battle was just beginning. "Our people have been fighting many 'Goliaths' throughout history, and I claim the promise of David when he said, 'The Lord delivered me from the paw of the lion and the paw of the bear, and he will deliver me from this Philistine giant.' You'll see, Zeev, God will defend us."

As soon as the words left his mouth, six of the Russian heavy personnel carriers strategically dropped to an altitude of 13,000 feet, then opened their rear cargo doors, allowing the Russian paratroopers to jump and rapidly descend into the city of Jerusalem. Gunfire erupted from jubilant Palestinians firing into the air celebrating the sighting, adding confusion to the unfolding drama when Israeli ground forces began shooting at the descending enemy. Zeman was somewhat relieved when the bombers flew out of the Jerusalem area, thinking that at least the historical and archeological monuments would be preserved. Within minutes, however, he heard them drop their payloads over the air bases outside Bet Shemesh to the southwest and Noqdim to the southeast. All Israeli fighter aircraft were aloft, but their landing fields were quickly destroyed.

Once the paratroopers were on the ground, five Russian Mi-26, eight-bladed military transport helicopters, appeared on the horizon and rapidly landed on the Temple Mount. As they were offloading, four Israeli F-117s suddenly dropped out of the sky, locked on their targets, and destroyed all five Russian helicopters with air-to-ground missiles. Follow-up strafing killed off any surviving personnel. Then they took on the Russian MIG-25s. Although the Russian MIGs were superior fighter aircraft, the Israeli pilots were, once again, fighting for their survival, and within eight minutes, all six MIGs were shot down. Simultaneously, the remaining Israeli fighter jets headed south to take on the bombers as they flew out of range of the SAMs. The Israeli pilots left the Russian paratroopers to the IDF ground forces to deal with.

At command central, Drori rushed to Zeman and handed him a phone as he announced, "Colonel Delman on the phone from the Mount. He wants to give you a report."

"This is the prime minister," Zeman said, attempting to control his rising anxiety."What is your situation, Colonel Delman?" Delman was the grandson of Moshe Dayan, the famous general and statesman known for his black eye patch. Delman believed his savage determination to see his homeland survive any Arab conflict to be the direct result of his grandfather's blood that ran hotly in his veins.

"Sir," Delman said fiercely through frantic gulps of air, "the Russians are at the Wall setting up gun emplacements...really digging in while..." his voice faded slightly as gunfire erupted in the background, then suddenly his voice came back strong, "...the Palestinians—mostly Hamas, are all cheering and firing upon our men! It's a massacre!"

Zeman made a command decision. "Pull your men back to a safe position, Colonel, and wait for further orders." The urgency of the situation began to take its toll on Zeman. He motioned to an aide to bring him a glass of water and with the other hand waved Drori over to the status boards. "Where are the Arabs now?"

Drori took out his handkerchief and erased the lines and arrows showing their former positions, then quickly drew new arrows and arcs to reflect their present locations. Emulating great military commanders poised in front of their status boards about to make command decisions, he took out a cigar from his jacket pocket and propped it in his mouth without lighting it and said, "We're being attacked from two sides at present. The Russian infantry are coming in over Lebanon and Syria in the north, the Syrians and Iranians from Syria on our western border, and we're holding our breath, hoping we can hold off the Egyptians from the south."

Quick to appraise events, Zeman nodded, then pointed to the Mediterranean Sea on the western side of the map of Israel. He tapped the push-pins on Tel-Aviv and Haifa. "So far, we're safe here. Obviously, the military targets are their first priority, but it won't be long before they attack our shipping center at Haifa and our capital."

He stepped to another map that depicted the entire Mediterranean basin and carefully surveyed it before asking, "Where is the American Sixth fleet right now?"

Drori gave the nod to Weinstein, who pulled a top-secret document from the U.S. Naval Central Operations Command in Maryland and handed it to Zeman. Then he moved several magnetic markers on the map. "The nuclear-powered aircraft carrier *Harry S. Truman* just passed Gibralter en route to their station off Naples. The rest of this segment of the Atlantic battle group is already on station, performing trial maneuvers off Italy."

It was time for Zeman to see who his friends were. It was time for America to stop straddling the fence between the Arabs and the Israelis and stand with the only democratic nation in the Mideast. It was time for Israel's political friends to recognize that oil wealth has catapulted radical Islam to terrorist states and what was happening to Israel now is what will happen to any other nation that rejects their theology and ideology out of hand. "Put me through to President Reynolds immediately," he ordered. "We're going to need their help if we are to survive."

A messenger handed Drori a sealed envelope marked *Classified.*

"Sir," Drori addressed Zeman after examining the material, "the casualty reports are coming in now."

"And...how bad?" Zeman asked dolefully.

Drori needed to be both diplomatic and sympathetic to his prime minister at a time of crisis. "Our air force is doing well," he began optimistically. "No fighter aircraft have been lost so far and they have taken out five Russian transport helicopters, six fighter MIGs, and two bombers. In our eastern corridor, our fighter jets took on and demolished six Iranian transport helicopters."

He paused and shook his head woefully. "But our IDF ground forces right here at the Wall are taking heavy hits." He consulted the chart in his hand. "We've lost between 250 to 300 men already. The fighting at the Wall is very intense. We're not only dealing with the Russian elite paratrooper forces, but the Hamas now feel they have the opportunity to settle their score and are using every smuggled weapon from the Arab states they have—including those Russian SA-7 Strella anti-aircraft missiles and every Molotov cocktail and every rock they can find to kill Israelis."

"How close are they to seizing the Wall?" Zeman knew that any invader of Israel had to secure the Wall first in order to begin the process of conquest and demoralization of its people. The Wall represented to Israelis what the Statue of Liberty, the Lincoln Memorial, and the World Trade Center meant to Americans. The conquest and subsequent devastation of these heroic sites was tantamount to ripping the heart out of the nation.

"We're reassigning troops from our eastern frontier to help defend the Mount, but that is going to leave us vulnerable against the Syrians. We're not sure we can get them there in time since the Syrian tanks are within five miles of Jerusalem as we speak."

Zeman slammed his fist down on the status board. "Tell the CO at Zefat to launch two IRBMs at military targets inside Syria, and two into Iran at once! They want to play hardball, then that's what they'll get. We will not just lay down and die!"

Drori saw the fury in Zeman's eyes. He looked like a cornered animal looking for an escape route as his eyes darted back and forth between the status boards as they were constantly upgraded every five minutes. A feeling of dread washed over him as he began to see his prime minister take steps to defend his nation that could very well bring an end to all civilization unless God did something soon.

"Sir," Drori replied with eyes pleading for understanding, "are you sure you want to do this?" Drori knew launching four intermediate-range ballistic missiles into Syrian and Iranian airspace would be an irreversible action that would have international consequences.

A tear appeared in Zeman's left eye as he replied in somber tones as if he were reading a divine oracle, "Zeev, our times are in God's hands. We are fighting for our survival. Give the order."

Drori nodded silently and hurriedly stepped to his command console to give the command.

"Mr. Prime Minister," Weinstein shouted as Zeman wiped his eye, "President Reynolds is on the secured line for you."

Zeman paused momentarily before picking up the phone to glance over at the picture on his desk of both him and President John Reynolds embracing at the last summit meeting at Camp David. He remembered discussing the issue of the Arabs taking revenge on both the U.S. and Israel for the disgrace they suffered in the Desert Storm Gulf War. *September 11, 2001 certainly qualified for their retaliation against America,* he thought, *so now it's our turn.* When he thought about the Russians, he figured this would be their way of making up for their failures in Afghanistan as well as making a firm claim on Israel's mineral reserves in the Dead Sea region and their strategic location as a land bridge into Africa.

126

He rubbed his stomach to soothe the ongoing discomfort and determined in his mind to set aside his ruminations for the moment. "John," he began after pressing the speaker phone button, "have you been watching what's happening over here?"

"Bennie," President Reynolds affectionately called him, "we are receiving both intel and satellite reports every fifteen minutes. My staff has already met for an emergency meeting."

Zeman felt a modicum of relief. To know that his only real ally apart from the Brits was monitoring events brought a degree of consolation at this time. "Well, things are really ratcheting up over here, and we may need your help if we are to win this one."

"You can depend on us for any material needs you have," Reynolds allowed. "We have all the equipment you may need at your disposal."

Zeman winced at the thought that Reynolds was saying something else, only he wasn't getting the message. "We may need troop reinforcements if we cannot turn this thing around within the next four hours, and we know that your battle group and nuclear carrier *Truman* is off Italy with your fighter jets being just 30 minutes away." He sighed as the events of the day began to drain him. "If things get dicey over here, can we count on your help?"

A pause of interminable length followed. Finally, almost reluctantly, Reynolds spoke up after clearing his throat. "Bennie, when my staff met, the consensus was that we will take a defensive posture to protect American interests over there in the Mediterranean and supply you with armament if needed, but we cannot cross the line and involve military personnel at this time. To put it plainly, we cannot commit any troops."

Zeman began to perspire profusely. He loosened his necktie, then unbuttoned his shirt collar. "Mr. President," he began sharply, using Reynold's official title to mark the sudden change in their relationship, "let me see if I understand you and your administration correctly. Now that we are asking America to make a choice between right and wrong and help us from being annihilated by these invaders, you are saying that you can only give us material aid—bombs, rockets, and such?"

He raised his voice an octave. "Are you not caving in to the political pressure put upon you by the Arab, petrol-rich countries that you have been attempting to curry favor? Do you not remember Ariel Sharon's words to your Congress that 'Jerusalem belongs to all the Jewish people—we in Israel are only custodians of the city...Jerusalem will remain united under the sovereignty of Israel forever'?" He took a deep breath before uttering, "If our sovereignty is threatened, we *will use* every available means to protect our nation!"

"Bennie," Reynolds scolded, "don't talk like that! We will not stand by and allow your nation to be destroyed. We always have options!"

But what options? Zeman thought. Reynolds' hands were most likely tied by his cabinet and the capricious American sentiment toward Israel. Zeman thought carefully before responding. He knew that American retaliation against terrorism was in fact, really a Christian crusade against Islam, and that Muslim-Americans would always choose loyalty to Islam, but what about the *real American* people?

"Mr. President," Zeman replied, reaffirming his discontent with the decision and the way the conversation was going, "what do the *American* people say about this attack on us? What do your constituents say? Are they for us or against us?"

"Our people are still in shock over the attack," Reynolds replied in lame defense.

"But there are no outcries over the injustices committed against us, are there? All of your Muslim-Americans are like mutes when America or Israel is being attacked, but if we dare defend ourselves by ferreting out an Hamas bomb-making enclave in the West Bank, and kill one of their leaders who authorizes the killing of innocent civilians, the cry of 'foul' is heard throughout the land and broadcast on CNN for weeks."

"This is true, unfortunately, Bennie, but remember, we have a tremendous Muslim population here in the States, and they have a voice as well; that's part of our foundation of freedom."

"Well, then let them stand up and be counted as Americans!" Zeman replied intolerantly. "Before you wind up having the same misguided loyalty problem that we have over here between Israelis and those Arabs who distort ownership claims to the land." Zeman was referring to Islam's claim in the Qur'an that Solomon and David as builders and planners of the Temple were not Jews, but Muslims, and therefore Arabs own the Temple Mount. "And might I ask about your Jewish population? What are they saying?"

This was a real concern that Reynolds had to take care of before his term expired: reviewing the revitalization of American patriotism throughout the ranks of immigrants, especially among the Arab population, who, unlike the Jewish, the Irish, the British, the Europeans, and the Indians, once they acquired citizenship, were as loyal to U.S. interests as native-born Americans. "They are screaming for justice along with the American people," Reynolds placated, "and they will see it, just as soon as we sort out this mess."

This is a stall, Zeman thought, *a colossal "hanging out to dry" until the shooting stops. But by then, it will be too late. Then America will offer their Red Cross to help bury our dead, lest they offend the Arabs.*

Once again, the realization that Israel had to look to God for survival came crashing down upon him. Zeman swallowed hard, resolved to getting as much aid as he could from America. "Mr. President, we probably will need supporting air cover. Can you supply us with a squadron of fighters from the *Truman* if we need them?"

Reynolds was now in a tough place. He couldn't say no to his friend, yet, if he committed his Navy fighters, it was tantamount to aligning the U.S. with Israel against Russia and the Arabs, when it wasn't America's fight. "We will move our battle group to international waters off Tel Aviv immediately," he replied earnestly. "Then we'll watch and see how you make out. Our presence should make a statement. Meanwhile, I will try to muster up support with the Joint Chiefs to give you troops."

It was pure unadulterated bluster, and Zeman knew it. "Our people appreciate anything you can do for us," he said in somber tones as he grit his teeth. "But remember, we have the right to defend ourselves, *and we will do it,* no matter what it takes."

Zeman deliberately omitted any valediction. He simple reached over and pressed the speaker switch to end the call.

In the White House, President Reynolds became increasingly alarmed as he thought on Zeman's words.

"Get Jodi on the phone at Yattir, please," Zeman said to his secretary through his desk phone intercom. It was times like this that he needed to hear a friendly voice, especially from his wife of 37 years, a woman whose keen sense of political and spiritual discernment was irreplaceable when in government office.

The connection to the top-secret location was made within ten seconds, then Jodi was on the phone.

"When are you leaving to get down here?" Jodi asked frantically. "The CO down here advises us that Russian paratroopers together with the Palestinians have seized the Mount, and that it's just a matter of time before they push outward and join up with the Syrian forces and capture all Jerusalem. So you cannot stay there any longer!"

"We're all right for now," Zeman said as the smile on his face from speaking to his wife began to fade. "However, that could change drastically within the next several hours if additional aircraft threaten us." He shot a look over to his family's picture. "Is Marty okay?" Zeman had a great love for his 28-year-old son who had just been diagnosed with Parkinson's disease.

"He's right here with me, Benjamin," Jodi replied, casting her eyes on her son, who stood busily reviewing the incoming military reports from all bases scattered throughout Israel. Then, knowing her husband's mindset, she suddenly realized he made a major omission. "Benjamin," she asked hesitantly, "what's become of the Americans? What did President Reynolds say about helping us?"

Jodi knew that the crisis warranted an immediate response from the U.S., and that both heads of State would have conferred by now.

Fortunately, Jodi could not see her husband's eyes fill up with tears. "He said they can support us with materials—munitions, tanks and the like—but no troops at this time. He cannot get approval from Congress."

Employing the discernment for which she was so well known, Jodi replied. "I'm sure it's because they don't want to 'offend' the Arabs, but remember, darling, our salvation is from God. He has unswervingly demonstrated that, so don't let this setback destroy your outlook. We're praying down here that you will make wise decisions and that we will be delivered, once again, from our oppressors."

Zeman shook his head in dismay. *What a gift!* he thought. *This woman truly edifies at the most crucial times, and is my best friend when I need her.* "I'll call you back within the hour," he said wistfully, then replaced the phone.

Thunderous sounds of RPGs and small-arms fire coming from television monitors receiving a live feed from news journalists inside the Old City arrested his attention. As the video cams panned the area, his eyes darted to the pictures of columns of smoke rising upward from the Temple Mount. On another TV, a real-time broadcast coming from the air base at Palmachim graphically showed the destruction of the tower, runways, and hangers from Syrian MIGs. Zeman shook his head in disgust just before he turned in reflexive alarm when another TV monitor flashed a division of Soviet-built T-272 Syrian tanks barreling down the David haMelekn causeway on their way to the Old City of Jerusalem. Within the hour, enemy forces would surround the city.

"God, help," he muttered. "This is becoming unmanageable."

Both Drori and Weinstein stood watching Zeman from across the room of the command center, waiting for the appropriate time to approach him. They sensed his pain and anguish in the moment. After several minutes, Weinstein nudged Drori and motioned toward Zeman. Then they both walked to him and stood silently at his side, waiting to be recognized. After many years of service to their prime minister, they knew well enough to hold off on any bad news until the appropriate time.

"What's the latest?" Zeman asked as he rolled up his sleeves after the moment of meditation.

Drori and Weinstein traded looks, then Drori waved several status reports. "Mr. Prime Minister, this invasion is rapidly taking on prophetic dimensions," he began methodically. "We have several squadrons of Syrian MIG-26s that entered Ramallah airspace and engaged our fighters, only to have them use their air-to-air missiles and destroy seven of ours. Together with the SA-7 anti-aircraft missiles the Hamas is using against us, our air force is in a desperate state. Then it seems that Jordan has been a part of this, allowing the Russians to use their base at Madaba for their short-range bombers. Our radar counted ten of them on their way to our west coast." He forced a smile and inserted the only positive element in the report. "Our IRBMs and bombers into Syria and Iran have rendered some collateral damage, but nowhere near as much as we're receiving.

"The combined forces are firing salvos of scud missiles into two areas: our IRBM base at Zefat, destroying our capabilities to launch any further missiles, and killing innocent civilians walking the streets of Tiberias near the Sea of Galilee." He paused and nodded to Weinstein, who handed him another report. "Colonel Delman at the Mount said he was waiting to hear from you, but could not hold on any longer, so they have retreated to the Valley of Hinnom outside the city walls." He handed the reports to Zeman and added woefully, "The Russian bombers that did evade our jet fighters are pounding our armored division outside Arad to the south..."

Zeman held up his hand in a halting motion to stop the flow of information. Suddenly Winston Churchill's remark about the reality of war came to mind: *"If you don't look the facts in the face, they have a way of stabbing you in the back."*

"I have made up my mind, gentleman," he said with heightening resolve. "The facts speak for themselves. We are on the brink of annihilation, and I, as your Prime Minister, cannot sit by idly and let it happen. If we cannot kill these giants with conventional 'stones' or weapons, we will resort to the only weapons we have left!"

Drori's hand began to shake as he listened to Zeman pronounce Israel's death sentence. Weinstein simply squeezed his eyes closed in an effort to shut out the unfolding horror.

"Ben-jam-in," Drori stuttered, "I mean, Mr. Prime Minister, are you asking us to prepare our nuclear weapons?"

Clamping his hand down on Drori's shoulder, Zeman replied calmly, "I'll remind you that the Russians have an estimated 2,000 nuclear warheads on high alert on mobile launchers and on top of silo-based SS-18 missiles—not counting their Severodvinsk class nuclear attack submarines fitted with SS-N-24/6 missiles lurking around in international waters that can fire a devastating projectile at any point on the planet, certainly within the capabilities of leveling every city here in Israel. And all but one of the Arab nations engaged in today's attack have thermonuclear weapons as well. Now, what makes you think that if they can invade us without any nation coming to our rescue that they won't hesitate to use *their* nukes to finish us off?

"Now listen carefully. Here is what I am ordering you both to do." Zeman stared at the status boards, then took a deep breath to signal the making of a command decision, knowing that what he was about to order fell within the scope of authority of the three men present. "Direct our secret missile base at the Hever Caves to prepare three ICBMs (Intercontinental Ballistic Missiles) with Multiple Independently-targeted Re-entry Vehicles (MIRVs) with five 10-kiloton thermonuclear warheads each to launch at my command to the following targets: Moscow, Tehran, and Damascus. We will deal with Egypt and Jordan next."

With looks of astonishment that life as they knew it could possibly end before the day was over, Drori and Weinstein stood inert for several seconds. Together they glanced over at the status boards to note the convergence of enemy armies upon their land, then silently turned and walked toward their command stations to set the order in motion.

TEN

Nuclear Power Plant, Yeroham

Outside of Zeman's immediate circle of advisors, Ravitzky was the first to learn that the prime minister had ordered three thermonuclear warheads to be placed on standby, ready to strike selected cities of the invading armies at his command. Drawing on his background knowledge in warfare, Ravitzky realized that there were no winners in a nuclear exchange. Fragmented pictures of the vast devastation wrought by an atomic bomb from his earlier Mossad training courses began to filter through his mind. A vivid collage of the material damage caused by a 10-kiloton bomb gave him heart palpitation when he thought about the horrific event.

An Israeli Defense Department spokesperson had once explained to him what happens when a nuclear bomb is detonated. The vary rapid expansion of the bomb materials produces a high-pressure pulse, or shock wave, that moves suddenly outward, accounting for most of the damage to buildings and other structures. The wind generated by the blast can be greater than hurricane force, often resulting in a tremendous vacuum or backpressure that persists after the wave front has passed. A modest-sized 10-kiloton bomb would level any wood-frame house to a distance of more than one and one-half miles from ground zero. The extremely high temperatures attained in the nuclear explosion brings on an incandescent mass of gas or fireball that would be about 1,000 feet across, while the flash of thermal radiation emitted spreads out in an area roughly equivalent to the fireball. Then firestorms like giant forest fires consume anything flammable while the thermal radiation causes flash burns on exposed skin.

Rapid nuclear radiation, or fallout, that occurs immediately after the blast, consists of neutrons and gamma rays that travel over several square miles and can penetrate solid matter, often contaminating water sources and wind currents that can spread for thousands of miles. Delayed fallout can bring catastrophic global effects on the climate through dust and smoke ascending into the atmosphere that can block off sunlight for several months, killing plant life and bringing on sub-freezing climates until the dust is dispersed. The ozone layer that screens out the sun's ultraviolet rays can also be affected. If these results were prolonged, all human life would perish.

Ravitzky shook his head in disgust. *Enough of this depressing rubbish!* He checked his wristwatch. It was now three hours into the takeover and invasion. He walked outside of the command trailer and stopped to look off into the distance at the power plant, wondering what was going on inside.

With his hand hovering over the red phone with a direct line to Jodi at the Yattir secret military reservation, Zeman carefully pondered his nation's predicament. *Should I allow the carnage to continue, or should I authorize the missile deployment? Should I allow my people to be destroyed? Will I preserve our nation by killing several hundred thousand Russians and Arabs?*

He picked up the phone as Drori and Weinstein started to walk up to him. They needed a decision. He raised his other hand and waved them off for now. *I'm not ready.*

He lowered the phone onto the cradle. "What was it that the French scientist Berchelt pronounced about the apocalyptic future back in 1860?" he whispered to himself. "Oh, yes, I remember now," he continued in monologue. " 'Within a hundred years of physical and chemical science, man will know what the atom is. It is my belief that when science reaches this stage, God will come down with His big ring of keys and will say to humanity: 'Gentlemen, it's closing time.'"

Zeman smiled at the fateful irony, then picked up a nearby lined pad to scribble some notes. He wrote the name *Hamza*, the Iraqi scientist who defected to the West back in 1994, who described Saddam Hussein's nuclear arsenal as nearly complete with their casting furnace and fuse components in place. The explosives and initiator for the nuclear reaction, he also reported, was in place, but they lacked the fissionable material to complete the doomsday bomb at that time. "That was then," Zeman muttered to himself. "And our present intel, along with the info gathered during operation Enduring Freedom, has proven that his nukes were operational. Zeman then wrote out *liar,* when he thought on how successful Hussein was in disguising the nuclear bomb plants from the United Nations Arms inspectors. *How much greater, now,* he shuddered to think, *is the ominous threat from Iran and their neighbors.*

Next he wrote out *counterstrike.* The very idea of nuclear retaliation by his Arab neighbors gave him a chill down his spine. *God, he thought, I would not want to lose any of my people to a nuclear exchange, but I must defend our land.* It was a fact, strangely enough, that the Islamic radicals directing the Arab invasion thought the exact opposite. Their thinking was to blow Israel into the Mediterranean Sea, with absolutely no regard to human life since an Israel counterstrike would cause perhaps millions of Muslim casualties.

Is this not simply a matter of self-defense? His mind was made up. He would give the order.

I need to talk to Jodi, he thought once again, *if only to hear her voice before I sign the E.O.* He lifted the phone a second time.

"Mr. Prime Minister!" Drori said, interrupting his thinking and pointing to another red phone by the status boards. "There's a Gregory Kavidas on our secure phone. He said he is a head of state and that he must talk to you immediately!"

Zeman froze for a moment in time. He had totally forgotten about Kavidas. With his mind filled with the invasion, Kavidas' visit had been squished into the inner recesses of his mind. He scratched his head. *Was it actually only seven days ago?* Suddenly segments of their discussion leaped forward to his memory. *What was that he said about a "storm" coming out of the very nations we have been fighting all along? Was that some kind of warning? a prediction?"*

Zeman rushed to the phone.

"Mr. Prime Minister," Kavidas said numbly before Zeman could utter a word, "please forgive my intrusion at this desperate hour, but I had to convey my concern and offer you my help."

"No, you don't understand, *I* needed to hear from you," Zeman replied, almost apologetically. "I can use whatever help you and the EU can give our nation!"

There was a pause. "What happened to the Americans? Are they going to assist you?"

Zeman glanced over at Drori and Weinstein, pacing back and forth, then did a roundabout in his chair to avoid their piercing stares. "I can't count on them," he said ruefully. "Their battle group is stationed nearby, but they only offered us material support. No forces."

"They are not taking any chances, are they?" Kavidas replied tersely. "Maybe they are hesitant to act until the smoke clears from their last attack on that cruise ship by the al-Qaeda network."

"That could be," Zeman replied, bristling at the thought.

Kavidas was referring to the terrorist attack on a luxury liner out of the port of Miami the month before. The *King Dolphin*, with 2,300 vacationers heading for a Western Caribbean cruise quickly sank in deep water 75 miles west of Key West after a bomb containing about 40 pounds of C4 high explosive blew a 23-foot hole in the bottom of the hull. Only 45 passengers and crew survived. The preliminary U.S. Coast Guard and FBI investigation showed that apparently scuba divers stealthily attached a powerful underwater explosive device magnetically to the metal plating under the engine compartment when the ship was taking on stores while tied up to the pier. Strategically utilizing the powerful force of water pressure, the explosion caused the ship to sink in 30 minutes. To date, the United States had not retaliated.

"The carnage, Mr. Prime Minister, must stop immediately before Israel is destroyed!" Kavidas said with controlled fury.

This man knows the magnitude of our peril, Zeman thought. "You're right, but what can we do? We do not have enough military resources to fight on three fronts—!" He paused to regain his presence of mind. "This is why we must..." he choked up, "...why we must take drastic steps to keep our nation from being annihilated. We will not be driven into the sea without a fight, and we will leave an everlasting testimonial to our pledge that our forefathers made at Masada. If we all have to commit suicide to prevent the enemy from claiming victory, we will do so with honor."

"Mr. Prime Minister, there is no need for another Masada!" Kavidas pleaded.

At last Zeman had arrived at the place where he was ready to wager his nation's survival at any price, Kavidas thought, a glimmer in his eye. *Desperate men don't think rationally.* The prime minister was at the "drop dead" moment to take one last drastic step to protect his land before giving it over to the enemy.

"Let me help your people before you give the final directive," Kavidas told Zeman.

Uncannily he knew that Zeman had decided to order the nuclear strikes that would engulf the entire Mideast and part of Europe in the greatest conflagration ever witnessed by man.

"How?" Zeman asked.

"Just hold off and you will see."

Kavidas hung up the phone.

It was Hatem who first noticed a change in Arav's demeanor. He couldn't quite put his finger on the change, but in his gut he knew something was different. At first it was Arav's unexpected reaction to the news on the plant TV covering the ongoing invasion. There were several facial expressions of unbelief, followed by what seemed to be contained rage. Then there were the leering glances that led to sneers when Saideh spoke to him as he watched the core temperature monitor.

Is he still in with us? Hatem wondered. No, he would not take any chances and trust this Jew who had no principles, who had betrayed his people for a price, who had sold his soul to satisfy a vendetta.

Hatem nodded to himself in confident affirmation of his reasoning, then patted his gun and walked to Arav's station, where he began to study the display housing the vessel coolant controls. He decided he'd better oversee the Jew's every move.

Arav began to perspire heavily the instant Hatem began to stand behind him. His eyes darted back and forth between the coolant vessel controls and the flash drive on the mainframe computer access port. He silently shot a prayer to God, feeling somewhat unworthy, yet penitent enough to ask for help.

"What's going on?!" Hatem yelled out.

Arav knew. There was a flash drive in the USB port, and the auxiliary electric generating power station that provided the emergency backup power to the coolant system pumps was back online. Arav had surreptitiously deleted the computer virus, allowing the reactor core to return to normal.

Without warning Arav spun and kicked Hatem in the groin while grabbing his gun. Hatem groaned in excruciating pain before falling to the floor in a fetal position. In one quick move, Arav immediately clicked off the safety on the AK-47, then pointed it at Hatem and fired two rounds into his chest. Hatem's body convulsed several times, then fell inert. Two seconds later Arav heard Saideh scream from behind, "Arav! Step away from the console!"

Arav immediately assessed his situation as he slowly stood up at Saideh's command. He started to squeeze the trigger on the AK-47 but realized he had no chance of winning against a trained assassin holding a gun at his back. "I must undo this evil," Arav said remorsefully as he lowered the gun to his side while simultaneously inching his other hand to the red alarm button on the console. "I had no idea that my part in this would contribute to a massive invasion of my country," he added with tears streaming down his face.

"Save it for somebody that cares!" Saideh cried out intolerantly as a crazed look came over his face.

"Your people are consumed by hate and driven by rage," Arav said while slowly shaking his head. "To think I willfully agreed to this act that led to the slaughter of my people revolts me. I am ashamed of myself."

"You didn't seem to care about *your people* when you came in with us," Saideh argued, "because in your heart you know, as the Qu'ran says, that Islam is the original religion from which all other religions—including Judaism and Christianity eventually developed! That is why the great Saddam Hussein once said, 'We are on the side of God.'"

Arav snickered. " 'On the side of God'? Are you serious? Do some research, and you'll find that you Palestinian Hamas terrorists learned your tactics from the Nazis! Your one-time leader, Yasser Arafat, on his mother's side, was related to Faisal Husseini, who allied himself with Hitler and planned with the Nazi war machine to exterminate the Jews here in Palestine. So is it any wonder that Islamic law dictates that you terrorists should reclaim land you think you are entitled to through jihad, the killing of Jews?"

"You dirty—!" Saideh breathed as the truth reached his ears. He pointed to the TV screen, displaying the progress of the invasion and yelled, "We now have powerful allies that will help us reach our goal! Jerusalem will be *our capital,* and *we will* reverse Jewish sovereignty over the Temple Mount."

"You are a bunch of fools!" Arav replied sarcastically as he shot a look to the TV screen, then over to the core temperature gauge that was steadily dropping. "Your *friends* the Russians have always strung you Arabs along like puppets. Do you really think they will allow the goal of Islam to rule all mankind to come to fruition? They are simply using you Arabs to accomplish *their goal*—to rid the land of Jews by destroying Israel! That's why over the years they have supplied all the Arab states with arms, so that you guys will do all the dirty work, and then—" he paused and pointed to the TV—"they just come in and mop up. Then they will take control. Watch and see."

"I've heard enough of this tripe," Saideh said in disgust. "Now move away from the console!"

Arav heard Saideh click off the AK-47's safety, so he slammed his hand down on the red button, setting off an ear-splitting siren. Saideh, suddenly disoriented, pivoted in place to locate the loudspeaker as Arav elevated his gun and fired a burst directly at Saideh. Saideh fell against the wall behind him and dropped to the floor with his head drooping to one side.

Seconds later three men in S.W.A.T uniforms from Mossad appeared in the doorway. Arav had the presence of mind to throw the gun to the floor and raise his hands. "It's over!" he yelled at them over the blare of the siren.

The team leader motioned to Arav and shouted, "On the floor!" He quickly obeyed as the team leader ran to him, then kicked the gun out of Arav's reach. Another scrambled to Saideh and placed his hand on his carotid artery. He shook his head. The other S.W.A.T member performed the same duty on Hatem. The team leader then keyed his two-way radio and advised Ravitzky that the terrorists were neutralized and the standoff was over.

Five minutes later, Zeman received the call from Ravitzky that the nuclear power plant at Yeroham was secured. Operation *Harakat* had failed.

At the same time, amidst the embattled zone at the Temple Mount, some 650 meters due east of the Old City of Jerusalem at the top of Har Ha-Zetim, the Mount of Olives, two men with the names Nocham and Qadar stood alone in front of a sycamore tree with outstretched arms to the sky, praising the God of Israel, and invoking his divine intervention into the madness of man.

Thirty-four miles underground, geodynamic frictional pressure suddenly accelerated, reaching the critical stage within minutes, causing the rock strata to fracture, provoking the main tectonic plate of the Afro-Syrian fault line to shift, overlapping the fault plane. The unleashing of the titanic subterranean forces generated massive vibrations on the earth's surface that rapidly gave way to violent tremors, sending seismic jolts emanating from Jerusalem through Israel and into the Mediterranean Sea and beyond. With the epicenter at Jerusalem, the strike-slip produced enormous shock waves that would not abate until the earth's crust convulsed. After several seconds, a major uplifting then rapid falling of the floor of the Ayyalon Valley, northwest of Jerusalem, a giant rift that ran for nearly one mile suddenly cracked open.] Hundreds of yellow plumes of noxious gas began to ascend from the newly formed crevasse and slowly drift toward the city.

Just west of the city, the low-lying earth surrounding Eitan Mountain, with an elevation of 788 meters, began to tremble violently until the ground around the mountain caved in, dropping the mountain into what looked like a huge pit with only half of the mountain protruding outward. To the southeast, Hordus Mountain, soaring some 758 meters into the sky, suffered a similar fate.

From Jerusalem, including Hebron to the south, Tel Aviv to the west, Nablus to the north, and the Jordanian border on the east, giant fissures resembling mammoth chasms in the earth's crust suddenly opened, swallowing the Russian and Arab war machines. From the tanks, heavy guns, and military transports of the Syrian army to the Russian gun emplacements, all evidence of man-made weapons succumbed to the tremendous force radiating from the internal engines deep inside the planet's core. The sustained jerking and quavering of the earth's crust extended over a period of 256 seconds before finally stopping, rendering never-before recorded destruction for over 55 miles in every direction.

Then, from the sky and from the bowels of the earth, came another great indignation.

Swirling black clouds appeared along Israel's coastline on the Mediterranean Sea, seemingly emerging from hundreds of violent vortexes caused by a deep seaquake. The clouds rapidly ascended into the upper atmosphere in what looked like a series of nuclear fallout mushrooms until they accumulated vast amounts of water vapor, then within seconds, the water vapor turned to ice balls.

142

Several miles east of the Mediterranean, natural underground reservoirs in sinkholes that crisscross the land to feed lakes, rivers, and canals, burst forth, pouring pressurized water onto the land in pulsating waves. The releasing of the colossal volumes of water from the giant underground cisterns immediately inundated the areas of conflict surrounding the vicinity of Jerusalem, creating flash floods that overflowed every street, every hill, and every mound of dirt within a radius of ten miles.

"Mr. Prime Minister," Drori shouted at Zeman with his eyes riveted to the TV monitors relaying satellite information into command central, "you must see this!"

Zeman dashed to Drori's side, then started to cry as he watched the screens displaying unchained cataclysms destroying Israel's enemies. Moments later he turned to Weinstein and said, "Get me to the surface immediately. I must see this with my own eyes."

Adjacent to the helicopter pad on the top of the Knesset building, a remote command post with three IDF sentries standing watch provided the ideal observation post for Zeman. Accompanied by two Mossad agents, Zeman, Drori, and Weinstein exited the elevator, then climbed the small staircase inside the armor-plated lookout to see firsthand what devastation had occurred.

Immediately Zeman and his staff noticed the black clouds almost directly overhead. They apparently were settling over certain parts of the city. Then without warning, the insidious cloud layer began to rumble and bellow slowly as rapid-fire lightning strikes shot to the ground. Simultaneously, huge hailstones the size of oranges began dropping like sinkers, crashing through building roofs and cars, leveling all trees and shrubs, targeting the adversary. Zeman grabbed a pair of field glasses from Drori to see firsthand the tragedy unfolding before his eyes. He pointed toward the Temple Mount and yelled out, "Praise God! Any of the Russians or Arabs who escaped the flood are being pelted by tons of hail!"

"What's that smell?" Drori gasped as he held his handkerchief to his face.

"It's some kind of sulfur gas," Weinstein said as he pointed across the city to one of the crevasses opened by the earthquake where yellow smoke continued to ascend as if it were coming from an infernal furnace.

The lightning and thunder, along with the avalanche of ice from the sky intensified until the horizon was no longer visible. Zeman could see the surviving enemy attempting to shield themselves from the onslaught from heaven, but to no avail. Twenty-five minutes later, the assault from nature subsided when a great darkness fell over the land. It was almost as if God had blacked out Earth from his view so he would not have to view the great death and destruction inflicted upon his creation once again.

Then came the cleansing. The tremendous outpouring of underground water, together with the water from the melting of the hailstones, began to return to their subterranean reservoirs, creating a massive ebbing that swept away the blood of the enemies of Israel.

Twenty hours after the cessation of the attack, Zeman convened his cabinet to assess and evaluate Israel's condition. Zeman, along with Drori, Weinstein, and other key staff members sat at his conference table with numerous briefings, charts, and photographs arrayed in the center.

When Zeman stood to address his staff, his eyes filled with tears. "My friends," he began, "we have been spared annihilation!" He pointed upward and continued, "By the mercy of God, we have been delivered from our enemies, only to have them slain in our streets by a loving, yet vengeful God who will not allow his people to be destroyed!"

Dabbing his eyes with a napkin while shaking his head, he added, "I am very grateful to the advisors who exhorted me to hold off on executing the command to fire our thermonuclear weapons into the enemy's homeland. If we had, the devastation throughout the Mideast would have been incalculable."

He lifted a report from the table and went on to say, "The destruction caused by the earthquake was enormous, being greater than any other convulsion of nature ever experienced here in Israel. Seismologists at the Nablus geodetic center have revealed that the earthquake had a magnitude of 8.5, spiking to 9.2 on the Richter scale.

"On the other hand, this calamity greatly contributed to the undoing of the rat-assassins determined to obliterate our people. The quake, along with the other unusual meteorological events, may be explained away by weathermen as 'bizarre,' but they were, in my estimation, nothing short of supernatural, intended to stop our enemies in their tracks."

He gestured out the window to the sun. "It was almost like Joshua's battle against the five Amorite kings at Gibeon. Remember how the Lord slowed the earth's rotation to allow for a longer day so that Joshua's armies could avenge God's people? How the Lord threw the enemy into confusion, then hurled hailstones on them—killing more than by the sword? Yes, it was almost as miraculous as that.

"The important thing I propose to say before I hand the meeting over to Defense Minister Drori for his evaluation of the military outcomes, is that our people are safe once again. While it's true that we have sustained major casualties, our enemies have experienced defeat. As I promised at the outset of these attacks, David has killed the Goliath." He stopped and nodded to Drori to add his report.

The baggy eyes and deeps furrows in Drori's face gave telltale evidence of the strain he'd endured over the past two days. Despite the fatigue, he said happily, "Gentlemen, to put it mildly, we *have* been blessed by a miracle. Even though we have suffered major losses, our land is still *ours*." Reaching for a brief to read off the statistics in order of ascendency, he added, "Our preliminary reports show the following causalities: at the Yeroham NPP, we lost four security guards, one technician. Our air force lost a total of 14 fighter jets with their 24 pilots and navigators. Our missile site at Zefat suffered heavy bombing; we lost 35 men and women there. At the Temple Mount, our IDF lost 475 soldiers. Our civilian losses from the bombings are still coming in, but at last count, there were over 640."

He stopped to pick up another report that recorded the material damage to military equipment and civilian buildings, but as he opened the file, Zeman waved him off. "We can get to that later. Tell us the good stuff—what happened to our enemies."

"It is a fact," Drori continued, "that the PLO/Hamas started this thing on the basis of drawing other Arab nations into the fray—that has been their plan from the start. Then came along 'big brother' to finish us off. But they, once again, forgot who they were dealing with—Israel is on the side of God!" Stopping to point to each of his fellow constituents, he added, "It is now a confirmed fact that terrorism requires sovereign sponsorship, and to prove this, we now have physical proof of what we have been claiming all along, that the Russians and Iranians have been supplying Islamic fundamentalists with military hardware and weapons targeted for our annihilation.

"This is why I am delighted to report to you that the Russian armies and their armaments, together with their paratroopers, the Iranian army contingent, along with most of the PLO/Hamas here in Jerusalem, have been killed. There may be pockets of resistance that we will have to attend to in the future, but for now, the enemy has been defeated. It seems that both the quake and the inundation from the underground water sources created great confusion, bringing many to fire upon their own troops. Whatever enemy equipment has survived can be refurbished and used by our military in the future." He stopped momentarily to retrieve a classified file then went on. "Our initial 'kill' count is Syrian and Iranian forces 437,350; Russian regular and special ops. forces, 28,200."

"What about survivors? POWs?" Weinstein probed.

Drori nodded. "Any survivors along our eastern border have retreated back into their holes in Syria. Any other survivors will be handled humanly according to Geneva Convention guidelines, which is far better than I could say for any of our POWs captured by the Arabs." Dropping the file he concluded, "As far as our IRBMs into Syria and Iran are concerned, satellite images show extensive damage to their military facilities. We assume there are proportionate casualties." Drori then sat down, handing the meeting back to Zeman.

Zeman stood and addressed Weinstein. "I want the IDF and the

Mossad to oversee that any and all Hamas and their PLO subsidies are immediately deported to Lebanon, Iran, or any other Arab country who wants them," he ordered vehemently. "We shall no longer tolerate their existence in this nation!"

Feeling that deportation of Israel's enemies should have been done decades ago, every head nodded in agreement.

Zeman looked over his cabinet members and asked, "Anything further?"

Drori raised his hand. "What do we do with all the dead bodies? The vultures and buzzards are gathering quickly. With our people preoccupied with rebuilding our cities and getting their own lives back in order, we anticipate that it will take at least seven months to bury them."

Zeman walked to his flip maps on a wall stand and selected a metropolitan map of Jerusalem. He pointed to the Kidron Valley, also known as the Valley of Jehoshaphat, situated between Jerusalem and the Mount of Olives. "In ancient times this was both a garbage dump and a burial place for the enemies of God," Zeman said trenchantly. "I think this would be an ideal cemetery for our attackers."

On his way back to his chair he motioned to another member of his staff. "Let's get our unemployed involved in this. We will pay them to bury the dead." He paused to take a poll. "Do we all agree?" Everyone present raised a hand to affirm their consent.

"And the small-arms weapons?" Drori asked wearily.

"What do you mean?" Zeman replied curiously.

"According to Colonel Delman and our other field commanders," Drori noted, "the Arab coalition were using advanced weaponry. The solid-state laser guns seemed to be the firearm of choice, leaving us with several million tons of munitions that we have no use for."

"What do you mean we have no use for them?" Zeman queried.

"Well," Drori explained, "the laser guns by Ratheon were made to be extremely lethal, lightweight, and versatile, but there appears to be one big problem, a glitch they didn't count on—"

Zeman gestured to Drori with his hand to speed up the report. "And that is?"

"They don't work after being submerged in water for an extended period," Drori added with his thumbs-down. "Obviously the electronic circuitry fails once moisture infiltrates the components."

Zeman connected the dots. Made of a mixture of synthetic carbon and fiberglass, the advanced weapon worked well in combat conditions on dry land, but with the flooding, the guns were rendered inoperative and unsalvageable. "So, what do you want to do with them?" Zeman asked with hands raised.

Weinstein raised his hand and suggested in a monotone, "The enemies of Israel have been vanquished. As a token of their defeat and our victory, let's use the worthless carcasses of their weapons to provide our people with heat by shipping them to the electrical generating plants to use for fuel instead of burning oil. There should be enough to provide supplemental electricity for Jerusalem for the next seven years."

Zeman immediately saw the irony in the outcome of the battle. The very thing the Arabs have used for decades to catapult them to world prominence and leverage against the West, oil, has been replaced in Israel, the archenemy of the Arab world, by the very weapons they purposed to destroy God's people with. He raised two fingers in a victory sign and said, "Perfect."

Once in solitude, Zeman carefully ruminated on the past 48 hours that had nearly brought his nation to ruin.

Once again, O Lord, he prayed silently, *You have seen fit to preserve your people, but what vehicle or person did you use? Did the destruction of our enemies come at your hand, O God, or did you send a emissary by the name of Kavidas to intercede for us and bring the calamities upon our adversaries?* The timely resolution at Yeroham, together with supernatural catastrophes that destroyed the invaders, could not be relegated to chance. No, there was some connection with the supernatural...that Zeman was sure of.

ELEVEN

Mount of Olives, Jerusalem

Despite the resplendent sunshine breaking through the array of puffy altocumulus clouds hanging over the city, the fetid reek of death and human spoilage from the plague and war was overpowering. One could only inhale and exhale out of sheer desperation. It was imperative that the corpses of the enemy be removed to the burial site as expediently as possible to avoid contamination of the living. Any Israeli dead would be buried in the cemetery of the Righteous at Peace Forest south of Jerusalem.

"It is an unwelcome sight," Nocham said to Qadar while shaking his head and overlooking the burial crews carting away the bodies.

From their vantage point high up on the Mount of Olives they were able to survey the entire Temple Mount and Kidron Valley area. Bodies, debris, weaponry, and trash lay strewn everywhere. From high ground, the receding water mixed with blood working its way into the crevasses from the earthquake heightened the eeriness of the scene.

Qadar nodded woefully, then pointed his right hand toward the center of the city and cried out, "Destruction has been decreed, overwhelming and righteous. The Lord, the LORD Almighty, will carry out the destruction decreed upon the whole land."

Having made the pronouncement, they began to slowly walk down the mount toward the Knesset building.

Zeman sat on the steps of the Knesset building intently watching his people rally to rebuild their nation. Large contingents of volunteers, along with military personnel, formed a united front to reclaim their land and their heritage from the attacking invaders whom God saw fit to disgrace and humiliate. A great sense of accomplishment and fulfillment came over him as he pondered the words of the old sage who said that man unites when fighting a common enemy.

We will restore our country, making it better than before, he thought with a strengthening resolve. Remembering the words of Emerson, he nodded toward his city and said to himself, *"Every wall is a door."* Any obstacle can be overcome.

Standing up to enter the building, he was suddenly approached by two men who walked up to him and pointed a finger in his face while wailing, "Woe unto you, Prime Minister Zeman, who has made a covenant with the evil one when you should have trusted in the Lord your God! This nation will undergo seven years of testing until they mourn for him whom they have pierced, Yeshua, the Son of God!"

Zeman's mouth dropped in horror as he gawked at the two men before him. They were dressed in hooded garments made of what looked like the coarse sackcloth used for potato bags, each with a leather belt around their waist. Their faces were somewhat obscure, being in shadow by the hood that extended over their heads.

"Who are you?" Zeman asked after swallowing hard. "And what do you want?"

Two seconds later Zeman rotated in place to see members of the IDF security force who guarded him at the doorway of the building with guns drawn. He motioned for them to holster their weapons. "Who are you," he repeated while looking closer at their faces, "and what 'covenant' are you talking about?"

They raised their hands over their heads and in unison gave out what became a loud dirge. "We are the voices of the God of Israel, who has sent us to watch over his people for a time, times, and half a time!"

Then the taller one removed his hood and reached over to clasp his hand on Zeman's shoulder. He peered into his eyes. "We have come to warn God's people. To give you insight and understanding of the judgments to come. Therefore consider the message and understand this declaration: God has determined that the next seven years will bring great cataclysms to the world. There will be seal judgments. There will be trumpet judgments. There will be bowl judgments. Each progressively worsening until God's people, Israel, cry out for the return of their Messiah by saying, 'Blessed is He that comes in the name of the Lord!' " Turning toward the city he raised his arm and with a sweeping motion proclaimed, "The Lord has raised up these enemies to chasten Israel and prepare his people for their Messiah! This battle has come at the hand of God to signal the beginning of his intervention into the lives of men, to seal up the time until the return of the Anointed One."

Zeman glared at the middle-aged man, who was bald, had piercing eyes, and a scraggily beard. He had a black complexion, as if he were of African descent.

"What do you want from me, and what 'covenant' are you talking about?"

The man gave a nod to the shorter man, who removed his hood and answered, "You have angered the Holy One because you have sought protection by covenant with the enemies of God! Hear and understand: 'I have come in my Father's name, and you do not accept me;' the Holy One has said, 'But if someone else comes in his own name, you will accept him.' Yes, you have accepted him!"

Bewildered, confused, and lacking spiritual discernment, Zeman shook his head. "What in the world does that mean?" He turned aside and motioned to the IDF guards behind him to come forward.

The taller man stepped up to Zeman and warned, "Israel must repent of her falsehoods, mourn over her sin and return to the Lord their God!"

With that the two IDF guards grabbed both men by their hoods and started dragging them away from Zeman.

The shorter, stockier man reacted by immediately pulling himself free. Pivoting in place, he raised his hand toward the two IDF men. He pointed to them both, then yelled out, "So that you may believe we have been sent by the Lord of Hosts—!" He stopped to look toward the sky, as if to get permission from God, then stared at them before snarling, "No man will harm us!"

Without warning two steady streams of liquid fire, like napalm, erupted and shot forth from their outstretched hands, igniting the two IDF guards where they stood.

Zeman stumbled backwards, then fell on the ground as flames engulfed what little remained of the guards. "Aargh!" he moaned as he shielded his eyes. Seconds later when he looked again, two small piles of ashes were all that remained of the incinerated bodies. Zeman staggered to his feet and reached out to hold onto the side of the building to steady his wobbling legs. He stood numbed and speechless; his mind seized up in panic.

The stocky, fully bearded one with furrowed eyes ablaze with fury turned and pointed toward Zeman and gave out with a shrill wail, "The Lord has decreed: There will be neither dew nor rain for three and one-half years!"

Having prophesied, slowly and silently the two men walked away into the daylight.

By the time Zeman managed to reach his office, Drori and Weinstein had already heard of the melee. They rushed to his side as he sat at his desk, first checking on his physical condition, then inquiring of his emotional state, recognizing that he didn't respond too well to the incident. At first Zeman simply looked off out the window with a glassy stare, then after a short interval of time he became aware of his surroundings and his accompanying staff. He turned to the two men before him. "What happened—?" he choked out.

Drori fetched a wet washcloth and quickly applied the refreshing therapeutic rub to Zeman's neck. "You were accosted by..." He trailed off, thinking of an appropriate term. "...two weirdos in costume who performed some magic trick like some two-bit circus fire-eaters—"

Zeman shook his head as he began to rally then tapped Drori's arm to interrupt. "What about the guards?"

"Dead," Drori replied grimly as he shot a look to Weinstein. "We reviewed the security videotape. They were incinerated right where they stood."

Shaking his head in disbelief, Zeman slowly rose to his feet as adrenaline swept through his body to meet the new crisis. "What they said," he began with a flinch, "about the invasion and the judgments for seven years, a drought for three and one-half years, was really upsetting and..."

"All nonsense," Weinstein put in with increasing volume, hoping to bring a favorable response from his Prime Minister, who heretofore responded gallantly to any threat that came upon him. "They were nothing less than crackpots." He looked over at Drori for approval. "We have the Mossad looking for them right now. We'll find them and bring them to justice for attempting to assassinate you and for executing the two guards."

Zeman nodded lazily while pondering the event, thinking that procedural guidelines for threatening a head of state should be followed, yet in his heart believing for some unknown reason that they would never be apprehended. "What do you think they meant by a *covenant* and *cataclysms?*" he asked as a chill went down his spine. Then he remembered something else. "And what about their claim that God is preparing his people for the Messiah?"

Both Drori and Weinstein exchanged glances before retiring to the stuffed chairs flanking Zeman's desk.

"My guess," Weinstein postulated, "is that these two idiots decided to take advantage of the frenzied mood pervading our city following the invasion and like any of the other 'doomsday' prognosticators—" he paused to nudge Drori—"and we've had our share of those, haven't we? Those who have predicted judgments, and droughts etc., etc We simply chalk it up to mass hysteria." He formed a summary explanation, then added, "We'll probably have many more of these psychos walking around before the month is out!"

Not convinced by Weinstein's exegesis of the ordeal, Zeman shrugged before turning to Drori for his wisdom and advice. "Zeev, what's your take on this?"

Drori represented the conservative side of Zeman's cabinet, always looking for cause and effect. Taking his position as defense minister as his personal mission in life, he scrutinized every threat to his prime minister or nation from the perspective that Israel has always been the hotbed of radical Judaism, Christianity, and Islamic thinking. This volatile thinking has resulted in Israel being the only nation where more wars have been fought than any other nation in the world. Accordingly he weighed every military action against his people very carefully.

"I'm not sure where this development leaves us," he began. "However, I am of the persuasion that these two characters should be taken as a possible threat to national security. The power they exhibited could be relegated to some bizarre form of pyrotechnics, parlor magic, the demonic, or on the other hand, they could be God's messengers. In that case, we are compelled to listen."

"Do you *really* think there is any credence to their claim that the invasion came *at the hand of God* and that we should expect cataclysms that will prepare us for the Messiah?" Zeman asked incredulously, then added as he scratched his head, "they claim it's all in preparation for the Messiah, whom they called Yeshua or Jesus."

Weinstein shook his head and answered impulsively, "We have been invaded many times over the centuries, and of course we could say that *it was at the hand of God!* History has attested to the truth of the prophets Jeremiah and Daniel, who predicted the Babylonian and Medo-Persian invasion, the Greek invasion, followed by the Roman invasion and occupation. Yet," he pontificated, "were they in preparation for the coming of our Messiah? No! Listen, if this were a genuine fulfillment of prophecy and the coming of the 'real' Messiah, not some imposter like Jesus, then our learned rabbis would have told us."

Weinstein's rationale made sense, bringing a wave of relief to wash over Zeman. But he wiped his brow as other lingering thoughts came into his mind. "What about that babble of 'coming in my Father's name...when someone else comes in his own name, you will accept him.' What do you make of that?"

"It sounds like a quote from the Bible," Drori said while fixing a penetrating stare out the window. "But I wouldn't have a clue as to what it means." Turning to Zeman with a puzzled look he asked, "I'm curious. What do you think that he meant by a 'covenant'?"

Throwing his hands up in the air, Zeman said, "Who knows? Did we sign a 'covenant' with any nation? No! Did either of you men sign any document on my behalf?" They both shook their heads. "So, what we will do," he ordered, "is to alert our law enforcement officials to watch for these two culprits—who should be easy to spot—and arrest them before they commit any further crimes."

Drori and Weinstein construed Zeman's last statement as the prelude to ending the meeting. They exchanged looks as Drori waved to Zeman on their way out the door. "Talk to you later."

Once alone, fragments of the encounter with the two men meandered back into his mind. *I was there*, Zeman thought, *and the fire thing was no trick. How could they have pulled that off, I wonder? And what about cataclysms? That is such a scary word. Cataclysms in Israel come and go, right? What was it my rabbi always said before he quoted Moses in the book of Exodus? Oh, yes, "Israel will always be eternal." Remember Moshie's words now: "But the more they afflicted them, the more they multiplied and grew."*

"Well, if the drought comes," he sighed and whispered to himself, "I'll pay a little more attention to what they said. If not—"

European Union Building, Luxembourg

Adjacent to the 17th-century Gothic Cathedral of Notre Dame at the *Le Republicain Lorrain* Restaurant, Gregory Kavidas sat reading the *Letzebuerger Journal*, the principal daily newspaper of Luxembourg while he waited for Mort Stein to arrive. The German paper, written in Letzeburgesch, gave a fluid account of the invasion of Israel, complete with first-page photographs of the earthquake devastation, the ongoing burial campaign, and vivid pictures of the immobilized war machines being used by Israeli children for playthings. Several interviews with

Israeli officials, along with Prime Minister Zeman's perspective on the invasion graced the second page.

Kavidas carefully read the article on how the *Masterlink* ID/credit system was rapidly replacing the Eurodollar. The article highlighted the Treaty on European Union, known as the Maastricht Treaty, in 1992 as being the forerunner to adapting a common currency for the member nations, yet quickly becoming obsolete from the confusing rate of exchange that undermined the intent of the EU to create a strong bond of identity across national electorates. Having the same currency in 15 member nations made it easier for travelers, but citizens soon tired of the hassle of losing money from purchases out of their country, unless it was put on a credit card. With *Masterlink*, the conversion discount was front-loaded so that the differential in the currency exchange when a foreign purchase was made was applied at point-of-purchase. This catapulted the *Masterlink* network to the number one financial system in Europe.

Kavidas looked up from the newspaper when he heard Stein approaching. Over the years, he'd been able to detect Stein's unmistakable walk, which included a skipping pattern, out of any other pedestrians on the sidewalk. "Good morning, Mort," Kavidas greeted with a nod as he folded up the paper and hailed a passing waiter.

Stein put in his order, then reached over to pick up the paper to glance at the headlines. "The plan is coming together."

"We are right where we need to be in our timetable, Mort," Kavidas replied with a curt nod.

"What's next?" Stein asked as the waiter brought his beverage.

Pointing over to the Cathedral of Notre Dame, Kavidas thought it colorful to mention some of the city's background. "See this town, Mort? This whole area was under German occupation during both World War I and II, bringing Germany in 1942 to proclaim the grand duchy a part of the Third Reich." He paused to clear his throat then whispered, "We aim to finish what the Germans started."

Stein cracked a smile as he thought on the prospects of Kavidas' remark. It was what Hitler called the "final solution"—ridding the earth of all Jews. Yet Stein's conscience remained untroubled because he differed from other Jews in his regard to the Third Reich. While the mere mention of Adolph Hitler and his Nazi party brought revulsion to the Jew, he saw the Reich as achieving a certain purpose in the annals of history. As in times past, whether it be Nebuchadnezzar the Babylonian, Antiochus Epiphanes the Syrian, or the Arabs with their PLO, Hamas, and Hezbollah, God allowed these enemies to antagonize and bring Israel into subjection because, he reasoned, they must have done something very terrible in the past. So in his mind, the treatment of the Jews was deserved. How he would explain these sentiments to his family or other Jews who portrayed him as traitorous was of no concern since nobody but Gregory Kavidas would ever get close enough to discover his true heart.

Discarding the newspaper, Stein turned to Kavidas and asked conspiratorially, "What are we to do with the two *performers* who accosted Zeman?"

Kavidas blinked at the characterization, marveling at Stein's intelligence network that kept him informed of every entity, person, or event that threatened their mission. He pursed his lips and stared at a point in the air as he pondered his answer. The mere fact that the two *performers,* as Stein put it, emerged in Jerusalem right on schedule confirmed the entire players' roles in prophecy. *The line in the sand has been drawn,* Kavidas thought. *It's us against God.*

"I'm not that worried about them this early in the game. Let's leave them be for now, since we have other elements in our equation that must be factored in immediately. Namely, Zeman." Reaching over to pour himself another cup of gourmet coffee, he said calculatingly, "I want you to go to Beirut and initiate the next phase in our program. You will need to make contacts there among the Hamas and Hezbollah who have been deported by Zeman and appoint a leader who will form a counter organization that we will help finance and equip for the day when they can return to Israel. We need this insurgent group to facilitate our cause."

"You mean to employ the same subversive tactics the Arab bloc states used?" Stein queried with a tinge of sarcasm.

"Yes," Kavidas explained. "In time we will need these Arabs to help us bring down the leadership in Israel."

Stein relished the thought of the day when the Israeli

administration would be under Gregory's control. "When will you be leaving for Jerusalem?"

"Tomorrow morning," Kavidas replied. "I plan to meet with Zeman, to feel him out, and determine the next course of action."

They locked eyes, then clasped hands and went their own way.

What Kavidas failed to consider, however, was the truth that the two performers were mounting their own defenses and that their forces included God.

Remembrance is a key theme of modern Judaism, and Jerusalem has ample memorials to testify of the potent events that have irreversibly altered the course of Jewish history. On the western ridge of the city are testimonials commemorating the two most significant, the Holocaust and the creation of Israel: Yad Vashem and Mount Herzl. Yad Vashem is the official memorial to the six million Jews who perished in Nazi-wrought Holocaust in Europe between 1933 and 1945. Mount Herzl pays tribute to the Viennese journalist, Theodor Herzl, who became the founder of the Zionist movement from 1897 to 1904. The Avenue of the Righteous, another vibrant memorial, connects the two.

The Avenue of the Righteous is lined with trees planted in honor of the individual Gentiles who helped Jews at the risk of their own lives during the Nazi regime. It is here that Oskar Shindler and others are remembered for their gallant efforts in preserving Jews from the gas chambers during World War II. It was here that Kavidas asked to meet with Zeman.

Upon arrival at the memorial site, the two newly appointed IDF bodyguards assigned to Zeman, with guns at the ready, meandered off some 20 feet to allow him private conversation with Kavidas. Zeman pushed himself up on one of the retaining walls, sat on his hands and shook his head.

"I'm still in shock over what happened last week," he began in tones that implied Kavidas was now a friend he could consider confiding in. "First the invasion, then the attack by those two hooded freaks—it's enough to give anybody a heart attack."

Kavidas put his hand on Zeman's shoulder and said consolingly, "You've navigated through some troubling waters, that's for sure. That's why I've been so anxious to meet with you, you know, to be with you in a time of need." He turned and looked him in the eyes. "Don't worry about the two *freaks*." Then, as if quoting a divine oracle, he recalled the words of Gamaliel in his advice to the Sanhedrin: " 'Leave these men alone! For if their purpose or activity is of human origin, it will fail. But if it is of God, you will not be able to stop these men; you will find yourself fighting against God.' "

Zeman looked intently at Kavidas, desperately trying to determine his genuineness...if it was real. *Can I truly trust this man, who I believe you, God, may have sent our way?* he prayed.

Yes, he would leave the matter of the two men with God. *Trust this Gentile?*

He was swiftly reminded of a passage in the Christian Bible that he had the occasion to read years ago when he was in college. It was about the Roman centurion stationed in Capernaum during the time of Jesus who had the sick servant and asked the Jewish elders to send this prophet, Jesus, to heal him. The elders reported to Jesus that the centurion was worthy of his attention since *he loves our nation and has built us a synagogue.* When Jesus approached the centurion's house, he was greeted by friends on behalf of the centurion who advised him that he need *only say the word and his servant would be healed.* Jesus then applauded the centurion's faith, claiming that it was rare in Israel. When the centurion returned home, his servant was cured.

Yes, Zeman thought, *Gentiles can be trusted. And like the centurion, Kavidas loves our nation.* "I appreciate that, and you," Zeman replied. "That's why I thought this a fitting place for us to meet, here at the place where Gentiles are honored for their contribution toward the Jewish cause, the survival of our people."

He then returned the gesture and placed his hand on Kavidas' shoulder. "I really believe you would have helped us last week during the invasion if I took you up on your offer."

If you really knew what the master plan was, you would not be thanking me, Kavidas thought to himself. He merely nodded. "We were ready to help out in two ways: first, although our defense force is still in the development stage, we do have a EuroArmy that is comprised of at least three divisions from each of the 15 member nations. These troops could have been deployed to help meet your need over here. Second, the EU does have significant financial leverage in Mideast countries. We were prepared to implement censorship, trade embargos, and travel constraints to Russia and the Arab bloc countries to force them to capitulate."

"Maybe sometime in the future, we may have to call upon the EU to do those very things," Zeman replied optimistically. "But for now, I would like to take you up on your offer to repatriate many of the Jewish residents living in Europe. You see," Zeman went on to explain, "in the invasion, we had many Israelis casualties. What's more, we want to fill the void created by the deaths and deportation of the Hamas and Hezbollah with Jewish settlers." Eyes glistening with tears, the prime minister declared, "We shall *never again* allow the Arabs to possess as much as a parcel of Eretz Israel, the land of Israel!"

Zeman was unable to discern the secret joy that filled Kavidas' heart when the hatred between Jew and Arab became so apparent. Kavidas knew the Bible's clear prediction in Genesis where God said the Arab would be like "a wild donkey of a man; his hand will be against everyone, and he will live in hostility toward all his brothers."

Kavidas smiled internally when he saw the plan coming together. The plan where all nations would come against Israel in the greatest war to come upon the earth. "The EU has already agreed to initiate the repatriation," he said. "So we can begin the process within the next three months."

Diplomacy was only one aspect of politics. Cunning ability to know when to use deception to further one's cause was another. While Kavidas was endowed with this trait from birth, many politicians must wait years to acquire it.

160

Standing up to stretch, Zeman smiled at Kavidas to signal their evolving friendship. "I've been thinking of proposing to our legislature," he said while engaging in good-natured back-slapping and bravado, "that they open a position for you to represent Israel to the Gentile world. Perhaps in the capacity of 'special advisor.' "

He paused to circle Kavidas and regroup his thinking. "I'm very confident that our cabinet would agree that you would be an invaluable asset in our government to stem the tide of anti-Semitism. With your political and financial expertise, not to mention your world acclaim, Israel would stand to gain immensely in the global arena."

Kavidas chuckled to himself as the hand of destiny moved another key member of the chessboard into position toward the inevitable checkmate position. "I am deeply flattered and grateful to you for the offer—" he stopped short and rubbed a tear from his eye—"but I must decline" he argued. "You see, I am committed to the EU to see their role in the marketplace come to fruition. If I were to vacate that position now, I'm afraid their dreams would be dashed."

Taken aback by his response, Zeman modified his appeal. "By joining us, you're making a statement that the EU stands with Israel, and hopefully that will bring other nations full circle to that much-needed mindset. And then there's the God thing."

That caught Kavidas' attention. He shot a look at Zeman, then gazed off into the distance. *The game is getting interesting.* "What does that mean?"

"You know the part in Genesis where God promised Abraham, 'I will bless those who bless you, and whoever curses you I will curse.' Well, you want to be blessed, don't you?"

Kavida cracked a smile to indicate his surrender. "Well, if you put it that way, I would be a fool to go against God, right?"

Zeman nodded with a grin. "Then you'll consider it?"

"Yes, I'll consider it."

On his flight back to Luxembourg, Kavidas outlined how he would gracefully make the transition from the President of the European Parliament to the cabinet position in Israel's Knesset. Once he was installed as a cabinet member, he knew his rise to prominence would be greatly accelerated.

TWELVE

Mount Zion, Jerusalem

ragments of reality, merging with pieces of the unknown, drifted into Paul Douglas' mind. He attempted to grasp the meaning of the unfolding drama, but reason and rationality continued to elude him. The question of his sanity flashed into his mind as he clutched his chest to confirm his breathing.

Yes, I'm still alive, he thought.

Then a collage of his precious family danced into his mind. He immediately recognized his mother, Kathy, and his father, David, and his brother, Alan, his sister, Hillary, along with a scene of himself walking up the stairs to the Jerusalem University, where his father taught Old Testament Biblical Studies.

But then a strange twist of reality occurred. He saw two unidentifiable men in sackcloth searching the city for him. At first, the vivid images of them knocking on doors until they reached his apartment floated toward his consciousness. Then, not finding him home, the two spectral personages departed. He saw them crying out into the night, "Paul Douglas! Paul Douglas!"

Seconds later, closeups of their faces with their haunting eyes appeared before him. One shouted out as he pointed to him, "Paul, the Lord has need of you!"

Paul bolted upright in his bed with his hands shaking uncontrollably, his body writhing and dripping with perspiration.

"What in the world is wrong with you?" he whispered to himself. *A dream*. He reached for his cell phone.

"It's the middle of the night. What's up?" Jonathan said wearily.

With a shake of his head Paul answered, "I had this terrible dream about two men in hooded outfits coming after me. It was really scary!"

"What did they want?" Jonathan, knowing that dreams are often prophetic.

"One of them simply pointed to me and said, 'Paul, the Lord has need of you.' The rest of it didn't make any sense."

"Do you think it had anything to do with the invasion and earthquake?"

Paul nodded in contemplation. "Quite possibly, quite possibly."

Thirty-five minutes later, Paul drove through the Hinnom Valley that leads to the college where his father taught. On the road to the upper plateau of the mount he could see the lush gardens encircling the Mount Zion campus of the college off in the distance. It was times like this that he praised God for His providential hand in shielding him from the ensnaring hand of Kavidas by setting him aside to work for the kingdom. As he neared the stairs of the faculty office of the graduate school, he paused.

Should I be waiting for something to happen? Is this déjà vu? Suddenly a mysterious cloud appeared before his eyes with flashes of light arcing out toward him. He stopped to look into the cloud and saw the exact dream he'd had had the night before being projected within the cloud. He stood mesmerized for what seemed like 15 minutes, but in reality only several seconds transpired.

"Hey, buddy, are you all right?" he heard several voices ask.

He turned to see many students looking curiously at each other. He shook his head, then rubbed his neck momentarily as he face flushed with embarrassment. "Yes, I'm fine." With that the students smiled at one another before rushing past him to their class.

He took one step then heard from behind, "Paul, Paul!" He stopped short, then stiffened as he slowly turned around. In his heart he knew something strange and inexplicable was about to happen.

"I am Qadar," the taller one said as their eyes met. "We have been looking for you."

In rapid succession, the other one spoke in a booming voice, saying, "I am Nocham. You and your companion, Yair, have been appointed to join us in our ministry of judgment, repentance, and preparation for the King."

Qadar stepped forward. "Therefore, bring your companion, Yair, to meet us at the Temple Mount in two days' time."

Paul blinked and they were gone. Vanished. Seized by the terror of the moment, Paul stood motionless as more students ran by him. Instinctively, he turned and slowly walked back to his apartment. He was unable to think clearly the remainder of the day.

Petra, Southern Jordan

When the sentries atop the rose-colored sandstone cliffs heard the roaring sounds of two motorcycle's exhaust pipes resonating off the canyon walls, they immediately called ahead by cell phone to the compound commander and warned of the intruder. The riders approached the lofty perpendicular cliffs that surrounded the ancient city called Sela (which in Greek was *Petra,* meaning "rock") or Bozrah, then stopped at the Ashaft or Sik, the entranceway to the mile-long corridor that leads to the fortress.

Seconds later the cyclists was met by two security guards that immediately recognized them and escorted them through the shadowy winding gorge that provided natural security against would-be invaders.

Once they cleared the narrow passageway leading into the sprawling valley, Paul once again became awestruck by the city's extraordinary beauty and impressiveness.

"Paul!" a voice yelled from across the valley.

Paul and Jonathan propped their bikes up on their kickstand, then rushed to Levi's guardian, Yair. Paul gave him a warm embrace, then held him at arm's length and said with a broad smile, "Yair, this climate really agrees with you! You look terrific!"

Seconds later Levi came running from one of the ancient buildings presently used as a church meeting place, followed by one of his playmates. Paul smiled at Levi, then held out his arms as he ran to him. "My, my," he exulted as he rotated to take a panoramic view of the city, "this *is* a national treasure!"

"Remember me? I'm Jonathan," Jonathan said.

"Of course," Yair replied, "You were with the group that came here right after the disappearance, right?"

Jonathan nodded and pointed to Paul. "We're working together."

Yair smiled. "You're riding motorcycles now?"

"Saves on gas," Paul quipped.

"You're just in time for lunch, 'Uncle' Paul," Levi said as he skipped past them.

"So, what's the important meeting all about?" Yair asked as he began to walk them toward their living quarters in one of the many mobile homes brought in by the Jordanian Bureau of Antiquities. As a Sabra, a native-born Israeli, Yair knew a great deal about Israel's struggles, and was quickly learning about the struggles with Kavidas and Stein.

"Hold on," Paul said, pulling Yair to a halt. "Let me see what's been going on here." Although he had visited the city in the past, he never ceased to marvel at the splendor of the ancient fortress. The ancient stronghold boasted several temples, a 3,000-seat theater, a treasury building, and tombs all hewn with great skill and infinite pains from solid rock, all being preserved over the eons of time from the clawing hands of deterioration.

Yair tugged at Paul's hand to continue in their walk to the trailer. "The Jordanian government renewed our lease as custodians of their monuments here," he began. "So as long as we treat their national park with care, we, as the caretakers, can also use the city for our purposes."

He pointed off in the distance at the village of tents and makeshift shelters used by many Bedouin families that also shared the fortress with them. "Since you were here last, the Bedouin community has increased somewhat." Turning toward the large assemblage of mobile homes on the opposite side of the canyon he added, "Over the past five weeks we have recruited nearly six hundred Jews to both help us here with tourist trade and work the maintenance of the park."

He stopped to whisper in Paul's ear. "And, more importantly, for us to use as a 'pool' for God to draw his 144,000 Jewish evangelists from!" He grinned and poked Paul in his side. "This is our real purpose here, to provide the breeding ground for God's chosen when the time comes."

Paul looked him squarely in the eye. "How is it *you* know of such things?"

Yair smiled. "I started reading the Bible after your last visit, and came to realize where we are in the scheme of things. Frankly, I was very frightened. I guess you could say the Lord scared the 'hell' out of me. That fear brought me to read about Christ the Messiah in the Tanach and soon afterwards I prayed to trust him as my Messiah."

"That's fantastic!" Paul marveled as he embraced him in fellowship. He was beginning to understand why he was told to bring Yair to the mount.

"Strangely enough," Yair continued, "I mentioned it to Levi one morning and he said he already knew it would happen."

Paul looked over at Levi. "Yes, he is showing many signs of a prophet of some kind. Perhaps one of the 144,000. Only we don't know what his calling would be at his age or how it will all happen." Inwardly, Paul could see a divine plan coming together. It was exciting.

"What about your friend?" Yair asked innocently while motioning with his head. "Where is he with the Lord?"

"Um," Paul started, "I'm not sure. I believe he's searching, but the strange thing is..." He paused momentarily once they arrived at the trailer and said as he gave Jonathan a hand signal, "Jonathan, I'll meet you inside." Once Jonathan was out of view Paul added, "Now that you're one of us, I can talk plainly to you about my recent dream and visitation, but I want to share it with the others as well since it includes Jonathan."

"Sounds big," Yair said in wonder. "God is going to do something big, I just know it."

"No doubt the time *has* come for God to move. He is even at the door."

Furnishings inside the mobile home were modest, but the atmosphere and tone of the setting was of God. As Paul looked at Yair and Levi and the way they were getting along in the nurture and admonition of the Lord, he was truly inspired. "God is pleased, Yair. I just know it," he remarked while putting the finishing touches on his dessert and coffee. "Remember, 'he who honors me, I will honor.' You'll see, God will bless your efforts and bring you much fruit of your labors."

Yair was just reading that portion of Scripture in I Samuel. He smiled broadly. "So what brings you here?"

Paul pushed aside the dishes. He looked at his watch, then explained, "About this time yesterday, I was at the college in Jerusalem where my dad taught. Two men in sackcloth suddenly appeared and 'commissioned' me to join them in their ministry of—" he paused to recall their words, " 'judgment, repentance, and preparation for the King.'" He stopped to stand up and hold onto the back of the chair. "This meeting with these two 'men' came the morning after I had a dream of these very men coming to me!

"I have come to the conclusion that these things are very mysterious, if not providential. For instance, they were dressed in biblical clothes with a message of 'judgment, repentance and preparation.' Next, they came immediately following the invasion and subsequent earthquake."

Yair held up his index finger. "Wait one minute," he said and stood up to walk to an end table to grab his Bible. "We know that the invasion was predicted in Ezekiel chapter 38 and that the Russians and their Arab allies would be destroyed by a divine cataclysm—the earthquake." Everyone nodded. "But as far as the two," he asked while thumbing through the Revelation, "did they tell you their names?"

"Yes, Nocham and Qadar," Paul replied curiously.

After a moment of page turning and another of reading in the concordance Yair said, "That figures. The Hebrew meaning of *Nocham* is "repentance" and *Qadar* is "to mourn in sackcloth." Turning to Revelation chapter 11 he read, " 'And I will give power to my two witnesses, and they will prophesy for 1,260 days clothed in sackcloth.'"

Suddenly, everyone at the table exchanged glances, then fell into utter silence.

"Then it's started," Yair intoned. "The time of Jacob's trouble; the seven- year Tribulation period, the unleashing of God's wrath. What has happened in the past week with the removal of peace in the Russian-Arab bloc invasion, then the earthquake, and the hailstones—"

"That's seals number one and two!" Paul interrupted. "As I remember Scripture, that means Nocham and Qadar had to have called down a drought as well."

Everybody nodded slowly as the realization of prophecy being fulfilled before their eyes became so frightening.

As Paul pondered the ramifications of their discovery, he clenched his fist and dropped it on the table. "You realize, of course, this means Kavidas and Stein are now back in the picture, moving the timetable along."

Another momentary hush descended over the group. Then Yair suggested, "Paul, Levi and I have noticed a distinguishable absence of an awareness of God since the invasion. Have you observed any such change up there in Jerusalem?"

Paul rubbed his chin in reflection. "Now that you mention it, I have noticed a kind of lawlessness on the news broadcasts. It's almost as if everybody is doing what they think is right in their own eyes. There's no longer any standards. Wrong seems right. I'm sure there are other signs of the absence, making it harder for us to work."

"This must be part of God's program," Yair ventured. "We will probably see more evidence of his absence now that the Restrainer has been removed."

Jonathan turned to Paul in heightened alarm. "Does this mean the Holy Spirit is gone, Paul?"

Paul shook his head. "No, it can't be. In my limited knowledge of the Bible, I believe if the Holy Spirit were to be removed, there would be no salvation during this period. The Holy Spirit is needed to bring one to repentance—I know that firsthand. No, it means that God's restraining hand on evil has been removed. That means man will now show what his depraved nature is capable of doing, and God will let it happen without restraining him."

Dead silence.

"That's scary," Jonathan said.

Paul scanned their faces. "We have nothing to fear. God will protect us."

They exchanged glances of affirmation.

"Speaking about work," Paul noted with a chuckle to break up the somber tone, "I almost forgot to tell you the best part. Why I came."

"Uh-oh." Yair gulped.

Paul took a deep breath, then put his hand on Yair's shoulder. "Nocham and Qadar told me to bring you to them tomorrow. We are to meet them at the Temple Mount. So I thought this would be a divine opportunity for you to bring Levi to see them."

Yair could feel his palms sweat. He hadn't been in Jerusalem for some time and with the rise of Kavidas and Stein, the specter of conflict was heightened exponentially. He swallowed hard while strengthening his resolve by equating the unfolding adventure to king David fighting Goliath. "When do we leave?"

"As soon as you can get your backpacks together," Paul replied. Yair then nodded to Levi, who headed into his bedroom to assemble his knapsack for travel.

"Yair," Paul spoke just above a whisper and turned to make sure Levi was out of earshot. "Are you prepared for the next seal?"

Yair gestured to Paul that they should leave the trailer before he would answer. Walking erratically in the direction of the Bedouin community, he jerked his thumb over his shoulder and said, "I didn't want to discuss this in front of Levi, but, yes, we're prepared for the famine. In a way we're like Joseph in Genesis. We have been storing canned and dehydrated food in one of the on-site caves for the past three years. Some of the deeper caves are quite cool, providing our 'refrigeration.' We have underground springs that feed the giant cisterns, so even in the drought, we should be okay." He pointed to an area in the northern part of the compound. "We also have plenty of livestock that should give us adequate fresh meat. Once a week several of our men will travel north to Lake Galilee for fish."

"It sounds like you've given this considerable thought and

planning," Paul replied, looking relieved. "Of course you know that our world is headed for some serious troubles, but with God's help, the righteous shall prevail."

"Honestly, it's not my planning, but your dad's," Yair answered. "He's the one who put this plan in place. We'll follow his blueprints and we should be all right. I'm very excited as to what God is going to do...now what about this group *Koinonos* your dad used to talk about? That resistance group formed several years ago back in the States after Kavidas and Stein initiated their attack against him."

"My dad told me we have ten sleeper cells here in Israel—twenty in the U.S." Paul halted in front of one of the ruined bridges. "I'm sure these two men in sackcloth will advise us to mount up our forces, so we've already activated them. The time has come for us to plan our counterattack."

"Good afternoon, Yair," they heard from behind.

When they turned, a big-framed Bedouin holding a shepherd's staff stood at attention.

"Oh, hello, Mibsam," Yair replied with a smile. He put his hand on Paul's shoulder. "This is my friend, Paul Douglas, the son of David and Kathy."

Mibsam Azib, a 24-year-old from a nomadic tribe out of Yemen gave Paul a salute, then shuffled off toward a flock of sheep outside the Bedouin compound.

Yair turned to Paul and said cryptically, "I'm taking a chance telling him who you are since I've known him for a while. I hope he can be trusted. Truthfully, I really don't trust *anyone* outside of our *own* group, so it's better that we exercise caution with our names around here."

Paul nodded in assent, then asked innocently, "These Muslims don't present a threat to you?"

"No. They're harmless gypsies that come and go as the wind blows. We pay them to tend to our livestock and help us with the custodial tasks around here. Besides, they add to the local color when the tourists come." They heard Jonathan calling them back to the mobile home.

Fifteen minutes later Paul and Levi, along with Jonathan and Yair, were riding their motorcycles back to Jerusalem.

The Temple Mount, Jerusalem

It was early morning when they all climbed up the ancient stairway adjacent to the Wailing Wall, then abruptly stopped upon reaching the upper level platform as the nearly completed Temple came into view. They reveled in joy as they gazed upon the remaking of the magnificent structure that Israelites had longed to see for nearly two thousand years. Turning to one side, some of the bulldozed remains of the Dome of the Rock were still visible.

Paul motioned to the rest of the group to follow him into the new construction site to where the northern section of the new sanctuary was being built, the location where the Holy of Holies would be. He pointed down to a massive 12X15-yard rock that has been preserved for centuries. "Supposedly, this is the very rock where Abraham was about to sacrifice his son, Isaac, formerly called the Rock of Moriah, just before the Angel of the Lord commanded him to stop and instead slay a ram caught in a bush. The Muslims have corrupted the Scriptures, claiming it was Ishmael who Abraham was going to sacrifice, all to support the claim that the Mount belongs to them. They also claim that Mohammed ascended to heaven in a night journey from this rock."

Yair and Jonathan had studied some of what Paul had said, while the portion about the Muslim claims was all new to him. "What do they do about the book of Hebrews in the New Testament that authenticates Abraham's offering of Isaac?" Yair asked curiously.

"They do what many others do," Paul explained as he expelled a sigh. "They either deny it or claim that 'God didn't really mean that. This ungodly principle of *eisegesis*, adding to the text, can be applied to just about any truth or doctrine the Bible addresses."

A burst of light flashed in front of them.

Suddenly the light turned into a whirlwind that erupted right before their eyes, sucking all the nearby debris from the construction site into a spiraling vortex that emitted a loud drone. The group fell to the floor, cupping their ears as the vortex accelerated to where it began, dragging some heavy equipment toward it.

"Hold on to something solid and shut your eyes!" Paul shouted above the frightening noise.

Yair couldn't find anything close, so he grabbed hold of Levi's leg with one hand and squeezed his eyes shut. Seconds later, the whirlwind slowed to a stop. When they opened their eyes, Nocham and Qadar stood before them.

Paul was the first to respond. "Y-you can do that," he spluttered frantically, "appear out of a whirlwind?"

"The Lord had given us authority for the next three and a half years to do whatever is necessary to protect his elect while keeping the balance to avoid evil from triumphing," Nocham declared solemnly.

Paul nudged Yair and whispered, "Remember when Philip was teleported over twenty miles from outside Jerusalem to Azotus after witnessing to the Ethiopian eunuch?" He pointed to Nocham and Qadar and added, "They were just 'beamed' in!"

Yair cracked a smile.

Qadar motioned toward the exterior of the Temple. "Please follow us." They proceeded to walk outside the construction site to the adjoining steps of the Temple then stopped. Qadar held up his arms toward the city of Jerusalem and began to weep, then cried out, "O Jerusalem, Jerusalem," he began as if quoting the Most High, "you who kill the prophets and stone those sent to you, how often I have longed to gather your children together, as a hen gathers her chicks under her wings, but you were not willing. Now you will cry for me, but you will not see me until you say, 'Blessed is he who comes in the name of the Lord.' "

Then he turned toward the Mediterranean Sea and continued, "To the world that rejects grace, I can only bring peace through judgment! You are totally darkened and no longer capable of displaying moral judgment! You are not capable of governing by any sense of ethical or moral restraints, but have become characterized by increasing deceit, treachery, merciless cruelty, and a total lack of justice. Therefore, I have removed *my* restraining arm so that your evil may run unabated!" He dropped his arms and took one step back as Nocham stepped forward to add his portion of the divine pronouncement.

"Any nation that rejects God forfeits His protection and invites enemies upon themselves!" Nocham yelled out with intensity. "You have been weighed in the scales and have been found wanting. A quart of wheat for a day's wages, and three quarts of barley for a day's wages, and do not damage the oil and the wine!"

When they finished their announcements, they both turned to Yair and Paul. "You have been appointed by the Lord as Jew and Gentile serving together to join us in our ministry," Qadar said as he lowered his hood. "Call upon your forces therefore and be vigilant to carefully observe the evil forces that are emerging. They intend to bring in their harvest as they see the day approaching."

They turned and walked over to Levi and, with a nod, Nocham said, "My son, your day of anointing is coming." They slowly walked off a short distance, then were gone.

It was several moments before Paul was able to speak to Yair and the others.

"That, my friends," Paul stated tersely, "was our commissioning ceremony!"

Levi looked at Paul. "Uncle Paul, they will be back for me."

"Yes, I know." Indeed, here was added proof that Levi held a special place in God's plan.

"I wonder where that leaves me?" Jonathan asked under his breath.

"Unbelievable." Yair remarked with a shake of the head. They all dusted off the steps they were standing on and sat down. "Quite an indictment against both Israel and the nations. What do you think Qadar meant by his decree?"

Paul started drawing figures in the dust. "I believe they are warning that the next seal, the third one, is going to first bring the prophesied famine and with it bring great economic strain to the world—you know, horrible inflation leading to a severe depression. The other part seems to fit with—" he paused to meditate—"probably something to do with medical care, since Jesus mentions the good Samaritan used both oil and wine when bandaging the robbery victim."

"Hmph," Yair uttered in amazement. "I can see it now. 'There will be famine and earthquakes in various places,' " he quoted, then added other interpretation, "medical insurance premiums for the ongoing hospital and drug care for all the AIDS patients that require treatment for many years will drastically contribute to that new judgment together with the woe of the drought." He shook his head and said wearily, "Things are going to get hairy around here."

Paul snorted in agreement, then looked beyond the city to the horizon. "I remember my dad telling us that when he was in seminary he had to do a research paper on the End Times and recalled reading about C.S. Lewis affirming that 'fear or pain of judgment is God's megaphone to reach a deaf world.' Then he reminded us that Ray Steadman went on to elaborate on the theme:

> Judgments force us to face unpleasant facts about ourselves. Judgment strips away our illusions, they restore us to reality. We plan more carefully; we live more thoughtfully. Judgments humble us. We begin to see that we are not really in control. We do not run everything about our lives. We are not autonomous creatures. We are not little gods, capable of making anything we want to of ourselves, as the media keeps trying to tell us. We are not in charge.
>
> God does not like judgment either. He keeps it as brief as possible. He gives ample warnings before it gets unbearable. He sends anticipations of it, forceful reminders that this kind of thing can happen so that we might pay attention and act before it gets out of hand. God must judge in order to eliminate evil once and for all from his creation.

Yair looked at Paul in amazement. It seemed like Paul's knowledge and memory was growing by leaps and bounds every hour. *It must be a divine thing that God is doing as he raises him up to be a leader.* "You and your dad memorized all that?"

"He would discuss his seminary debates with me," Paul replied. "It was all part of his course work." He chuckled. "We would banter back and forth, so I never forgot it."

With that Paul closed his eyes to reflect on the theme of *judgment* coming upon the earth. He knew in his heart that it was warranted. With America acting as a representative slice of the world's societies, God would have to bring judgment in order to uphold his holy Name. Consistent with a nation in spiritual decline would be the action of

America's Supreme Court that ruled that state-organized prayer was unlawful, then there was the denying of the posting of the Ten Commandments in classrooms and the removal of God from the Pledge of Allegiance. Is it possible that God could bless any nation that indulges in these atrocities? No, Paul affirmed, it is not consistent with His attributes. The erosion of spiritual values had become very apparent over the past three decades where abortion—the throwing of children into the burning yaw of the god Molech—the deliberate sacrificing of the unborn became legal, being funded by tax dollars. Humanist and environmentalist values that dictated the protecting of the life of the snail darter, the sea turtle, and the manatee, while society murdered innocent children, could not be overlooked when judgment came. Defending the rights of groups that promote child pornography on the Internet or upholding the rights of homosexuals citing First Amendment liberties, when this behavior is condemned in both testaments, cannot be overlooked or excused by God.

No, Paul thought, *the judgment is deserved.*

Yair's voice broke him away from his thoughts. "Paul, the work crews are arriving. It's time to go."

"Let's roll."

Beit Hanun, Gaza Strip

Five miles south of the Erez border crossing at Beit Hanun, Naphish Azizim paced the floor nervously as he waited for his new contact. *Life has become increasingly difficult,* the Hamas leader thought, *so we must stay on the move to avoid the house-to-house searches by those Jews.* Azizim was determined to see that his people were vindicated, regardless of how long it took or how many sacrificed their lives to achieve Allah's goal for Islam. *Do not the Ulama (Islamic for "learned") interpret the Jews returning to the land and my people's uprising as fulfilling Muhammad's prophecy, setting the stage for the final battle between Islam and those illegitimate Jewish dogs?*

175

"Yes," he said aloud. This past battle was not the final battle! He raised his fist to mock the God of Israel and with a vengeance cried out, "Your followers—the Jews and Christians—commit acts of terror out of *disobedience*, but we kill in *obedience* to Allah!"

The 28-year-old criminal from Israeli justice checked his weapon for readiness, then shoved it in to his belt for safekeeping. Then he put the rest of his belongings into his overnight bag while cursing the Jews for blowing up his home, killing his fiancé, and forcing him to live as a homeless person. Relegating him to live the life of a fugitive in the underground. *It is only temporary*, he thought to appease his anger. *Then we will return in power and might!*

There was a knock at the door.

Azizim first checked the street below his second floor hideout for IDF or Mossad, then looked through the peephole in the door. It was his contact.

Just to be sure, he pulled out his gun, held it up as he switched off the safety, then slowly opened the door. Spotting the gun, his eager contact took a step back before Azizim recognized him as a Bedouin, then Azizim smiled and pulled him into the apartment. Azizim carefully studied the bullish looking man standing before him, surprised that a member of the nomadic gypsy tribes known for their unkempt and grubby appearance could clean up so well. "You are the Mibsam Azib that called me?" Azizim asked suspiciously.

The enterprising would-be terrorist, mildly intimidated by the gun-wielding professional killer before him nodded sheepishly. "Yes, sir."

"What is it that you have to report?"

THIRTEEN

Tel Aviv

The KLM flight from Luxembourg circled the Tel Aviv airport for over thirty-five minutes before landing. While aloft at 5,500 feet, Kavidas was able to see layers of aircraft stacked in holding patterns waiting for the tower to give them clearance to land. Once on the ground, he realized the heavy air traffic was the outworking of the very repatriation plan he inaugurated. Thousands of European Jews were now relocating and settling in Israel every day.

A black Mercedes Benz sedan blinked its lights at Kavidas as he stepped out of the terminal. Seconds later the vehicle pulled up to the curb, then both the chauffeur and Stein jumped out to greet Kavidas. The chauffeur grabbed Kavidas' luggage, rapidly inserting them into the trunk of the car while Stein opened the rear door for Kavidas.

"Good flight?" Stein asked as he gestured to some disgruntled Europeans hailing cabs to stop yelling at the cabdrivers in Portugese and Greek. They were now in Israel.

"Excellent flight. In fact, things are moving along in an *excellent* fashion," Kavidas chortled. A moment later the Mercedes pulled out into traffic heading for Jerusalem. Kavidas gazed out the one-way window and added, "I'm looking forward to a rewarding stay here in Jerusalem."

Accommodations for Kavidas would be at the expense of the Israeli government, affording him a luxury apartment at Independence Park on Hillel and Agron Streets, reserved for diplomats and heads of state.

With a gesture to the chauffeur, Kavidas pressed the button to close the window partition behind the driver's seat to ensure privacy. "Mort, tell me what you accomplished in Beirut," he said with precision.

"Better than expected," Stein replied trenchantly. "A rogue element of disenfranchised Arabs, mostly Hamas and Hezbollah, were looking for leadership to rebuild their infrastructure to mount their terrorist war to pay back the Jews. They have a real *attitude* and a score to settle. So when I showed up with your checkbook and a plan, they welcomed me like a second Yasser Arafat. It only took me seven days to establish a network of trustworthy persons who are ready to move at my command."

As they neared Jerusalem, flatbed trucks with tarpaulins covering the bodies of the war dead slowed down the traffic to a mere crawl. When Kavidas looked off into the distance, the near-complete Temple stood as an imposing testimony to the fulfillment of Bible prophecy. A fulfilled prophecy that would personally involve him and the nation of Israel over the next three and one-half years. "Good work," he said as he patted Stein's knee. "You being a Jew, tell me how you were able to convince them."

"Very easily," Stein replied with a wide grin. "I simply reminded the leader about David in the Tanack when he ran from Saul and defected to the Philistines. You know, a Jew turning against his own! It's been done before. They only raised their eyebrows and held out their hands. As I started to write out the *expense* check, I told them that I was a Jew in name only." He snorted in a muffled laugh. "They didn't care. As long as the check could be drawn on a EU bank and they could buy their guns and bombs, it didn't matter."

Kavidas nodded. Things were falling into place. "What about the Zeman plan?"

After drawing a deep breath, Stein explained, "The point man in this operation out of Beirut is an Arab by the name of Farouk Abdeel. His father is a Syrian, his mother a Palestinian, born here in Israel. They raised him, in a typical Islamic fashion, to hate Jews. He's perfect for the job. And, best of all, he did security work for Hamas, so he knows all the men close to Zeman as well as all his hiding places. When we're ready, it's a done deal."

For the promise to let the Palestinians back into Israel, Kavidas would get Islamic suicide squads who would do double duty to fulfill

178

their Qur'anic command of jihad. For the payment to buy guns, Kavidas would achieve *his* initial objective, terrorism against the Jews, while the Arabs thought they were achieving theirs, the completion of the Jerusalem Project—the plan adapted back in 2001 to win total Arab Muslim control over Jerusalem. Then, instead of dividing Jerusalem between Jew and Arab and dismantling Jewish settlements, Kavidas would see that Hamas' demands were met in total—to the extent that his long-range plan, the annihilation of the Jew, would be completed. Yes, Kavidas was content with the preliminary negotiations that would lead to his reigning in Jerusalem very soon. "I want to know the details of your plan," Kavidas said after a moment of contemplation. "But I cannot risk any complicity in this. Understood?"

Aware of the serious ramifications that would endanger the master plan, Stein took every precaution to protect Kavidas' anonymity. "I've set up a meeting for tomorrow with the principals at a neutral location," Stein answered with a nod. "You will in no way be implicated or even mentioned for that matter," he assured. "Once the players are in place, I will give you all the details."

Kavidas smiled, then proceeded to look out the window in silence, enjoying the scenery.

Botanical Gardens, New Granot

Stein watched with stirring interest a golden eagle majestically circling above the pine forest just south of Jerusalem, a short distance from where he stood at the Botanical Gardens at Newe Granot. Once the eagle flew out of view, his attention was drawn to the colorful mosaic of lichen upon fallen logs only inches from his feet. Behind the logs were lush and colorful growths of wild oleander and thick groves of myrtle. He looked into the distance and took a deep breath to inhale the smell of nature. He felt exhilarated.

"Mr. Stein?" he heard from behind. He turned to see two men dressed in European clothes approaching him at a rapid pace. Farouk

Abdeel from Beirut, the overweight man with a stump for a left pinky finger, he recognized immediately. The other was an unknown. Stein nodded at Abdeel, then looked with piercing eyes at the other man who had the hardened face of a serial killer and the hands of a stonemason. He looked like a paid assassin. "This is Naphish Azizim, Mr. Stein," Abdeel said. "He is our man here in Gaza. He is well trusted and has been briefed on our operation." He put his arm on Azizim's shoulder and added, "Naphish has a natural instinct, a sixth sense if you will, that tells him when Mossad or IDF is near. He has only been captured once, and vowed never to be captured again."

That combination in a man was perfect for Stein's assignment. Inwardly he was ecstatic whenever he located a man who was willing to die for what he believed in. *In all probability, that is your destiny*, he thought, but didn't say that.

They swapped handshakes as Stein said, "It's good to meet you, Naphish. Are you ready to go to work?"

Azizim responded with a reserved nod.

"Good," Stein said. But before he would review the critical assignment for Azizim, he had to get the expendable stuff out of the way. Turning to Abdeel he asked, "How long before your people will be ready to move to reclaim your place here in Jerusalem?"

"We are fragmented right now," Abdeel explained, "but our spirits are high. We are looking forward to—" he created imaginary quotation marks in the air—"the *resettlement*." Everyone grinned. Then Abdeel summarized, "We calculate four weeks before we can attack, assuming all our munitions and access points are in place."

"Naphish, will you be ready in four weeks?" Stein asked the newcomer.

Another reserved nod.

Stein then asked the critical question. "Naphish, you know who your target is, right?"

Another nod, this time with penetrating eyes.

"You have him marked and the day designated?" Stein probed with increasing irritation. With that, Azizim walked to Stein and handed him a piece of paper with the target's name and the date when he would perform the task.

"Location?" Stein asked, looking askance at Abdeel.

"At a Christian holy site," Abdeel replied.

Stein clapped his hands. "Outstanding choice!" Turning to Azizim, he inquired impatiently, "You're okay with that, Naphish?"

One more nod.

Stein poked Abdeel in the side. "Doesn't this man talk?"

Azizim's eyes bored into Stein's face. After several seconds he said somberly, "When I have something important to say."

Strange people, these Arabs. Always suspicious, always looking for a fight, Stein thought. *Just do your job; that's all I require of you people.* "Impressive," he remarked sarcastically.

Azizim reached over and clasped Stein's arm. "There is something *important* you should know," he began mysteriously.

"What is it?" Stein replied anxiously.

Azizim explained, "I have been in contact with a migrant Bedouin who thought I should know that an American by the name of Paul Douglas came to visit the custodian hired by the Jordanian Bureau of Antiquities at Bozrah. Although he had no idea what it was about, he thought it was unusual and thought the information would be profitable. I like to take care of our people, so I gave him a reward, not knowing the value of the information."

Stein froze when he heard the name *Paul Douglas*. The association with David Douglas meant a great deal to Stein. By extrapolation he made a quick judgment call that Paul was indeed David Douglas' son and no doubt a cunning adversary. "I see. Well, any information about them would be appreciated." Stein then clasped Azizim's arm and said with intensity, "Keep me informed of their every move."

The meeting was over.

Independence Park, Jerusalem

Kavidas' lavish apartment was consistent with political power brokers. Sparing no expense to accommodate the newly appointed special advisor, Zeman made sure Kavidas' needs and wants were fully met—a chauffeur and a full-time housekeeper being part of the benefit package afforded to diplomats. The penthouse apartment boasted of an expansive view of the Old City, and from his vantage point, Kavidas was able to see over the city, clear through to the Mount of Olives. The place where biblical prophecy dictated the Messiah would return...a rendezvous place and appointment he would sooner forget.

"Mr. Kavidas, Mr. Stein to see you," his housekeeper announced as Kavidas stood pensively surveying the panoramic scene before him. It was early morning.

Kavidas waved to the housekeeper, signaling his consent to show Stein in.

Stein, dressed in vacation garb and carrying an attaché case, quickly browsed the apartment, then shot his eyebrows up in approval. "Nice."

Kavidas dismissed the housekeeper. He sat on the leather sofa and placed his feet on the ottoman. "Bring me up to speed on the *Zeman Plan*."

Stein liked the idea of coining the operation. The *Zeman Plan* sounded like a legislative bill that promised some kind of reformation. In a way, Stein thought, the operation would lead to one of the greatest reformations Israel would ever experience. "We will have the elements for the operation in place in four weeks," Stein explained carefully. "We have a point man out of Gaza to handle Zeman, and another out of Beirut to handle the reclamation."

Kavidas simply pursed his lips. "Security?"

"Very tight." Stein replied. "These men are seasoned contractors with heavy credentials. They will disappear into thin air once the mission is accomplished."

Timing is everything, Kavidas reminded himself. Four weeks would place him right where he wanted to be when the *Zeman Plan* was implemented. "Good," he replied, showing his favor. "By the way, do these 'contractors' recognize what we are helping them to achieve?" he asked benevolently.

Knowing that the use of the Arabs to further their purpose would ultimately mean their destruction, Stein assumed Kavidas was simply being sarcastic. "They only think short-term, never long-term. This is why they resort to terrorism rather than peaceful negotiations. Negotiating a settlement would take too long to iron out the issues, so they employ street tactics—force—looking for instant results. So we'll let them enjoy themselves, thinking they're in control of their destiny as they help us fulfill ours, then we'll pull the plug."

Kavidas snorted when he heard that truth. The fact that half of all terrorist groups in the world were united in Islam only underpinned their future hopes for *Khilafah* in Israel, the ideal Islamic state where their religion became pandemic, controlling all. But he knew that would never come to pass as long as he was on the planet. Nor would the dream of Yasser Arafat—that Jerusalem would become a Islamic capital—come to pass. It just was not meant to be.

What will be, Kavidas reminded himself, *is that the Mideast problems will continue to act as a platform for my ministry—the destruction of Israel.* "Agreed," he finally said after a moment of rumination. Then he pushed the ottoman away and clasped his hands. "What about the progression of *Masterlink?*"

Stein reached into his shirt pocket and pulled out what looked like a blank credit card with a black disc the size of an aspirin in the center. On the reverse read *Masterlink, your link to the future!* with a small plastic bubble containing the emollient cream that enabled the skin to absorb the microdisc in a painless fashion within a matter of moments. He proceeded to peel off the disc, placing it on his top of his right hand. Then he simulated breaking the bubble, extracting the cream and rubbing it over the disc. "This is the *Masterlink* microdisc system that is already in use in many places on the globe. It carries the GPS tracking system and the entire medical, credit, and employment information we need to maintain control. Our system is virtually doing away with all cash and check transactions. In fact, we're looking at one year before we go worldwide with the system where no one will want to use any other form of monetary exchange to buy or sell anything."

Kavidas gave him a curious look. "You've put a new spin on it. Very interesting."

Stein grinned. "What we are about to implement in *Masterlink* is far superior to the personal identification number system (PIN), secret access codes used by automatic teller machines already in use. Within three weeks we will activate the hidden asymmetric encryption device in these microdiscs. This method will employ a complex transposition and transformation procedure under the control of a 74-bit key that controls 21 stages of polyalphabetic substitution, each alternating with 20 stages of transpositions. Essential and unique to our security is the long message being totally random and never reused. This is a public key cryptography technique that we developed in Athens over the past two years. This system uses one key for encryption and a different key for decipherment. So when *Masterlink* central receives a message, we are the only ones who can decipher the code.

"This asymmetric encryption system is virtually 'bulletproof,' being secure from all prying eyes except our inner circle at *Masterlink*. It will be used for authentication of nationality for travel, doing away with passports, list any international violations so we can monitor terrorist groups, contain vital information such as the recipient's political party, including who they vote for, their religious preference, confirm or deny credit, and verify electronic signatures for every transaction known to man."

Stein opened his attaché case and pulled out a modern hand-held computer, then waved the computer's wireless scanner over the microdisc to demonstrate its ability. The computer flashed into life, and began to read the sample microdisc containing fictitious information. Stein then pressed a key on the computer and turned the screen for Kavidas to see. "I have selected a racial profile: Mideastern men under the age of 38. Now watch this."

He passed the disc under the scanner and the screen read the microdisc of the fictitious person. Vital information from every government, civil, medical, educational, and financial institution, along with date and place of birth, employment/job classification, criminal and religious history appeared on the screen.

"With this," Stein gloated, "we can access information on every man, woman, and child on earth. We then categorize them any way we want, depending on what screening device we choose."

Kavidas was impressed with the innovative improvement. "And with information comes control," he added with a devilish guffaw.

"Isn't that our objective?"

The housekeeper entered the room. "Mr. Kavidas, are you ready for your coffee now?"

Kavidas waved her on.

"We have a development that requires your attention," Stein began to explain with a degree of reservation. Any group, person, or *glitch* that potentially could jeopardize the mission was looked upon very seriously.

Kavidas' eyes suddenly brightened. "Go on."

Stein set aside the remnant of his chocolate éclair and crossed one leg as he straightened his back. "I have received word through one of my contacts that David Douglas' son has come out of hiding."

Kavidas' demeanor radically changed. He squeezed his eyes shut as if suddenly undergoing flashbacks of the encounters with Douglas, episodes that severely thwarted and nearly brought his mission to failure nearly three years ago. "Here in Israel I presume?"

A curt nod conveyed the answer.

"What do you think he's up to?"

Part of Stein's role and purpose in their relationship was to supply Kavidas with information, be it of a spiritual, military, academic, or commercial nature, and then to integrate that information into biblical prophecy that directly affected their crusade. Then he was to make recommendations to protect their crusade regardless of the costs. "I have a hunch that he is going to join forces with the two *performers* that attacked Zeman, then marshal all their confederates against us."

"We can handle whatever they throw at us," Kavidas replied resolutely with a shake of the shoulders.

Stein felt the hair rise on the back of his neck. In his mind's eye, he projected out three and one-half years into the future, seeing the end result of the two *performers*, but he could not envision what would become of Douglas and his group.

"You're sure?" he asked in a tone that seemed to apologize for his lack of faith.

"You can trust me on this," Kavidas said emphatically. He lied.

Office of the Prime Minister, Jerusalem

The 16-foot-high, silver-plated Menorah, the seven-branched candelabrum opposite the Knesset building, reflected the bright sun directly back into Zeman's eyes. The blazing sun reminded him of the ongoing drought. He turned away from the window and walked to his desk. Seconds later he looked at his two advisors, Drori and Weinstein, and shook his head while holding up a confidential memo. "The month-long drought is getting serious, gentlemen. This report from the national water bureau shows the levels in all fresh water lakes has dropped over 28 percent, and unless we receive rainfall within the next 30 days we risk salt-water intrusion into our water supply from the Mediterranean. At present, the water pressure to the consumer has been reduced 15 percent, and mandatory water restrictions are now in effect. No washing of cars, no lawn watering, etc."

Drori shot his hand up and said impulsively, "The sale of individual water purifiers has skyrocketed. People are taking water from canals, their swimming pools—wherever they can find it, and boiling it for drinking water. Of course the price for any bottled water has quadrupled."

"We do have water in emergency underground reserves hidden in ancient cisterns if needed," Weinstein inserted calmly. "They could supply our nation for at least six months. Then with snowmelt on Mount Herman, we could last another three. But after that, if the drought continues, we'll have to begin desalinizing the Mediterranean."

As serious as the drought could be, Zeman didn't consider it a crisis at this point when the only credibility of the so-called drought fell into the domain of those two crackpots who predicted it. And for that matter, they could have conjured that notion up for all he knew. Time would tell. Zeman then tabled that part of the meeting and lifted another file together with Israel's newspaper, *Maarriv*. "Michael, what's the story on this inflation; it's going through the roof!"

Weinstein was a Rhodes scholar who had a photographic memory.

"Mr. Prime Minister, we thank God he protected us through the invasion," he began optimistically. "But now the bills are coming in for the war damage—military, commercial, residential, etc." His eyes went glassy, and his mouth formed a scowl as if he were reading an obituary column. "Then there's the soaring cost of medical services because of the AIDS epidemic. Together with the medical insurance companies relentlessly passing on the escalating costs to the consumer, the figures are becoming frightening. It's not going away." He shook his head and added grimly, "The price tag of the war is $67 billion so far, with the AIDS problem adding another $1.3 billion this year alone. This has impacted the economy so that the purchase power of our currency is down now to one-eighth of what it used to be." He stood up to fetch himself a glass of water and noted, "If it's any consolation, the AIDS problem is not just here in Israel, it's worldwide."

"At least the cost for electricity to the homeowner has dropped since we've been burning the weapons at the generating plants," Drori mentioned acidly. "Another way of sticking it to the Arabs. Of course they pay us back by blackmailing the world with their control of the oil reserves."

Zeman simply nodded at the influx of information that did not sit well with him. His jaw tightened as he said gruffly, "For the past 2,545 years that separate the destruction of our city to the Babylonians in 586 B.C.E. to our recovery in 1967, over 20 conquerors from various empires have ruled over Jerusalem. I am standing before you to say that no matter what calamities or armed forces confront our nation, we will never surrender." Using the key word *surrender* as a trigger he added, "Winston Churchill once said, 'The greatest advances in human civilization have come when we recovered what we had lost: when we learned the lessons of history.' Well, we have learned plenty since 1967 and we have advanced in quantum measures! Yes, in particular we've learned that anti-Israel sentiment is alive and well, and we cannot depend on any nation to help us in the time of crisis. Some have called it anti-Semitism, but if anybody knows anything at all, then let it be known that anti-Semitism leads to anti-Godism and eventually to anti-Christism! So let the Christians stand up and be counted as well!"

Drori and Weinstein traded looks as their prime minister paused in his venting. "Coffee, sir?" Drori offered.

Zeman immediately recognized his negativity, an indulgence few leaders can enjoy. "Yes, please."

"Mr. Prime Minister, I understand the relocation of the Jewish settlers from Europe is going well," Weinstein said in a lively tone to change the gloomy atmosphere. "The program has much promise and should help the economy in view of the inflation. We'll bring in plenty of EU credits!"

Zeman nodded and replied with fresh vigor, "That reminds me, Michael, we need to bring this *Masterlink* program before the next parliament. If we are to continue to bring in these EU immigrants who are all using this financial system, we need to get on board or we'll lose more money in exchange rates." Zeman reflected on Kavidas' military offer and added, "By the way, with this invasion and earthquake stuff, I did not have an opportunity to tell you gentlemen that this man Kavidas offered to send us EU troops during our war. That, I'll remind you, was more than the Americans were willing to do."

"We owe him," Drori replied.

Weinstein looked intently at Zeman. "We will lend our approval to the Knesset to appoint him as *special advisor* to the Prime Minister."

"I believe that will be in the best interest of our nation, gentlemen," Zeman concluded.

Soon after Zeman met with his advisors he called Kavidas to his office.

At 1:30 P.M. Kavidas arrived at the Knesset building to keep his appointment with Zeman. He was pleased to find that IDF security assigned to the building had been notified of his appointment and permitted him easy access. Once inside, he was escorted by military police to the prime minister's office.

The atmosphere was extremely cordial. Refreshments on a corner table along with Zeman meeting him in a sports shirt signaled a change from an official state of anxiety to a mood suggesting relaxation and approval. Kavidas concluded that his nomination was a done deal.

"My people are very grateful to you, Mr. Kavidas, for all your support during our crisis," Zeman began as he gestured for him to meet him at the refreshment table.

"I appreciate that," Kavidas replied humbly. "I hope to do more for your nation in the future."

Zeman raised his right index finger. "*Our* nation," he corrected. "This is just as much *your* nation as it is ours," he added emphatically. "And in that regard, my advisors and I have agreed to bring the matter of your office of Special Advisor to the Prime Minister before the parliament at our next meeting to be held next Monday. Frankly, it's just a formality."

"It will be an honor to serve under you, Mr. Prime Minister," Kavidas said.

With a wry expression, Zeman observed, "I have noticed that since the thwarted invasion, we have gained a tremendous amount of respect in this hemisphere. Naturally we can attribute it to God vanquishing our enemies, but somehow I must give some credit to you."

In an attempt to be modest, Kavidas replied, "This reminds me of the fear that came upon the enemy at Jericho before Joshua and the Israelites conquered the city."

Zeman snapped his fingers. "That's right! It's just like that now. I've read in my international reports that many rogue or hostile states are thinking twice about their foreign policy toward us. They no longer consider us the 'wimp' on the block. We feel very secure now."

Kavidas was enjoying the interplay. It amused him. "You will see even greater respect in the days ahead," he pronounced as if it were a divine oracle. "Because we have a vast number of European Jews relocating here, thus bolstering up the nation's population, we also have the total resources of the EU at our disposal. So we're in a good position to command admiration."

It had been a long time since Israel received admiration, Zeman realized. He turned toward Kavidas as a puzzled look came over him. "We do have a problem with our economy, however. This is what we need to discuss."

Acting surprised, Kavidas simply responded with, "Oh?"

"Yes, with the price tag of the war and our medical costs constantly rising, we need help. So I'd like you to put together a *Masterlink* feasibility study for me to present to our parliament next week."

Kavidas' heart raced at the prospect of Israel, one of the last vestiges using currency, to finally install his electronic monetary system. In fact, he had to call upon his inner resources to suppress the overwhelming joy he felt at the prospects of such a venture.

It also reminded him that Bible prophecy cannot be altered.

FOURTEEN

Mount Zion, Jerusalem

The amber wing dragonfly hovered over a dry blade of St. Augustine grass, then slowly descended and drooped its wings once it came to rest atop the tall grassy lookout. The dragonfly lingered momentarily before flying off to another clump of grass on the other side of the lawn, only to repeat the cycle in vain.

The observer watched the dragonfly searching for moisture amidst the arid landscape and sighed. *Where have my green grass and colorful garden gone?* he thought. He stooped down on the lawn that once boasted of vibrant growth and ran his fingers through the soil. The green grass had mostly burned up, leaving only patchy knobs in soil mixed with sand and coral dust. He stood up and looked at the palm trees at the edge of his property that had also fallen prey to the drought. Their leaves were brown and limp, their trunks decayed and infested with insects feeding on the dead tree. He shed a tear when he cast his eyes off in the distance as a stray dog lay dying from starvation outside his neighbor's front door. Everywhere he looked, there were signs of drought and barrenness bordering on desolation.

"Paulie," he heard from behind. He turned toward the voice and saw his sister, Hillary, running toward him, holding a small bouquet of dry flowers she had picked from their garden.

He put his arm around her and tried to hide his concerns for what he saw happening to the environment. He realized the weather conditions for the entire earth were radically changing. "What have you got there?" he asked with a smile that spoke of his deep love for his sister.

"Just some flowers I picked from our yard. Do you like them?" she asked curiously.

He looked at his innocent little sister, holding a cluster of desert rose with their colorless stalks and their lifeless petals and shot a prayer to heaven. *Lord, protect her in the days ahead.* "Yes, they are pretty," he said with a tone of resignation.

Then from behind a mosquito flew over Hillary's shoulder and landed on one of the roses. "Aahhh!" Hillary gasped and threw the cluster to the ground. Her brother flounced about, trying to swat the elusive insect, only to see it fly off out of sight. He reached over and embraced his sister to reassure her that he would guard her safety.

Paul stood dazed as he came out of the vision and immediately went into prayer asking God for understanding over what he thought was a terrible foreboding revelation.

"Your vision only confirmed the fragmented reports from America that we've been watching on the TV," Yair noted while they sat down to breakfast. "Having your sister in the vision is simply a fragment left over from your emotions upon realizing that your family was suddenly taken from you to heaven."

"Yes, but to see Hillary and myself in front of our old house in Coral Springs and to see our old neighborhood in a state of desolation was really scary," Paul replied with a shake of the head.

"The mosquito?" Jonathan asked. "Why such a violent reaction?" Jonathan had an insatiable quest for information. His inquisitive nature constantly sought facts and figures.

"It can only mean that insects like mosquitoes and ticks that carry the AIDS virus have mutated once again," Yair noted with increasing alarm. "Naturally, they not only bite humans, but they also bite animals and birds, bringing AIDS to the animal kingdom."

With a nod Paul agreed. "Which would lead to a more potent strain. We've known for some time that the virus could be transmitted by insects, but this seems to point to the fact that the virus has become biologically integrated into the bug indefinitely, being excreted during

192

further blood-sucking meals. This makes it much more difficult to get rid of them, because the bug goes from one person or animal to another. That makes the virus almost impossible to eradicate."

Paul remembered various accounts when they lived in Florida, where health officials were hesitant to declare the truth that mosquitoes with the AIDS virus were showing up more frequently in random tests and that they showed signs of immunity to insecticides. The mosquitoes that once carried the West Nile virus transmuted during the epidemic were now carrying the virulent AIDS virus unchecked. The fact that the AIDS virus continued to mutate made it extremely difficult to find a vaccine. The specter of animals carrying AIDS and how that would impact the food chain was almost too unbearable to contemplate.

"What prophetic implications do you see?" Yair asked.

Paul pulled out his pocket Bible and turned to Revelation chapter nine. "It seems this is symptomatic of a greater problem that will continue to the end of the age—until Christ returns. Listen to this verse: 'Nor did they repent of their murders, their magic arts, their sexual immorality or their thefts.' This prophecy, which occurs during the period in which we are now living, shows there is a continuous rise in frequency of these sins, especially homosexuality—without any sign of repentance—and accordingly, God is bringing greater judgments on the world until mankind gets the message."

A full-scale discussion mushroomed when Jonathan commented on Paul's vision. "Doesn't the cost of the drugs to treat AIDS have anything to do with the spiraling inflation?"

Paul looked at his friend Jonathan with admiration. He had recently discussed that very issue with his father only weeks before the disappearance. "Yes, in Revelation 6, there's a verse that scholars believe refers to what was then future medical care costs and is now present with us. I'm confident that AIDS-related diseases are partly to blame for the expensive medical insurance and drug prescriptions that have led to the extremely high cost of living."

"Does that mean we won't be able to eat?" Jonathan asked inquisitively.

Paul came to realize that the plagues of drought, famine, and the

AIDS epidemic would lead into the next judgment, death. The famine would be a cause of much of the deaths. But he didn't have the heart to explain that to his friend now. "Our God has promised to provide all of our needs according to his riches in Christ, so don't you worry about eating. God will see that we are fed just as he fed Elijah during the famine. You'll see."

When Jonathan left the table, Paul motioned Yair aside for a meeting, leaving Jonathan with Levi.

"Your ongoing visions appear to be in keeping with the prophecy in Joel 2," Yair remarked.

"You mean where it says, 'your young men will dream visions,' " Paul replied with a broad grin as he poked Yair in the side. " 'And your old men will have dreams, right?'" Paul reveled in his heart that the alchemy between him and Yair was quickly resembling a modern version of Paul and Timothy. An important element during times of tribulation.

"Something like that," Yair replied lightly.

"When your visions come, we will celebrate," Paul shot back with a sobering tone.

Paul hadn't thought about the rest of the prophecy that said, "Your young men will see visions." There was a distinction between dreams and visions. Dreams occur during sleep, while visions most often occur during waking hours. "Yes, I guess I had better watch out while I'm driving since I could suddenly have a vision and cause an accident."

"Well, we'll trust the Lord on that one." Yair clucked approvingly.

The Douglas apartment was an ideal place to organize their strategy. While Jonathan worked part-time in the college library across the Kidron Valley, Simon worked on his BA degree in archeology at the

Hebrew University just three miles away.

"In view of your vision," Yair suggested, "I think now is a good time for us to contact Brandon Lane in Florida."

"I agree," Paul affirmed. "His info from the States will supply us with an ongoing status of the effect of the judgments over there, as well as an exchange of ideas on how to cope with them."

With that Paul opened up an envelope, pulled out a *Masterlink* invitation card, and dropped it on the kitchen table. "Get a load of this," he said with a fading smile.

"Where—?" Yair gulped.

Paul waved off his question with a ready answer. "I'm still in contact with some of my neighbors here in Jerusalem. Yesterday I stopped by one of them for a visit and he told me he received it unsolicited in the mail. I warned him of the implications, and he gave it to me."

"It looks to me like *Masterlink* will soon have a foothold here in Israel," Yair said ruefully as he examined the card with the microdisc and emollient attached in a neat and attractive package. "In all probability the Israeli government has given preliminary approval, and Kavidas and Stein are moving forward by taking a pulse on the market response."

Paul pulled out of his wallet a *Koinonos* ID card and placed it on the table next to the *Masterlink* card and said emphatically, "This is the only card we will carry!" The *Koinonos* project incorporated a bartering system implemented by Christians in America several years ago where their closed group exchanged services for food or vice versa to avoid the *Masterlink* system created by Kavidas and Stein.

The project emerged from the Douglas' study in *gematria*, the method of disclosing the hidden meaning of a biblical text by reckoning the numerical equivalents of the Hebrew or Greek letters. The study led to the discovery that Kavidas' name, Gregory A. Kavidas, was in fact a cryptogram for the number 666, the secret symbol of the ancient pagan mysteries connected with the worship of the devil, and the number ascribed to the Antichrist, the "Beast" in Revelation 13. Douglas' attempt to spread the revelation and warn the public met with disdain, contempt, and unbelief. The system met every security and financial need to modern man, eclipsing any degree of caution. To fight against the system was just not popular. The Douglases were then obliged to leave man to his own devices.

Yair rummaged through his wallet and pulled his card out as well. "This means we had better accelerate our *Koinonos* project over here and in the States, since it will not be long before our buying and selling transactions will terminate unless we have a *Masterlink* ID. Then, when we begin to feel the effects of the famine, we will be able to get by until we're forced to hide out in Petra."

Paul gazed out the window to digest the new development, then said in an eerie pathos, "I remember reading a quote by Sir Isaac Newton that he wrote nearly three centuries ago: 'About the time of the end, a body of men will be raised up who will turn their attention to the prophecies of the Bible, and insist on their literal interpretation in the midst of much clamor and opposition.' I guess it's exciting to say we're living in the very days he described. Isn't it, Yair?"

Yair stared at his friend and detected a glimmer of doubt. "You're not doubting God's promises to us are you, Paul?" Yair had to be strong for his partner, knowing the day would come when reciprocity dictated he may need words of encouragement to pull him out of a doubting session.

"No," he replied, "I know that doubting God is the death knell to faith." He picked up the *Masterlink* card. "It's just that this card is another reminder that the Tribulation period is from God, designed before the earth began to prepare Israel and the world for the return of Messiah Jesus and that these judgments upon unbelieving man must come to pass to accomplish that end."

Yair put his hand on Paul's shoulder. "Missing your family is part of it, right?"

Paul nodded at his companion.

Seconds later the daylight in the living room was greatly overpowered by increasing brilliant white light that caused every object to disappear from view. Paul glared at Yair, then they reflexively shielded their eyes from the refulgent light. When they sensed it diminishing, they turned in amazement to see two figures emerging. It was Qadar and Nocham.

"Blessed is He that comes in the name of the Lord," they greeted in unison.

Paul and Yair instinctively jumped up and stood erect at the table out of respect for God's messengers. "We are your servants," Paul offered humbly.

Qadar spoke first. "In two days' time you are to meet us at Golgotha with your companions. There we shall unlock the Fourth Seal."

Nocham reached over to Yair and touched his right hand. "Be sure to bring Levi."

They vanished before Paul's and Yair's eyes.

Yair started trembling. "This is really getting scary."

Paul took a deep breath. "Fitting location," he said dryly. "Golgotha, the place of Christ's death—the Fourth Seal, death. Fitting day, too, Friday, the day of Christ's death."

Yair stopped shaking just in time to choke out, "What do they want with Levi?"

Paul blinked. "Maybe it's time for his commissioning?"

Yair spun around. "At five years old?"

"God has a plan," Paul reminded meekly.

Botanical Gardens, Newe Granot

There's something soothing to the human soul when surrounded by nature, Stein thought as he waited for his people to show up. He sat on a concrete bench strategically placed within the hollow of a string of bougainvillea bushes and stretched his arms and legs while experiencing the fullness of the garden. *Time is moving quickly*, he thought. *It's been four weeks since our last meeting. Things should be in place now.*

Promptly at 1:00 P.M., Abdeel and Azizim walked into the garden area with obvious signs of success. Abdeel gave Stein a double thumbs-up while Azizim simply grinned. Either one was acceptable to Stein. He waved them to his bench, then motioned for Azizim to stand watch a short distance away. As Abdeel sat down, Stein noticed he had acquired a pinky ring that fit snugly over his stump. "Tell me we're set to go," Stein ordered curtly.

"We're ready," Abdeel affirmed. "Our *resettlement* troops are armed and ready to enter *our* city of Jerusalem as soon as I signal them. My signal will come immediately after we've taken care of Zeman. Then we will regroup with other Muslim pockets of resistance that have been hiding out since the invasion."

Stein estimated that the Hamas and Hezbollah hideouts numbered about three thousand give or take several hundred, with the Muslim Druze community adding another four thousand. Then the six thousand or so Ethiopians living in Israel who vowed allegiance to the Arab cause also threw in with the Hamas. Together, a formidable army, although rag-tag in nature, would be assembled to retake the city.

"Good, that's what I needed to hear." He waved Azizim over to their huddle and added, "Now listen carefully. Tomorrow, Friday, the eve of the Sabbath, is the day that has been designated for the attack. You know the place, so let's get our people in position tonight so we're ready for tomorrow."

Everyone agreed.

"One thing…,"Azizim said in staccato to Stein, "before you go… my friend in Petra called me just one hour ago."

"Oh?" Stein said, pausing, "And…?"

"He said that young Douglas arrived very hastily and rushed his friends and a young boy out of the fortress and raced away like a gazelle with his butt on fire."

Stein stifled a laugh at the metaphor. "Thanks for the tip." Deciding to sort that out later, he simply nodded to his fellow conspirators and walked away as discreetly as the mood allowed.

Stein closed the door of his car, then pressed the speed-dial on his encrypted cell phone and within ten seconds had Kavidas on the line.

"Everything is in place," he began dispassionately. "Your tour with Zeman will take you to three holy sites. First the Via Dolorosa, then the church of the Holy Sepulcher, and then, although it's a moot point, to the Temple Mount."

Kavidas had his phone equipped with a scrambling device to avoid detection. "Good work," Stein heard a mechanical voice announce. *Click.*

Stein pocketed his cell phone then bit his lip as he thought about Azizim's report of young Douglas. *Now what could these irritants be up to?* He wondered. He made a mental note for tomorrow: be prepared for the worst.

Looking down at the phone then out the window of his apartment, Kavidas marveled at Stein's masterful ingenuity to assemble such a plan. He used the age-old method of securing information—the same method used by the Mongols during the Ming dynasty to breach the so-called impregnable Great Wall of China—bribery. Two thousand EUs surreptitiously placed into the hand of one of Zeman's aides provided Stein with his complete itinerary for the day that would end up changing the course of Israel and the world.

Yes, tomorrow, Israel will be mine.

The Church of the Holy Sepulcher, Jerusalem

The Church of the Holy Sepulcher is considered the most sacred site in all of Christendom as it stands over Golgotha, the place of the Crucifixion and the tomb where the body of Jesus was laid. Hadrian, in A.D. 135, attempted to obliterate every vestige of the Jewish religion and the Christian religion as a Jewish sect by destroying Calvary and the tomb of Jesus by building a Roman temple dedicated to Jupiter at this high point in the Old City. This blasphemous act had the opposite result, for instead of desecrating the place, he permanently marked the site and preserved it until the fourth century, when Helena, the mother of Constantine, identified the tomb of Jesus and built a church there. The Persians later destroyed the church. Later under the Crusaders in the twelfth century, the present church was built. The overwhelming size and complexity of the church often bewilders tourists with its various Christian .communities sharing the church under a decree by Turkish rulers in 1852, each maintaining its own chapels and altars, conducting services according to its own schedule and denomination.

The magnificence of the church is found in the section built over the hillock, a bald, round skull-like mound, where the crucifixion took place. The hillock is named the "place of the skull" (in Hebrew, *Gulgoleth*; in Latin, *Calvary*) because of its peculiar arresting points of resembling "eyeholes" with a rounded top. Other accounts attribute the name to a place where the heads of condemned criminals were cut off, thus obtaining the name of Calvary, that is, "beheaded."

At present there are two chapels at the top of Calvary. One is believed to be the site of the Crucifixion and belongs to the Greek Orthodox Church; the second is believed to be the site where Jesus was stripped of his garments and nailed to the cross, and this belongs to the Catholic Church. One-third of the platform of the two chapels rests on the actual rock of Calvary. The rock is the central attraction of the faithful. Miraculously, no part of the structure had suffered damage during the recent earthquake.

At 10:00 A.M. four nuns from the Sisters of Zion convent opened the South gate at the Church, bowing toward the multiple crowds to signal their permission to enter the grounds. Within minutes, hundreds of pilgrims began to funnel into the courtyard as waiting charter buses opened their doors to unload passengers eager to run to their designated tour lines. Both outside and inside the Church grounds, souvenir and postcard hawkers recognized their open season and began to sell their

wares. Freelance "guides," clustered around the doorways, offered to show visitors around for an unspecified fee. Construction workers on scaffolds and artisans on ladders began their perpetual repairs amidst competing hymns and multiple aromas of incense arising from the ongoing prayers and incantations of the priests. After fifteen minutes, the church chapels, vestibules, outdoor verandas, rooftops, and gift shops were all full with 20-minute waiting lines. Despite the oppressive heat, the driving force to experience the sacred memorial kept everybody's spirits high. And despite the bustle, the church seemed to maintain its own unique magnificence.

Paul and Yair were the first to notice the huge assemblage of people as they neared the main gate. Recognizing the potential peril in great crowds, Yair motioned for Levi to huddle near him as Jonathan clasped Levi's hand securely.

"What are they giving away here?" Jonathan quipped to Paul. "Man, look at all these people!"

Paul gestured for him to be quiet.

Yair, the self-appointed point man, joined in. "Paul, look at the TV and news reporters with the video cams lurking about."

Paul visually panned the area and noted an unusual amount of media personnel roaming around, waiting for something. He just had no idea what. With concern, he bit his lip in a vain effort to subdue the escalating anxiety coming upon him. "Everybody stay together," he warned. "There is a great volume of people here."

He began to direct the group through the inner courtyard toward the area called Golgotha when Yair stopped him and poked him in the side. "We don't know exactly where to wait, so maybe we should stay out in the open. They will find us."

Paul nodded at the suggestion and motioned for the group to rest in place.

"Paul!" Yair gulped as he pointed to the rooftops. He turned Paul's head toward him and whispered, "I see men with Uzis up there!"

Paul carefully raked the rooftops with his eyes. "They're Mossad," he said in a calming tone. They must be making a security sweep."

"Somebody important must be going to stop by," Yair replied curiously.

"I know of two important persons who are going to stop by," Paul replied with a chuckle. "And it looks like there is going to be quite a show."

Standing in the shadows inside the lofty bell tower, Azizim trained his binoculars on the only road to the holy site. He grinned expansively when Zeman's limousine came into view. It was right on schedule. Seconds later he signaled Abdeel by cell phone, waiting one-half mile down the road in a canvas-covered transport truck filled with Hamas and Hezbollah personnel, each sporting weaponry fit for the assignment. Flanking Abdeel on each side were six other trucks equipped in the same fashion. In total he had over two-hundred trained terrorists and one gifted assassin to accomplish the mission. On Azizim's word, Abdeel set the plan in motion.

Once Zeman's limo came to a stop in the outside courtyard, two IDF guards instantly emerged from the vehicle with their hands on their side arms as a precautionary measure. Zeman stepped out first, then extended his hand to Kavidas and said, "Number two on our tour, Mr. Kavidas, the Church of the Holy Sepulcher." Then he pointed toward one of the IDF guards and added, "It will also be of interest for us to visit the alleged place of Golgotha as a sidebar."

The guard acknowledged Zeman's plan.

Zeman's view of Kavidas was blocked by the roof of the car as he moved to exit, but had he seen his eyes, he would have wondered why they seemed to glisten with glee when he said *Golgotha*.

"I would be *very interested* in seeing that important part of the Christian faith," Kavidas said in a tone vibrating with intensity. Moments later their small entourage moved from the outer courtyard into the entrance vestibule of the Church to begin their excursion.

Yair tapped Paul on the shoulder and with eyes surveying the ocean of people mulling about said in wonder, "Do you hear the crowd? There's a certain 'buzz' rising out of excitement. Something's going on."

Signaling for Jonathan and Levi to stay put, Yair pushed his way to a security guard standing on a perch overlooking the mass of people who suddenly flew into commotion. He tugged on the guard's uniform and yelled out, "What's all the fuss about?!" He pointed toward the entrance vestibule and added, "Who's over there?!"

Paul observed Yair nodding, then slowly making his way back to where they were stationed.

"Well?" Paul asked with increasing volume to combat the noise of the crowds. "What's going on?"

Yair gestured for a huddle and announced, "You're not going to believe this, but as we speak, Prime Minister Zeman is visiting the Church with some other dignitary. That's all the guard would tell me!"

Paul shook his head in disbelief. "This event is rapidly unfolding...unbelievable...then with Nocham and Qadar coming here, we're—"

"Paul!" Jonathan blurted out with eyes flashing as he pointed off in the distance, "I just saw a man up in that bell tower peek out with a rifle in his hands!"

Paul and Yair spun around just in time to see the sun's reflection off a metallic object, then it faded into the shadows. "Could be anything!" Yair replied reflexively.

"Probably Mossad," Paul concluded while motioning with his hand for the group to remain calm.

Twenty minutes passed before Zeman's group completed the abbreviated tour of the east wing; then they came outside into the inner courtyard to enter the west wing to visit Golgotha. The crowds began to roar and applaud as the group proceeded with two IDF guards leading the way.

Suddenly Paul cried out as he pointed to Zeman, "God help us! Look!"

Yair, Jonathan, and Levi immediately rotated in place to see what Paul saw.

Jonathan's eyes flashed in astonishment. "That's *Kavidas* with

Zeman!"

In the frenetic environment, neither Paul Douglas, Yair, nor Jonathan could think rationally. *What in the world was Kavidas doing with Zeman?*

Thoughts of some kind of colossal plot unfolding crossed their minds. Instinctively they froze and scanned the crowds, then the wall, then the rooftops, until Yair spotted what looked like a man taking aim with a scope-mounted rifle in the bell tower. Yair grabbed Paul next to him and yelled in his ear, "Jonathan was right! There *is* someone up in the bell tower, and it doesn't like Israeli military or Mossad!" He gulped. "I have a bad feeling about this!"

"So do I," Paul croaked out and began to draw their group toward the nearest wall for some semblance of security.

Seconds later, Zeman and Kavidas began walking by them amidst a throng of people when suddenly a loud *crack* from the bell tower was heard. Simultaneously, Kavidas jumped in front of Zeman.

"What the—?" Azizim, the man in the bell tower, muttered in amazement as he stroked the rifle barrel.

Nearly every eye turned to see a small plume of smoke emerge from the shadows. When they looked back at Zeman, Kavidas lay on the ground with his head in a pool of blood, with blood pulsating from the exit hole in his right temple. The people scattered in every direction.

"Shot fired!" one IDF guard screamed out as he frantically wrestled Zeman to the ground. The other guard pulled out his pistol, then dropped to a S.W.A.T position to look for the shooter.

Taking advantage of the hysteria, Azizim carefully calculated the distance between the heads of the IDF guard and Zeman, then calibrated his scope accordingly before firing two more rounds at Zeman. Both rounds found their mark: one in his forehead, the other in his chest. Zeman groaned as he grabbed his chest and fell limp.

Instantly, three Mossad agents zeroed in on the bell tower with their Uzis and let loose a barrage of gunfire. Azizim switched off with his rifle and started shooting with his own Uzi machine gun. Hundreds of tourists on the ground ran or jumped to safety as bullets ricocheted off both the ground and the tower wall in a fierce battle.

The Mossad realized that Azizim had the edge with the two-foot thick walls and the narrow openings in the tower, affording him a vantage point ideal to continue to snipe out his targets. After 20 seconds, the shooting stopped but the coordinated attack continued. Horns blasting and tires squealing outside the church signaled the sudden arrival of Abdeel's transport trucks to the church compound.

Paul turned to Yair in horror as the army of terrorists rushed into the courtyards to quickly set up their perimeter. "This is an invasion!" he yelled out.

Levi, flushed with fear, broke away from Jonathan and ran out into the courtyard. "Yair!" Jonathan screamed as he gained speed. "Get Levi!"

Yair started to leap toward Levi when suddenly a spiraling ball of fire almost fifty feet in diameter appeared a short distance from where Paul's group stood. It hung suspended in the air like a miniature star that no man was able to look upon. Yair stopped short as the fireball intensified to what resembled a blast furnace, an fiery inferno—searing the ground and singeing the clothes of nearly everyone in the compound. As the temperature in the courtyard soared, every living creature tried to shield him or herself from the conflagration, only to be incinerated if too close or to break out in huge body blisters if fortunate to be at a distance.

The Mossad retreated to safety while the few unharmed sightseers cowered in the far corners, crossing themselves for protection. When Paul looked at the intruders, the Hamas and Hezbollah invaders, every one of them lay dead, burned beyond recognition. Even their vehicles were nothing but burning skeletons.

"Where's Levi?" Paul cried out.

Levi was nowhere to be seen. Paul and Yair leaped forward to search for him when all at once a great calm came over the courtyard as the scorching temperature began to drop and the fireball began to diminish. Out of the center of the glowing fireball stepped Nocham and Qadar with their hands outstretched. Yair and Jonathan looked at each other as they realized their group was untouched by the blazing fires.

Nocham cried out his greeting, "Blessed is he that comes in the name of the Lord!" Then he turned quickly and looked upward while pointing toward the bell tower. As he opened his hand, out shot flames like a blowtorch that ascended rapidly, encircling the tower until Azizim emerged, holding his Uzi and rifle up in the air.

The flames surrounded Azizim as he screamed, "Allah be praised!" He held his finger on the Uzi trigger until the clip was spent, then dropped in a heap at the ledge of the tower as the fires consumed his body. Seconds later he fell to the ground below in a smoldering pile of charred flesh.

Nocham then looked directly into a media video cam and shouted out as he pointed to Azizim's remains, "Such is the fate of the enemies of the Lord!" Raising his hands to heaven, he cried out, "Behold, the Fourth Seal has been opened!"

The remaining crowds frantically dug their fingernails into the church walls or anything that resembled insulation from the fires. Paul glanced over at Zeman and Kavidas' bodies, only to be sure that his mind was still registering reality. Their bodies remained inert, as well as hundreds of innocent bystanders who were in heaps or pressed into corners or dangling over the guard rails—all exhibiting evidence of a ghastly form of death—burning.

Qadar stepped away from the glowing spiral as it began to fade, then looked behind him and held out his hand as Levi suddenly walked out from the center.

"How did—?" Paul mumbled to himself.

"Levi!" Yair yelled as he ran to him.

Qadar stepped in front of Yair and held him at arm's length while firmly locking Levi at his side. Then with a booming voice he yelled, "This child has been selected from the tribe of Levi to join with his brothers in the war against evil!"

Paul latched onto Yair's shoulders and held them from shaking and said, "Be strong, Yair!" he breathed. "Be strong!"

Nocham walked to Qadar and in full view of the onlookers they joined their left hands while placing their right hands on top of Levi's head.

"They're laying hands on him! They're going to anoint him!" Paul yelled to Yair.

Both Nocham and Qadar raised their eyes toward heaven as little

Levi calmly stood between them with only a look of anticipation on his face. He was not afraid.

"Look at his face!" Jonathan shouted. "It's beginning to glow!"

"Lord, you have been our dwelling place throughout all generations," Nocham and Qadar prayed an invocation aloud, "before the mountains were born or you brought forth the earth and the world, from everlasting to everlasting you are God." As if receiving minute-by-minute instructions from on High, they suddenly paused as the people stood spellbound, waiting for their next word.

Yair shot a look at Paul, who began to cry uncontrollably.

Nocham glanced over at Yair, then back to Levi, and cried out to the Lord in prayer, "O Lord my God, let this boy's life be a perpetual testimony to your people! Grant him wisdom and boldness from above, enabling him to preach the word with power. This we ask in the mighty name of Yeshua ha Mashiach, the Holy One of Israel."

Qadar reached into his cloak and pulled out a small ram's horn containing olive oil. He held it above Levi's body and poured a portion on his head while saying, "Go forth proclaiming the truth in the name of the Father and of the Son and of the Holy Spirit."

Suddenly Levi's body began to shake and convulse as God's Spirit began to infuse him. He looked down at his hands and quickly realized his body was changing. He was growing older as if he were thrust into some celestial time machine accelerating him into the future. He was maturing into a man in clear sight. Yair's eyes remained riveted on the little boy as he was suddenly transformed into what looked like a teenager. His clothes too, miraculously transformed. His shorts, polo shirt, socks, and sneakers glistened brightly until they disappeared, being simultaneously replaced with a one-piece garment made of a dull white material.

Levi was now anointed as a tribal leader of the 144,000 Jewish missionaries.

Overcome with joy, Paul and Yair fell on their knees in praise.

FIFTEEN

Biqqur Holim Hospital, Jerusalem

F our IDF officers together with six Mossad agents and the director waited anxiously for the ambulance carrying Zeman and Kavidas to arrive at the emergency room at Biqquor Holim Hospital. In the parking lot outside, a man in a black Mercedes was also waiting. It was Stein, watching for the vehicle that would bring his fallen leader to the appointed place where together they would take a quantum leap toward their predestined place in history.

Stein lowered the driver's window, then turned off the engine when he began to notice his surroundings were changing. It was only midafternoon, yet the sky was mysteriously darkening. He checked his wristwatch. *It's beginning to take effect,* he thought. *It won't be long now until the day is shortened to only 16 hours. Then one-third of the day and night will fail.* "The prophetic calendar cannot be altered," he whispered toward heaven with mocking reverence. "Yes, 'for the day of the Lord is coming. It is close at hand—a day of darkness and gloom,' " he quoted with a smirk. Seconds later his reverie was shattered.

With siren blaring and lights flashing, the ambulance carrying Zeman and Kavidas arrived, escorted by three IDF military vehicles. All the security personnel waiting inside the hospital rushed out to assist. Following them at a reasonable distance were several news reporters.

Stein ran to the ambulance, only to have the Mossad, with guns drawn, stop him cold. "Gregory Kavidas is my business partner and companion," he pleaded. "You must let me see him!"

Mossad supervisor, Moshe Ravitzky, stepped in with a halting gesture. "This is a matter of national security, you must leave the area!" As the paramedics rushed to unload the two stretchers, he waved over

208

two Mossad agents, who quickly went to his side. "Please escort this gentlemen out of the hospital zone immediately!"

The very second Stein was manhandled, his eyes fixed on the two agents with a penetrating stare. "Move on!" Stein commanded them in a guttural snarl.

As if suddenly overpowered by some invisible force that began governing their minds, the agents dropped their hands at their side, turned, and walked away into the chaotic frenzy behind them.

Stein then clasped Ravitzky's hand and gave him a lethal stare. Ravitzky's eyes pleaded for understanding, then all at once a blank look came over his face. "Lead me to Kavidas!" Stein demanded.

Silently and mechanically, Ravitzky chaperoned Stein into the hospital, through the security guards, and led him directly to where Kavidas lay in ER #3.

Ravitzky motioned for the ER doctor and the two trauma nurses to immediately leave the cubicle where Kavidas lay covered. Once alone with Stein, Ravitzky pulled back the sheet covering Kavidas and turned to Stein, shoulders slumped, and said tonelessly, "He's dead."

"He's not dead, he's sleeping!" Stein boomed as he pulled the sheet down to Kavidas' feet.

Ravitzky turned suddenly as the cubical curtain was abruptly pulled back. Two doctors rushed to Kavidas upon hearing Stein shouting.

"Leave us!" Stein clamored. They backed out, closing the curtain behind them.

Ravitzky looked down at Kavidas' distorted, bloodstained face, and pointed to the exit hole in his right temple. "How could he be sleeping?" he gasped. "With a hole—?"

Stein spun around with tears stinging his eyes. "He's sleeping, I tell you!" he screamed in Ravitzky's face. With that he shoved Ravitzky aside and climbed on top of Kavidas as he lay on the gurney. He stretched himself over Kavidas' body, then turned his head and cried out, "Master in heaven, bring life back into this body so he may accomplish your will!"

Nothing happened. Ravitzky wiped his brow as he began to become aware of his surroundings as if he were coming out of a trance.

Then Stein climbed off the gurney, grabbed Ravitzky by the throat, and breathed, "You do not believe—leave us!"

Ravitzky nodded and slowly backed out as well.

Climbing on top of Kavidas once again, Stein placed mouth to mouth, eyes to eyes, hands to hands. As he stretched himself on him, Kavidas' body began to grow warm. But Kavidas remained still. Dismounting once again, Stein walked back and forth in the cubicle for several minutes, praying and invoking his god to intercede, then climbed on top of Kavidas one more time as before.

Several minutes passed before Stein raised his head and closed his eyes as he wept aloud, "Mighty one, ruler of earth, hear my prayer and renew your servant's life." Curiously, as if receiving instructions, Stein placed his palms over the fatal head wounds and blasphemously prayed again, "I am thankful that you have heard me. I knew that you always hear me, but I do this for the benefit of the people who do not believe, that they may believe that you have sent us."

When Stein opened his eyes, the wounds in Kavidas' head were closed. Both the skin and hairline looked untouched.

He jumped off the gurney and yelled out, "Gregory, come alive!" Within seconds, Kavidas' eyes fluttered. His chest began heaving, followed by his hands shaking. Then he grabbed the sides of the gurney to pull himself into a sitting position and looked at Stein.

Ravitzky pulled the curtain back and blanched in astonishment as Kavidas turned toward him. Then Ravitzsky fell into the nearest chair. The ER doctor following Ravitzky simply darted his eyes back and forth between Kavidas and Stein, remaining speechless. After several seconds, he turned and yelled for a nurse, "Stat!"

As the nurse entered, Ravitzky rose from the chair and held on to the walls as he walked out into the ER lobby.

Minutes later, the media broke into the cubicle as Kavidas and Stein stood, expressionless, looking into the cameras.

Across the hallway lay Prime Minister Zeman, pronounced dead by two staff physicians who were equally shocked when everybody's attention was focused on Kavidas' resurrection.

"Yair, come quick!" Paul yelled into his kitchen. "You're not going to believe this. Kavidas is alive!" Yair raced out of the kitchen with both Jonathan and Levi shuffling their feet behind him. Simon, Shlomo and Shira rushed into the living room to join in the group. They all stood in front of the TV as it televised scenes from the church of the Holy Sepulcher and the hospital. Then it showed the incredible scene of Kavidas and Stein standing together in the ER cubicle.

"But he was dead!" Jonathan gulped. "We witnessed the shooting! Paul, how can this be?"

To engage the newly full grown teenager in an adult conversation, Yair reached over, put his arm around Levi, and said to the group with a slight shake of his head, "We're living in End Times. Anyone can see that our daily news is coming from the book of Revelation!"

Paul pointed to the TV. "Specifically, the thirteenth chapter!"

"Paul," Jonathan asked, "you mean—?"

Paul nodded, "That's right, Jonathan, Revelation 13 predicted that the Antichrist would be fatally wounded, then be raised from the dead." He retreated to the sofa, then added, "Satan is attempting to make a mockery of the Scriptures by counterfeiting the ministry, miracles, and resurrection of Christ."

"And he has many more tricks up his sleeve," Yair added. "Look at this, Paul!" Yair said in alarm, pointing to the TV.

Replays of Kavidas jumping in front of Zeman after the assassin's shot was fired filled the screen. Live interviews with Defense Minister Drori and Chief of Staff Weinstein, along with renowned surgeons, popped up. Discussions on the probability of surviving such a head wound were being debated along with comments from both religious leaders and psychics as to how the supernatural element was overpoweringly present. The evidence was piling up that Kavidas was being hailed as some kind of savior who attempted to take the bullet for Zeman, and for his reward, God saw fit to bring him back to life. Then pictures of Stein who claimed credit for healing Kavidas came into view. He was being saluted as a modern-day Elijah or Elisha, the Old

Testament prophets who raised people from the dead. The nation of Israel was galvanized with the event, seeing it as their chance in time to once again rise to being a great nation like they were in the time of Solomon. Finally, the mortality table was exhibited in the form of a chart: 3 IDF military; 2 Mossad agents, 350 civilian tourists, and 207 Hamas and Hezbollah terrorists, including the point man, Farouk Abdeel, and his assassin, Naphish Azizim, exclusive of the wounded that numbered 135.

Paul reached over and turned the TV off. He waved the group into his dining room to sit down at the table to discuss the developments. He began by opening the Israeli paper, *Maarriv*, with its front-page photo of Zeman lying dead at the church with Kavidas fatally shot at his side. "This is what we're dealing with," he began to explain. "The fulfillment of prophecy right before our eyes. But what are we going to do about this dynamic duo that has now captured the hearts of every Israeli here in Palestine? That's the question before us."

Shira needed to clear her head. She shot her hand up in the air. "Paul, help me to understand this," she said with a quizzical look. "Are you saying this whole thing with Kavidas diving in front of Zeman and taking the bullet was staged so he would emerge as a national hero?"

Paul took a deep breath while preparing himself to explain the theodicy that was unfolding in Israel. Drawing upon his father's Bible studies was quickly becoming an art form with him.. He grabbed a piece of paper and drew a circle in the middle. "This circle represents Israel in God's timetable," he began. Then he drew lines radiating out to connect to a larger circle. The drawing resembled a wheel. "These spokes signify the different nations and events in the last days of history. The entire wheel is a depiction of the Bible. In short, all prophecy is central to Israel, and we are fortunate to be here 'on location,' so to speak, during these last times.

"Now when we look at the events we see some key players, namely Kavidas and Stein." He picked up the newspaper and pointed to Zeman's photograph. "That includes this poor man, Zeman, who was used as a pawn on Satan's colossal chessboard to bring Kavidas here to begin his 'ministry.' The invasion, Nocham and Qadar, and even the attack by the Hamas and Hezbollah at the church falls within the sovereignty of God, who allowed the prophets to predict in outline form what was going to happen before Christ returns to set up his kingdom."

Jonathan raised his hand for a follow-up question. "You're saying that when 'N & Q' proclaimed the Fourth Seal, death, that the body count at the church was part of that?"

Paul nodded when he heard Jonathan refer to Nocham and Qadar as "N & Q." "What's more," he ventured, "the Fourth Seal includes other plagues that we must prepare for."

"Like what?" Shira fretted.

"We should not be frightened, Shira," Paul said, "because as I said before, God will protect those who belong to him. But we must be prepared for difficult times that lie ahead." Paul nodded to Yair, who picked up the cue.

"With the Fourth Seal there seems to be an increase in severity," Yair began methodically. "This judgment affects one-quarter of the earth's population—a horrible number of people—with bizarre deaths from domestic armed conflicts, plagues, probably from pestilence, and then there's the—" He broke off his commentary to defer back to Paul.

"Wild beasts," Paul added as he nodded to Shira. "Frankly, I believe this has something to do with the AIDS epidemic..."

"...Shira, please get me a cup of coffee," Yair interrupted while giving Paul a distressing look. "You don't need to hear this."

"What do you mean?" Jonathan inquired as Shira left the room.

Paul rubbed the back of his neck as he ventured into uncharted territory. "If you remember I once said that my dad's research found that many scholars believe that the AIDS virus originated in Africa, where men were having sex with animals—bestiality. This abhorrent lifestyle led to the virus mutating and crossing the barrier from the animal kingdom into humans. For many years these virulent AIDS strains have continued to change into unpredictable germs that only now have come to light. Then with the advent of mosquitoes carrying AIDS and in turn biting animals, we have animals with AIDS. And in some form of crazy irony, I am of the persuasion that animals with AIDS will go wild where God will allow the plague to go full circle. It started with men having sex with animals; now the animals will turn into wild beasts and ravage the earth to seek revenge."

Everyone looked at each other, not saying a word as Paul finished explaining one of the most frightening prophecies ever to be unveiled to the world.

Manhattan

Several hundred cockroaches suddenly emerged from behind the refrigerator in Rami Khouri's kitchen as he sat eating his lunch. "This place is driving me crazy!" he yelled out.

He slammed the rest of the sandwich down on the table, then rushed to the cabinet under the sink to retrieve a bug killer. He quickly sprayed the invading insects in the open, stepping on as many as he could, then pulled out the refrigerator from the wall to inspect the source, being careful not to disturb the picture of Louis Farrakhan meticulously exhibited in a place of honor.

"Blasted roaches!" he exclaimed as he looked at a water-soaked hole about three inches wide, where streams of cockroaches were pouring out from between the kitchen floorboard and the ceiling below him. He sprayed the area with the insecticide then stuffed a dishtowel into the hole to stop the flow of the filthy intruders. Apparently the refrigerator drip pan had developed a leak, allowing moisture to weaken the floorboards so as to provide the perfect environment for the age-old pests to build a huge infestation.

Once the crisis subsided, Khouri went back to his sandwich, wondering if he'd ever seen so many roaches in one nest before in his life. *A bit unusual*, he thought.

Moving into his dingy living room, the 38-yearold Muslim-American walked over to his worktable, picked up the TV remote, and clicked on the news. Khouri considered himself somewhat of a news junkie, watching live feeds and continuous newscasts nearly every hour that he worked on his projects. Each project was a masterpiece, carefully engineered to produce the maximum amount of damage to both life and property. While the wiring and soldering could at times be somewhat tedious, with the insertion of the circuit boards being somewhat hair raising, watching the news seemed to relax him. That is, until he saw the footage coming out of Israel broadcasting the slaughter of the Hamas and Hezbollah brethren at the church of the Holy Sepulcher. The linking of the assassin and the point man to Muslim fundamentalists by the media infuriated him. He hated it when journalists exposed Islamic radicals in a bad light.

He stood up from the table and walked to the sofa to watch the details on TV as they became available to the public. After one hour, he walked to open the only window in the apartment. A wave of blistering heat wafted over the sill and hit him flush in the face. He crashed his fist against the wall and swore. "This incessant heat!" He turned and sat on the sill to face his worktable and began to think about his new mission.

Within two minutes, his back began to itch. He reached behind himself to scratch the areas, when he suddenly remembered the CDC warnings about the mutated mosquitoes carrying a new kind of virus. He quickly shut the window and inspected the walls of his solitary abode, where he came across two mosquitoes resting comfortably next to Farrakhan's picture. He looked closely at the bloodsuckers and sure enough, their rear appendages were red.

"Digesting my blood?" he muttered angrily. *Swat! Swat!*

A wave of satisfaction washed over him that led to a deep sigh. He had made his mind up. *Allah will be pleased*, he thought, *and I will be rid of this rotten apartment once and for all.*

Rising early in the morning, Khouri adhered to his usual routine. He made his usual pot of coffee and ate his two jelly donuts, then walked to and sat down at the worktable, where he usually assembled the primary and secondary stages of the bombs he had been trained to build. All this he accomplished every day before reporting to work as a conductor on the BMT 14th St. Canarsie line subway train.

His function within his cell was to complete the primary stage, the ignition circuit and the secondary stage, the initiator circuit, with the final stage, the addition of the explosive, being completed by a member of a different cell group. One that he knew nothing about, except for their name: *Flame.*

But this morning would be different.

He reached down under his worktable and lifted up one of his creations, placing it carefully on the workbench before him. Then he walked to his bedroom closet to retrieve an insulated shoebox kept hidden under several loose floorboards. This box was his "private stash," as he called it, to be used only in an emergency. The box contained three pounds of Semtex wrapped in a food storage bag, and it was the culmination of four years of hard work in making the right illegal connections to obtain the goods. None of the other cell members knew about this. Over the years Khouri had dreamed that since Allah had not seen fit to give him a wife and family, he would cherish this prize for the day when he could make a statement with his life. One that would be remembered long beyond any progeny he might enjoy through a family.

The extremely stable and powerful explosive Semtex had the texture of Plastercene and was like kneaded dough, with bouncy elasticity. It was odorless and had a low level of fumes when dormant, making it difficult to detect with normal "Sniffer" machines and animals. It was capable of passing undetected through the X-ray luggage screening devices installed at airports. It was often used in the manufacture of accelerants for detonating larger, more lethal bombs. It had only taken about six ounces of Semtex to bring down the Pan Am 103 Boeing 747 that had exploded over Lockerbie, Scotland.

Khouri removed all the tickets, transfer stubs, and punches from his railroad attaché case and discarded them. *Won't be needing these anymore*, he thought. *Flame will find another mission for me, far away from here.* Then he connected the ignition circuit to the board containing the initiator circuit and carefully set it into the case. After that, he placed the entire batch of Semtex into one corner of the case and connected the explosive to the two boards to complete the assembly. Stopping to make an internal assessment, he thought, *Now I just have to press the time delay connected to the detonator when I reach the location, and I'm home free.*

He pressed several layers of bubble wrap over the assembly to secure the device and closed the case. Protruding from the handle of the case was a micro-switch, once thrown, that would trigger the timer set for fifteen minutes. *Plenty of time*, Khouri thought.

He walked from his apartment on 6th Avenue to the Union Square station where he flashed his ID card to a fellow conductor then boarded the 5:15 A.M. eastbound train that traveled through a tunnel that ran under the East River. It would take seven minutes for him to reach his destination on the far side of the river.

The jostling of the train relaxed him. His mind went back to 1990, when an Egyptian immigrant to the United States named El Sayyid Nosair was arrested and charged with murdering Rabbi Meir Kahane in Manhattan. *Nice target*, he mused. The subsequent police investigation in his home had disclosed 47 boxes of papers related to conducting assassinations and attacks on aircraft, as well as plans and formulas for making bombs. A note was found that said:

We have to thoroughly demoralize the enemies of God by means of destroying and blowing up the towers that constitute the pillars of their civilization, such as the tourist attractions and the high buildings of which they are so proud.

Khouri cracked a smile as he thought about Nosair. *A warrior. I, too, shall be a warrior*, he consoled himself. *Working toward the ultimate battle against the government of the harlot.*

The train came to a stop. He looked out the window at the sign that read *Bedford Avenue*. He was on the other side of the river, right where he wanted to be. The subway doors opened, allowing the passengers to disgorge where he hesitated on the platform for the commuters to leave the station area. He meandered over to the end of the platform by the staircases leading to the street and stood for several minutes while the few remaining passengers left the area. He checked his watch, realizing it would be six minutes before the next train arrived. *Just enough time. Okay*, he thought as he surveyed the platform one more time. *Time to go!*

He climbed down the utility staircase that led to the tracks and hurriedly walked the one hundred yards to the target area, directly under the East River. There, in a darkened area under a support truss, he placed the case. He looked back at his path to ensure his return, then leaned over and flipped the switch. Then he pressed the button on his stopwatch and began to run along the tracks out of the tunnel.

After 40 yards he slowed his pace, then turned halfway around to check the site when suddenly his foot caught in a switching rail. He cursed and checked his watch. He still had plenty of time—four minutes.

Then a green light flashed in the distance. "Allah be merciful!" he gulped when he realized what was about to happen. A westbound express was coming in from Long Island and would be rerouted automatically to the track where he was.

You idiot, he cursed himself. *You forgot about the express schedule!* Then the switching rail quickly closed on his foot. The pain was excruciating as the powerful electric solenoid pulled the rail in, severing his foot from his leg. He fell over on the tracks, narrowly avoiding the electrified third rail and began to scream as the train came barreling down the track.

The engineer of the 5:22 A.M. out of Lorimer Street never heard the screams.

At 5:41 A.M. the timer completed the circuit to the detonator that exploded the bomb.

At first the powerful explosion shot plumes of fire over two thousand feet in both directions from the blast site, igniting everything in its path. Then the concussion resonated off the subway walls, producing a deafening echo, followed by the crashing of the interior support trusses. Once the support trusses collapsed, the ceilings and walls of the tunnel began to crack. Then they began to rupture.

Within 35 seconds of the initial blast, the ceiling of the tunnel burst, exposing the outer support shell that was also severely damaged from the blast. The tremendous weight of the East River above was no match for the weakened tunnel. Once a fissure developed in the outer shell, millions of gallons of water began to violently flow into the tunnel until the entire tube was filled.

Of all the commuter trains during rush hour that were trapped inside the tunnel, there were no survivors.

Jerusalem

Paul Douglas walked out of his bedroom holding an E-mail up in the air. "Listen to this everybody," he announced to the group busily discussing Bible prophecy. "I've just received an urgent E-mail from Brandon Lane in Florida. He wants me to send him an Instant Message so we can talk over the Internet."

Paul had been working for several weeks on an encrypted language to be used by *Koinonos* to avoid detection by any corrupt law enforcement network or subversive organization, especially *Masterlink*. Although there were still several bugs in the rudimentary encryption system, he was confident it could hold its own. He sat down at the computer terminal and began typing on the keyboard that was in turn connected to a language synthesizer with software he'd developed that converted the words from English to the cryptic text. Across the Atlantic in Miami, Brandon's computer had the same equipment to decode the message.

[Sending]
Hello, Brandon, this is Paul in Jerusalem. We were going to contact you three weeks ago, but unfolding events precluded that effort.

Several seconds passed before the response read:

[Incoming]
Thank God you are safe! There is utter chaos over here in the States, and I hear in Israel as well. While we just learned about Prime Minister Zeman being assassinated and Kavidas being raised from the dead, you no doubt heard about the terrorist attack in the Manhattan subway today.

[Sending]
We have not listened to the newscasts from the States today, so no, we didn't hear yet.

[Incoming]
Well, here is what happened: The FBI, along with the ATF services, announced that an African-American of Muslim persuasion who worked for the Transit Authority in Manhattan detonated a huge bomb in a subway tube under the East River. Over 1,750 innocent commuters and workers were killed. Islamic radicals here in the States took responsibility for the attack, threatening a string of them in retaliation for what's going on in Israel, even though the USA has backed away from supporting them. Now, as the Bible predicted, men are fainting and committing suicide like never before out of panic and dread of the next horrific event. This is what America gets for not opposing evil things when they were small. Now evil is rampant and uncontrollable throughout the land.

[Sending]
We feel your pain over here. We just witnessed the opening of the Fourth Seal: death and the outworking of it at the Church of the Holy Sepulcher, where 560 people were killed. Your subway incident is just another of the many catastrophes to come upon America and the world as the judgment spreads throughout the earth. Another part of the judgment, and I believe there is ample proof of this, is the AIDS epidemic reaching unprecedented proportions. How is the problem with the mosquitoes and ticks carrying the virus? Is there any change in the behavior of domestic or wild animals? By the way, I had a vision about this just the other day where the mutant mosquitoes were biting animals, causing them to lash out at humans.

[Incoming]
With the decrease in daylight hours and the increasing heat, people are afraid to go outside. Rarely do people go shopping in stores anymore; they buy everything over the Internet so they don't have to be exposed to the outside elements with the unbearably hot, dry weather, or the possibility of being mugged. It seems the degree of thievery has reached unprecedented proportions. In fact, nobody goes to the grocery store without an escort for protection. Society is living in fear.

The reduced daylight and drought has affected plant growth, so now vegetables and fruit are not ripening correctly. They are turning brown and dying before they can be harvested. We are most decidedly beginning to feel the effects of the famine judgment over here. Regarding the animal kingdom question, I have heard and read several reports where house pets have been turning on their masters and even birds, both domestic and wild, have been bitten by the mutant mosquitoes and are carrying the AIDS virus now. Stories of exotic birds, like macaws and cockatoos, gnawing through their cages and attacking their owners are becoming very common over here. It probably won't be long before a great ferocity comes over all the animals. This has only added to the mass hysteria taking place.

The terrorist attacks, the change in the climate, and the mutant mosquitoes have caused other bigger problems as well. It seems that it has had an effect on the psyche of the American people. They are very despondent—on the verge of losing hope, and accordingly, there is a major increase in drug and alcohol use. This, in turn, has brought a sharp increase in immorality, where the statistics on teen pregnancy and children out of wedlock has been eclipsed by abortions, homosexuality, incestuous relationships, and of course that which you already know, bestiality. What's more, it seems that all religious and civil restraints have been thrown off, and an "anything goes" atmosphere is prevailing. It is disgraceful to think that the liberals have gotten their way, and we are now living in the wake of liberality.

But God will not be mocked, for whatever man sows, that he will reap. It seems that God is visiting us with a strange kind of divine retribution in another form, one that I hate to mention because it is very terrible. He is striking America with a plague that appears to be targeting the long-standing right-to-abortion laws. The American Medical Association, the CDC, and other regulatory agencies are keeping it under wraps so as not to scare the public, but because of my drug company, I have access to this information. What is happening is increasing at an alarming rate. It is the birth of conjoined twins to non-Christian couples. The ratio of conjoined twins to normal births now is a staggering 1 out of every 10 births. And the conjoining is occurring at extremely difficult places. Most of the twin births are *Cephalopagus*, joined at upper trunk and head, with *Craniopagus*, joined at the head, following closely. Those with extensive connections, the *Dicephalus*, twins joined with one body and two heads, are still rare, but their numbers are rapidly increasing as well. The enormous medical challenges facing these deformed, yet exceptional children are keeping pediatric surgeons very busy. Many professionals in the medical field are looking at the use of the "quick-abortion" drug, RU-486, as the possible cause.

I am convinced that God has not been pleased with the ethical and moral choices America has made over the years because they have not properly chosen which liberties were worthy of protection. Now we are suffering for those choices. Our only hope is that this nation would repent before God. May God have mercy on us.

As the group read the last response from Brandon Lane, their hearts began to sink with sorrow.

[Sending]
We shall continue to pray for America in the same way we pray over here for Israel in accordance with God's Word. Namely, the verse in 2 Chronicles 7:14. We will E-mail you again several days from now. Blessings

Paul turned the computer off as the group sighed in relief. The news from the States was very taxing, raising their awareness of the global scope of God's judgments to come upon the earth. "Let's have a cup of coffee and recall God's promises," Yair suggested. "We can all use a little fellowship about now."

On the way into the kitchen, Paul pondered the weighty E-mail from Brandon. It was apparent to him that the plagues and calamities occurring in Israel and in the States were representative of the tribulation being inflicted on the entire globe.

God was making sure there would be no escaping the judgments.

SIXTEEN

Renaissance Jerusalem Hotel

T he Renaissance Jerusalem on David Wolfsohn Street was Stein's
hotel of choice. Heralding a mixture of the European and Middle
Eastern culture surrounding it, it offered modern European
architecture, furnishings, and hospitality. Also to his liking was the
hotel's Emerald restaurant that boasted of rare elegance with its exotic
European menu, crème-de-la-crème environment, and elaborate prices,
dedicated to the epicurean community. To their Israeli clients, a kosher
menu was also available.

Diplomats working at the nearby Knesset, visiting dignitaries, and
charter members who could afford the dinners dined in awe as they sat
amidst the enchanting Chihuly glass sculpture exhibits. Replicas of his
glass installations that adorn public parks, tourist attractions, and
national monuments set the Emerald off from any other restaurant in
Jerusalem. It was the perfect place for Kavidas to dine with Stein to
celebrate the greatest triumph of their lives, the raising of Kavidas from
the dead.

Walking toward their secluded table that had been especially
reserved for the occasion, Stein stopped at an ornate metal basket
suspended by a gold chain from the ceiling with several Chihuly glass
eggs decoratively placed inside. He looked around, then picked one up
to examine it. "A work of art," he commented, meticulously replacing it
and moving on.

Kavidas simply paused to allow Stein the indulgence. Once the
wine order had been placed, Stein reached over and held Kavidas' hand
as a solemn look appeared on his face. "Gregory, you know at times I
can be somewhat of a pragmatist, but you must tell me what it was

like," he began as he shook his head in wonder. "In those first moments and the time following your death experience," he said with a grimace, "what did it feel like to be shot in the head?"

A look of bewilderment that quickly changed to irritation came over Kavidas. "You want me to go into that now? In a restaurant?"

Stein withdrew his hand as a wave of embarrassment washed over him just as the waiter brought the wine. The discerning waiter carefully set the wine in place, then opened the menus and politely left them on the table and walked away.

Kavidas lifted his glass to toast and said, "To the one who made this all possible, may his name be exalted in the earth." They tapped glasses and sipped the wine.

Seconds later, Kavidas looked deeply into Stein's eyes as if to read his heart. He was able to identify areas of faith that bordered on unbelief. Especially those matters relating to death and what lies beyond the portal into eternity. Spiritual matters being understood by spiritual people.

Kavidas was not readily inclined to recount his excursion to the internal regions of the supernatural, believing it to be a private matter between him and his lord. But if it would bolster Stein's faith and lend cohesiveness to their relationship, then he believed it would be worth the investment. Finally, he nodded at Stein and a strange expression came over his face. It was as if he were suddenly traveling down a path to relive the event that changed the world.

"As soon as I lost consciousness," Kavidas began as he gazed at an imaginary spot in the air, "I saw what looked like the figure of a man beckoning me to follow him as he stood at the entranceway of a cavernous tunnel where light radiated outward for a great distance. The light in the tunnel was so intense I had to shield my eyes. As I drew closer I was able to see more clearly. The figure took on the appearance of an angelic being with two full-length wings that had reared up above his head. He looked very beautiful, yet his presence was very overpowering. His only audible words were, 'The master awaits you.'

"Before I stepped into the tunnel, I looked back and saw myself lying on the pavement at the church with a glassy stare on my face and the blood pulsating out of my temple. I knew I was dead, yet I was able

224

to feel myself as if I temporarily abandoned my corporeal body and acquired a spiritual one. Strangely enough, I was able to pass my hand right through other parts of my body. I felt transparent.

"As I followed him into the tunnel, a warm tingling sensation came over me. I could feel the bright light as it enveloped my newly acquired spiritual body. I stopped before I went too deep into the tunnel, and looked back again and saw myself in the hospital with you over me. In reflection, I know that my physical body was being healed while this was going on. The light suddenly brightened, going from brilliant to dazzling as I walked through to the other side. That's when the majestic spectacle of the throne room came into view.

"It was a magnificent scene. The great Angel of Light, the Prince of the power of the air—the anointed cherub who once walked in Eden, sat on his throne. The resplendent light emanating from his being was shooting out into space finding its place among the stars. He had four wings extending from the rear of his body—two were extended outward while two remained closed, almost obscuring his face. Then those wings slowly opened, revealing his splendor.

"I fell down before him in praise. 'O morning star, son of the dawn,' I said, 'your servant awaits your command!' Oh, the gloriousness! Oh, the loveliness! Oh, the beautifulness! Surrounding him was a great angelic host with beautiful satyrs that stood as silent sentinels guarding him. The host sang incantations that invoked worship while a great multitude of his followers paraded before him.

"As I stood in wonder, he called my name to come forward and approach him. Awestruck, I obeyed. While standing before him I realized that any pain that I suffered on his behalf or anything in my life that meant anything, paled into insignificance. I stood as a nothing before his glory. Then, I was commended for my service to him and granted life. I turned and walked through the tunnel and woke up in the hospital."

Kavidas came out of the daze and eyed Stein. "Now I know what it was like for Lazarus before Jesus raised him from the dead."

Stein closed his eyes and put a palm to his forehead. Kavidas' recounting was so utterly fantastic and moving that he could not contain himself. Several tears streamed down his face. Moments passed before he spoke. "Believing this, why is man so afraid of death?"

Intensity suddenly arose from within Kavidas. "It's because of the lies coming from the other side, that's why! The other side claims that 'man is destined to die once, and after that to face judgment.' They also claim that death has a 'sting' or that it is painful. That on the other side of the door leading to eternity there is perpetual punishment unless—" he made imaginary quotation marks in the air—" one makes their peace with God by receiving Jesus as Savior.' That's what they preach, literally scaring the hell out of people! But in fact after we close our eyes in death, there is no pain, no anxiety or longing to return to life and share our experience with the living. No, we awake in a spiritual wonderland filled with majestic angelic beings that serve us for all eternity. It is another world designed to satisfy the desire of every living creature. A place filled with inexpressible things that bring happiness for all eternity. It's the paradise promised to the faithful where our loved ones who have gone before us greet us at the end of the tunnel that takes us from death to life."

Stein sighed as Kavidas fell silent and reflected on his experience. He longed for this blissful place that Gregory described.

It would be several years, however, before Stein would learn the truth: Satan, the Father of Lies, had created this colossal delusion for Kavidas to convince him of his purpose and reward. Designing to thwart the purposes of God, the Liar projected a false reality and duplicated God's miracles to deceive him and all of man into thinking they are safe without Christ.

The real truth is that Kavidas walked through the valley of the shadow of death into the black darkness of the abyss, the domain of the dead, the bottomless pit, even hell where there is only howling and the gnashing of teeth from those being imprisoned, scorched, and tormented until their appointed time of judgment to which they will be cast into the everlasting lake of fire. It was there that Kavidas was temporarily held captive until God saw fit according to the appointed time revealed in Scripture for him to be revived so he would continue to fulfill his destiny predicted in the divine prophecy.

When the waiter returned, Stein was famished. He studied the menu for several minutes before saying to the waiter as he pointed to the flyer stapled to it, "What does it mean 'menu modified due to environmental conditions'?"

The waiter cleared his throat and said apologetically, "Mr. Stein, due to the drought and the increased difficulty in securing quality food, the management had to make some adjustments. Now many of our items are taken from deep freeze or are synthetic in nature."

Stein looked off into the front of the restaurant and realized how few patrons there were. The famine and drought was radically impacting business. He turned to Kavidas, who shrugged and flicked the side of the menu. The realization that the curses were affecting them personally suddenly dawned on them. "Bring me the fish of the day," Kavidas finally ordered.

"Same," Stein said with a snort. With that he stood up and walked to Chihuly's glass exhibit of the upside down teardrops on the opposite side of the room. From there he meandered along the adjacent corridor until he came across Chihuly's red spears and spiny tree models. He gingerly fingered them, still fascinated with their abstract message, all the while dwelling heavily on Kavidas' recounting of his death and testimony. He needed to clear his head if that were possible. Ten minutes passed and hunger pangs suddenly overcame him. He returned to the table as Kavidas watched him with curious eyes.

"Are you all right?" Kavidas wondered.

Stein nodded and took a deep breath. His brief interlude of diversion was over.

"We need to discuss where we go from here," Kavidas redirected.

Twenty minutes later their dinners were served. The celebration soon came to an end.

Slowly pacing back and forth in his new office, Kavidas noticed the portrait of Golda Meir, the former Prime Minister, hanging on his wood-paneled wall. It was slightly askew. He smiled in contempt and walked to it, saying vehemently as he adjusted it, "You were wrong when you prophesied, 'There will be no peace in the Middle East until the Arabs stop teaching their children to hate Jews.' There will be peace as long as I am here! And the Arabs can still teach their children to hate Jews because that fits my purpose!"

From there he walked to his first-floor window and looked in the direction of the Temple. Although it was obscured from view, his mind registered the fact that the Temple construction was now complete. With a view toward his future role in the Temple he thought, *Now would be a good time to galvanize the people.* The word *dedication* came to mind. *Yes*, he thought, *it would be good to celebrate while at the same time introduce myself in another role.* With a view toward the distant future he said to himself, "It won't be too much longer, Gregory, before the praise due your name is shouted from the rooftops."

There was a knock at his door.

Seconds later Drori and Weinstein walked in. Kavidas glanced at his watch. They were right on time. Unfamiliar with his demeanor, they nodded respectfully at him and waited for his lead.

"Gentlemen, have a seat," Kavidas said as he cordially pointed to the two antique chairs consistent with the Byzantine decor of the room. "It is so very good of you to come. We have much to tend to at this crucial time in Israel's history." He began by holding up the front page of the *Maarriv* with its full coverage of Zeman's funeral and said in a somber tone, "Let us start our relationship off with a word of praise for our fallen hero. It is men like Benjamin Zeman who rank among the great statesmen of this nation, be they Theodor Herzl, David Ben-Gurion, Chaim Weizmann or of late, Yitzhak Rabin, Menachem Begin, or Benjamin Netanyahu, that we can credit Israel's existence!" He closed his eyes for a moment of silence out of respect for Zeman's memory.

Drori and Weinstein exchanged looks, then bowed their heads.

"We want to thank you for your endearing words at the Prime Minister's funeral," Drori said as he nodded toward Weinstein in agreement. Zeman was buried in the cemetery of the martyrs at Ramat HaSharon, where other fallen leaders of Israel's struggle for recognition as a nation were memorialized. "Our nation was truly touched by your eulogy and the ongoing tribute you paid to his name. We are very grateful, too, for your stepping in at this critical time and lending your experience, your political influence, and your financial support to help revive our nation that is still reeling from the terrible blows of nature and the attacks of the Arab coalition."

Kavidas noticed Drori stopped short of mentioning the other plague assaulting the nation, the two *performers*. He postulated their omission was simply to postpone the discussion on the troublesome duo until his role in Israel's government became clear. *Fine with me*, he thought, *I have my own plan on how to handle them*. Kavidas purposed to employ his gift of persuasiveness, subtlety, and craft now that he was in a position to influence the leaders that shaped the laws that governed the people he came to rule.

"Regarding the Arab coalition," Weinstein said, bristling, "we have uncovered the masterminds behind the assassination. Key members of the Hamas and Hezbollah exiled to Lebanon were the ringleaders, along with other elements holding out in pockets here in Israel. Mossad and IDF will continue to hunt the dogs down until every last one of them is dead."

"No Muslims should be allowed to remain in Israel," Kavidas suggested in an attempt to attenuate their pain. "Their creed is that violence and the sacred are inseparable, a creed that goes against everything a nation under God believes in."

Weinstein nodded in affirmation and joined in. "What is to prevent the Arabs from acquiring a portable nuke and terrorizing us again like they did at Yeroham?" He turned to Drori and added, "Nuclear weapons in the hands of the Brazilian government is not the same as in the hands of terrorist states like Saudi Arabia, Syria, Egypt, or Iran! No, the U.S., the Chinese, and what's left of the Russians, along with other major players need to sanction the sale of nuclear technological equipment to terrorists states. Any nation that trades with terrorist states must choose between them and us here in Israel and our counterpart in the West, the Americans. No, these barbarians cannot be allowed to threaten us ever again!"

"On a brighter note," Kavidas reminded to move the agenda, "the European Jewry replacement plan is working well. The influx is helping the nation's economy as well as filling in the gaps in the work force for all those slain in the attack and making up for all the PLOs who no longer work here."

Drori raised a hand. "What do you suggest we do with the non-combatant elements that remain? I'm talking about the Muslim Druze and many Ethiopians who are still friendly toward Jews."

Kavidas had a plan that he would not divulge to anybody. That plan included the Muslim remnant. "Israel has conquered many enemies lands in the past, bringing the captives into subjection while allowing them to remain in the land. I see no great urgency to remove those harmless Arabs who can serve us well in the future."

A smile came across Drori's face. "You mean like during the time of the Judges when Israel pressed the Canaanites into forced labor?"

"Something like that, only into domestic labor. Housekeeping, gardening, and such," Kavidas replied softly.

Weinstein paused to take a hard look at the man before him. A man who suddenly came across Israel's sky like a shooting star who was obviously blessed of God in miraculous ways and endowed with amazing abilities. His financial support to his nation, his plan to bolster Israel's population with Jewish immigrants from the EU, and now with his political wisdom...*It was almost supernatural,* he thought, *especially when one considers his astonishing recovery from the head wound. In reality, it appears that he is rapidly becoming more of a religious figure than a political one.*

"Mr. Kavidas," Weinstein finally said after several minutes of thought, "we know that our parliament in the Knesset would have a difficult time accepting a Gentile as a Prime Minister. A majority of the 120 seats is needed to vote you in and probably we could only get about 40 right now. In the future that number will change as the nation and its policymakers get accustomed to you.

"But under the present circumstances, and with your overwhelming acceptance by the public, I am going to propose that we officially nominate you as 'special advisor' on a permanent basis. The position will carry with it all the force and authority as any of the other elected officials here in the Knesset with the exception of the Prime Minister that requires a popular vote as well. Unofficially—" he paused and nodded toward Drori—"and of course Zeev and I have discussed this thoroughly. We will defer important matters and decisions of state to you until our national election next year. This way we can maintain a working government."

The plan was both enchanting and flattering to Kavidas but lacked the needed impetus to place him where he needed to be in Israel. It was time to become more dialectic by ratcheting up the political role they imposed upon him. He would introduce the critical ingredient necessary for any international leader to soar above the traditional; he would become their religious figure to capture their spirits while still retaining a semblance of the political in order to capture their minds. The alchemy would intrigue the masses. This was how David, the giant killer turned warrior-king accomplished his popularity and won the hearts of ancient Israel.

"I accept your gracious offer," Kavidas said with a cryptic smile as he walked to the window. He pointed toward the many pedestrians walking the sidewalks on Ruppin Street and said with a heightening sense of satisfaction, "One has only to look at the man in the street to know they are tired of fighting. They are tired of the inconveniences of the blights on our nation—the drought, the scarcity of food, and so on. We should take the completion of the Temple as an opportunity for a national celebration. The dedication will act as a catharsis, a discharging of the pent-up tensions and anxieties our people have endured the past two months."

"That's a great idea!" Drori announced with a clap of his hands. *He's uncanny. It's almost as if he read my mind.* He reflexively turned to Weinstein and said, "Michael and I will set it all up."

Kavidas gave him a wink and a nod. They had given him the kind of response he was looking for.

Stein lounged on his living room sofa, watching yet another segment in the ongoing analysis and commentary on Zeman's assassination brought to the public on the INN 24-hour news station. Every nuance, detail, and supposition, along with continuous profiles and interviews of political and military advisors cluttered every hour. It was nearly impossible to gather any news from other parts of the world unless one had satellite TV. Becoming increasingly bored, he reached into the bag of chips in his lap and stuffed a handful into his mouth.

The phone on the end table next to the sofa rang.

"Mr. Stein," a woman's voice said, "this is Zelly at the front desk. There is a well-dressed Bedouin by the name of Mibsam Azib down here who would like to speak with you."

Stein closed his eyes momentarily. *Mibsam Azib? Who is he?* "What does he want?"

"He is rather insistent. Can I put him on the phone?"

"Fine."

"Mr. Stein," the deep nasal voice said. "We have a mutual acquaintance. A man by the name of Farouk Abdeel. I would like to talk to you about his mission."

"Put the receptionist back on the phone," Stein said immediately.

"Yes, Mr. Stein?" the receptionist asked.

"Send him up."

Independence Park, Jerusalem

The diminishing daylight hours disturbed Stein as he walked up to Kavidas' apartment. It was only 4:15 P.M., yet darkness was rapidly sweeping the land as premature nightfall overpowered the light. He noticed the darkness that now came by night was surreal, a darkness that could be felt. He shuddered when he related it to the ninth plague that came upon the Egyptians at Moses' behest. *Put it out of your mind,* he commanded himself. *No unpleasantries.*

Kavidas welcomed Stein with a warm embrace.

"Congratulations," Stein began with an expansive grin as he walked into the living room. "Your discussion with Drori and Weinstein went well. They confirmed your appointment as Special Advisor."

Kavidas paused and reminded himself of Stein's clairvoyant powers. He already knew everything about the meeting. "Yes, it went well," he affirmed. "Yet I'm prepared to take action should they suggest anything that will be at cross purposes with our mission."

"Your plan to have a national celebration at the Temple dedication was a good one," Stein said hesitantly. "But I respectfully suggest that I believe it will be used as a platform for the other side to make a statement. What's more, I am convinced there will be a serious confrontation."

"I already thought of it, Mort," Kavidas said resolutely. "However, I'm not too concerned. We can handle whatever they throw at us."

"I'm not just referring to Douglas and his batch," Stein replied with eyes pleading for understanding, "but to the two *performers* who will most definitely make a showing there."

"They could be troublesome," Kavidas admitted as he turned his head in a moment of thought to draw upon his knowledge of the Bible. "But you and I both know that although they wield great powers now, their time here is very limited. We'll just have to leave the dilemma with the Master and trust him for the outcome. He's been doing a good job so far."

Stein couldn't argue with the truth. "You're right." He walked to the kitchen for a drink of water only to notice the pressure coming out of the faucet had been greatly reduced. It only trickled out. He ignored the inconvenience. "I received a visit from an Arab Bedouin while you were meeting with Drori and Weinstein," he ventured. "A very enterprising man, I might add. A would-be brut who can help us."

"How?"

"It seems he is the contact that Abdeel, the Palestinian, used to gain information about Douglas and his troupe of players," Stein explained. "He knows all about their fortress in Petra."

"He can be useful when the time comes," Kavidas replied with increasing interest.

Stein gave him a thumbs-up. "Very useful. In fact, I've taken the initiative to commission him to work right now. I am going to use him to organize a new wave of the remaining Hamas and Hezbollah dissenters together with all the Druze and Ethiopians presently adrift in splinter groups here in Israel. They will regroup with the Arabs in Lebanon and other states outside of Israel to form a united front. We need to have Israel's enemies gather momentum so they can be used as our rod of correction in the future."

Kavidas, once again was impressed with Stein's preparedness and his ability to organize and govern the domestic security concerns that would leave him free to concentrate on the issues he was ordained to control: the spiritual, emotional, and physical welfare of the world. "Explain to me the mechanics of the plan."

"I first warned him that this undertaking to organize whatever fundamental Islamic forces he could would be of monumental importance. Namely, that the Arab-Israeli conflict will play a big part in the world in the days ahead and they need to maintain solidarity. He seemed to understand he could be instrumental in bringing that about. From there I went on to remind him that the day will come when we will need inside information on the Christian hideout in Petra; that a future altercation with those Christians and their allies who reside there is inevitable. He, being an Arab, would like nothing more than to see them get forcibly ejected from there. Then I rewarded him."

"Reward?"

"A special kind of reward," Stein noted with a chuckle. "I 'baptized' him with a *Masterlink* microchip with a credit of 10,000 Euros. He was impressed with the way the emollient ointment permanently affixed the chip to his right hand. I explained that this would be like his own private access port that will finance his operation while at the same time provide spending money to enjoy some of the perks that go along with being a part of our organization. When I get his progress report each month, he gets another 10,000 EU credits transferred to his account. He was enraptured."

Kavidas nodded with a blank look. He began to nibble on his lower lip as he contemplated his role in the upcoming Temple dedication celebration. *This is really going to be interesting,* he thought. "Good," he said.

Stein blinked, then just shrugged at Kavidas' doxology.

King David Mall, Jerusalem

Men and women in the advanced stages of AIDS standing outside the grocery markets begging for money and food was quickly becoming a way of life in Jerusalem. Homosexual behavior and drug abuse, being so amply documented in all epidemiological literature addressing AIDS, proved this conduct to be an extremely efficient agency of infection, second only to direct intra-vascular viral injection. The AIDS victims were easily identifiable with their broken or inflamed skin that oozed with body fluids—a gaunt and sickly appearance that told of their weakened body and spirit. Many shoppers were repulsed by the development and sought their groceries and foodstuffs elsewhere, while others took pity and acted compassionately and benevolently as they entered the store.

Panhandling was prohibited inside the supermarket, but the fact that there were human beings walking the sidewalks slightly over 75 feet away who were on the verge of death made for bad business. Storeowners, along with the mall managers, quickly grew intolerant of the condition and hired security guards to "politely" escort the outcasts off the mall premises. Relying upon the public's sympathy for support, however, the victims continued to reappear in larger numbers.

But the AIDS victims were not the only deterrent to shopping. The wild dogs were also a problem. Domesticated dogs were apparently infected with a bizarre virus that many attributed to the resurgence of bestiality. The dogs prowled the parking lots, with many lying in wait in the coolness of the automobiles' shadows, looking for food in garbage receptacles or ready to pounce on an unsuspecting shopper with a bag full of groceries. Numerous incidents where the wild dogs mauled the shoppers to death were also reported. Often the managers would put stale dated meat in the rear of the stores to distract the dogs away from the customers. Other store managers posted employees in the rear of their stores with .22 caliber rifles to kill them and throw their diseased carcasses in the dumpster.

For Yashur and his wife, Estelle, from the *Koinonos*, the worsening societal change signaled another aspect change in the Fourth Seal, death, and provided yet another opportunity to distribute gospel tracts. The store owners and mall managers viewed the tract distribution as a possible solution to the widening enigma with the mindset that if the AIDS victim were to "find religion," the church to which they would attach themselves would take them off the streets.

"Look at these vegetables and fruits, aren't they disgusting!" Estelle said to Yashur in dismay. She held the sample produce up in the air as a demonstration. The tomatoes were unripened and wormy and looked somewhat deformed, more like gourds. The oranges and bananas were still very green from the lack of sunlight needed to mature them. Somehow the public was beginning to accept the mutations as being normal.

"If you think that's bad, look at the prices!" Yashur snapped while holding up a package of beef hamburgers. "How are we supposed to afford the basics?" The cost of meat had risen four times in the past month.

Within minutes they were both heading toward the checkouts with the few items they could afford. Estelle looked at the waiting lines and gasped. Despite the escalating prices, the public was scooping up and hoarding food out of fear of shortages. It reminded Estelle of the days when the Hezbollah in Lebanon waged war on the civilian population in northern Israel. In a panic, residents flocked to the stores to buy up food, bottled water, and plywood for their windows. Many stores had to limit customer purchases to accommodate the frenzied population.

Estelle pointed to an express checkout with a short line and said, "Let's split up the order." She grabbed a shopper's basket and separated the items in her cart to bring their orders under the limits.

"Please wand your *Masterlink* ID," the woman checker advised the man in front of Estelle after the items passed through the conveyer belt scanner. He nodded and placed his right hand under the reader. "How are you, Mr. Rosen?" the checker asked as she read his name off the monitor. He replied and smiled as Estelle stood on her toes to peek at the monitor. The monitor was full of information that she couldn't read from her vantage point. Within one minute, the man cleared the checkout and was on his way.

"I'm paying with Eurodollars," Estelle announced as she loaded her order on the conveyer belt. The checker gave her a dirty look and pointed to a sign above the register that read, *Masterlink Only.* Estelle looked behind her to see several disgruntled shoppers showing their contempt for the delay. "I'm sorry," she said half apologetically, "but I don't have a *Masterlink* ID, and I don't intend to get one!"

"I'm sorry too, lady," the checker snarled back, "but you'll have to take your order to the rear register." With that she jerked her thumb over her shoulder to point to an area at the back of the store. It was obvious that store policy encouraged the use of the newly accepted credit system while discouraging the use of cash. It was also obvious to Estelle and Yashur that unless the *Koinonos* group implemented their bartering system soon, Christians would be going hungry.

Ben Zvi Cultural Center
Ararbanel Street, Jerusalem

The Ben Zvi Cultural Center was carefully selected by Yair and Levi as a prime location to distribute gospel tracts. Located in the heart of the Jewish community while remaining a considerable distance from the tourist areas, the center represented neutral ground. It was the perfect environment to engage the Sabra, or native-born Israeli, with the truth of Jesus Christ while they explored the roots of their heritage—the Messiah, being the Root, and base reason for their existence and purpose. Other elements such as low visibility by law enforcement officials and being a reduced traffic area contributed to their decision.

"Our world needs good news!" Levi shouted to several patrons as they descended the steps of the center. "Would you like to read of some good news?" He approached them with tracts in one hand and a pocket Bible in the other and added, "Yeshua is the Messiah, the Son of David. Believe on Him and you will be saved!"

Yair looked on in admiration at Levi's ongoing spiritual development.

"Fool!" a man shouted back as he grabbed the tract out of Levi's hand and threw it to the ground.

"Yeshua is not the Messiah; he was crucified! The Messiah must bring in the kingdom!" a woman yelled back as she walked away.

"Now that the Temple is built, the real Messiah can come! Read your Bible, you'll see!" another said in a huff as she stormed off.

Levi simply shrugged and walked to Yair in confidence. "My ministry is to proclaim; God's is to claim."

Yair smiled. "I like that." He put his arm around his shoulder and affirmed that truth. "We can only cast the seeds of the gospel, God will bring the increase."

Levi nodded at his comrade's resolution. "You know, Yair," Levi said with conviction, "when the others come forward, the harvest will be great. For now, I will just be obedient and do as you say: 'Cast the seed.'"

Levi's reference to the 'others' reminded Yair that the remaining divinely selected individuals from the twelve tribes of Israel to make up the rest of the 144,000 Jewish witnesses were yet to emerge. "Your spiritual nourishment, Levi," Yair encouraged, "will come from your diligence to share the truth with the world. That sharing will fulfill your calling." Reminding him that their spiritual food came from spreading the Gospel, he added, "C.S. Lewis once said, 'A wise man can't always be defending the truth, there must be time to feed on it.'"

Levi turned and walked to the entranceway of the center to greet the next batch of visitors making their way down the front stairs. Time to repeat his introduction. "Our world needs good news!" he yelled out again as he proceeded to hand them tracts. "Would you like to read of some good news?"

All at once he happened to glance back at Yair and realized that he was experiencing something weird, perhaps the supernatural. Yair was lying on the ground. Thinking Yair was dead, Levi ran to him. Then he realized his comrade seemed to be sleeping soundly. Levi immediately recognized that his comrade must be having a dream since his facial expressions were changing rapidly.

Yair was dimly aware of his surroundings until he was transported in the Spirit to a place that he seemed to remember. He found himself standing a short distance from a great wall that had a doubled arched doorway in it. Engraved in the stone above the doorway was the word *Beautiful*. He felt himself and knew that he was still alive, fully awake and conscious. *This is the Gate Beautiful or the East gate*, he realized. But he knew the Turks had walled up the entranceway, yet he knew that when Messiah returned, He would enter the city through this gate. *The time is near*, he thought. *The time is near*.

Then a figure of a man clothed in white linen robes with huge glistening wings on his back began to materialize before him. His presence became increasingly overpowering. *This was no ordinary angel*, Yair thought. *This angel is of the high hierarchy in God's army of messengers*.

Yair fell to his knees before the angelic being and began to extend his arms in obeisance when suddenly the heavenly creature cried out, "Stand up! I am only one of the chief princes of the Most High God. I am Michael, the watchful guardian of Israel who stands in the presence of God. He sent me to give you insight, guidance, and direction for the days ahead."

Michael raised his arm in a majestic fashion as dazzling light shot out through the doorway obscuring the background. Yair squinted and shielded his eyes as Michael clutched his hand to escort him through the entranceway. Once in the doorway, Michael stopped and turned to Yair and said, "God's people, Israel, will go through a time of great distress such as has not happened from the beginning of nations until now. But all those whose names are written in the Lamb's Book of Life will be delivered. Those who are wise will shine like the brightness of the heavens, and those who lead many to righteousness, like the stars forever and ever." Michael then stepped aside to allow Yair to see what lie beyond the doorway. "Now see and understand."

Yair immediately recognized the immense structure that came into view. Over the past three years he had been watching with great anticipation the magnificent building project, waiting for its completion. It was the New Temple. But as his eyes began to survey it he realized that his view was a few years into the future because the outside shrubbery was now fully grown and several weathering stains on the walls were visible.

Then Michael nodded to signal a scene change to which hundreds of thousands of people appeared on the Temple Mount. The innumerable crowds were overflowing out of every doorway, spilling over into the entrance ramps and platforms. Revelry and merriment seemed to be prevailing as if they were waiting for a great event to unfold. Off in the distance several groups of men dressed in priestly uniforms seemingly lined up to be called into the sanctuary to perform their duties as intercessors before God.

In another corner of the Temple Mount were stalls containing scores of animals to be slain on the altars of sacrifice. *It looks like they're celebrating the feast of Yom Kippur, the Day of Atonement,* Yair thought. It was readily apparent the sacrificial system had been renewed and operational for years. Michael motioned with his arm once more to change the perspective, and Yair suddenly found himself gliding over the top of the ground as if on some invisible people mover until he landed inside the Temple courtyard. He was then escorted to the central building, the Holy of Holies. From there Michael walked him into the inner chamber where a replica of the Ark of the Covenant was situated. Several moments of silence passed before the high priest walked in with a man who, when Yair first saw him, he was taken back in shock. It was Gregory Kavidas. Yair looked in unbelief and disgust at Michael, who stood expressionless as the horror continued to unfold.

Kavidas walked to the high priest, who bowed before him as if he were a god. Then Kavidas clapped his hands repeatedly until two other priests walked into the holy chamber. He nodded to them and they, in turn, walked out, only to return seconds later carrying a man-sized gold idol. Walking ahead of the priests was Mortimer Stein, who appeared to lead the procession. The two priests then shoved the Ark of the Covenant into a corner and placed the gold idol in its place.

"It is no longer needed!" Kavidas shouted. As they retreated, Yair looked at the idol's face and gasped. It was the face of Gregory Kavidas!

The high priest walked to the idol and bowed down before it. The other priests reluctantly joined in as a broad smile of satisfaction came over Kavidas' face. Then Stein fell prostrate on the floor before the idol. This was the moment to which Kavidas was born. The high priest motioned for the other priests to alternate their worship between the idol and the real Kavidas. To their astonishment, Kavidas received their worship.

Stein then stood up as the priests looked on and bowed before Kavidas. Stein then turned to the idol and laid his hands on its head. The priests looked on in utter disbelief as the idol began to open its eyes and mouth. Then the idol spoke. "I am God! Bow before me!"

Yair Kaplinsky gasped again and instantly covered his mouth in horror as the blasphemy continued. The ultimate sacrilege by the man of lawlessness, the perpetrator of the colossal lie, was now being revealed before his very eyes. After a brief interval of time, Yair could not stand in the presence of the desecration any longer. He turned to Michael to pull him out of the Holy of Holies and walked with him outside to one of the exterior platforms of the Temple where he lingered for several moments. Suddenly one of the high priests from the Holy of Holies came out shouting, "False Messiah! False Messiah!"

Thousands fell to the ground to pay homage to the false messiah, while others began to panic and run from the Temple, trampling countless numbers of worshipers as the melee heightened. The hundreds that ran in search of the real Messiah were screaming the Messianic greeting, "Blessed is He that comes in the name of the Lord! Messiah Yeshua, the Son of David, save us!"

Yair blinked his eyes and suddenly he was transported in the Spirit to his home in the fortress at Petra. He saw both himself and Levi at the mouth of the entranceway that led into the city as those hundreds of Jews who ran from the Temple desecration poured in. "Save us from the false messiah," they shouted in unison, "save us!"

Michael touched Yair on the shoulder and said, "Now go your way, Yair. The prophecy is sealed up until the appointed time."

"Yair, are you all right?" Yair heard. "Wake up!"

Yair's eyes fluttered as Levi continued to rub his neck. "I guess...," he muttered slowly.

"You looked like you were unconscious," Levi said. "You looked like you were out cold, but you were seeing something because your face kept contorting."

"I had a dream, "Yair replied, his voice vibrating with intensity. It was about the Temple and—" he stopped short and grabbed hold of Levi's arm—"we have to get back to Paul's house right away."

The recounting of Yair's dream to the group rivaled the early days of storytelling where an aged narrator sat in a stuffed chair in front of a fireplace on a snowy night with a host of open-mouthed children firmly planted at his feet, eagerly anticipating his every word.

"God must be setting a precedence," Paul said trenchantly after Yair explained his dream. "These are the Last Days and the prophet Joel did say that 'your old men will dream dreams, your young men will see visions.' "

"Yair, why do you think God had Michael present the dream?" Jonathan asked.

"Because Daniel predicted that in the Last Days the archangel Michael, who is the guardian angel of Israel, would come forward," Yair replied. "This is just a reaffirmation that the time in which we are living is indeed the Tribulation period."

Paul leafed through several chapters in his Bible then explained, "The core of your dream has to do with the Temple, and both Christ and Daniel did prophesy that there would be a desecration in the Holy of Holies that would eclipse that of Antiochus Epiphanes. It is apparent Kavidas is going to fulfill what is known as the Abomination of Desolation when he sets up his own idol in the sanctuary. Then all Israel will discover who he really is, the false hope, the idol shepherd, the false messiah—the Antichrist." He paused and shook his head, then said ruefully, "But by then, a great deal of damage to the nation will have occurred. "

"How does the idol talk, Paul?" Shira asked curiously.

Paul rubbed his neck to ease the building tension. "It's not by ventriloquism, Shira, but by demonic powers."

"Isn't some ventriloquism considered to be demonically inspired?" Simon asked. "I mean, I've read several books on demonic abilities, and ventriloquism is way up there with astrology, clairvoyance witchcraft, and hypnosis, as a means of communicating with evil spirits."

Paul nodded. "Yes, it can be. And this is why Christians shouldn't mess with that stuff."

Yair gave Paul a cryptic look. "What's your thinking on the Jewish people storming Petra?"

"What we do know," Paul explained, "is that various prophets proclaimed that after the desecration of the Temple, the Antichrist, Kavidas, will be unmasked. This will drive the Jewish nation out of Jerusalem to find refuge from the wrath of God that follows in the remaining three and one-half years of the Tribulation. This explains the part of the vision where they flee to Petra. Jewish people know about this because it is recorded in Isaiah and Micah, as well as in Revelation."

"Well, let's just get the word out to everybody as to who Kavidas really is!" Yair said with a clenched fist. "God will protect us as we spread the news!"

Paul smiled at his companion's zeal, but shook his head. "It's not that simple. We're dealing with two satanically energized persons with great powers, whom God has ordained to be the very instruments that will bring Israel to its knees in preparation for the return of Jesus Christ, their Messiah. Their national day of humiliation and defeat is fixed in the future on God's calendar and cannot be changed. This has been recorded in prophecies that were penned over three thousand years ago. For now, we can draw upon the resources God has provided and try to reach as many individuals as possible with the truth."

Shira looked at Paul inquiringly. "What does lie in the future?"

Paul added, "We can expect in the days ahead that Kavidas will take credit for the promises of God to Israel by performing some amazing feats."

"You mean like raising from the dead?" Jonathan interjected.

"Yes, that and many more things that will defy physical laws, logic, and belief," Paul continued. "All these satanic powers will be used to deceive the people of Israel, and to a great degree the outside world, much like Hitler did in the early years of his conquest. He used Germany and the people to achieve his purposes. In like manner, Kavidas will use Israel, the Jews, and the Arabs to accomplish his goals."

"To draw everybody away from Christ's plan of salvation by offering a counterfeit one through himself," Levi instructed. All eyes turned toward Levi after he made the pronouncement. They were amazed at his newly acquired spiritual discernment.

"Exactly," Paul affirmed.

"So Kavidas' rise to stardom, so to speak," Shira added sarcastically, "will culminate at the Temple when he claims that he is the Messiah."

"Right," both Paul and Levi agreed.

"Well, it appears to me," Yair said emphatically as he addressed the group, "that our task is to proclaim Christ to his people Israel and the world, while tripping up Kavidas and Stein as much as possible. Is that the way you see it?"

Everybody nodded in agreement.

"Then we and our K-group need to get to this Temple dedication ceremony and make a bold statement and expose this Kavidas for who he really is!"

Everybody exchanged glances.

SEVENTEEN

Temple Mount, Jerusalem

Many Bible scholars believe that King Solomon received divine inspiration in order to build the temple in Jerusalem that would bring to his God the just honor he deserved. Scholars add that Solomon built the temple in 960 B.C., according to an original pattern that is in heaven. Solomon hired a Tyrian architect, Hiram, to oversee the building project that was characteristically Phoenician in style. The construction of Solomon's temple took seven years, employing 183,000 workers, who used precision-building techniques where no hammer, chisel, or any other iron tool was heard at the temple site. This amazing engineering feat was augmented by the fact that the entire cutting was performed off-premises to preserve the sanctity of the holy Mount.

God directed Solomon to build the Temple on Mount Moriah, the very place where Abraham offered up his son Isaac as a sacrifice to Jehovah some twelve hundred years earlier, and the very place where over one-thousand years later, God would offer up his own Son, Jesus, on that very place that was renamed Mount Calvary.

Throughout the ages, God clearly has been making a statement that the Temple Mount has a very special place in his heart.

In fact, the magnificent Temple of Solomon stood as a silent memorial to Israel's God for over 400 years until it was destroyed by the Babylonian king, Nebuchadnezzar, in 586 B.C.

So what happened to cause such destruction?

Down through the years, the people of Israel misplaced their worship with idolatry and began to view the Temple as a good-luck charm, considering them inviolable as long as they worshiped in their own way at the Temple, with little regard for the God of the Temple. This led to deeper idolatry, desecration, wickedness, and sinful behavior that God could no longer tolerate. He spoke to Israel through Jeremiah the prophet and warned them to repent of their sins and return to Him, but their callous hearts would not listen.

To punish them, God sent the Babylonians to demolish the Temple and take Israel captive.

Seventy years later, Cyrus, king of Persia, authorized the return of the Jewish captives to Jerusalem to rebuild their Temple as recorded in the book of Nehemiah and Ezra. This became known as the Second Temple or Temple of Zerubbabel, and was smaller than, and inferior to, Solomon's. According to the Talmud, a Jewish commentary on the Bible, Zerubbabel's Temple lacked five things that were in Solomon's Temple—namely, the Ark of the Covenant, the sacred fire that came down from heaven and consumed the sacrifice, the Shekinah or God's glory, the Holy Spirit, and the Urim and Thummim, the high priestly device used to communicate with God.

King Herod, an Idumean, sought to appease his Jewish subjects by refurbishing the Temple. In his zealous reconstruction project, he doubled its extent by lengthening the walls and adding monumental stoa with magnificent stairways. He also added enormous, ornate, white marble columns and massive stone walls that enclosed the Temple complex on an earthen platform high above the floor of the Kidron ravine. The walls had numerous gates; one gate in the north wall, one in the east wall, two in the south wall, and four in the west wall facing the city.

The construction on the Herodian Temple began in 19 B.C. and was the very Temple where Christ denounced the merchants and moneychangers as they haggled patrons for a good price for a Temple sacrifice. The Roman general Titus in A.D. 70, as prophesied by Christ in Matthew 24, later destroyed this Temple.

The children of Israel still did not learn the lesson that they should not be preoccupied with the Temple itself, but with the spiritual principles it illustrated.

The Temple Mount then became a battle ground between Jewish, Gentile, and Arab forces. In A.D. 132-135, after the Roman emperor

Hadrian reneged on his promise to rebuild the Temple, the Jewish zealot, Bar Kochba, led a rebellion that ended with Hadrian desecrating the Temple by erecting pagan idols. Later in A.D. 135, the Roman governor, Rufus, plowed up the Temple Mount to signify the destruction of Jerusalem and initiated the birth of the city as the Roman colony called Ailia Capitolina.

In A.D. 326, the Byzantine emperor Constantine built the Church of the Holy Sepulcher to overlook the Temple ruins to emphasize that it was no longer a Jewish memorial but a Christian site.

Years of conflict passed until, in A.D. 637, Muslim Caliph, Omar, conquered Jerusalem and discovered that the Temple Mount was covered in centuries of dung and debris. This led to the Caliph Abd al-Malik building the Dome of the Rock on the Temple Mount in A.D. 691.

When the Crusaders conquered Jerusalem in A.D. 1099-1118, they transformed the Muslim Dome of the Rock into a Christian church, until Saladin recaptured Jerusalem in A.D. 1187.

Turmoil over the Temple Mount continued until A.D. 1917-1948. During such time the British, who mediated between the Jews and the Arabs over the Temple Mount, were in control. Then, on May 14, 1948, Israel declared its independence from Britain and conquered Jerusalem. However, they did not gain access to the Dome of the Rock or the Western Wall.

In 1967, during the Six-Day War, Israel liberated the Temple Mount with the purpose of rebuilding the Temple, only to have their hopes dashed when Defense Minister Moshe Dayan ordered the Israeli flag removed from atop the Dome of the Rock and granted the Wakf, the Supreme Moslem Council, sovereign control of the Temple Mount with the proviso that Jews can have access to the Mount, but cannot conduct prayers or religious services.

With the ownership of the Temple Mount in the balance, in September, 1981, Yeshiva students, under orders from Rabbi Getz, broke down an Arab wall inside the Rabbi's Tunnel that runs underneath the Temple compound, claiming that the treasures of the Temple, including the Ark of the Covenant were hidden within a lower chamber accessed by the tunnel; Arabs clashed with Jewish students, bringing the police to seal the entrance to prevent any future Israeli intrusions.

Concerning the geographic orientation of the Temple, needed to facilitate the construction of the third Temple, the March-April, 1992, issue of *Biblical Archaeology Review* published an article by the famed archaeological architect, Dr. Leen Ritmeyer, who successfully verified the exact location of the ancient sanctuary.

Then in 2003, Islamic fundamentalists, armed with high explosives, blew up the Rabbi's Tunnel that runs under the Temple Mount after they learned that the Ark of the Covenant had indeed been discovered there, hidden in an ancient cavern. It was later learned that their goal was to remove any evidence of ownership by the Jewish nation.

Unfortunately, the nefarious act undermined the foundation of the Islamic Dome of the Rock, and since it was discovered that the Islamic radical group, Hamas, was responsible, the Arab League permitted the Islamic mosque to be dismantled. Now, years after the destruction of the Arab mosque that was subsequently dismantled and sold off to various Muslim enterprises, the New Temple, built under the supervision of the Temple Mount Preservation Commission, was ready to be dedicated.

It was ten minutes past noon with the Temple Rededication Program about to begin at 1:00 P.M. Both Kavidas and Stein stood next to a pillar on the east porch that overlooked the outer court. Stein realized that the Temple Preservation Commission scheduled the event at this time to allow a little over four hours of ceremony and celebration before the shortened hours of daylight brought darkness to the city. Despite the world's ongoing efforts to overcome their reduced daytime activities, it was still difficult to become accustomed to.

"Are you all right with Drori and Weinstein speaking?" Stein asked Kavidas while flicking the side of the program.

The program listed them as speakers followed by the high priest, with two lightweight dignitaries in reserve if needed. Kavidas would be the last to address the nation.

"I don't anticipate anything other than complete loyalty to me, if that's what you mean," Kavidas replied in a robust tone. "In time I will have to deal with their insubordination, but for now, they know their place."

Stein nodded as the prophetic seed to future conflict took root in his mind. The thought of high-profile government employees demonstrating insolence unnerved him. He strolled to the terrace that overlooked a courtyard, then looked up at the blackening clouds that hung suspended over all Jerusalem. The clouds, resembling bellowing puffs of black smoke, ran all the way to the horizon.

"Don't you think it's quite eerie seeing this cloud cover, knowing that rain will not fall?" he asked Kavidas rhetorically.

"You need to steel yourself against any physical and emotional ties connected to what's happening in our environment as we move toward our goal," Kavidas said in a mild rebuff.

Kavidas found himself having to reassure Stein more frequently as time and commitment toward their mission advanced.

"Remember, Mort, each time a seal is opened, the world will be fraught with a new set of problems to deal with, be it drought, darkness, famine, or whatever!" He paused to point upward in a mocking fashion and added, "But we, with help from above, shall persevere! Isn't that what the Bible-thumpers always say?"

Stein cracked a smile at Gregory's attempt at humor. He then checked his wristwatch and nodded toward the reception area. As they walked off, he asked, "What shall be the order of the day?"

What shall be the order of the day? Kavidas repeated in his mind. "I shall employ all the resources at my disposal to convince 'God's people' that they can trust me as their political advisor as well as their spiritual leader," he replied.

Stein clapped his hands. "This is going to be very interesting."

At 1:30 P.M. the group arrived at the number 6 parking field of the Temple Mount with twelve couples from *Koinonos,* or K- group as they had come to be known. Shuttle buses were already in full operation, transporting droves of Sabras, native-born Jews, as well the newly arrived Euro-Hasidim with their eighteenth-century *kapotas,* coats, and *shteimel,* hats, to the disembarking lot adjacent to the Mount over one-half mile away. Neo-orthodox Jews, and Gentile proselytes were rubbing shoulders as they too joined in the pilgrimage to the Mount. Once they arrived at the drop-off zone the crowds climbed two flights of stairs to the exterior courtyard that was especially equipped with many thousands of folding chairs for the ceremony. Based on the volume of buses and cars in the parking lot, Paul Douglas estimated that the crowds numbered in the tens of thousands.

A loud horn blared over the PA system, radiating throughout all the parking fields and into the surrounding community.

"Paul!" Yair shouted above the noise of the crowds as he pointed toward the southwest corner of the Temple Mount. "That's the priest blowing the shofar from the trumpeting stone to announce the upcoming ceremony!"

The group turned and peered off in the distance to see the priest in all his official garb slowly rotating to every compass point and blowing the ram's horn to signal the commencement of the rededication ceremony. In the First and Second Temple period, the priest blew a trumpet to announce a gathering, but for today's rededication, the commission insisted on the vintage shofar.

Paul nodded at Yair's observation, then stopped to direct the group to a secluded vantage point to begin their survey of the Temple from a distance. They had all agreed that they would walk the half-mile while discussing some of the more interesting engineering and architectural aspects of the Temple.

"As we look at the splendor of this magnificent structure," Paul began while referring to his notes, "remember, this pales into insignificance when compared to Solomon's original Temple built on this very site. For prophetic purposes, we could call this the Third Temple, the Tribulation Temple, with one more to be built in the future." Paul drew from his father David's studies that referred to the prophecies in Revelation and Ezekiel that spoke of the Millennial Temple that would last for one-thousand years during the earthly reign of Christ.

"Paul, what's that smell?" Simon asked curiously as he held his nose.

Paul and Yair took a quick whiff of the breeze blowing their way.

Yair was the first to respond with the horrific truth. "That's the smell coming from the cemetery. Many more dead bodies from the invasion remain to be buried." The smell served as a reminder of their purpose at the ceremony, namely, to expose Kavidas as the false messiah that would bring many more deaths.

"It's disgusting!" Shira added as she skewed up her nose.

"Hopefully, the wind will shift and carry the stench out to sea," Paul said.

Everyone agreed.

Paul then ran his hand horizontally in the air and continued with his explanation of the Temple Mount. "What you see laying before you is the largest man-made platform left over from the ancient world. When Herod the Great expanded the Temple Mount during one of his ambitious campaigns to win over the Jews, he extended the nearly rectangular plot to the size of 30 football fields, approximately doubling the size of the Temple Mount from Solomon's original boundaries. The ancient retaining walls were deliberately left in ruins by the Romans to serve as a testimony to the destruction of the Jewish state. This Temple is smaller in proportion, but rebuilt on the same site."

"Wasn't the Holy of Holies in Herod's Temple built over the Even Shetiyyah, foundation stone, the Rock, the very rock that Abraham offered up Isaac, and the very rock where the Ark of the Covenant was placed?" Jonathan asked.

"Yes," Paul and Yair affirmed.

"But then after Herod's Temple was destroyed in A.D. 70, the Dome of the Rock replaced that in A.D. 691," Paul continued. "This Temple is oriented in the exact location as Solomon's and Herod's Temple." Paul's face contorted slightly. "It is also the place where the Antichrist will desecrate the Temple."

"Where did they put the rock, Paul?" Shira inquired innocently.

"It's still in the same place," Paul replied with a smile. "It's a little bit too heavy to move around."

The largest single building stone ever discovered in Israel, the Rock is located on the Temple platform. It weighs 600 tons and was set in place to stabilize the Temple structure during earthquakes. By comparison the Rock is much larger than any other stone.

"How did the Israel government determine ownership of the Mount? I mean, wasn't that a big deal with the Arabs?" Simon asked after he had read through the Dedication program, searching for the answer.

"A very big deal!" Yair explained. "Since 1967, Muslim Wakfs, who had governing authority over the Mount, set up stringent rules that prevent access to the Temple Mount by non-Muslims for religious purposes. They made it a crime to, in any way, desecrate a holy site, and any archeological excavation would certainly violate that law. And since ownership can only be determined by excavation, the problem was unresolved.

"In 1973, however, Leen Ritmeyer, an archeological architect, who succeeded Brian Lalor, who was continuing the work of Benjamin Mazar from the Hebrew University team who began excavation south of the Temple Mount in 1968, uncovered conclusive evidence of Israeli Temple ownership. Much of their work relied upon history books and the work of an English engineer named Charles Warren, who surveyed the Temple Mount back in the 1860s. Later, another English engineer by the name of Charles Wilson faithfully recorded the mysterious caverns, caves, tunnels, and cisterns that are underground beneath the Temple Mount.

"Then when the Ark of the Covenant was located in the Rabbi's Tunnel located under the Temple Mount in the early 2000s, the overall evidence was quite convincing that God gave the Mount to the Jews. Further, after the invasion, the then Prime Minister Zeman, ordered all Muslims out of Israel. This allowed Israeli archeologists to have a field day exploring the subterranean caverns under the Mount. Naturally, every discovery pointed to Israeli ownership dating back to the time of David in 1,000 B.C."

"How did the builders know how to build this Temple like the old one?" Shira chimed in.

Yair put his arm around her shoulder. "That's a good question. They used various sources in addition to Warren and Wilson's surveys. There was existing evidence on the Mount itself, and from the first-century A.D. Jewish historian, Josephus, and an important Jewish document called a *tractate*. The tractate of the Mishnah called the *Middot* furnished archeologists and contractors with the necessary descriptions and information to rebuild the Temple as close to the ancient one as possible."

Paul nudged Yair to move along. The group agreed and walked on another few hundred yards toward the Temple Mount, then paused to once again hear Paul and Yair's narrative.

"How did they transport and lift those massive stones?" Shira asked as she pointed toward the Temple walls.

"In modern times we use heavy transport vehicles and hydraulic cranes to bring building blocks to a construction site and set them in place," Yair explained. "But in ancient times the quarryman would extract the stone from the limestone pits and then square the stone for transport. While smaller stones were placed on wagons, the larger stones—like the cornerstones that weighed some 50 tons or more—had to be transported on special wooden rollers. Many of the stones were specially shaped by the masons with 12-inch long projections on opposite sides of each stone. These projections were fitted with ropes for pulling and were later removed. But for transport, ropes and treadmill-powered cranes fitted with winches lifted the stones on one side and lowered them onto the rollers. Oxen could then pull the stones with ropes placed around the projections.

"The historian Josephus claimed that over 1,000 oxen were used in the construction project of building the Temple. The nearby quarries in the vicinity of the Mount were quite elevated so the masons utilized the downhill force of gravity to aid the transport.

"At the completion of each course of ashlars, or squared building stones especially cut to permit a very thin layer of mortar joints, the area within the retaining wall was filled in with cartloads of marble chips and broken stones, up to the top of the latest course. Thus, the stones, some weighing over 80 tons, were not lifted, but lowered into place."

"That's amazing!" Jonathan exclaimed with a nod. Paul then gestured for the group to advance further along toward the Mount. They had very important business with Kavidas to attend to.

As they neared the Mount, Paul noticed there were scores of men patrolling the wall with marksmen rifles and Uzis. Upon closer inspection he saw they were both IDF and Mossad. *I would think security would be at an all-time high for the Temple dedication*, he thought. *We need your protection, Lord; watch over us*, he prayed.

Once they were at the Mount, the grandeur of the Temple became increasingly obvious. The Western Wall had been resurfaced, with two new gates to the inner courts, while still retaining the original stones left over from the Herodian Temple. Out of respect for the Wall that had represented Judaism for centuries, a group of Hasidim had gathered for prayer. They were clearly people who had zeal for God, but like the Pharisees of Jesus' time, lacked the knowledge to recognize the Messiah. Some of them wore startling robes of fawn, belted at the waist like dressing gowns, while many were veiled entirely in dusty black, thin, long coats, and wide-brimmed hats. Their unshaven beards and their ringlets, curled around their ears, typified their devotion to their culture and tradition. From where Paul stood, he could hear their plaintive cries to Jehovah to restore Jerusalem to its rightful place in the world.

The remaining three walls each had four gates allowing entrance into the interior courtyards. In addition to the gates, arched bridges attached two of the walls and stairways that allowed pedestrians access to the upper courtyards. One of the arched bridges spanned the Tyropoeon Valley that bordered the Temple Mount on the west, giving the priests and nobles direct access from the Upper City to the Mount. In Herodian times an aqueduct also ran over this archway, bringing water from a pool near Bethlehem to the huge cisterns or reservoirs that lay beneath the Temple platform.

Carved into the bedrock below the landing platforms of both the Western Wall and the Southern Wall were dozens of shops, ritual bathhouses, and two council houses. An imposing staircase atop the wide plaza in the center of the Southern Wall served as the main entrance that led to the Double Gate where pilgrims would enter and exit.

Adjoining the Double Gate was the Triple Gate, where members of the priestly order could reach the storerooms where the wine, oil, flour, and other items needed in connection with the Temple service were kept. From there, they could reach the Temple platform. The exterior wall and lintels featured stone-carved decorations that boasted of floral and geometric motifs that conformed to Jewish law that forbade the representation of human or animal figures.

The Royal Stoa, a long exquisite hallway atop the Southern Wall that graced the Herodian Temple was not rebuilt, but a modern version resembling a covered outdoor patio with elegant limestone pillars, so highly polished that they resembled marble, evoked deep awe from the worshipers as they approached the Temple.

Once the group climbed the stairway from the parking fields to the south entrance of the Temple Mount they arrived on the plaza where they were then directed to another staircase with ten steps that would take them to the main entrance of the Double Gate. As they ascended the staircase, a section of the ancient wall where the ancient shops had been was preserved and exposed to allow the public a view of the ruins.

"Yair!" Paul called as he pointed toward the clear acrylic shield protecting the monument, "look at the burn mark imprinted in the Temple Mount wall!"

Yair paused to observe the phenomenon. It was a ghastly reminder of the burning of the Temple by the Romans in A.D. 70 when they overran the Temple and its precincts, taking brushwood and placing it inside the archways and setting it ablaze. The intense heat reduced the limestone to powder, causing the arch to collapse. But before the arch collapsed, the fire burnt into the back wall of the chamber, leaving the imprint of the arch as a symbolic testimony to the dreadful inferno.

When they passed through the entranceway into the gate building on the upper level they were surprised to see a large wall with photographs, illustrations, and diagrams of the subterranean passageways and cisterns that formed a complicated labyrinth beneath the Temple Mount. Paul waved to all the male members of the group to flock to the wall to study the findings of years of exploration by renowned scientists, engineers, and archeologists. Shira gazed off into the crowds, looking for someone she might recognize.

The charts explained the complex network that few pilgrims or tourists ever knew existed. One chart diagramed the location of all the underground cisterns that were cut into the limestone bedrock. Another computer-generated illustration explained how the quarrying of these cisterns provided the stones used for some of the Temple buildings on the surface.

Pictures of the cisterns were captivating. One large E-shaped cistern with the capacity to hold over 700,000 gallons of water could easily supply ancient Temple militia with ample drinking water in the event of a siege. Another photograph and diagram described the gigantic underground cistern known as the Great Sea with its giant finger-like openings, cut 43 feet below the level of the Temple Mount and located beneath the site of the former Akra fortress. It could hold an estimated three million gallons of water.

After ten minutes of examining the display, Shira summoned the men to her aid. The crowds were becoming very rambunctious, and they wanted to get to the dedication site inside the courtyard.

Their eyes widened like saucers once they arrived on the great court, intended for the use of the people. The sidewalls of the great court were covered with carved work, representing cherubim, garlands, palms, and opening flowers. The doors by which the people and the priests entered the great court were made of polished bronze with stunning reliefs of seraphim. Above the walls were porticos that ran all around it with three sides having triple piazzas. The porticoes were covered with roofs of cedar supported by marble pillars paved with mosaic work.

The area where they stood, the outer court, could be frequented by Gentiles and unclean persons, and had on its inner side and extending all around a rampart surrounded with a stone parapet, the top of which was reached by a flight of fourteen steps. In each corner was a room,

256

used respectively for storing the wood deemed unfit to be burned on the altar; for those affected with contagious diseases to wash themselves; for storing sacrificial wine and oil; and for the cooking of the flesh of the consecrated sacrifices. The stalls and holding pens for the red heifers and other clean animals used for sacrifice were kept in the lower level.

The inner court, used exclusively as the court of the Israelites was at the western gate of the outer court and was reached by a stair of fifteen steps. This court surrounded the Temple, and against its wall were chambers for storing the utensils required for the services. In this court stood the altar of burnt offering, made of unwrought stone. Between the altar and the porch of the Temple stood the round bronze laver used for ritual washing.

The exterior of the Temple proper area could be seen from Paul's vantage point, but the interior was concealed from view. The Temple stood much higher than the court of the priests and was approached by a flight of twelve steps. The Temple was built over the Rock and stood upon massive blocks of white marble, richly ornamented with gold both inside and out. The two-story building was in the shape of a T, with the porch of the building, forming the cross member of the T, boasting of a vestibule that ran 150 feet in length.

At the back of the vestibule were the main double doors that led into the Holy Place, where ordinary rituals took place. Inside the Holy Place were the table of showbread, the seven-branched lamp stand, the altar of incense, and the utensils used for sacrifice. In ancient times the Holy Place was divided from the Holy of Holies by a curtain that stretched from floor to ceiling, but the curtain was torn in two pieces at Christ's crucifixion and therefore lost its Judaic significance and was never replaced. In this Temple, a symbolic blue veil was used. The inside of the Holy of Holies that was at one time occupied by the Ark of the Covenant and the Mercy Seat, now remained empty.

Scores of ushers were busy escorting the worshipers to the rows of chairs that filled the outer court. As Paul's group walked toward the seating area, a man carrying a sack of handbills approached him and stuffed a flyer in his pocket then moved on to another patron. Paul looked at the handbill that read:

MOSHIACH HAS ARRIVED!
Draw Your Own Conclusions...

THE MOSHAICH MUST
RISE FROM THE DEAD!

Russian and the Arab-bloc nations
have been humbled,
and the people of Israel
have emerged victoriously!
Daniel's prophecy of the Temple Rebuilding
has been gloriously fulfilled!
With European Jews returning,
the prophecy of Ezekiel is being fulfilled!
We are living in extraordinary times...
where we are at a state of peace!

**The Moshiach who will usher in
the final redemption of our people...
has arrived!**

He will set Israel up as the head of all nations!

Draw Your Own Conclusions...

"Who do you suppose they're talking about?" Shira asked Yair as he looked on. In her heart she already knew the answer.

"It's quite obvious to me Kavidas is the only candidate that currently fits this description," Yair said, bristling, as further proof of Kavidas' acceptance was being circulated. "Undoubtedly this flyer is pointed at the skeptical and unbelieving faction of Hasidim and other sects of Judaism that have rejected him since he's a Gentile, but that will change in time."

Both Paul and Yair knew that Kavidas' rise to messiahship would be marked by miracles and further victories for the nation of Israel, thereby convincing every Jew of his blasphemous claim to the throne. He would capitalize on their expectation of the Messiah being, first, a political and military leader that would free them from Gentile oppression and, secondly, a spiritual cleric that would direct them in worship. This erroneous reasoning is what led the spiritual leaders of Jesus Christ's day to reject him since he did not demonstrate any military or political prowess. If they had correctly understood prophecy, they would have accepted him as Messiah who came to liberate them from the oppression of sin with his second coming to establish Israel as the head of all nations. In this sense, Kavidas was an anti-Christ, one who opposes Christ, to the Gentiles, while to the Jews, he was a type of Messiah who, like Joshua, would free them from their enemies as they inherited the Promised Land.

It was at times like this Shira began to question where she stood with God. *Could this Jesus really be the Messiah?*

"Paul, look at all those harpists!" Yair blurted out as he pointed to the section of the courtyard cordoned off for the Temple orchestra. There were 25 harpists along with other ancient musical instrument players practicing for the ceremony.

Paul had read that the Temple Institute was preparing scholars and local artisans for this very day. They were making priestly garments and implements, including the special Amizrak, used to transport the blood for the sacrificial ceremony, and a 24-carat gold crown, or mitre, for the high priest. Many of the plans for the priests' facilities in the rebuilding were gathered from the Temple activist movement known as the *Atara L'yoshna*, dedicated to restoring Jewish life to its former state.

Paul turned toward the inner court and replied, "Look over there at the priests filing out of their chambers with their woven linen garment, robes, and headdresses." Now that the Temple would be fully operational, the worship services would be attended by the priests, with the high priest, the Kohen-Gadol, officiating over all.

Once they were seated, Jonathan turned to Paul and said, "In a way this is very exciting, as we witness the way they performed the temple worship service back in the time of Christ." Paul knew that this Temple in no way compared with the splendor of the Solomonic or the Herodian Temple, but the actions of the priests and the musicians would be similar.

Yair tapped Paul on the shoulder, then pointed toward a group of news reporters that were concentrated in one section of the stoa that stood high above the crowds. Paul could read two banners that hung below the makeshift booth that read *Maarriv* and *Haaretz*, two of Israel's leading newspapers. It reminded him of a stadium featuring a sports event with the journalists sequestered high up in a cubicle, overlooking the athletes who were trying to outwit and overpower their opponents. He wondered if that would happen today.

What Paul didn't know was that the Temple Preservation Commission had instructed the news media that only coverage showing the ceremony in a positive way should be televised.

As Paul studied the program a sudden attack of acid indigestion came over him as he realized that he had been swept up in the fervor of the moment—the celebration of the dedication—while their real purpose in attending the event was not to commemorate the dedication of the Temple, but to expose and disgrace Kavidas and his evil plot before he duped countless others. His indigestion, inherited from his father, only acted up when his anxiety level increased. He perceived that it would be at an all-time high today. He popped two antacids into his mouth, then nodded to Levi to brace himself for what might happen next as two of the speakers walked out of a side room unto the large, ornately decorated, bronze rostrum that contained three lecterns.

Paul recognized them as Defense Minister Zeev Drori, and Chief of Staff Michael Weinstein. The center chair reserved for the keynote speaker was vacant.

"It's game time!" Paul whispered in Yair's ear.

Yair gave him a reassuring nod.

Paul looked over at the rest of the group to see if they were prepared for the event. The look he saw on their faces was one of controlled fear.

The service began with ancient Temple worship music that lasted for ten minutes before two rabbis and the high priest walked to the lecterns to call the multitude of worshipers to prayer. After the prayer, six priests accompanied the high priest into the Temple proper area and to the stone altar where they lit the firewood under the carcass of a red heifer. Then the high priest carried the mizrak used to transport the blood into the Holy of Holies, where he symbolically sprinkled the blood on the mercy seat of the Ark of the Covenant. He remained in the inner sanctuary for several minutes then walked out with his hands raised triumphantly in the air. Shortly afterward, when he appeared before the multitudes with the six priests, he again raised his hands to signify God's acceptance of the sacrifice and the forgiveness of the nation's sins. The crowds cheered and cried openly as they realized God had shown them favor by reinstituting the sacrificial system.

The high priest, along with the six other priests, bowed to the crowd then retreated to the priest's chambers as Defense Minister Drori and Chief of Staff Weinstein rose to their feet and walked to their respective lecterns. Weinstein nodded to Drori who, in turn, greeted the masses with hands raised. "Shalom, and welcome to our dedication ceremony," he said warmly into the microphone. "We are here today to celebrate the momentous occasion of the Temple rebuilding and to recognize a great political leader that loves our nation. Firstly, let us thank God for his benevolent watchful care, which saw fit to deliver us from our enemies! Our nation's existence is a continuing tribute to the God of Abraham, Isaac, and Jacob! He will never slumber, nor will he sleep. It is at his command that we, as a nation, draw breath."

The crowds cheered thunderously.

"Secondly, we must thank those who sacrificed their lives in the invasion to which God saw fit to use them as a testimony to their patriotism and love for their nation." He made a sweeping gesture with his hand, then pointed toward the Temple proper. "Now, for the first time in over two thousand years, we have been privileged by God to build a sanctuary to honor him. This Temple is the fulfillment of Daniel's prophecy that predicted the Temple must be standing in order for Messiah to come. Well, the Temple is fully operational, and we are at peace in the land! Now, knowing this to be true, can the Messiah be far off? Could he indeed be among us today?" He stopped to nod to Weinstein, who picked up the cue to continue, but the crowds erupted in a jubilant uproar, chanting, "Kavidas! Kavidas! We want Kavidas!"

Paul nudged Yair with his elbow. "I was afraid of this. The crowds are behaving like religious fanatics. Add Kavidas' political stratagem, and he's got them right where he wants them. The amalgam of religion and politics by evil forces always seems to gives rise to totalitarianism. Listen to the way they cry out for Kavidas!"

Yair nodded in assent at Paul's observation as his stomach began to knot up while the groundswell that began with Drori started to take on frenetic proportions. He glanced up at the top of the wall surrounding the Temple compound and realized that Mossad and IDF forces were systematically patrolling the perimeter, carefully watching the crowds for potential troublemakers. A wave of foreboding came over him. He knew in his heart that things were not going to end well this day.

"My fellow countrymen," Weinstein began as he gestured the crowds to silence. "Never before in the annals of Israel's history have we been so fortunate to enjoy God's blessings as we have today. With that in mind, what could be the greatest blessing God could bestow upon our nation? His Messiah!

"In our nation's past we have been visited with many who claimed their right to the throne of David. There was a Jesus, a Bar Kochba, a Rabbi Shneerson, and countless others who have come and gone over the centuries. And each time a so-called 'messiah' rose up to vanquish Israel's enemies, they were either found out to be a counterfeit, were miserably defeated, or were prohibited from ascending the throne by divine Providence—until today!"

Weinstein looked at Drori. "As our Defense Minister Drori mentioned, the sequence of events points to a time when the Messiah should appear. A Messiah who would galvanize our nation spiritually, politically, and I might add, militarily." He hesitated once again, but this time raised both hands in the air. "The event the prophets foretold would distinguish the true Messiah from all others has happened before your very eyes—his rising from the dead!" Weinstein then bowed as if he were standing before a god as Kavidas walked on the platform.

The crowds jumped to their feet, waving their hands in the air and shouting, "Blessed is he that comes in the name of the Lord! Blessed be his holy name!"

Above the deafening cries, Yair pulled Paul's head toward him and said in his ear, "They deliberately neglected to make mention of the plagues, the seal judgments, that are devastating their nation all around them! They are doing what the false prophets did during the time of Jeremiah—proclaiming a false reality, a false peace."

Paul simply shook his head as the realization of that truth settled in. Then he shot a look at Levi, who was very quiet, seemingly entranced by what he was experiencing.

Kavidas walked to the middle of the platform and called for the high priest to join him at his side. Paul noted that Kavidas attempted to duplicate the very position Solomon had taken at the dedication of the first Temple—standing on a bronze platform in the middle of the Temple courtyard. He wondered what other elements in Solomon's dedication Kavidas would attempt to credit to himself.

As the high priest approached Kavidas, Paul suddenly noticed Stein was conspicuously absent. His eyes searched the area behind the platform, the preparation rooms off to the side, then the crowds. Finally Paul spotted Stein sitting down in the front row with a smug look on his face. Paul knew Stein would be near, and he knew he would be exultant. *Now with Satan alive and well here in our midst, we have the phony trinity complete,* he thought.

"I have asked our high priest to accompany me today," Kavidas began as the crowds fell silent, "because this is a highly charged religious event in the life of our nation and he needs to be a part of it. Historically, the high priest has always acted as the mediator between

God and his people; representing the people in the Holy of Holies; bringing the blood of atonement before the throne of grace while confessing the sins of the nation." He paused to put his arm around the high priest's shoulders. "But that dispensation ended with the destruction of the Second Temple and the dismantling of the priesthood.

"I am delighted to inform you that while the priesthood is now fully operational, they are only acting symbolically in the capacity of the high priest because the priests are no longer needed. However, with the Temple being operational, we must carry on the tradition of the priesthood and utilize them as the Gentiles do in their church services when they celebrate communion. Their communion is symbolic of their belief that Jesus Christ died for their sins. When they participate in communion they are remembering that event. Now in our time, the priests will perform their priestly duties as in the past, but it is only representative of our heritage because—" he came to an abrupt stop and held his hands up in the air while he hung his head in mock humility— "God has appointed *me* to mediate and intercede on behalf of this great nation."

The audience jumped to their feet and began clapping.

Levi grabbed Yair's arm when he heard Kavidas' claim and with fury in his eyes said, "This is blasphemous! He just put himself in the place of the Jesus the Messiah, who *did* die for sin!"

Yair patted Levi's hand as the roar of the crowds reached a fever pitch. "God will not allow our Jesus to be ridiculed, you'll see," he soothed. But Yair's attempt to appease Levi's righteous anger failed.

Moments later, as the crowds were swept up in the religious fervor of the moment, a supernatural quiet suddenly overpowered the entire Temple compound. Paul sensed a flurry of demonic activity was taking place, as if divisions of evil spirits had emerged and were beginning to influence the people. He shot a look at Stein, who appeared to be praying. He turned to Yair and said in his ear, "Look at Stein! He's calling up the forces of darkness to control the people!"

Then the masses began to move their chairs out of the way so they could kneel on the ground. During the stirring of the chairs, Levi began to stand up as anger seized his heart, only to be pulled down by Paul and Yair. He forced himself away from their grip and with tears stinging his eyes said haltingly, "I will not stand by idly and let them blaspheme my Lord!" With determined strength he pushed his way to the center aisle and stood there. With the people sitting or on their knees, Levi was the only one standing.

Paul looked at the top of the walls to see that the Mossad and IDF agents had their rifles trained on Levi, watching him as a hunter follows his prey. "Don't do anything foolish!" he whispered aloud. *Lord, if there were ever a time to send your witnesses, Nocham and Qadar, it's now. Hurry!*

Kavidas sensed Levi as an enemy, yet he masterfully controlled the scene by nodding to Stein, who returned the signal and started to walk toward Levi, while motioning to the Mossad and IDF agents that they should stand down.

A strange atmosphere pervaded the entire compound, for not even one person—outside of Paul, Yair, and their group—noticed Levi standing. The Temple devotees were in a state of trance-like worship.

As the quiet permeated the Temple Mount, the high priest laid his hands on Kavidas to pronounce his blessing as Kavidas knelt on the platform with his hands spread out toward heaven. The high priest then cried out, "Praise be to God who has given rest to his people Israel just as he promised. May he never leave us or forsake us. And now we thank you, God, for sending us the Moshiach, the anointed one, who will act as our new David to rule our nation politically, as well as our Messiah who will lead our nation spiritually. May his reign never end as—"

"HE IS NOT THE MESSIAH!" Levi screamed out while pointing his finger at Kavidas.

The outburst caught the high priest unaware. He quickly released Kavidas and shot his hands up in the air as if to surrender. Kavidas jumped to his feet and gestured toward the men on the wall. Then Stein reached Levi and grappled him to the ground as many of the Mossad and IDF agents on the wall dropped to one knee to assume a ready stance.

"DON'T SHOOT!" Yair yelled out as he pushed his way through the crowds. Suddenly Paul and the rest of the group found themselves rushing along with Yair to Levi's side as he squirmed his way free from Stein. Once he was free, Levi bolted with a vengeance toward Kavidas.

As the crowds broke out of their mesmerized state, their eyes darted back and forth between Levi and the guards on the walls. Several people yelled out, "Run for your lives!" The crowds panicked and began fleeing down every staircase.

Levi and Stein reached the platform at the same time. Levi flew at Kavidas and began throttling him as Stein attempted to pull him off. The high priest, along with Drori and Weinstein, joined in, but they could not overtake Levi's hold on him.

"YOU ARE THE ANTICHRIST!" Levi screamed out as his hands tightened around Kavidas' throat.

"I can't get a shot! I can't get a shot!" Paul heard from the wall as he neared the platform.

Stein managed to pull Levi away from Kavidas momentarily, but a supernatural strength allowed him to regain his grip. By then Paul and his group were at the scene.

Several sprays of bullets began to splatter all along the platform. Everyone froze as if paralyzed from fear. The firing stopped. Everyone but Kavidas and Levi backed off, leaving Levi alone in the open with just one hand clutching Kavidas' neck.

A single shot rang out from the wall.

Seconds later Levi moaned as blood began spurting out his neck. Then he fell to one side and released his grip on Kavidas.

The frenzy worsened as the *Koinonos* group, who was also attending, lost their sense of reason and attacked both Kavidas and Stein. Paul and Yair and their group had the presence of mind to clear away from the platform area, but the *Koinonos* members flew into a rage. They knocked Stein, Drori, and Weinstein to the platform on top of Kavidas and began violently kicking them.

Gunfire erupted once again.

The sharpshooters on the wall began killing off members of the *Koinonos* group one by one until all twenty-four of them lay dead.

Several minutes after the shooting ended, the inquisitive crowds slowly began to return.

Paul looked at Yair in horror, then started toward the platform

266

when a loud gush of wind was heard. Then a giant whirlwind suddenly erupted in the middle of the courtyard. The speed of the whirlwind accelerated, creating a violent vortex that started sucking the chairs into its throat until Nocham and Qadar stepped out of it. Nocham raised his hand and the whirlwind began to slow until it simply became a whisper of rotating air. Paul looked into the fading whirlwind and thought he saw what looked like a team of white horses pulling a fiery chariot back to heaven.

Qadar looked down upon the piles of dead bodies, then up to the wall. Paul noticed a visible change in his countenance to one of anger as he raised his hand and cried out, "Those who live by the sword, shall die by the sword!" Lightning bolts shot out of his hand, striking every guard on the wall who carried a weapon. Their flaming bodies slumped and fell off the wall into the courtyard below.

The returning crowds were stunned as the drama unfolding before their eyes. Many screamed out in fear, while others just dropped their mouths open in utter disbelief and searched for something tangible to hold on to. Then Qadar turned his wrath on the idol worshipers. As several hundred stood near the east wall, shuddering in fear, he cried out once again, "If the Lord is God, follow him; but if Baal is God, follow him—to your grave!"

Then he pointed his finger at the worshipers, and fire burst forth like a flame thrower. The flames shot across the courtyard, incinerating the worshipers as they stood in horror. Nothing remained of them but smoldering embers.

"Stay here!" Paul and Yair together yelled to their group as they dashed to the platform.

As they started pulling bodies off the pile to reach Levi, Qadar latched onto their collars and yanked them off, saying, "Stand back!" Paul and Yair exchanged looks as their faces contorted with the pain of Levi's death and the terror that seized their hearts.

Nocham's watchful eyes were focused on Kavidas and Stein. As they began to slip away, he stretched out his hand to them and cried out, "Stand fast!" Their bodies immediately became immobilized. Then Nocham turned to the high priest, who was hiding behind Drori and Weinstein. He stared at them for several seconds, then stretched out his hand at them, but they suddenly turned and ran off the platform, seeking refuge behind a stone column.

Qadar motioned to Yair and commanded, "Bring Levi to me!"

Yair blinked in recognition, then reached into the pile of corpses and pulled Levi's limp body out into the open next to Qadar. Nocham then joined Qadar, whereupon they both laid hands on the lifeless Levi.

Yair retreated several steps as every eye in the Temple compound was riveted on the two witnesses from God. When he shot a look back at Shira, Jonathan, and Simon, they were on their knees sobbing and praying. Only Shlomo remained standing.

Nocham pulled a vial of oil from his cloak and poured a small measure on Levi's head while Qadar pressed his hands around Levi's neck. They both turned their heads toward heaven and closed their eyes as they prayed in unison, "Lord Jesus, the Giver and Sustainer of life, we entreat you to bring life back into your servant, Levi. Through the limitless power of your Spirit, we claim the promise proclaimed in your Word that your witnesses may call upon You to raise the dead!"

Levi's eyes fluttered. Then color returned to his face as life forces were being renewed second by second by the power of the Living God. Yair looked down upon his charge and saw Levi's chest heaving as his lungs began gulping in air. Levi spit up blood as he coughed several times, then he touched his neck and said through a muffled gag, "I'm alive!"

Yair jumped up in the air and quoted Christ jubilantly, " 'For I am the resurrection and the life. He who believes in me will live, even though he dies!'" Paul ran to his side and helped him lift Levi to his feet.

Nocham turned to Paul and Yair and ordered, "Leave the Mount now!"

Moments quickly passed as Nocham and Qadar waited for them to clear off the platform. Then Qadar pointed toward the dead members of the *Koinonos* group and cried out with a vibrating voice, "Four seals have been opened! Now behold, the Fifth Seal!"

Douglas heard the loud decree and knew immediately that the Fifth Seal was the martyrdom of the saints, a grizzly image when he thought on the carnage that lay upon Kavidas' altar.

Qadar raised one hand and the whirlwind began to materialize out of thin air once again. Then with the other hand he pointed toward an exit gate. As he pointed toward the gate, all the chairs and any onlookers were immediately swept to the sides to create a path for Paul and his groups to escape. Paul realized the opportunity and motioned to Yair to hasten the evacuation out of the area. Within minutes they were all off the Temple Mount heading toward Paul's home.

When Kavidas became conscious of his surroundings once again, he realized that something drastic had to be done in order to stop the assaults on his ministry by these two witnesses and their followers.

He would have to call upon greater forces than himself to accomplish it.

EIGHTEEN

Tartaros, The Subterranean Abode of the Fallen Seraphim
Somewhere Near the Euphrates River

The unregenerate souls and spirits of mankind will never be permitted into the infernal regions of the subterranean prison assigned to those fallen angels who abandoned heaven in a vain attempt to corrupt the messianic line to Christ by having sexual intercourse with antediluvian women. No, the unregenerate spirits of mankind who have rejected God's truth are held captive in a separate dungeon where the light of this world does not shine, where perpetual darkness prevails, where the unending burning and pain from the unquenchable fires never ceases. That place of torture and torment where man is forever alienated from God is called in the Hebrew, *Sheol,* or *Gehenna;* in the Greek, *Hades;* or in English, *Hell.* It is situated in a separate dwelling compartment of the nether world somewhere in the bowels of the earth where unrelenting flames sear, singe, and scorch, yet never consume.

Hell is that place where heat and noxious fumes smother every chance at life for those who have turned aside from God's plan of salvation. The place where the shades or pale reflections of the men and women that had once been dwell in endless regret. This Hell, one foreordained day in the future, will be cast into the lake of fire, where the smell of burning sulphur fills the nostrils of the dead, where the dead will spend all eternity. But for now, Hell—that blasphemous place where demonkind rule—is reserved for those angels that followed Satan, and for the departed souls of men who believed his lie. The place where those evil angels who have followed Satan dwell and are allowed transport to the surface to inflict untold miseries on man.

Not far away from Hell is the underground chamber of confinement called *Tartaros*, where the upper hierarchy angels belonging to the evil company of angels called the *Techaspith* are imprisoned. Here, ordinances unlike those in Hell are binding on the incubi. In Tartaros, the seraphim or *chayoth*, in the Hebrew, who mated with woman six millennia ago are now chained together, waiting for that fateful day when the gate that holds them will be opened. Opened in that day by a divine decree to permit them passage to the surface where they will kill one third of all humanity.

To facilitate his plan for the ages, however, God in his limitless counsel, would permit the release of one seraph to wreck havoc on the earth for a brief period.

Accustomed to the utter darkness, Abaddon, the custodian of Tartaros, felt his way toward the dungeon where the seraph abides in solitary confinement. Over the centuries he had methodically cut into the cavernous walls certain markers to guide him as he traversed the busy labyrinth that connected his abode with the prison cell of which he was the keeper.

If it were possible to have shadows in darkness, his penumbra would reveal his composite profile of both human and animal parts that make up his species of demonkind: a human-like head and face with sight, smell, and voice that is also capable of thought, volition, and temperament, as well as that which is necessary to carry out evil machinations. His cunning, malignant mind was dissolute and devoid of holiness, dedicated to the sole purpose of undermining the promises of God through deceit and wantonness. His memory, however, was fully conscious and recalled his joyful habitation with the Holy One until sin was found in their leader.

Abaddon had an animal-like body that was brutish and immense in size with arms and legs grotesquely out of proportion, as well as oversized wings that form the frame of this superior angel. His six wings, in three pairs, covered his face and feet while also providing flight to travel within the allotted arena of his designated domain.

As the custodian of this underworld, devoid of God's loving kindness, Abaddon grasped the key to the confinement room ever-so-tightly as he slowly walked the passageway channeled from his footsteps over the eons since his imprisonment. As he neared the cell he heard the sound of chains dragging hastily on the rocky ground as if the inmates heard his approaching. He could hear the dragging sounds come to an abrupt halt as they reached the gate. In a way, he experienced a kind of absolute power, knowing that he alone possessed the single key that could unlock the gate that would release the seraphim from the never-ceasing agony they had endured over the centuries.

The creatures waited at the gate in hopes that the day of their temporary release had come, only to slowly retreat in agony and disappointment as Abaddon pointed to the one he admired—Asmodeus. His predilection for Asmodeus was determined because of the creature's pernicious nature toward Israel and propensity toward death and devastation of the inhabitants of the earth.

As Asmodeus walked through the gate to his temporary freedom, he renewed his hatred for mortals, who were offered salvation while angels were deprived of such. Resolute in purpose, he would take on the challenge of blocking and destroying any living soul from discovering and following the Truth.

"Here is your written assignment and limits of authority, Asmodeus," Abaddon instructed in a language known only to angels.

Asmodeus opened the parchment and made a fist in triumph as his deformed wings attempted to extend behind his body. This signified victory, for he would be allowed to bring death to the nonbeliever. But as he read further, his wings quickly retracted, signaling defeat,for he would only be permitted to harass the true believer. *Alas*, he thought, *I shall make the best of my assignment and bring honor to the one I worship.*

Independence Park, Jerusalem

Kavidas looked at his reflection in his bathroom mirror as flashbacks from the Temple Mount incident came to mind. *How dare they come to the celebration and disgrace me like that! Yes, but they are very powerful,* he reasoned, *capable of greater miracles than we can perform—especially raising the dead. We can only imitate that type of spectacle. That blasted Douglas and Kaplinsky! And oh, the setback to our purpose! But that's all right, because what we have in mind will eclipse anything that they can design.*

Instead of dwelling on the humiliation, Kavidas would, by a deliberate act of his will, consider it merely a temporary reversal and keep going. He bolstered himself by the thought that man's propensity and desire for evil would enable his cause to ultimately triumph, and that his purpose would be to continue to feed that tendency until their minds reasoned in favor of the flesh and gave in.

Ah! he thought, *there is where the victory lies!* He sighed in relief and continued in the diatribe with himself. *Let those two so-called witnesses be damned! But you know that their powers are virtually unlimited; then again, their time on earth is indeed limited. Yes, just a little more than three years, and we'll be free of them. We'll just have to work around them, that's all. What to do with leaders Douglas and Kaplinsky, then? We'll gather support from those authorities and powers that are at our disposal. That's what we shall do with them!*

He managed to crack a smile as he steeled himself against defeat and resolutely determined in his heart to turn the Temple Mount incident into a victory.

He walked out of the bathroom and glanced out the living room window as the approaching darkness caught his attention. He looked at the clock on his bedroom dresser and thought, *It's only 4:00 P.M., yet nightfall is approaching.* An eerie and foreboding feeling came over him as the realization that the seal of darkness was not only pervasive, but also progressing. It was another reminder that they had no time to waste to accomplish their mission. *Stay focused,* he reminded himself, *stay focused.*

The phone rang and he knew it was Stein.

273

"Gregory," Stein said. "I have given the order."

Kavidas nodded in relief and ended the call. Moments later, invigorated with the news from Stein, a feeling of ultimate conquest came over him. He really felt good. Then the credo of Hannibal, the Carthaginian conqueror, suddenly came to mind: *"I find a way or I make one."*

Paul Douglas' Apartment
Hativat Yerushalayim Street

The atmosphere at Paul's apartment at dinnertime was bittersweet. While Paul and Jonathan were concerned with the future welfare of their group, Yair was reveling in the joy of the Lord with Levi at his side. The mundane conversation helped to divert the tension of the Temple Mount incident, until after a moment of meditation, Jonathan asked, "Paul, if Nocham and Qadar are acting in the spirit of Elijah like you said, then why doesn't the Lord just have them call down fire from heaven and wipe out those villains, Kavidas and Stein? After all, God knows that they're the Antichrist and false prophet!"

Paul looked askance at the muted TV as continuous coverage of what had been labeled *The Temple Mount Massacre* inundated regular broadcasting throughout the day. "Because the time of their judgment is yet future. That time being when Christ comes back, a little more than six and one-half years from now." Paul felt a wave of confidence come over him the moment he uttered those words. *To think*, he thought, *that we know just when He is coming back is unbelievable. Yet, the timetable was unalterable. What a confidence!* "Until that time, they are immortal; they can't be killed," he added ruefully.

"So until then," Jonathan asked, following up his question with another as the conversation began to engage the others around the table, "we just have to tough it out?"

Jonathan's question raised other questions in Paul's mind. *How do the survivors cope with the death of members from the K-group, as well as countless others who will perish in the years to come as a result of the judgment of the Fifth Seal?*

"In a way, yes, we just have 'to tough it out.' While we must oppose Kavidas and his evil forces, we must also be vigilant to evade his tenacious grasp. We must rely on God's protection while doing everything possible to slow him down." He paused to point upward. "We do have resources from above to help us for the next three years—Nocham and Qadar—and after that we once again will need to rely solely on the Lord for direction."

"The way I see it," Yair joined in, "we are in a time similar to the Old Testament economy of the kings. Whenever the Lord wanted to chastise Israel or one of its rulers, he raised up an enemy as a rod of correction. One that comes to mind that continuously acted as an irritant with their constant border skirmishes and raids was the Philistines."

"Are you making a corollary to Kavidas and his crew along with Hamas, Hezbollah, and the Arab nations?" Shira asked curiously.

"Absolutely," Yair asserted. "Our sovereign God knows exactly what he's doing. He has allowed the emergence of these enemies to bring about the reformatory measures needed in the world to bring in his kingdom. Then they will be judged and get what's coming to them!"

"I remember my dad telling about an article by John MacArthur that he read when he was in Bible college," Paul said. "It was about the different kinds of wrath God can bring upon man. There's the *eternal* wrath, where one suffers everlasting punishment in hell. Then there's *apocalyptic* wrath, where massive disasters and calamities are poured out upon mankind in the last days of the world. Then there is the *cataclysmic* wrath where God brings an end to a city or even a civilization such as in the case of Sodom and Gomorrah or in the days of Noah's flood. But the worst kind of wrath is that of *abandonment*, where God gives people over completely to their own sinful desires. He steps back and lets it rip. They want their sin so badly that God lets them wallow in it without hindrance. He simply withdraws his restraining grace."

A moment of silence permeated the room as the weight of that truth settled on the group.

Mustering up the courage to break the silence, Shira asked, "Where are we now, Paul?"

Paul shot a look at Yair, then swallowed hard and shook his head. It was a sobering revelation that they were experiencing the worst kinds of wrath. "Both the apocalyptic and abandonment, I'm afraid to say. The recurrence of the world's lack of repentance toward sin being the major cause."

Upon hearing the ominous sentence, Shira turned her head toward the kitchen window, only to notice something strange. She walked to the windowsill and began to examine the Christmas cactus plant that was blooming. *Flowering three months early?* she asked herself. It was just another reminder that daylight hours were shortening, playing tricks on nature. *The plant thinks it's December since it gets dark so early.* Slightly numbed, she returned to the table and listened to the ongoing conversation.

"We should be making preparations for leaving Jerusalem," Yair warned. "Kavidas must be really 'ticked' after being embarrassed at the Temple Mount. I would really love to be a 'fly on the wall' at his place when they discuss the raising of Levi. That must have really bummed him out!" He sighed. "We can expect retaliation of greater proportions than what he's been dishing out so far." He turned to Paul and suggested, "I think we should move some of the surviving members of the K-group to Petra to be safe. We must protect a remnant."

"I think it's a wise decision," Paul replied. "You and I will organize other men from the K-group, then wait on Nocham and Qadar for instructions. The Lord will use them to be our protective shield."

"With the drought and food becoming scarce and ridiculously expensive, timing is crucial," Shira urged as she put her hand on Levi's shoulder. "Will you remain here in Jerusalem with Yair?" she asked as her breath caught in her throat.

"I must!" Levi answered succinctly and emphatically.

Paul and Yair nodded in agreement. "The Lord has need of Levi at this time," Paul soothed. "He'll be safe with us; you needn't worry." Turning to Shlomo and Simon he said, "You should prepare to leave within three days." *Or sooner if Kavidas begins to move in*, he thought, but he didn't say.

Even with the assurance of protection, Simon nibbled on his fingernails as his apprehension for Levi's safety mounted. "Be sure to stay close to Yair," he warned.

Levi smiled in return for his concern. The little gesture meant a lot to him.

Jonathan happened to look over at Paul's computer monitor and noticed a pop-up message. Seconds later it announced an incoming E-mail. "Paul, we have what looks like flash encryption E-mail coming in from Brandon Lane in Florida." Paul and Yair rushed to the computer monitor to read the E-mail.

[Incoming]
Hello, Paul, Yair, and the group. I gather things have been hectic over there, and you've been unable to write. That's okay, I understand. The incredible news about Levi and the massacre at the Temple Mount just came across the news ticker on the bottom of my TV screen while I was watching our local all-news channel. It read as if it were censored; therefore I wanted to get the truth from you. What does this have to do with Kavidas and his bunch?

[Sending]
I am sending you an encrypted file with all the details of the Temple rededication massacre that you can download. I'm sure that Kavidas now has control over the news going out of Israel, so this way you can read the unbiased truth for yourself. As far as Levi is concerned, we are all praising God for sending Nocham and Qadar. They are the two witnesses that God sent to bring condemnation upon Kavidas and his people, while all the time being a wall around us. If it weren't for their protection, we probably would all be dead by now.

It has become much too dangerous here in Israel due to an escalation in the conflict between Kavidas and our group, so we are sending the many of the K-group to Petra while Yair and Levi stay here in Jerusalem with me. Together we will direct the rest of the K-group with the help of Nocham and Qadar. It has been decided in view of the turn of events to move our base of operation to a secret location. We shall keep you advised of our whereabouts. Now, tell us what is going on over there in the States.

[Incoming]

We have been experiencing God's wrath in rapid succession over here, yet, never a hint of repentance; no, not even a moment of national prayer for guidance. When there was simply a reduction in food supplies and rampant inflation, the current administration chalked it up to environmental and economical disturbances. It seems that society just rolled with the punches.

But once the judgments worsened with the plague of AIDS going off the charts and unprecedented amounts of birth defects, unrelenting weird insect pestilence, and the domestic animals turning against their masters thing, the powers-to-be have begun to look at several possible causes. One, they looked back in history and have now been saying that many of our problems are the result of our treatment of Israel. There was a column on page three of the *Sun Times* two days ago that hinted that President Reynolds regretted not helping Israel out during the invasion, and these bizarre happenings are God's way of paying America back. If only he knew about the divine principle of Genesis 12:3 and God's judgment on immorality, we could have avoided much of our trouble. Two, the "powers" have directed some of the nation's churches to warn the people that moral turpitude leads to a decadent society. So they were advised to preach on moral restraints. As if that were really the problem.

The liberals, on the other hand, have been blaming all the trouble on the Christians and their *Koinonos* groups. They maintain God is punishing America because the Christians have been judging and condemning them before God. So, since they can't get back at God, they're taking it out on the Christian church. There have been "witch hunts" by vigilante groups, where pastors and many of the church faithful have been ridiculed and punished by lawsuits and other forms of prejudices. Then there are the secret killings that are going on that the news networks are silent about. It reminds me of the many criminal atrocities committed by the gays on straight people and how the media played it down so as not to offend the homosexual community. I see it all as an outworking of the Fifth Seal, the martyrdom of the saints that was predicted by Christ in Matthew 24, and John in Revelation 6.

If that weren't bad enough, we have the ever-threatening U.N.-Funded Commission on Global Governance over here that is mandating laws that are playing right into the hands of Kavidas and his purposes. They are using global warming, ozone depletion, and ecosystem destruction as primary reasons for mandating global governance that is nothing more than a new world "ethic" or religion called the Earth Charter. This Charter states that the rights of nature are defended first and foremost on the grounds of the intrinsic value of animals, plants, river, mountains, and ecosystems rather than simply on the basis of their utilitarian value or benefit to humans. This creates a mechanism to switch from the threat of war as a means of controlling society to something that would work in peace. It's called an environmental holocaust.

They are using this arena as a unifying principle by labeling these threats as a new enemy to unite the people against people themselves since the Commission states that these dangers are caused by human intervention, making the real enemy humanity itself. This, then, gives the government a hammer to force the people to give up their rights, whittling away national sovereignty. They're doing it by claiming that the eco-crisis is a global threat so great that it threatens life on earth. Add to that the judgments by God and you have the Commission claiming that the crisis should be controlled by a partnership between government and business, operating under a central super-agency to regulate environmental issues without any control.

But, you see, their goal is nothing less than to create a world system of financial control by a pseudo-private enterprise, namely Kavidas' *Masterlink* system that will dominate the political structure of each country and the economy of the world as a whole. This, in turn, will create a world government where the state is sovereign over its subjects, and where freedom and rights are granted at the pleasure of the state, not as inalienable, God-given rights envisioned by our Founding Fathers. As we speak, our Economic Security Council is meeting to incorporate the world economy and the International Monetary Fund in a central bank operated under the governance of *Masterlink*.

What is being concealed from the public is that global warming is a fraud—scientific facts show the atmosphere is actually cooling— and that these conservation biology issues are based on the pantheistic belief that God is in all things of nature and that they are essential to the survival of the earth itself. Of course, with America's weakened spiritual discernment; the Commission is adopting these corrective measures into law. This gives new meaning to the bumper sticker, *Save the Baby Humans.*

Several moments passed while Paul and Yair, along with several other onlookers digested Brandon's report. Based on the report, it was obvious that the spiritual conditions prevalent in the States were being mirrored around the world. It would take an act of God to change the course of events.

[Sending] Let us covenant to pray for each other as the Seal judgments worsen.

He signed off with the benediction:

Blessings from Paul Douglas and your friends here in Jerusalem.

Paul turned off the computer just as Simon walked out of the kitchen with his hand on his side. "Paul, I have bumps on me," he said curiously, "and they hurt."

Paul escorted him to the bathroom to investigate his claim, then quickly walked back out. "Yair, come look at this! Hurry!" he said with heightening alarm.

Paul and Yair examined Simon's back and saw that boils of some kind were erupting and rapidly progressing to cover his entire body. They appeared to be starting as welts, then hardening into boils filled with some kind of fluid. Paul asked Simon, "Have you eaten anything that could have caused an allergic reaction? A bug bite?" He knew the bubonic plague had subsided, so it couldn't be that.

Simon shook his head. "No," he replied as tears began to fall.

Paul was perplexed. He called Jonathan and Shira in and asked for their opinion of the outbreak, but they too were mystified.

"Let's get him to a doctor," Paul said with a tone vibrating with intensity.

Yair then wrapped Simon in a blanket. Within moments they were in his car on the way to the Biqqur Holim hospital emergency room.

Four miles from the house, Yair reached over and held Simon's hand. His hand was ice cold. He began whimpering and appeared to be visibly shaking from some kind of attack. "Let's have a word of prayer on the way," he said softly.

Simon nodded and squeezed his eyes closed.

"Lord God, we ask even now that you come and meet with us through the power of your Holy Spirit. We bring Simon before you and place him on your altar of mercy, asking you to heal his body because of the blood of our Lord and Savior Jesus Christ!"

A noticeable change in the temperature inside the car suddenly occurred. It was no longer cool, but warm. Yair then turned the air conditioner on just as Paul said, "Yair, pull over! The boils are going away!"

Seconds later Yair pulled the car to the curb and quickly got in the back seat. Paul lifted Simon's sweatshirt for Yair to see for himself what was happening. The swelling and inflammation from the boils was reversing. When he touched one of the boils, it was no longer hard, but soft. On his belly, the boils had totally disappeared while on his back and neck, they were visibly shrinking before their eyes.

"This is amazing!" Yair said in wonder. He sighed in relief and embraced Simon. "This is a miracle! The Lord healed you."

On the way back to their house Paul pondered the ramifications of the phenomenon he had just witnessed. When he looked in the rear-view mirror Simon was smiling, but his heart continued to be very unsettled.

Rear Patio, Renaissance Jerusalem Hotel

A Jew meeting with an Arab under the new regime in Jerusalem was not all that popular. Stein, looking to be as unobtrusive as possible, arranged a surreptitious meeting with Azib behind his hotel in a far corner of the pool area.

Stein was surprised that the hulk of man that stood before him produced such an impressive plan to move their objective of organizing a counteroffensive forward. He apparently possessed the brains of a brilliant strategist while maintaining the tenacity of a pitbull. He calculated that the combination would raise the enterprising Azib to a high-ranking terrorist in the days to come.

"I thought you might like to know," Azib began with a devilish grin, "that I've been keeping close tabs on that group at Petra, and it looks like there is some kind of build-up taking place."

"A build-up?" Stein countered.

"Yes. In addition to an increase in food shipments—staples, meats, etc.—there has been a significant increase in personnel. I'm not just talking about service people, but mostly Jews and some Gentiles that are moving in and taking up residency there. It's almost as if they were forming some kind of base and fortifying it. The women and children seem to be settling in and making it their home while the men who come on the weekends appear to be performing drills and preparing for some kind of military action. Strangely, they don't have any weapons."

Stein rubbed his chin as he pondered the development. He knew that prophecy dictated tPetra would be one of the last vestiges of resistance before the Christ returned, but for them not to arm themselves or prepare for conflict sounded unrealistic. Unless, he thought, they were thoroughly trusting that their God would deliver them from the enemy. *Preposterous!*

Stein nodded as he processed the data. "Keep me informed. What else have you got?"

Azib pulled out a Palm Pilot from his shirt pocket, keyed in his password, then looked at Stein, who had a curious look. "Surprised to see that we Bedouins are connected to the Internet?"

"Frankly, yes," Stein replied.

"Well, the West better to get used to it. We Arabs are no longer the 'sand diggers' the Americans claim we are. We are now people of means! Allah put *oil* under our 'sand' and we are going to profit from it until every drop is extracted and we have suppressed every last Jew," he added with stinging sarcasm.

I'm not going to engage this fool in an argument about Arab rights, Stein thought. *Even though I'm a Jew, this is not my fight.*

Stein knew that the Qur'an taught that Muslims were not allowed to make peace with non-Muslims and that Islam's goal was absolute supremacy throughout the world. He chuckled to himself when he remembered that prophecy prohibited such a victory. *But as long as they can dream about it, I can use them to work our plan. Their ideological zeal will be their undoing.*

"Fine. Knock yourself out!" Stein retorted. "The plan, please?"

Azib studied his Palm Pilot for several minutes to refresh his memory, then crossed one leg over the other as he prepared to give the report. "Since our last session I have met with many leaders. First, there are the Hamas and PLO survivors. They are totally with us. Then, secondly, there are the Hezbollah and Wahhabisi in Lebanon who are amalgamating their forces to face off with the Zionist dogs. To date, we have over 25,000 zealots, not counting splinter groups, who will fight!"

Stein scratched his head. "Who are the Wahhabisi? I've never heard of them."

"The Wahhabisi are African-American proselytes who have been recruited from American prisons and are now hiding here to fight along with us." He looked askance at Stein. "You're serious? You've never heard of them?"

Stein shook his head.

"Sort of uninformed, aren't you," Azib reminded Stein with a dig. "Well, there are Islamic clerics that have been trained in Saudi Arabia to go into the prisons in America and convert large numbers of Afro-Americans, not only to our religion, but also to our political ideals and objectives. And since many of the released prisoners need a platform to 'pay back' for perceived injustices done to them by white America, they are perfect for the Wahhabisim movement. By the way, 70 percent of the 2 million man prison population are Afro-American."

Stein was astounded at the numbers Azib brought to the table. His astonishment overpowered the impulse to slam the irritant with a sarcastic mouth that sat before him. He decided to let it go. "What else?"

"There is tremendous interest in the Arab world to form alliances with any nation, Muslim or non-Muslim, that will fight against Israel. I have secured reliable contacts in Afghanistan and Pakistan, along with other African nations such as Libya and Algeria and eastern countries such as China and Japan, who have demonstrated interest in mounting radical forces that will help us in our war against the Jews."

Azib closed his eyes, then began reciting what sounded like a prayer. " 'The Jews are smitten with vileness and misery and drew on them the indignation from Allah. The true Umma—the community of Islam—fight in the way of Allah; all infidels in the way of idols. So true Muslim, fight the friends of Satan. Then in the day of peace there will come a sudden overturning and the oppressors will come to naught.' " He opened his eyes and added, "The Qur'an 2:61; 4:78; 26:228."

"Impressive." Stein noted that when Azib quoted so passionately from the Qur'an that it had been years since he had heard a Christian quote from the Bible with equal intensity and enthusiasm. Turning aside, he gazed off into the hotel's garden to think on the prophecy of Armageddon in Revelation 14 and 16 and how this mule, Azib, just unwittingly voiced the preliminary line-up of the countries destined to come against God in the final war on the plains of Megiddo. "You earned your pay today, Azib," Stein said with a grin and a pat on the back. "I will see that 15,000 EU credits are transferred to your account before the day is out. The extra 5,000 is a bonus for your inventiveness."

"May Allah bless you," Azib replied gratefully with a bow. Seconds later he slipped out of sight.

Petra, Southern Jordan

Partly cloudy skies dominated the morning light, periodically muting the little bit of sunshine that managed to infiltrate the soaring cliffs that surrounded the fortress at Petra. The stronghold appeared to enjoy divine favor with God because, as the residents attested, there was more sunshine and daylight at Petra than in all of Israel. Perhaps even the rest of the world. But, despite the clouds, there was no rain.

Directly across from the magnificent Temple of the great Nabataean king, El Khazneh, was the 3,000-seat theater that once hosted the ancient city's athletes who later were drafted into the king's army to fight the Roman forces of General Pompey and Emperor Trajan. But now, as Yair and Simon sat on the stone benches scarred from centuries of battle and environmental corrosives, they could only imagine what happened in the past. More importantly to Yair was what God had planned for the future.

"Just imagine, Simon, what it will be like when this whole city is filled with the 144,000 Jewish preachers!" Yair exulted. He turned and pointed systematically to the ancient stairways, storehouses, and other monuments carved out of the reddish sandstone. "All of these buildings will be filled with God's people, both Jew and Gentile, waiting for his return."

"What will they all be doing, Yair? " Simon asked.

"Well, if I understand the Bible correctly, they will be going out into the land to proclaim Christ while at the same time condemning Kavidas and all those who follow him."

"What will Kavidas do to get even?"

An astute question coming from a young man, Yair thought. "He will try his hardest to stop them, and unfortunately, many others will join in the resistance and will be killed. That's why this safehouse will be mightily used of the Lord to harbor those fleeing from his evil wrath."

Distracted by sighting his brother and Shira exploring the rock tombs across the valley, Simon waved and yelled out, "Jonathan, Shira, we're over here!" They simply waved back and continued to investigate the site.

When Simon looked back at Yair, he was doubled over in pain. "What's the matter, Yair?!"

"I suddenly don't fell so well," Yair groaned while holding his stomach. Then he fell limp on the stone bench.

"Jonathan, Shira!" Simon yelled across the valley. "Come quick! Yair's fainted!"

It took all of one minute traveling at high speed to traverse the distance from the rock tombs to the theater. But when Jonathan and Shira arrived, Simon too, was in a dead faint.

Jonathan reached over frantically, lifted one of Yair's eyelids, then held his wrist. Then he repeated the procedure on his brother. "They're alive! They've fainted!"

"Maybe they've been poisoned!" Shira ventured aimlessly.

Jonathan lifted his brother up in his arms to carry him as Shira yelled out, "Somebody help!"

"Shira, get Yair and carry him to our quarters!" Jonathan instructed mechanically as he lumbered along with his brother in his arms.

Shira attempted to lift Yair as Jonathan suddenly came to an abrupt stop. "What are you doing?!" Shira asked roughly.

"Something's wrong here!" Jonathan realized. He nodded toward Shira and said, "Lay him back down again."

When both Yair and Simon were lying on the stone bench, Jonathan put laid his hands on them and said to Shira, "Join with me in prayer right now!"

"Pray?" said Shira.

"Yes, you may not believe, but you can still pray," Jonathan replied frantically.

Shira looked at him and felt a niggling discomfort in the pit of her stomach. "Since when did you cross over 'to the other side?' "

"You mean come to believe on Jesus?" he shot back.

Shira nodded.

"At the Temple compound when N & Q raised Levi from the dead," Jonathan added quickly. "Couldn't deny it any longer."

Jonathan placed his hands alongside Shira's on Simon's and Yair's heads. Jonathan then closed his eyes as he turned his face toward heaven and prayed fervently, "Lord Jesus, thank you for giving us the presence of mind to stop and call upon You. Because of the power of your blood, we now command any evil spirits that may be oppressing Yair and my brother, Simon, to depart in Your name!"

When Jonathan and Shira stopped praying and opened their eyes, both Yair and Simon were smiling and looking at the clouds going by.

Paul read the number on the caller-ID of his cell phone and adrenaline swept through his body like a flash flood. There were to be no calls from Petra except in an emergency since unfriendly agencies could easily track the number to its source. "Jonathan, is anything wrong?" he answered with heightening alarm.

"Paul we've had a problem here with Yair and Simon. They fell into a faint, but praise the Lord, they're all right now. So don't worry!"

Paul took a deep breath. "Jonathan, explain what happened." Jonathan gave him a quick reprise of the incident, then hesitated toward the end of the story. Paul sensed something else. "Put Yair on the phone," he instructed.

"Yair is resting right now, Paul," Jonathan replied cautiously.

"Simon?"

"He's outside walking around in the compound. He'll be all right as well."

"What do you think caused them to faint?" Paul asked. "The sun? The heat? What?"

"Well, it could have been the heat, but then…"

"But what? Are you telling me everything?" Paul pressed.

"To be honest, Paul, I think it was some kind of demonic attack," Jonathan finally blurted out. "It had all the earmarks of some kind of harassment because once we went into prayer and I invoked Christ's blood, the assault suddenly subsided. Within minutes, they were fine."

Paul tensed up from Jonathan's assessment. His hands tightly balled at his sides as a wave of helplessness washed over him. He mentally linked the previous incident involving Simon and began to calculate the chances of satanic oppression. He knew evil spirits could not possess Christians, but they could certainly be subjected to abuse, and as Christ's return neared, that abuse would naturally intensify exponentially. In his mind, Simon's salvation or lack thereof was in question, leaving him vulnerable to attack. In Yair's case, it was demonic oppression of a high magnitude.

"Have Yair call me the minute he wakes up." The thought of waging a battle against demonic forces in addition to fighting Kavidas and his bunch revolted Paul. *But then again*, he thought, *aren't they all in one cesspool together?*

One hour later, Yair called Paul and assured him that they were safe and that he must continue his work. Paul was relieved, but the thought of another attack gnawed at him.

NINETEEN

F azlur al-Bashar methodically drove his rented car around the Central Baptist Church in downtown Miami three times before finally parking it in the five-tier garage across the street. From there he walked to the Biscayne Donut Shop on the opposite corner and ordered a cup of black coffee and a Boston cream éclair. Then he retired to a booth in front of the window that held the church in full view. He made note of the day, Sunday, and the time, 10:30 A.M., then carefully recorded the number of faithful congregants and visitors attending the worship service. He counted approximately 750 and decided that the figure would satisfy his superiors. His superiors had determined two months earlier that before the fast of Ramadan arrived that American Christians should be made to empathize with those who were suffering over in Israel since they have been long supporters of the Zionists. Al-Bashar ordered another coffee and éclair, then lit up a Camel cigarette and thought about his next visit to this church.

Salt Lake City, Utah

The chapel at Smith College was extremely full on Sunday mornings. Both faculty and student body of the Alliance Church who viewed their work as continuing ministry for God rarely missed a worship service. This provided the perfect target for Kamran Sayyaf. From his car parked across the road, he secretly assessed the schedule and expected

289

attendees for his assignment. Satisfied after one hour of concentrated study, he left the school to meet with his mission supervisor, who was also an expert in explosives.

Folsom Stadium, University of Colorado

It was an easy task for Abdullah Siddiqi to breach the security at Folsom Stadium during the week. Posing as a member of the facility maintenance group responsible for cleaning the aisles and concession areas after each Sunday sports event, he wheeled his trash barrel through several aisles picking up litter and refuse, then stealthily worked his way down into the air-conditioning equipment compartment to begin his work.

He retrieved two shoebox size units from the garbage barrel, set the timer in each for the following Sunday morning, and placed them underneath the air conditioning intake vents. Then he covered the boxes with two dust filters to conceal them. Next, he wheeled the trash barrel up to the concession stand, where he removed the plastic bag containing the litter he picked up, making sure that the two remaining units inside the barrel were synchronized with the first two units, then placed an empty bag inside the barrel to satisfy any security check.

Once his work was complete, he casually walked to the utility area of the stadium and flung the trash bag into the garbage dumpster. Five minutes later he was driving back home to meet with other members of his cell group.

Lane Drugs, Miami

It was the same Sunday morning when some internal prompting reminded Brandon Lane that his unfinished quarterly report to the board of directors was due the next day. It was a task he'd volunteered to complete after his father's disappearance. It therefore constituted an emergency that required an immediate priority decision. His conscience dictated that he should tend to the matter after Sunday worship service, but an inner voice urged him to apply due diligence and complete it before going to church. He reasoned that this would free his mind and thereby enable uncluttered worship. With over an hour to spare, he drove past the Central Baptist Church and noted that the parking lot was still mostly empty, mentally calculating that it would take about fifteen minutes to put the finishing touches on his report.

Plenty of time to bring me back to the church and still get a decent parking spot, he thought. *As a new seeker I can't expect a reserved space,* he reasoned, *but maybe I could ask for my dad's old parking place. Something to think about.*

He signed in at his drug company security desk, inquiring about the condition of the guard's sickly daughter, then proceeded to his office on the second floor that overlooked the church on one side and the popular shopping mall at Bayside on Biscayne Bay on the other. Moments later he was busily involved in determining the company's profit and loss margin on its TOI-VAX drug used to combat AIDS. On the one hand, it was obvious that Lane was losing money on the drug, with the cost of research and development the key indicators, while on the other hand, meeting the tremendous humanitarian needs of the public more than compensated for the cost. It was Lane's way of giving something back to the world. He believed along with his dad that the company was a platform for ministry and was delighted that his board was in complete agreement.

Time seemed to elude Brandon as he re-studied his report when he abruptly realized that he was late for the worship service, almost ten minutes in fact. *Rather than mess with finding a parking spot, I'll walk over.* With the walk of about seven minutes he would make the sermon and offering. *No problem.*

Seconds after he pressed the elevator down button, he heard a tremendous blast coming from what he thought was the direction of his church. As the elevator doors opened, the floor of the building shook violently. He dropped his briefcase and grabbed hold of the elevator wall and held on until the building stabilized five seconds later. After a quick jerk, the elevator door closed and brought him to the main floor. His mind could not readily accept what he saw as the elevator doors opened. The reception booth where the guard sat had been picked up and thrown against the far wall and lay in splinters covered with piles of debris. Hundreds of glass shards dangled like icicles from the front plate-glass window frames while intermittent sparks from the mangled ceiling fixtures threatened to ignite anything flammable. Lane had the presence of mind to rush to the reception booth, only to see his guard buried under layers of wood, sheet rock, and pieces of lobby furniture. He located his hand and checked his pulse.

"God," he cried heavenward, "what happened?!" Brandon shook his head as the picture of the guard's daughter flashed in his mind. "Sorry, friend," he muttered. "I'll be sure to take care of your daughter."

In the next moment, an electric arcing took place in the ceiling, then a live wire dropped to the floor next to the pile of debris where the guard lay dead. Sparks from the high voltage feed showered the area, igniting the pieces of wooden furniture. Seconds later the fire alarm sounded followed by the activation of the sprinkler system. As Brandon stood in shock surveying the damage, the water from the sprinklers hitting his face alerted him to his perilous predicament. He ran outside the lobby to safety.

Thank you, God, that today is Sunday and none of my other employees were here, was his first thought. Then he suddenly thought about the church.

As he rounded the corner to the church he cried out, "God, where *is* the church?!" Nothing remained standing where the church once stood. The area was leveled, with flames and smoke filling the air above the site. Even the steel girders that supported the stone structure were lying like pretzels on top of the mountain that once was Central Baptist church. Huge sections of the stone walls were scattered about on the street and as far as he could see, there was not a nearby building without a broken window. As if it were a memorial signaling the death of the church, a lone pylon teetering on top of the mountain of debris creaked back and forth as hundreds of Sunday bulletins floated lazily downward toward the earth. When the full realization of the disaster came over him, he stood inert for several minutes then turned around and walked dazedly toward his car.

Jerusalem

Paul immediately dropped to the floor of one of the remaining K-group member's living room and assumed an emergency prayer position once he realized what his eyes saw on the television. News reporters from *MSNBC* stationed in Miami, Salt Lake City, and the University of Colorado were simultaneously explaining to viewers that three terrorist attacks against Christian churches and organizations had occurred only 40 minutes earlier.

"Shaul, come quick!" Paul shouted toward the kitchen.

Shaul, a young robust believing recruit, was eating lunch while Paul was phoning other members of the group in preparation for their next offensive with Kavidas when the news alert flashed across the TV screen.

Shaul glanced at the TV as they entered the room, quickly assessing the situation, then joined Paul in prayer as the narration of the disasters continued. After several moments of petitioning God for help and mercy, they stood up to listen to the unfolding report. "...Authorities at Smith College report that at this stage of the disaster, 406 students and faculty members are unaccounted for and presumed dead in one of the worst college tragedies in the past 50 years. The National Guard has been called out and preliminary reports indicate that a powerful bomb was planted somewhere in the chapel building with the purpose of killing Christians meeting for worship this Sunday morning. FBI agents on the scene remarked that the attack had all the fingerprints of a radical Muslim terrorist group using the military explosive HMX."

Switching to the University of Colorado's Folsom Stadium, a circling news helicopter televised images of the ambulances inside the stadium with emergency vehicles outside. Using high-powered telephoto lenses, the video cameras focused on hundreds of body bags stretched out on the field in front of the platform that carried a banner that read, *Unity Church*. Then the camera panned to scores of medical personnel who were carrying victims on stretchers to the waiting ambulances that formed a long circuitous line to the outside of the stadium. "Today we are witnessing one of the worst terrorist attacks to hit Colorado, if not all of America," the newscaster aloft in the helicopter announced. "We are here at the Folsom, 50,000 seat stadium where the Christian group, *Unity Church*, was holding their quarterly rally. Estimates of as many as 23,000 men attending the rally have been given.

"Officials have reported that a large quantity of concentrated mustard gas in aerosol form has been released through the air-conditioning system that serviced the interior of the stadium along with a vast quantity that was released into the ventilating system that pumped fresh air to the bleachers under the stadium's canopy. Mustard gas, when it comes in contact with the skin, causes severe blisters and breathing it in brings extreme damage to the lungs and other internal organs. Since concentrated exposure can be lethal, the number of fatalities is expected to be in the thousands. Although no group has yet to claim responsibility, the CDC and a representative of the U.S. Army's Weapons of Mass Destruction division said the attack had all the markings of the al-Qaeda group."

The scene changed. Another newsperson began interviewing a survivor from the Miami disaster.

"That's Brandon Lane!" Paul exclaimed in shock.

Lane's distraught face was covered with white powder that apparently came from the blast debris swirling in the wind.

Archival pictures of what Central Baptist Church looked like several years before the destruction filled the screen with an inset of Brandon Lane giving commentary on the sequence of events that brought him to the site. When the newscaster questioned Lane, Lane's eyes filled with tears. Then he thanked God that he was spared a horrible death from a bomb blast, but added that he was very grieved to learn that Christians were killed and that his church was demolished.

"We'll wait a few hours before we E-mail Brandon," Douglas said ruefully.

Shaul just shook his head in disgust as the telecast continued to update the worldwide public with the horrific report. Then after several moments of intense listening he said numbly, "God is very displeased with America. This is what happens when the U.S. turns their back on Israel when they needed their support. Sure, there has been no official statement from the radical Muslims, but I know in my spirit that they're responsible for this."

He stopped to make a fist, then punched his other open hand before continuing. "And this is what the U.S. gets for not stamping out these radical Muslim pockets who are determined to destroy America and now its Christians as well. America has allowed their enemies to place their fanatical warriors in their country to eventually wreak havoc and destabilize their economy, their political and religious systems." He gestured toward the TV. "This is just the outworking of their master plan. Good 'Old Uncle Sap' is getting it right where he deserves it, in the gut! Now maybe the U.S. will change their immigration laws to keep these extremist Muslims out!"

For several moments he stood watching the TV, grinding his teeth as the photomontage of the attacks continued to assault his senses. With heightening rage he continued with his tirade. "Free people must recognize who picks all the fights these days; who systematically inculcates racial and religious venom among their youngsters, and whose religion teaches the destruction of the other! It's not the Americans or the Israelis—but the Arabs! The PLO, al-Qaeda, the Hamas, the Hezbollah, the Mujahadeen and every other descendent of Ishmael that you can think of!"

Paul put his hand on Shaul's shoulder in an attempt to ease his pain and stop the flow of resentment building up inside his fellow patriot. "This is also God's way of carrying out the judgment of the Fifth Seal, the martyrdom of the saints. There is no way to get around the prophecy. Don't you see that God is using the Arab nations to humble America and Israel until they repent and turn to him?"

Shaul nodded. He knew God's purpose, but it still hurt to see innocent people being slaughtered as they worshiped their God.

The question as to whether or not these victims were members of pseudo-Christian or true Christian churches was left with God.

"Paul, over 21,000 new Christians have just had their lives snuffed out by these blasted Arabs!" he said with tears stinging his eyes. "Is God just going to stand by and let it happen without some form of retribution? When do they get paid back?"

Paul knew that he had said it before. *Complete judgment for the Arab nations and their allies is yet future, when Christ returns. But God*, he sympathized, *couldn't they get a slice of your revenge and judgment now and make the Christians happy for a while? But no*, he reasoned as he thought once again on Scripture, *"Vengeance is mine, says the Lord."*

"We must leave that with God and fight the battles he places before us," he consoled. After a few moments of reflection, Shaul willfully suppressed his anger and in the unforgiving calculus of life, mentally gave the problem to God.

It would be only a matter of hours before the American brigade of the radical Muslim network, al-Qaeda, would take responsibility for the coordinated attacks that would eclipse any terrorist attack on U.S. soil to date. They boasted that this was their way of retaliating against their two most hated groups for supporting Israel, Americans and Christians. In the ensuing investigation it would be learned that the Florida, Michigan, and Colorado al-Qaeda operatives emerged from sleeper cells well imbedded in American citizenry that had implanted agents within each target. They were awakened by the command of an emerging leader who was successfully banding the fragmented Arab terrorist groups together under one cause. Further, the leader was thought to be based somewhere in Israel.

Three hours passed before Paul felt relaxed enough to sit at the member's computer terminal to write to Brandon. For 15 minutes he stared at an imaginary spot on the monitor until the proper words finally came to him. Once online he began his message that seemed to surface from numbed limbs.

[Sending]
Brandon, our senses were stunned, while at the same time, our hearts are breaking since we've learned of the cowardly terrorist attacks against America once again. It's hard to believe America

would be so hated by these groups that they would disregard every known convention and kill innocent civilians just to make a statement.

We saw you on TV, and I have to tell you that you've looked better! While we are enraged with the perpetrators, we are relieved and rejoicing that God providentially saw fit to protect you. On a more serious note, we're dreading the report of the final count of those who gave their lives for the cause of Christ. We have a hunch that there are many from *Koinonos* that perished.

[Incoming]

Hello, Paul. It was good to hear from you during these desperate hours. As you probably know by now, God had arranged for me to be out of the church when the bomb exploded, but a part of me blew up in smoke with the building. I was beginning to hear the message the pastor was preaching, and now I feel like those survivors from the 9/11 attack on the World Trade Center—there will always be a void in my life from now on. Whenever I think of Central Baptist from now on, the image of the devastation and the fallen heroes who died will be forever etched in my mind.

Regarding the coordinated attacks, new information has just been broadcast here on the local TV stations. Ironically, the *Masterlink* system helped track and nab the culprits through the GPS, Global Positioning Satellite network. Since nearly every American and foreign national has the chip implanted for economic and international passage purposes, it was easy to locate them based on information the FBI and the FEMA, Federal Emergency Management Association, were able to uncover. Since the catastrophe of 9/11, many of these agencies now are intermeshed, allowing for quick arrests.

However, and it saddens me to say this, I do not believe our law enforcement agencies will have much success in rooting out these subversive groups or operatives from America in the future because the Lord is just not going to allow it until the Christian church repents over their apathy and lethargy. Until that happens, the Lord will use the principle defined in 2 Chronicles 7:14 that addresses both covenant Israel and the Christian. Once "God's people repent and turn from their wicked ways," we can expect our land to be healed.

But until then, there will be no abating from the terrorist

attacks. There will be no victories fighting terrorists in foreign lands. God is using these people to chasten both Israel and America. And, unfortunately, mainstream America is not really interested in protecting the few new "Christians" since they view them as judgmental and in many cases hypocritical, and although they have not declared it publically, the man in the street probably blames Christians for the plagues and the other calamities that have hit planet Earth. I would think that this development will cause a great hardening of the world's heart toward God. People will lose faith. I guess this is what Jesus meant when He said in Luke 18, "When the Son of Man comes, will he find faith on the earth?"

Paul glanced over at Shaul, who was seated next to him as they read Brandon's last few sentences. Obviously Brandon's theology regarding God's dealing with Israel and America was the same as theirs. Shaul simply nodded at Brandon's evaluation and affirmed that as truth in his own heart.

Paul could discern that Brandon's heart was really troubled and in need of encouragement. But from 7,000 miles away, it was impossible to give him a warm embrace as a fellow Christian who just suffered a severe loss. But through the power of prayer, they could bridge the gap.

[Sending]
When you are in pain, as brothers in the Lord, we feel your pain. We shall call upon God's Holy Spirit to minister to you.

Paul then typed in his prayer for his friend, then moved aside and let Shaul type in his. Then they pressed *Send* together.

Convent of the Sisters of Zion, Jerusalem

On Monday morning an unusual degree of excitement came over Paul as 24 male members of the K-group led by himself and Shaul descended the steps of the Convent of the Sisters of Zion that led to the *Pavement*, or Lithostrotos in Greek—the place where Christ was publicly tried before Pontius Pilate. The *Pavement,* cited in John 19:13, is located nearly 25 feet below the floor of the modern-day convent. In Christ's time it was at street level. It was here that Pilate presented Jesus, had him scourged and said, "Behold the man," and here he finally washed his hands and condemned Christ to death on the cross.

The convent location offered both sanctity and seclusion for the group. Sanctity, because it was one of the few archeological sites in Jerusalem that was certified to be authentic and accurate, providing a nearness to God. Secluded because the custodians, members of the Greek Orthodox Church, closed the site to the public at Paul and Shaul's request because of a reciprocity agreement with Jerusalem University College where Paul's father had taught Old Testament Biblical Studies.

"This reminds me of the ancient catacombs," Shaul remarked to Paul as they entered the large underground room where a sense of enclosure prevailed. Paul nodded. In a way it did resemble an oversized catacomb.

Paul thought it appropriate to take a few moments and give the K-group a brief tour based on the information his dad shared with him when they toured the site. He turned on the overhead lights and pointed to the floor. The light revealed all the large crevices in the age-old precut slabs of rock caused by chariots and pedestrians breaking off large chunks over the eons of time until it was covered by earth for new construction by subsequent invaders. Many of the slabs that formed the pavement, that resembled a cobblestone driveway, were several tons in weight.

"Notice that this is the original pavement built by the Romans in the first century B.C." He pointed again to several channels in the pavement. "These are gutters that were used to collect rainwater off the pavement and direct them to vast underground cisterns used for drinking water." From there he walked the group toward the north end and turned on a light over a mosaic on the wall. The mosaic made of fine marble and ceramic tiles formed a picture of Christ carrying his cross with Roman Jerusalem in the background.

Pointing down once again, Paul continued his narrative. "Notice the striation in the rock slabs. These were cut into the rock to prevent the Roman horses from slipping on the pavement."

Many of the members simply shook their heads in amazement as they marveled at the preservation of the ancient roadway and its biblical significance.

"This is extremely interesting," Paul said as he waved them over to a far corner. Once he turned the overhead light on, carvings in the rock slab at their feet became visible. There were five carvings or etchings in the stone that resembled both animate and inanimate objects. There was what looked like a cube, a spoked circle that was approximately eight inches in diameter, a three-dimensional square, a smaller circle with an indistinguishable figure attached to it, and a small sphere with what looked like straggly hair around it. It could be compared to a scorpion.

"These drawings carved into the surface of the rock are what scholars believe are traces of games played by the Romans. One of the games played with dice, called the King's game, could have been used with Jesus as the subject according to Matthew 27."

Several of the men in the group lingered at the carved pavement as Paul called the group away to have their discussion. When he looked back at the men, two of them were sniffling as the realization of the truth of Christ's execution seized their emotions.

Once the K-group formed a circle and opened their meeting with prayer, Paul reviewed their dilemma. "We all know now that America has been hit hard by three simultaneous terrorist attacks by the al-Qaeda network. One of these bombings affected a personal friend of mine, Brandon Lane. Fortunately, the Lord saw fit to protect him.

"I believe this bunch is working with other factions in the Arab world determined to punish America for their support of Israel, as well as striking out at Christians because of their fundamental religious values that conflict with theirs. This certainly includes any stateside members of our K-group family. In addition, any Christian or American that supports the Jew is also fair game. This places us in a very precarious predicament. One that requires us to meet in secret from now on."

Neville, a British-born member of the K-group, asked, "Do you think Kavidas had anything to do with this?"

Paul shot a look at Shaul, then back at Neville. The members were catching on to the real threat facing humanity. "To be honest with you, we firmly believe that Kavidas and Stein have their hand in every action that threatens their ultimate plan, to bring as many souls into hell with them as they can. Naturally, any Christians in America, Israel, and the rest of the world represent a threat to their master plan. So, yes, they must be somehow involved."

"They will use any means to achieve that goal," Shaul appended Paul's remarks. "Especially the Arabs who figure prominently in God's plan." Making a sweeping gesture with his hand he added, "Later, Kavidas and Stein will bring in other forces from the West, the Orient, and Africa in an attempt to finish off Israel."

"What part do you think America will play in this final act?" Adam, a toughened K-group member from Canada, asked.

"Most experts in the field of eschatology believe that since America is in no way mentioned in Scripture, not even symbolically, that America forms an alliance with other nations, like England and other European nations, probably the EU, to become the kings of the West," Douglas replied.

Adam raised his hand for a follow-up question. "How in the world did America, a once-mighty nation for God, wind up this way?"

With a slight shake of the head, Paul replied, "America's collapse can be traced back to its abandonment of the three pillars that once made it great. The home, the school, and the church. Over the years these three God-ordained institutions have been attacked by every atheist, liberal politician, TV comedian, and sexual purveyor until the value system became so eroded that God has turned his face on America, waiting for national repentance."

"A far cry from where America once was," Richie from America put in. "As an American interested in history, I remember taking great pride in DeToqueville's depiction of the early years of my nation." He squeezed his eyes closed to recall the quote, then recited it. " 'Not until I went into the churches of America and heard her pulpits aflame with righteousness did I understand the secret of her genius and power. America is great because America is good, and if America ever ceases to be good, America will cease to be great.' " When he opened his eyes, a look of abandonment came over many of their faces.

Paul pulled out of his pocket the printed E-mail from Brandon Lane and waved it in the air as an exhibit to support Richie's argument. "America has sustained some heavy hits in the past several years. There were the terrorist attacks of 9/11/01, the assault on the cruise ship out of Miami, the New York subway bombing, and then the three attacks on Christian churches and organizations this past week. As a Christian leader and son of a seminary professor, I am expected to have at my disposal facts to support my views. Well, listen to this quote by George Mason, a delegate at the Continental Congress." Paul gazed off in the distance and quoted, " 'By an inevitable chain of causes and effects, Providence punishes national sins by national calamities.' You see, the national calamities the U.S. is undergoing is, once again I repeat it, nothing more than the outworking of their flagrant departure from the biblical mandates that once made America great. Short and simple!"

"Demon worship, resurgence of occultism, elevation of nature worship, apathy, lukewarmness, immorality, and the propensity to be more concerned with our pleasure than the kingdom of God," a voice from the rear of the group rattled off. Several "Amens" erupted from the group in affirmation.

"Naturally, these compromises in our religious and social systems has damaged other areas," Paul explained. "Confidence in decision-making regarding our political policies and military strategy has been severely damaged over these past several years. In many of the conflicts, like in Afghanistan and Iraq for instance, justice for the attack on the World Trade Center and other terrorist acts has not been exacted in any sense of the word. Our efforts to punish those responsible have been fraught with problems that resulted in nothing but frustrations for our armed forces. You would think that with our military superiority, advanced armaments, and technological expertise, that the U.S. would have had a decisive victory in a matter of weeks or months over those cowards who hide in caves, but alas, we have not. They crawled into holes or disguised themselves as civilians or women or were treated as heroes and given refuge by our so-called friends in that region—all to our embarrassment. As a result, the bad guys got

302

away once again."

Several men just sighed and shrugged as if to say that only God can mete out the justice due to these criminals. Paul read their faces. He had to agree and move the agenda along.

"For us here in Jerusalem, we must take an offensive position to erect roadblocks to slow up Kavidas and Stein. As far as the rest of the world's problems—including America—we must leave them with God to handle. In his time the enemies of the Cross will be dealt with."

"When Jesus returns, that's when Kavidas gets his!" Neville snapped angrily while making a fist. Several of the men gave out with a muffled cheer in agreement.

"Yes, but until then, things are going to get dicey around here," Paul warned. "The world has another two Seal judgments to go through, then a set of seven Trumpets followed by seven Bowl judgments. Whew! Believe you me, Jesus will be a welcome sight by that time!" He cracked a smile. "*But for the Christians*, we expect the Lord to protect us until he returns for us."

"The sooner the better!" Shaul praised aloud.

The crowd voiced a hearty amen!

A hand waved from the back of the group. Then a voice asked, "Paul, are the women and children safe at Petra?"

Paul opened his mouth to answer, but nothing came out. Suddenly a sound like the blowing of a violent wind came from somewhere within the great room and filled the space where they were standing. Paul looked behind him to see a rotating air mass forming as flashes of strobe-like light radiated from the vortex. Most of the men shielded their eyes as the whirlwind intensified and began to breathe heavily as the oxygen in the room seemed to diminish as if it were being sucked into the vortex itself. Gripped with fear, many of them fell prostrate on the floor. Paul recognized it was the signal that Nocham and Qadar were about to appear and peeked through his fingers into the swirling air mass to once again catch a glimpse of the fiery chariot and the team of white horses that transported them. His heart seemed to skip a beat as his adrenalin level surged when he saw this manifestation of God's power. He could not even imagine what the scene would look like when his Savior returned as King of kings and Lord of lords.

Several moments passed before the whirlwind slowed and faded, leaving Nocham and Qadar standing before the group of men. "Get up!" Nocham commanded the men on the floor who were seeing the two witnesses for the first time. "We are only your fellow servants. Worship God only!" The men exchanged looks as they stood up, but their knees continued to knock together.

"It has been decreed by the Holy One that many shall die for their faith since the Fifth Seal has been opened," Qadar explained with a bellowing voice that reverberated off the rock walls. "But great will be the reward for those who persevere to the end." He pointed upward. "Have no fear because the number of the slain has been fixed and that number is certain. It cannot be changed."

Our friends and K-group families. Are they safe? Paul thought but was afraid to ask.

Qadar turned toward Paul and nodded as he spoke words of encouragement. "All who seek refuge in the fortress at Petra will be protected from any attack by mortals by seven legions of angels designated as guardians. They will watch over God's people and keep them safe from harm as it is written, 'For in the day of trouble he will keep you safe in his dwelling; he will hide you in the shelter of his tabernacle and set you high upon a rock.' "

Nocham took one step forward and continued the decrees. "Beware, because as is it written, the man of lawlessness has been revealed who will work in accordance with the work of Satan being displayed in all kinds of counterfeit miracles, signs, and wonders, and in every sort of evil that deceives those who are perishing. They perish because they refused to love the truth and so be saved. For this reason God sends them a powerful delusion so they will believe the lie that man can be saved without receiving Christ as the Messiah and Redeemer." He stopped and pointed to both Paul and Shaul and added, "Be vigilant and be strong, for evil forces are working against your people to discourage them."

While raising his hand in a farewell gesture, Qadar said, "God is preparing his army of witnesses to assist you. Until they come, be faithful."

Within moments the whirlwind returned for them, removing

them out of sight.

"Just as I thought," Paul said as he swallowed hard. He mentally processed the both Nocham and Qadar's statements and discerned the warnings. "Those terrorist attacks were part of the judgment of the Fifth Seal."

"We can expect many more martyrs for Christ in the days ahead," Shaul added sharply.

"Yes, I'm afraid," Paul affirmed. Then in reflexive recollection he recalled the past two episodes involving Simon. "We should also expect an increase in demonic activity as well as a heightening of attacks from Kavidas, the so-called 'man of lawlessness' as the apostle Paul labeled him. But the 'safety net' has been clarified by Nocham and Qadar; all those seeking refuge in Petra shall be safe."

"But God is going to send us reinforcements!" Shaul chortled when he thought on the 144,000 Jewish witnesses.

The atmosphere in the room abruptly became charged with God's power following Shaul's edification. Several men began humming the hymn "Redeemed," then within 30 seconds, they began singing it. The voices that echoed off the wall were a sweet-smelling savor unto God.

Temple Mount, Jerusalem

As they drove into the Temple Mount parking lot, Kavidas motioned to Stein to take note of the low-lying clouds that hung suspended like soiled pillows over the entire sky and the horizon as far as one could see. He pointed up, then gave a thumbs-down in his effort to show contempt for God's judgment that lingered over the eternal city. Once they arrived on the Temple Mount proper, Kavidas went directly to the place of his humiliation. He strolled around as if he was reliving the contest between himself and the two witnesses from God, then abruptly stopped.

While he stood in the place normally occupied by the high priest, he said with calculated resolve, "I will never be disgraced in this place ever again! This will be the place where I'm honored before men."

Stein noticed a slight anomaly in Kavidas' demeanor when he made that statement. He immediately registered the signal in his subconscious as being inconsequential, yet in the back of his mind he knew that the day would come when God would indeed intervene and their reign of conquest would be over. The moment of reaching the pinnacle of fame and worship would terminate and all of his engineering and manipulation to turn mankind away from Christ would come to an end. *Could Gregory have had the same thoughts just now?* He wondered. *Put it out of your mind*, he commanded himself. *Until that time we will revel in our victories.*

Looking with admiration at his master, Stein immediately drew a parallel. He determinately recalled the point in Germany's history when Adolf Hitler conquered France and arrived in Versailles, a city outside of Paris. Surrounded by an entourage of his military officers and states persons, Hitler went directly to the palace of Versailles and walked to the monument commemorating the famous Treaty of Versailles of 1919-1921. It was that treaty that mandated a number of restrictive and compensatory measures for his fatherland, Germany, including massive demilitarization and financial reparations for damages inflicted during World War I. After viewing the memorial outside the palace that represented the symbol of Germany's humiliation, Hitler turned to his supreme commander and said, "Blow it up!" It was a moment of triumph for the house painter turned dictator.

Stein trailed behind Kavidas until he walked to a masonry bench outside the inner court area that overlooked the front of the Temple. He invited Stein to join him on the bench, whereupon they began to survey the outlying territory in silence. Kavidas continued to scan the countryside as he spoke. "Mort, you did a magnificent job in coordinating the three attacks on the American Christians. Whoever your point man is, he is to be congratulated." Without breaking his stride in his surveying of the scenery before him, Kavidas added, "A bonus for a job well done is in order."

"I will see to it," Stein replied without looking at Kavidas. He, too, was enjoying the scenery.

"Unfortunately, we have a long way to go before we break the spirits of these Christians," Kavidas instructed as he turned to face Stein. "So, we have reached that place in our timetable to apply greater restrictions on those doing business with them. I will give you the parameters; you are to set the particulars for *Masterlink*. First, I want to gradually put a spending limit on any individual, group, or corporation that overtly or covertly supports Christians. Secondly, any individual, group, or corporation that is supporting Christians should be put on notice that they will only be able to do business with *Masterlink* approved merchants or vendors. Thirdly, any individual, group, or corporation that is overtly or covertly supporting Christians should receive warning that their credit is in jeopardy. Continued commercial enterprise with those promoting Christianity will mean that in the near future they will lose their privilege to charge anything. Implement the credit rating system we discussed when we originally devised *Masterlink* so we begin to reward any person or company that follows our guidelines while at the same time we punish those who do not." He grinned and added caustically, "Offenders will be relegated to the ancient bartering system until they conform."

Stein stared off into the distance as he absorbed Kavidas' orders.

"My spirit testifies that your operation here in Israel to bring Douglas and his cohorts into subjection appears to have an edge on it," Kavidas said approvingly. "Keep it up, Mort. If we can divert them so they concentrate on their own survival instead of focusing on getting people—" he paused to mouth an oath, then spoke out the side of his mouth—"*saved*, we shall be doing well in accomplishing our mission."

Stein nodded as he soaked in the words of encouragement.

Kavidas stood up, then rested one foot on the bench as he nibbled on his lower lip. After several moments of concentration he said, "It is also time for us to implement restrictions on any and all access to the Bible. We have got to remove any vestige of a standard of Truth that can explain or thwart our plan. Keeping information from the masses has always been an effective means of control. The less they know about prophecy that can impact them, the better."

Stein once again looked up at Kavidas as a supernatural emissary who would change the course of human events for all time.

Renaissance Jerusalem Hotel

Stein defined leadership as having the ability to take one's vision and make it into reality. Having defined it, he lovingly applied the attribute to himself. He considered this part of his creative genius that few men possess. *I will engineer the next phase of our conquest by drafting up a plan to implement Gregory's vision as I did with Masterlink,* he told himself in the quietude of his apartment. Stein reflected on his accomplishments since he teamed up with Kavidas, then congratulated himself by sitting down in his living room with a large glass of Chardonnay, a soft rendering of Chopin's piano Concerto No. 2 on his CD player, a pen, and a large lined notepad. He would now assume the position of architect to draw up the blueprints to build on Gregory's verbal sketches for the next phase of their program. Then he would give the order to execute them.

Thinking back to his brainstorming episode, or "vision," as he called it, while in Cozumel several years ago, he recalled the formation and progression of *Project Renaissance*. *Project Renaissance* started out with *Redisearch*, from the mind of Stein, that provided commercial and individual credit clearance and background checks at an extremely low fee. After gobbling up a huge share of the credit market, he then built upon that platform to construct the next phase, *Medlink*. *Medlink* was a supplement to *Redisearch* that would provide confidential medical information such as the cardholder's personal physical description and emergency medical data needed for such conditions as diabetics, epilepsy or cardiac patients. *Medlink* was the predecessor to all health reform.

Then there was *Infolink*, the next stage in the sequence that simply combined the two in one card. Then finally came *Masterlink*, the ultimate form of identification that encompassed the other three stages, as well as adding all political and religious data. The final stage that included political and religious information was encrypted so that only official agencies had access. Naturally, Kavidas and Stein had access privileges. Within three years of the advent of *Masterlink*, the proposal to replace the card with an imbedded microdot system was overwhelmingly received by the public, law enforcement agencies, and commercial vendors. Stein's inspired vision was handsomely applauded by his partner, Kavidas. Very few realized it as the fulfillment of Bible prophecy.

Stein kicked off his shoes and raised the wine glass to his lips only to be interrupted by a smell that everyone in Jerusalem had become accustomed to. The ongoing fetor of the burning of the invasion weapons as fuel. Somehow the exhaust smoke from the electrical generating plants burning the flammable weapons had meandered up into the atmosphere and found its way into the air-conditioning ducts of his apartment. Stein mouthed an expletive in protest, then in the next breath, praised the Israeli military and the thousands of unemployed citizens hired to bury the war dead for a job well done.

He took a deep pull on the Chardonnay, then closed his eyes to concentrate on the task at hand.

An hour later five pages in his notepad were full.

TWENTY

Christian Fortress, Petra

Simon's spirit soared with exhilaration as he climbed the red rock canyon wall above the stadium ruins at the fortress at Petra to watch for new arrivals. Each morning he would look for the busloads of wives and children of K-group members and select proselytes who would travel the distance of some one hundred miles from Jerusalem to the ancient Nabatean city. Traveling southwest around the Dead Sea and down through the Negev, they then drove east to connect to the primeval Kings Highway, the important north-south route through Transjordan that ran past Petra in southern Jordan clear to the Gulf of Aqaba. In time this route would be blocked off by forces allied with Kavidas to prevent further buildup of what was quickly becoming a Christian fortress for those escaping his hypertrophying empire. But for today, the roadways were open.

The promontory of the fortress Simon chose as his lookout towered over 85 feet above the desert floor, affording an excellent view of the barren wasteland that surrounded it. Ongoing overcast conditions where the sun's reflection off the desert sand was minimal enabled Simon to see nearly six miles in each direction. Unofficially, he was regarded as the watchman of Petra, a title his mother reluctantly ascribed to.

Fifteen minutes after the day's passengers disembarked at the entranceway to the fortress, Simon, feeling relieved of his responsibility as watchman for the day, was suddenly overcome with an urge to explore the natural cave hewn deep into the backside of the promontory. It was a strange notion that unexpectedly appealed to him, one that he had overlooked in the past because of the likelihood of it being inhabited by bats. But today was different. Today, there was an unexplainable inner compulsion to investigate the unknown to see what kind of adventure lay therein.

He picked up a rock and threw it into the darkened cave to judge its depth. After three seconds of flight he heard a *thwack*. The rock had hit the cave's rear wall. He estimated the distance at approximately 35 feet and thrust himself into the opening. Once the sound of his footsteps echoed off the cave walls, he heard a loud *whoosh*. Knowing what was about to happen next, he quickly covered his eyes as clusters of bats erratically flew by him at enormous speeds responding to the disturbance. Then the cave went silent.

He peered into the rear of the cave and thought he saw some kind of intermittent illumination that piqued his curiosity. When the light began flickering, he thought he saw a large indefinable outline mixed with shadows on the cave wall. His heart rate accelerated as he extended his hand to touch the side of the cave to steady his path and took several steps toward the illumination. *What in the world is that?*

After three steps he abruptly stopped his movement and held out his hand to feel the air. The temperature in the cave was dropping rapidly. He noticed the moisture and slime on the wall were becoming icy and reflecting the flickering light back into his eyes. His eyes rolled momentarily, then an image of a naked girl caressing him flew into his mind. He slapped the side of his head to jog the sordid picture loose, then mumbled, "What's going on?"

He stood still to regroup his senses when suddenly he heard a voice in his mind say, *Come closer!*

"Who said that?" he gulped as he shook his head in disbelief. He raised his hand to his forehead and muttered, "That's what I get for standing in the heat for an hour." He looked around, took one step backward, then stopped again.

"Come closer!" the audible voice repeated. He froze in place, then turned his head from side to side to locate the sound. It was coming from the rear of the cave, where he first spotted the light. *Turn around and run!* he thought.

But the voice arrested his attention. It was drawing him in. "Come closer, Simon!"

"How do you know my name?" he asked with a quivering voice as his legs began to wobble.

"I know all about you!" the voice replied with a raspy edge. "Now come closer!"

Simon turned his torso to look behind him to see the light in the entranceway and decided to make a run for it, but his legs would not move. Fear seized his heart as the realization that he was in trouble washed over him like a tidal wave. "Who are you?!" he yelled out.

No answer.

He looked down at his feet for a loose stone, but he couldn't see one in the diminished light. He crouched down and felt around until he grabbed a sizable rock then stood up and hurled it at the place where the sound came from in a lame attempt to identify the source. All he heard was a loud *thwack* as the rock impacted against the cave wall.

"Simon, come here," he heard in his mother's voice.

Simon wiped his eyes and glared at the rear of the cave where the light continued to flicker, producing a grotesque shadow on the wall. "Mother?" In his mind, he knew his mother to be in Jerusalem with his father. *How can this be?*

"It's me, darling, come closer."

Simon suddenly began to writhe in pain as large boils erupted on his arms and legs. When he felt his face, there were several welts under his eyes. He winced and cried out, "Mother, help!" Seconds later he found himself lying prostrate and flaccid on the ground, moaning uncontrollably.

A loud rustling silenced him. He lay motionless for several moments until he heard another strange noise, the sound of a large mass moving across the cave floor toward him. He bolted upright and squeezed his eyes shut as he thrashed his arms about him. "Go away!" he screamed.

Suddenly an unseen claw grabbed him by the neck and began dragging him to the rear of the cave. His mind locked in terror. All he could do was yell out, "God, help me!"

Eerie mechanical sounds started up, then the claw jerked forcibly until he began to choke. "You are mine! God will not help you! Denounce this Jesus your friends believe in and you will live!"

Shock ripped through Simon's body as he gasped for breath. He dug his feet into the crevices in the cave floor to resist the movement, but the invisible thing defeated him. Then the thing broke out in a coarse laugh and mocked, "Your God is dead! Fear me!"

Simon let out a shrill wail, then cried, "Let me go!"

But the thing continued to drag him forward until it stopped in front of an enormous hole in the floor of the rear of the cave. Simon looked into the hole and saw what looked like burning coals with tentacles of fire scraping the sides, beckoning him to jump in. "Let me go!"

The thing lifted Simon off the ground and held him suspended over the hole. Suddenly he could see the thing's outline in the light of the fires. His body was not corporeal but immaterial and translucent. Simon gazed at his form, yet he could not grab hold of anything of substance. He could only see that it was not humanoid in shape but possessed a fiendish-looking body with multiple appendages that resembled mutated wings.

God, I need you! his heart cried.

A blinding light flashed in Simon's eyes as he heard, "IN THE NAME OF JESUS CHRIST, I ORDER YOU TO SET HIM DOWN!"

When Simon opened his eyes, he saw Yair holding a flashlight in one hand and a large stick in the other. He was positioned in an attack stance, ready to fight the invisible creature.

Simon's body jerked back and forth as the thing began to react to the command. Next, multiple squeals echoed off the cave walls.

The thing is recoiling! Yair thought.

Then, what sounded like a massive metal door opening rebounded off the walls of the hole.

He's calling for help! Yair realized.

The thing let out with a piercing howl, then threw Simon against the cave wall and turned on the voice that violated him. "How dare you interfere!" it yelled fiercely.

Yair looked intently where the voice emanated from and saw the thing's outline menacingly coming toward him. He shot a look at Simon, lying limp on the ground and began to step backward when he suddenly became flushed with unrealized supernatural power. He dropped the stick and held his hand up in a halting gesture and cried out, "I CLAIM THE POWER OF CHRIST'S BLOOD OVER YOU! WHAT IS YOUR NAME?"

The sounds coming from the hole immediately ceased as the thing began to materialize before Yair's eyes.

Yair turned his flashlight on the thing and grimaced in horror. The thing looked like a griffin with the body of a lion and the head and wings of an eagle, only this creature had six wings instead of two and they were deformed so it could not fly. Its bird-like head with its hooked nose seemed to rotate on an axis as it surveyed the room with piercing red and yellow eyes. With its claws it pawed at Simon's inert body.

"I am Asmodeus!" it reluctantly disclosed.

Yair drew strength from his internal reserves then glared at Asmodeus and bellowed, "IN THE NAME OF JESUS CHRIST, I COMMAND YOU, *ASMODEUS*, TO RETURN TO THE PIT FROM WHERE YOU CAME!"

The cave immediately filled with a pungent odor. Yair squeezed his nostrils as the stench of what smelled like sulphur began to overpower him. He began to feel faint when suddenly Asmodeus walked to the precipice of the hole and fell headlong into it.

Deafening screeching was heard for several moments, then the hole closed up right before Yair's eyes.

The cave returned to normal.

Yair rushed to Simon's side to see his strength finally returning to his numbed limbs. He scanned Simon's body with the flashlight as he stood up, noticing every exposed area of skin looked like it was badly sunburned. "Let's get out of here!" he said as he put his arm around his brother's waist and walked him out into the daylight.

After pouring the boiling water into the teacup, Yair replaced the kettle on the stove and turned to Simon, who was sitting at the kitchen table of their designated mobile home. It was the perfect forum to discuss the attack and rescue. Yair's eyes locked on Simon's, pleading for understanding. "Explain to me why you felt the need to wander off and explore that cave!"

Simon shrugged. "Adventure, I guess. I like to explore the caves around here, you know that. I never thought that some giant demon would be lurking in one of them. I never thought that I would be the target of some creature from the netherworld."

Yair shook his head in dismay. He walked to Simon and embraced him. Then with one hand he grabbed him by the ear and twisted it until Simon cringed under the pain. "Promise me you will never leave this perimeter again!"

Simon eked out a smile as Yair released his ear. "I promise." Then he turned and said, "How did you know where I was?"

Yair toyed with his flashlight as he explained. "When you didn't come down from your 'morning constitutional,' I decided to go up to the peak and look for you. When I didn't see you, I looked around and then noticed footsteps in the mantle rock and decided to follow them. I knew they were yours because—" he reached over to Simon's sneakers and turned one over—"you're the only one around here wearing Nikes."

"If you hadn't come when you did, that thing would have thrown me into the pit!" Simon said with a voice vibrating with intensity.

"As I was nearing the cave off in the distance I saw a huge cluster of bats came flying out and from that I knew you were inside," Yair said with a smile. "Then, as I walked deeper into the cave, I heard a screeching and I knew you were in trouble!" He twirled the Mini Mag Lite flashlight in his hand and added as he pointed to Simon, "Fortunately for you, I always carry this guy on my belt for just such an emergency."

"And you had the presence of mind to call out the thing's name? The demon's name?" Simon asked curiously.

Yair's eyes suddenly brightened as he fixed a penetrating stare at an imaginary spot in the air. Then as if he were instantly transported back to the cave, he said, "I remembered what Christ did in Mark 5 when he encountered the demon-possessed man of Gadara. Jesus asked him, 'What is your name?' 'My name is Legion,' he replied, 'for we are many.' Once I knew the demon's name, I knew I could command him to hell by the power of Christ's blood."

Seconds went by as Yair's eyes widened in astonishment. He then turned and gazed at Simon. He read his mind. He raised his hands in surrender and said, "I'm ashamed to say that I never even thought of calling upon Jesus to help me, Yair, much less his blood."

Yair's heart was pierced. He never took anybody's salvation for granted because their parents were Christians or their behavior was Christlike. No, biblical precedence dictated that was folly. But how could one account for another's failure to call upon the only One who could help him at a time of crisis, especially in the area of spiritual warfare. "Simon, are you sure that you belong to him?"

Fear rose up in Simon's heart. The kind of fear he experienced back in the cave. The kind of fear that often drives men to call upon their internal engines to perform dynamic feats of strength or the kind of fear that drives men to examine where they stand before God. Simon wanted to be exercised to righteousness by this experience, to draw closer to God, not to push away from Him; not to bitterness. Not to damnation.

"There is a level of doubt in my heart, Yair," he admitted as he began to fill up with tears. Yair's eyes probed deeply into Simon's. He reached out his hand to clutch Simon's as he prayed with him the sinner's prayer. He didn't realize that his eyes remained open as the doubts overwhelmed him.

Moments later, Yair's cell phone rang. It was Paul at a K-group home in Jerusalem. It took several minutes of reassuring him of their safety after the retelling of the attack to calm his anxious spirit. "This Asmodeus that you called out is no ordinary demon," Paul said cryptically, attempting to avoid alarming the group. "He is a savage and pitiless evil angel according to the Apocrypha. He comes from the second highest-ranking class of angels, the seraphim. He is known as one of the destroyers that comes from a company of fallen angels called the Techaspith, who are extremely hostile toward Jewish people and all those who love them." He whistled through the phone as a signal of relief. "Let's just thank God that you called upon Christ's blood to overpower him."

"I couldn't help but be unnerved over Simon's part in the battle. He never thought to invoke the power of Christ at a moment like that," Yair rejoined. "He cried out to God, but the demon kept coming."

"That's because believing in God is not enough," Paul reminded him. "Remember what James said, 'The demons also believe that—and shudder.' Unless one calls upon the blood of Christ during a demonic attack, they will not have victory...Yair, now that I think of it, are you saying that you don't think Simon is a believer?"

Yair didn't want to discuss the issue of Simon's salvation over the phone, but suddenly felt compelled to convey any news of encouragement to Paul at desperate times such as these. "He expressed such a doubt that we all prayed with him to receive Christ as his personal Savior." He sighed and whispered into the phone, "Only God knows for sure at this point."

"Then we'll leave it with him." Paul cleared his throat. "Now listen clearly. This attack on Simon is really a pivotal event. It means that someone called this demon out of the abyss from where he dwells to harass our group. The whole thing with Simon must be all his doing, I'm sure of that now. So this is what we must do: Because of the increasing danger of demonic activity directed at our group and the entire compound, no one should be permitted to leave the confines of Petra unescorted, and even then, they should be accompanied by several strong Christians to deal with any evil presence that may be targeting us. Understood?"

Yair nodded as he replied, "Understood. Now, what about you?"

"We are all fine. Tell the group Levi and I are remaining strong. Shaul is a real companion in the Lord to me. We work well together. Turning to the pressing matters at hand, we've just received a lengthy field report from one of our underground contacts that Kavidas and

Stein have implemented new phases with severe restrictions in the *Masterlink* system. Although I haven't examined it yet, rumor has it they've ratcheted-up their continuing effort to seize control of the world's economy while putting the squeeze on Christians at the same time. It's supposedly tantamount to the start of the Roman persecution of Christians during the first century. As far as we're concerned here in Jerusalem, we'll continue to use the resources the K-group has stored away, then when they are exhausted, we'll rely upon the Lord working through Nocham and Qadar to provide us with whatever we need." Knowing the state of provision in Petra, Paul simply confirmed their resources. "Your food stuffs are in good shape down there, right?"

"Uh, huh."

Paul sensed his friend's needs. "You okay? You sound tired. You need to rest."

"When can you come down for a visit?" Yair expelled a sigh.

Paul read Yair's signal. "I'll make arrangements to rotate out with Shaul so we can come down on alternate weekends. Okay?"

"Tell Shaul your weekend is first."

Paul smiled. "I will." The conversation was over.

The second Paul pressed the *End* button on his cell phone thoughts of the demonic attack on Simon filled his mind. *That was really a microcosm, a miniature model, of what is inevitably going to occur there at Petra.* He shook his head and rubbed his neck in anguish as the realization of that fateful day loomed in his mind. Fragments of scenes depicting Kavidas and his forces coming out against him, the K-group, and elements of the 144,000 Jewish evangelists filled his mind. Pictures of a great battle where the enemies of God with their military superiority and demonic alliances would be vanquished by the power emerging from prayer. The prayer of the faithful calling upon the Almighty to deliver his people who would fight with only the armor and weapons he had provided: the belt of truth, the breastplate of righteousness, the shield of faith, the helmet of salvation, and the sword of the Spirit, the Word of God. *Lord, thanks for the Spirit who brings encouragement to your people.* Paul turned aside and carefully scrutinized the *Masterlink* report. After one hour of hard study, he called Shaul at his home to meet him.

"This Phase I of the new restrictions is a broad stroke with several parts," Paul pointed out as he interpreted the report. "What it does is target the employers of Christians, and rewards them with *Masterlink* credits if they begin to covertly ease the Christian out of their jobs. To the Christian employee who is using another form of credit apart from *Masterlink*, their credit will be terminated. So the Mom and Pop store that extends credit to sell groceries to Mr. and Mrs. Christian until the end of the week will be warned that *their* access to *Masterlink* will be jeopardized. So any customers who want to charge their purchases in their store will not be able to do so. Unbelievable, right? Secondly, to any sole proprietor or corporation that in any way supports Christians, they are put on notice that they have restricted limits to restock and then, if they continue to violate the order, their suppliers and vendors will be notified and they are dropped from the network. In short order they will be out of business."

"It reminds me of the strong-arm tactics employed by the Mafia," Shaul noted sourly. As he pored over his copy he began squinting at the page when he realized the import of the Phase II restrictions. His face turned red with rage. "They can't do that! They can't keep people from reading the Bible or learning memory verses!"

"From what I gather," Paul said as he nodded gravely, "Phase II is engineered to ultimately expunge the Word of God from the planet. That will include all forms of the Word—written, electronic, etc. There will be worldwide ads in newspapers, TV, and all other commercial media that will give bonus credits on one's *Masterlink* account for those who volunteer to turn in their Bibles and other related study material for the convenience of accessing it online through the Internet, if and when needed. Ultimately this access will be denied, but the initial offering is like the situation in America when the gold prices began to soar in the '80s. Everybody that was holding on to their old gold jewelry, be it their high school ring or grandma's gold spoon for sentimental value, soon redeemed it for cash. The craving for cash quickly replaced all romantic and schmaltzy reasons to cling to the valuable metal.

"This phase of the program also includes a bounty system for those who turn in any die-hard that refuses to upgrade or comply. The reward bonus seems to be graduated based upon the magnitude of the person's position at the time the whistle-blower cashes them in. In other words, turning in a full-time clergyman who refuses to relinquish his Bible will bring a bigger bonus than that of a machinist who leads a Bible study during his lunch hour.

"Then there's the added clause to rid the land of the Word of God committed to memory. Obviously Kavidas' mastermind, Stein, has worked very hard at devising a system to erase every vestige of the Bible, including any memorized portions of the Scriptures."

"How does he expect to pull that off?" Shaul asked incredulously.

"Well, it will work like this: you'll remember how many commercial jingles you hear on TV stick in your head for weeks, right? I mean, people go around whistling the music and slogans to ads from TV and radio long after they've heard them. In some cases for years. How do the ad agencies work people's heads that way? They use mnemonics to infuse it into their memory. Studies have shown that people wake up in the morning and the first thing that fills their mind is a jingle they heard two weeks ago and can't get it out of their heads. After awhile people associate the jingle with the product, and *bam!* Their product sells like crazy! Well, that's the way Stein has constructed this part of Phase II.

"Through this very carefully calculated plan, his design is to first reach the youth of the world through their music. Music has been referred to as a direct viaduct to the soul, so what better medium should he use to reach their souls? The hard rock, rap, and hip-hop music of today is already stripping the youth of every vestige of morality, so it will not be a difficult transition to add subliminal messages and employ mnemonics to crowd out any remnant of Scripture they learned at home or in Sunday school. Then, just as couples living together without marriage started out in the younger generation and spread to the middle age and seniors, so too will this catch on and spread throughout the globe. You'll see. In the times that we're living today where moral standards are at their nadir, replacing Scripture with their music will be easy to accomplish."

"What's your opinion of Phase III?" Shaul asked as he surveyed the report. "It seems to have religious overtones to it."

"Admittedly, the report regarding Phase III is sketchy, and I suspect that it is because this falls into the spiritual realm, and this is something that Stein will inaugurate with a big showing. Probably in line or even greater than the stunt of bringing Kavidas back from the dead."

"What could be bigger than that?" Shaul marveled.

"Unknown," Paul said as he shook his head gloomily. "Unknown."

Independence Park, Jerusalem

Stein sat on the edge of the sofa in Kavidas' living room fiddling with his pen as Kavidas finished his telephone call. Seconds later Kavidas walked into the room and jerked his thumb over his shoulder as he said, "That was Drori on the phone. I'm not really sure that he and Weinstein have made the *necessary* investment in my office as Special Advisor that will satisfy me in the days ahead. A course correction may have to be implemented to rectify that if indeed it is true."

"Meaning?" Stein wondered.

"I mean that they appear to be questioning my authority and even my authentication as Israel's special leader. At this level it is only by inference and innuendo, but my spirit discerns there is more discontent and suspicion below the surface."

"Hmm, that could be bothersome."

Kavidas shrugged it off as a problem that he could easily solve if and when it materialized. He pulled up one of his stuffed chairs next to the sofa. "Bring me up to date on your progress. I sense you're disappointed. Is your plan for Douglas proceeding as scheduled?"

Stein gave him a palms up to signify defeat. "Greater powers have intervened. We'll have to use conventional might on them for now."

Kavidas nodded. Subconsciously he anticipated a problem when invoking support from spiritual forces that would join battle against Christians who knew how to use the power invested in them. It was the Christians who ignored that power who were easy prey. "I'll work with Drori to authorize the IDF and Mossad to launch an attack against Petra on the grounds that they're a subversive group threatening both Israel and Jordan's national security. We must eliminate them to ensure our success. Meanwhile, you get with your people to make an 'unofficial' raid." He shifted his weight to signal a change of agenda then asked, "Where are we with respect to your changes in *Project Renaissance?*"

Stein smiled since the implementation of his upgrades in the "project" was the only real positive thing he could share with him today.

Eve of Shabbat Ha-Gadol
Temple Mount, Jerusalem

The predominant feature of the Sabbath in Judaism is cessation from labor and business activity, being unprofaned by workday purposes and designed to raise man's life to a higher level, by affording him a day of rest and imparting to him the idea of human equality. The Sabbath festival preceding the Pesach, the Passover, is designated as the Great Sabbath, the Shabbath ha-Gadol. Both Kavidas and Stein agreed that the eve of the Shabbath ha-Gadol at the Temple Mount would be the perfect setting to unveil Phase III of *Project Renaissance.*

Moments after the high priest performed the liturgical Kiddush, the sanctification of the people, he reminded the large crowd of worshipers that the holiday commemorated the great miracle that occurred on the Sabbath preceding the exodus from Egypt. The celebration was based on the tradition that when God ordered the people of Israel to prepare a lamb on the tenth of Nissan for the paschal offering, the Egyptians were paralyzed with fear and could not prevent the offering of the Egyptian deity, the lamb. Another explanation, considered more plausible by modern rabbis, is that the holiday refers to the rule in the Haftarah, the Books written after the Torah, that Sabbath observance ends in the words, "Behold, I will send you Elijah the prophet before the great and terrible day of the Lord. He will turn the hearts of fathers to their children and the hearts of children to their fathers." Believing there was startling relevancy to his ministry, Stein selected this holiday to galvanize the people into one group of followers.

Impressed with his priestly regalia, Kavidas bowed before the high priest out of respect for his office as he walked with a deliberate step to the bronze rostrum with its three lecterns to make his presentation. After a nod to Stein, Drori, and Weinstein, who sat expectantly next to the high priest, Kavidas raised both of his hands and prayed before the huge crowd of worshipers. "God in heaven," he cried aloud, "you have sanctified us with your commandments. You have graciously given us your holy Sabbath as a heritage in remembrance of the creation, and now, as we begin to celebrate Passover, we invoke your blessing on the faithful and your nation, Israel..."

"Paul, come quick, something's cookin' at the Temple Mount!" Shaul shouted to both the TV and toward the bathroom. They were still sharing accommodations with a K-group member. "Kavidas is praying as if he's about to make a speech!" Paul immediately dropped his razor and rushed to join Shaul in front of the TV as Kavidas continued to captivate his audience.

"...your nation, *my nation*, has been subjected to many perils over the past eight months, and I've been asking myself, 'Why is this happening, and how can we get back into favor with God?' Well, after many agonizing days of examination and entreating God—" He paused to point to Stein, Drori and Weinstein—"and consulting with our nation's learned rabbis," he lied, "we believe we have 'been to the mountain' and have now made our peace with God."

Thunderous applause broke out.

Kavidas waved them to silence after one full minute of receiving their appreciation, then spoke into the microphone in a controlled voice. "Our world, notably here in Israel, has been subject to many calamities over the past eight months. These disasters have brought severe affliction to the land that I love. Great forces of questionable origin have been exerted upon humanity and I believe that the time has come to explore these forces that use aimless, merciless, and judgmental motives to harm our world."

He pointed toward the sky, then said in contempt, "The climate, the environment in which we live, the economy, and the people have been unfairly treated by—" he stopped short to scan the crowds, then shot a look to Stein who gave him a thumbs-up before he added, "a god who is cruel and unjust." He held up his hands in a halting manner and cried out, "The time has come for change! We, here in Israel, need to recognize that the god of this nation is also the God of other nations as well. He is also the god of the Hindus, the Muslims, the Mormons, the Jehovah Witnesses, and the Christians. Because he is a multi-faceted god, we cannot place restrictions on him by claiming that we have first-hand knowledge or revelation of him. Nor can we hold to the notion that the Bible is the only testament of who he is. No, there are many other accounts of this God as well as avenues to this god that should be explored at a time when divine intervention for the welfare of the people is so vitally needed."

At first there was a hush over the crowds as they digested Kavidas' blasphemous charge. Stein sat stone-faced with his hand fisted into balls at his sides. Many looked askance at Drori and Weinstein, who simply sat stunned in disbelief. Then a moment of murmuring preceded another outburst of applause.

"Paul," Shaul gasped in disbelief with his eyes riveted to the TV screen, "the crowd is eating this heretical tripe up in scoops! It's almost as if they're entranced with this Kavidas, ready to bow at his feet!"

"Now watch how he slips in Phase III," Paul predicted solemnly. He shook his head in disgust. "Remember what the French philosopher, Blaise Pascal said, 'Men never do evil so completely and cheerfully as when they do it from religious conviction.' What is happening before our very eyes is the delusion of humanity under the guise of a religion that is about to undergo a radical change."

"Never before in the history of man has there ever been a more opportune time than now to modify man's worship of his god," Kavidas explained. "In Christendom there is the goal of ecumenism to break down those church barriers that have kept Christians separated for centuries. But because of doctrines and dogmas, that goal was not achievable. Christians are still arguing over abortion reform, the rights of homosexuals, and even the deity of Christ." He slammed his fist down on the lectern and shouted, "Well, I'm here to say, let the doctrines and dogmas be damned! We need solidarity as a people without the restraints of doctrines and dogmas! We need to have a fresh view toward the worship of God never before experienced in the annals of time! We need a religion that embraces a form of universalism like ecumenism, but one that is unique! One that will put an end to separate forms of worship. One that will unite all of humanity under one form of worship." He stopped and waved Stein over to the rostrum. As soon as Stein stood up, the crowds began to applaud as they recognized him as Kavidas' right-hand man.

"Here it comes!" Shaul lamented as he wagged his head at the TV. "Here it comes."

With a determined gait, Stein walked to the second lectern and motioned the crowds to silence. "Many may consider what I have to say and do to be offensive, but nevertheless, it must be said and done in view of this momentous occasion. I believe this to be the proper time and format to advise you of this since this directly affects your form of worship. Further, I firmly believe that truth will prevail based on the facts presented before us today, and that any skeptic that denies the validity of our claims will be utterly convinced beyond all doubt and suspicion." He paused to give Kavidas the nod and waved over Drori and Weinstein. They unwittingly marched in a single file over to him.

"Drawing from our history, I will remind you of the great prophet Elijah who was mentioned in our opening prayer," Stein expounded. "Well, the Bible has recorded the period in Israel's past when both a famine and drought, such as what we have been experiencing for many days, was ravaging the land. It was a terrible three-year period when God was punishing the Israelites for their wrongdoing. Then along comes this Elijah the prophet, who defeats the false prophets of Baal at

Mount Carmel, then tells King Ahab to look toward the sea because rain was about to fall. Well—" Stein stopped short and bowed his head for several minutes in what looked like a prayer as the crowds gaped in wonder. "Behold, the spirit of the Lord is upon me!" he cried out as he raised his hands toward the sky. Kavidas looked up in expectation as Drori and Weinstein exchanged startled glances.

"Look, the clouds are rolling back!" a woman's voice from the crowd yelled out. News reporters immediately turned their cameras upward to give the viewers at home a live feed as the low-lying clouds that ceased to bring rain many months before began to part as if some gigantic knife were suddenly slicing them in half, then pulling them to the sides.

Once the clouds opened, bright rays of sunlight blasted the crowds, then fanned out and bathed the land as if it had been shielded by a lunar eclipse. The crowds shielded their eyes, many grabbing articles of clothing to cover their heads until their eyes adjusted accordingly.

"This is unbelievable," Paul exclaimed as he fell back into the sofa to watch the unfolding drama.

"So that you may believe!" Stein shouted. "Sun, go backwards!"

Once the clouds were folded back, revealing the blue sky, everyone held up their hands and opened their fingers slightly to shield their eyes as they tried to focus on the sun. Although it was not as radiant as in the past, the unexpected sunburst nearly blinded the onlookers.

Obeying the command, the sun suddenly arrested its east-to-west progression and hung momentarily suspended in the sky. The scientific-minded and the skeptics began studying their watches to calculate its movement as others simply gaped in awe at the astrophysical phenomenon. After ten minutes of watching, waiting, and whispering, suddenly hundreds of hands shot upward from the crowds and pointed as they screamed, "It's going backwards! It's going backwards!"

Hundreds of the worshipers fell prostrate on the Temple floor and began to chant, "God has come down to earth. The Messiah is in our midst!"

What seemed like an interminable period was really only 15

minutes where a noticeable reversal in the sun's movement was seen. The on-site TV cameramen were quick to zoom in on several worshipers' wristwatches to show their timepieces retrogressing before their eyes. Commentary from the news reporters included bizarre statements that this was "God's time machine" that paralleled the sundial going backwards in the time of Hezekiah, king of Judah.

As the chanting reached a fever-pitch, Stein spoke into the microphone, "Look toward the sea!" The crowds stood up to look over the Temple wall toward the Mediterranean to see a small cloud on the horizon. The puffy cloud had a tail-like funnel that extended into the sea. From the distance, many were able to see the cloud begin to swirl and the funnel begin to spin like a waterspout. Within seconds the small cloud began sucking up water from the sea and branching out and forming into great cumulus, water-bearing clouds, which rapidly swept toward the land while the former cloud cover was held back by some unseen force to allow this bizarre storm entrance into the holy land.

Moments later the worshipers were clamoring for Kavidas and Stein as they ran for cover from the heavy rains.

Shaul tossed the TV remote on to the end table and began to nibble on his broken fingernail as he reflected on the event the nation of Israel just witnessed. After a moment of contemplation he sighed with resignation and said to Paul, "Who is in control here? God or them? How can God allow them to perform these supernatural feats that validate their office while He just watches idly from heaven and lets it happen?" He sibilated softly then breathed, "I just don't understand it."

Paul poured two cups of coffee then walked to the sofa and sat down next to Shaul. "As a Jewish man, you may not have any knowledge of alleged miracles that occurred in the 1800s and 1900s in France and Portugal that resemble what we saw today."

Shaul raked his beard. "No, I don't have a clue. What do you mean?"

"Well," Paul explained, "my dad told me about an incident way back in 1917, in a small settlement in Portugal that is just north of Lisbon. The Virgin Mary was reported to have appeared six times to three children, a Lucia dos Santos and her cousins. During the visions, Mary urged them to pray the rosary, which would lead to the conversion of Russia. The Catholic church approved of the sighting and it is still a center for pilgrimages.

"Earlier, between 1844 and 1879, a Bernadette Soubirous, a French peasant girl claimed she had experienced numerous visions of the Virgin Mary and that Mary imparted miraculous powers of healing to the waters of a spring near a grotto in Lourdes. The visions were declared authentic by the Roman Catholic Church, and the Lourdes grotto became a shrine for pilgrims."

Shaul gave Paul a quizzical look. He attempted to connect the dots in the accounts, but needed help. "Are you saying that those sightings are similar to what happened today at the Temple?"

Paul cleared his throat as he attempted to postulate his theory. "What I am saying is that when we examine those sightings of Mary, we see that they were designed to promote the worship of Christ's mother and hence replace Christ as the mediator between God and man, which is a position only to be held by him according to 1 Timothy 2:5. Further, these alleged healing episodes raise serious doubts as well. They may have occurred, but in my mind I can only attribute healing to Christ and the first century apostles during the Apostolic age when the church needed authentication. Any miraculous healing since must be carefully weighed out, based on who the healing is pointing to. In other words, who is being glorified by the miracle, the miracle-worker, such as in the case of Mary, or Christ, who alone deserves our adoration and worship."

Shaul nodded as if he understood. "Let me see if I have this straight. You're saying that these appearances that have been documented by the Catholic Church are nothing more than a diversionary tactic designed to take people away from seeking salvation in Christ by directing worship to Mary?"

"It's all part of the master plan," Paul affirmed. "A colossal delusion, orchestrated by Satan from the beginning in Eden to draw innocent souls to himself through the medium of organized religion. What Satan did was simply to attach Mary and baby Jesus to the Madonna and child cult that originated in ancient Babylon under the name of Ishtar and Tammuz that is described in Jeremiah chapter 7 and 44."

"Now I remember reading that part. That's where Jeremiah berates the children of Israel with a scathing rebuke for worshiping the Queen of Heaven. Another name for the Babylonian goddess."

Paul gave him a thumbs-up. "Now you're getting it. This colossal delusion has been perpetuated throughout the centuries in organized religion, and we have just seen the modern version of it here on TV."

"Then Kavidas and Stein are using the same tactics, deluding the public through false miracles?"

"They appear real," Paul affirmed. "Remember, Satan is the prince and power of the air and the angel of light. This enables him to project false realities to dupe mankind. Of course this also embraces UFOs and extraterrestrials, but we won't get into that now."

Shaul sat up and took another slug from his coffee cup. "So this whole thing with the sun and the rain is all just an illusion like what happened at Lourdes and Fatima?"

"It appears so."

Shaul shook his head as the truth began to make sense. "That explains why Kavidas and Stein never really clarified their 'new religion,' because if they defined it, the people would recognize that it is a direct violation of the First Commandment and outright reject it. This way they simply employ the tool of syncretism and fool the unwitting public."

"Because *he* is the religion. The whole basis of this new religion is that it doesn't lead to worship of another god, but is the worship of *the man as god*. This is what Nebuchadnezzar did that alarmed Daniel's three companions, Shadrach, Meshach, and Abednego. He exalted himself as god. This is what the Roman emperors did. This is what occurs in the Japanese Shinto shrines, and what Lenin did to bring veneration to himself. In effect, this is man's attempt to fill the spiritual vacuum resulting from years of hedonism and narcissistic living."

Shaul slapped the side of his head to jog his memory. "This reminds me of the dream Yair had about Kavidas performing the abomination of desolation that occurs in the midpoint of the Tribulation. This is all leading up to it, right?"

"This was the authentication of Phase III," Paul summarized. "The new religion is now in place. In time he will fulfill that prophecy of polluting the sanctuary, yes."

"The emblem of unity in the religion being the *Masterlink* system," Shaul realized as he stared out the window. The truth that those without the *Masterlink* mark could be saved while those embracing the *Masterlink* mark could not be saved seriously troubled him.

Paul stood up and stretched his arms. He was on overload and unable to soak in any more theology for the day. "I need a break. I'm going to Petra to visit Yair and the group for the weekend. You E-mail Brandon and explain what happened at the Temple. Tell him we're gearing up for another battle."

Shaul saw the fatigue on his friend's face and decided to postpone any further discussion. He motioned for Paul to rejoin him on the sofa so they could pray. Paul sighed deeply as he sat down again, knowing that his spirit and soul urgently required it.

Two hours later Paul departed for Petra, leaving Shaul all alone in the apartment.

Thoughts of failure and abandonment by God assaulted Shaul for several moments until he remembered God's promise that he would never leave him or forsake him. Then their mission on earth, their purpose for living, came to mind. A purpose that God had ordained whereby they would be the very salt of the earth that would keep Kavidas and his team from overrunning the world with their axis powers of evil. Then Louis Pasteur's statement that Shaul had learned as a boy came to mind: *"Let me tell you the secret that has led me to my goal. My strength lies solely in my tenacity."*

"That's it," he exclaimed with a snap of his fingers. "We must go after this Kavidas with the tenacity of a dog on a bone."

He turned his head and his eyes connected with the screen-saver on the computer. It was an italicized text with a royal blue background. The text was slowly rotating in a circular motion. He peered at it for a moment as the force of the words began to sink into his heart. *It is better to light a candle than to curse the darkness.*

"Okay, Lord," he said to himself. "I get the message." He sat down at the console, then connected to the Internet to talk to Brandon in Florida.

[Sending]
Dear Brandon: I'm writing to you from a K-group member's apartment. We don't believe it's safe to return to Paul's apartment just yet. Paul asked me to write you as he is out of sorts and took off for the weekend to Petra to be with Yair, Levi, and the group. We had an unbelievable event here today. Kavidas and Stein have just put on a show at the Temple, and to my knowledge, there hasn't been anything to compare to it since Kavidas was raised from the dead. Paul believes that the demonstration of Stein's powers where the clouds rolled back, the sun moved backwards, and rain fell out of the drought-stricken heavens was nothing more than an illusion or localized event. I went online to the neighboring countries, and there is nothing mentioned in the news about the sun or rain or any supernatural event for that matter. What's your take on the "miracle"? Please advise.

[Incoming]
Apart from a small column on page four of an international newspaper, there has been no publicity of the incident. What's more, there has been no regression of time, or change of weather patterns here in the States, for that matter. I suspect that while part of the "miracle" about the sun could have been an illusion, the rain was probably real but only local, similar to the plagues brought on at Moses's hand while in Egypt. In connection with the rain, I would guess that the cessation of the drought judgment is only temporary. You should expect it to resume. Remember, those ten plagues in Egypt only affected the people within the confines of the land of Egypt, not the entire world. This may account for the news blackout.

Be sure to let Paul read this E-mail. There has been significant changes in the economy here in the States, and I believe it is representative of worldwide conditions. Namely, this Kavidas/Stein *Masterlink* system seems to be tightening its grip on any evangelistic methods, linking it directly to the population's pocketbook.

As of this week, any *Masterlink* patron who may have an inkling to embark on a search to find Christ is being denied credit. Some of my employees who are not Christians have been asking their fellow employees and *Koinonos* members who are Christians questions about the seal judgments and have expressed interest in salvation. Now when they attempt to use their *Masterlink* credit line, they are being denied. It seems the system is being tightly monitored and credits are being issued to any person who reports or "squeals" on anyone seeking information about becoming a Christian. So many of my employees are set against one another, bringing conflict into our midst. The bottom line is that people are becoming afraid to search for spiritual answers to their problems.

Another area that has undergone a radical change is in the area of recreation. While in the past Americans were enamored and preoccupied, even to the point of obsession with sports, video games, pornography, and sleazy TV shows that do nothing to build up our society, these luxuries are systematically replaced by survival courses and techniques. It seems that Americans have replaced their hedonism and narcissism with programs designed to survive the ongoing seal judgments and curry favor with God, and guess what is the underlying motivation for the survival? Moralism. Yes, that's right. There is now a huge push for Americans to preserve their 'moral' heritage and return to their religious roots. The hedonism is just no longer fashionable, if you can believe that. This, supposedly, is the way to change the hearts of the wayward and bring them back to God. No doubt Kavidas and Stein have joined with organized religions to bring this to fruition. Of course this is all a colossal scheme to draw people away from the real truth: their spiritual salvation in Christ and employing Christian ethics based on the Bible in their daily lives. As you and I know, that is the only way to bring about reform.

[Sending] We intercepted information on the *Masterlink* modifications you referred to that are known as improvement Phases I-II. We understand now that Phase III of this improvement is a totally new way of replacing the Bible and all evidence of its influence through a bizarre program of mental overwrites and mnemonics.

It seems that Kavidas and Stein are in this for the long haul.

TWENTY-ONE

Office of the Special Advisor, The Knesset Building

Defense Minister Drori, and Chief of Staff Weinstein, sat on the edge of their stuffed leather chairs in the Special Advisor's office waiting for Kavidas to arrive. They had both received an urgent call in the early morning hours to discuss an "imminent threat," as Kavidas put it, with the nature of the crisis remaining a secret. They were extremely unnerved. *Unprecedented* was the word Drori used when describing his feeling of the mystery crisis to Weinstein.

Drori impatiently meandered to the floor-to-ceiling window and separated the drapes to afford himself a panoramic view of the city when his concentration suddenly was interrupted by the outside weather. "Michael, come look at this," he said in somber tones as he tapped on the window. "Not only is the rain stopping, but it looks like whatever rainfall we did miraculously receive simply disappeared as if the drought were never broken."

Weinstein walked to the window and gazed off into the horizon to see the odd cloud patterns. Then his eyes raked the rooftops outside the window looking for evidence of the "miraculous" cloudburst and drenching rain. But there were no puddles or pools of water despite the overcast conditions. He did, however, take notice of the climate changing; it was getting colder. "This is the strangest thing," he marveled. "It's almost as if the 'miracle of the rain' just evaporated."

Drori scratched his head as a wave of suspicion came over him. "I wonder how many more 'miracles' performed by our—" he stopped short—"Special Advisor and his friend, Mortimer Stein, will evaporate in time."

"You better watch how you talk," Weinstein warned. "If Kavidas had heard that remark, your butt would be in the masher faster than you could say '*Oy Gevalt*, oh dear'!"

Drori cracked a smile. "I know I shouldn't say this, but I really am having a problem with him now. Especially after this last episode where his partner stopped the sun's movement across the sky. I mean, his ascendency to the position of Special Advisor seems to be built on the bones of our people here in Israel and things that are sleight of hand. If one were to trace his spectacular rise to public office, one would see that his career is fraught with wars, conflicts, mishaps, calamities, and magic!"

Just then the door flew open!

Drori and Weinstein froze in place, then turned in reflexive alarm as Kavidas stood in the doorway with one hand on the doorknob and the other tightly balled into a fist at his side. For what seemed like an interminable period, he stared at them both with penetrating eyes, then said perfunctorily, "Please be seated, gentlemen."

"Yes, sir," they said in unison. As they retreated back to their chairs Drori tried to steal himself against the building anxiety that he may have been overheard, but the fear wouldn't leave. *God forbid Kavidas was listening!*

"A situation has developed that is quickly reaching the place of threatening our national security," Kavidas began with muted bravado. "It is now in our best interest to squash this problem before it gets any bigger."

Drori and Weinstein exchanged glances. "Situation?" Drori queried. "What situation are we talking about? I'm not aware of any 'situation,' Mr. Advisor, unless you're referring to the never-ending problem with the Arabs or the environmental hazards we've encountered over the past eight months."

"The situation I'm addressing," Kavidas instructed with heightening volume, "is the conspiring group known as *Koinonos* that has a powerful foothold here in Jerusalem and is building a Christian fortress in Petra with the aim of launching a government overthrow in the near future. I expect you, Mr. Drori, to take immediate military action to thwart any possibility of a *coup d'etat.*"

Drori jumped to his feet. "Mr. Kavidas," he argued, "this cannot be true! My assets in the field have nothing to report as far as any subversive groups are concerned. What's more, there isn't a single shred of intel to point to them having even as much as one gun, much less any ordnance to engage in an attack! As far as Petra goes, the Jordanian government isn't the slightest bit concerned over their presence or they would have registered a complaint with us in a heartbeat. That area is subject to regular reconnaissance with military over flights and satellite surveillance, so believe me, if the Arabs thought they represented a threat, they would have their ambassador with one foot on our doorstep and the other on the United Nation's by now." He paced back and forth for a moment before turning toward Kavidas and asking reprovingly, "Mr. Kavidas, are you sure of the validity of your sources?"

Kavidas knew it would come to this. He bristled with anger, then pointed his finger into Drori's face. "Are you challenging me?"

Weinstein rose to his feet and motioned with his hands for them to calm down. "Why, Mr. Kavidas," he fumbled for words, "Zeev is simply trying to be cautious during a time when our nation has undergone tremendous difficulties. We would not want to engage our military in something unless it was proven to be a legitimate force that threatened our national security, that's all. I mean, surely you can't blame him for feeling that way."

"You needn't jump to his defense, Michael Weinstein!" Kavidas snarled as his eyes darted back and forth between them. "It so happens that I know your hearts, and you both think alike, but express it differently. You both doubt me. Neither of you have supported me from the beginning, apart from social appearances. The day of reckoning has come. My timetable is too short for defiance, and I can no longer afford any insubordination from men on my staff."

He walked to the panoramic window and glared up into the sky as Drori and Weinstein stood mute with their eyes following his every move. Collectively they felt every word like a whiplash on their backs. *Think fast. Appease him for the time being until his mood changes,* Drori commanded himself in an effort to attenuate the pain of the verbal assault.

When Kavidas turned to face them, there was a fury in his eyes they had never seen before. Drori didn't realize it at the time, but he would never regain the chance to overcome Kavidas' judgment of them. "Now, you listen to me," Kavidas demanded as he raised his right hand and pointed both his index and little finger at them both. "From now on, you will do as I say and when I say it! Clear?"

A strange force suddenly overpowered both their intellect and their senses as he kept his fingers directed at them. While they understood his words, their minds felt manipulated by an internal pressure that emanated in their brains and seemed to exert a strange control on their will. While reason dictated that they were being impressed in their minds by an unexplainable power, they were unable to fight or disagree with it.

"Clear," Drori said.

"Clear," Weinstein echoed.

Kavidas slowly lowered his hand while his eyes continued to penetrate and seize their minds. "Sit down!" he ordered.

They obeyed mechanically.

"Drori, you will dispatch to Petra an IDF expeditionary regiment of at least two battalions that will include your elite special forces. Attack unannounced by ground with adequate air support in a lightning raid to eliminate any potential adversary. Next, order your Mossad forces here in Jerusalem to ferret out every last one of these *Koinonos* members who are hiding and place them under arrest for sedition. We will hold them in detention indefinitely as potential terrorists until we can sort this whole thing out."

Having given Drori instructions, he turned to Weinstein. "Weinstein, you will contact the Jordanian Prime Minister and advise him of our situation. You will explain that these are predominantly *our* people who have barricaded themselves in the ancient fortress with the goal of building a subversive army to undermine the Israeli government." He stopped speaking and clapped his hands. "Let's get to it!"

They both nodded, stood up, and marched out of the office.

Kavidas then went to his desk and picked up the telephone. He pressed Stein's number on the speed-dial list.

Stein's cell phone rang.

"I have set in motion the plan to rid the land of the vermin at Petra," Stein heard over the encrypted phone network. "This plan should draw out any of the *Koinonos* groupies that have not been picked up by Mossad. They will probably try to rescue their 'fellow Christians' down there in Petra. You need to initiate a backup plan using your people in the event that the IDF or Mossad is met by some kind of resistance we haven't counted on. This insurance will guarantee success. Are we clear on this?"

The edge in Kavidas' voice caught Stein by surprise. "Um, why yes, we're clear." When the phone went dead he unwittingly scratched his ear and muttered, "What was that all about?" *Mounting pressure of his office, that's it!* At first blush he looked at himself as the cause. *I must be faithful to carry out my part of the mission so as not to put undue strain on him.* He then put a call in to Mibsam Azib for an important meeting.

What he didn't know was that Kavidas was suffering from an acute case of theophobia, the fear of reprisal from God.

Christian Fortress, Petra

The moment Paul's motorcycle cleared the Sik, or narrow passageway, leading from the desert into the fortress he was met by Yair, Jonathan, and Levi who greeted him with open arms. Their meeting had all the hallmarks of a blessed homecoming.

As Paul approached Yair's mobile home he marveled at the K-group's acceptance of the cramped quarters and the frontier-like setting of the compound. The mobile homes were very modest and unassuming, but they were cozy with two or three small bedrooms, a center room, and a breakfast nook. Once inside Yair's home, Paul's eyes immediately ran to the table in the breakfast nook as the aroma of his homemade banana nut loaf filled his nostrils. He smiled as the thought of the breakfast nook as the K-group's favorite place of fellowship and fun.

Paul bit into his peanut-butter and jelly-laden nut loaf and sipped his cup of coffee as Yair and Levi looked on in wonder. "Haven't members of the K-group been feeding you guys?"

With a broad grin he replied, "There's nothing like home cooking."

Yair poured himself a cup of coffee and sat down. He ran his fingers through his beard. "Paul, how did the world get to this place?" He took a sip of coffee. "I mean, our society—the world—has reached the place where our heavenly Father is bringing down judgments on mankind, Israel and the rest of the world are being unwittingly controlled by the Antichrist and his partner's financial system, they have now put Kavidas in the place of a god, and no one is bothering to ask why? They don't even look into the proverbial 'mirror' and ask themselves how did this happen?"

Paul swallowed his last piece of nut loaf and took a swig of his coffee before he attempted to explain the theodicy. "I guess one could say that it started when the God-given ability to choose right from wrong was replaced with situation ethics. This started back in the Garden of Eden, but has been kept in balance by the restraining arm of the Christian, exerting force by drawing from biblical values and the example of the Christ-centered lifestyle. But, in my purview the biblical value system and the Christian example has been compromised. Biblical values have been replaced with humanistic thinking. Even the staunchest believer has bought into much of the humanistic tripe being circulated in today's universities. The Christian moral and ethical example has been replaced by secular influence, so that the Christian wants to behave much like the non-Christian instead of the non-Christian being provoked to want to behave like the Christian.

"This trend took hold in the early '60s, when the liberals went virtually unopposed in their tactics of subtly and cunningly replacing local ordinances and federal laws that protected special classes of people that promoted and funded immorality and global governance that allegedly was to benefit society but in reality took us further away from

338

a sense of community and alienated the classes so that now we have the liberals against the conservatives. The moral right against the immoral left. Any spiritual codes we once embraced has been replaced by a code underwritten and approved by Satan, with sex and money being his chief areas of operation. It seems that our society has been reduced to those two key points of interest. In effect, virtue has been replaced by lust. It seems like it is the only code people want to live by today." He paused to finish his coffee.

"Your explanation reminds me of Martin Niemoller's quote regarding the Nazis," Yair explained as he opened up his Bible. "I keep this quote in the front of my Bible to prompt me in my responsibility to speak up against evil *as* it appears." He unfolded a small piece of stationery and read, " 'In Germany they came first for the Communists, and I didn't speak up because I wasn't a Communist. Then they came for the Jews, and I didn't speak up because I wasn't a Jew. Then they came for the trade unionists, and I didn't speak up because I wasn't a trade unionist. Then they came for the Catholics, and I didn't speak up because I was a Protestant. Then they came for me, and by that time no one was left to speak up.' "

Paul slammed his fist down on the table. "That will never happen as long as I can draw breath!"

Levi simply held his tongue as if he knew that the remedy for humanity was only greater tribulation. *The reason I was born*, he said in his heart. "I'm returning to Jerusalem with you, Paul," he said trenchantly. He knew he would be needed.

K-group Member's House
Kfar Saba, Jerusalem

"Your breakfast is ready!" Paul heard filtering through the bedroom door. The hospitality in the Greenbaum house was unmistakably unparalleled in all of the K-group member's network. It was one of Paul's favorite resting places.

He turned to the young man sleeping in the bed next to him. "Levi, time to get up."

Moments later they were both sitting on the edge of their beds getting dressed.

"Bathroom first!" Levi announced.

"Nice try!" Paul replied with a devilish guffaw.

"Paul!" Levi pointed to the wall in front of them. "Look!" The wall appeared to be detaching from the rest of the house and slowly moving backwards until it was about ten feet away, where it hung suspended in mid-air momentarily, then disappeared, leaving a mysterious blackness in its place. "What the—?" Levi blurted out in wonder.

Suspecting what would come next, Paul blinked and stiffened. "Brace yourself, Levi!"

Thousands of white twinkling dots appeared out of the blackness to form the backdrop of the theater-like stage that appeared before them. Then a ball of fire emerged out of the backdrop that remained rotating in the center. Next, several smaller, circular objects resembling a combination of large marbles and tennis balls that were intersected with arcs of white light materialized.

Levi pointed to the third small ball with eyes pleading for understanding and said, "That looks like the planet Earth!"

"It is Earth!" Paul affirmed. "That is our solar system, our sun!"

"Uh-oh," Levi said as a zooming effect magnified the ball of fire until it dominated the blackness. Seconds later what looked like a Quick-Time player began to show like a movie the surface of the sun being slowly overtaken by what looked like a malignant cancer until the light was entirely snuffed out. The scene changed, showing the effect on the third planet, Earth, along with its moon. They were completely enveloped in darkness. The only visible light came from the distant stars and their faint reflections off some remote planets.

Paul grabbed Levi's hand and said with a nod, "This is only part of what the Sixth Seal is going to be like when it is opened. God help us."

Levi's breath caught in his throat. "Of that we can be sure of."

Seconds later the wall returned to normal. The vision was over.

There was a loud bang on the door. "Your breakfast is ready, *gentlemen*!" Mrs. Greenbaum shouted through the door.

Twenty-five minutes later, when Paul had finished his cheese omelet, he raised his coffee mug to Mrs. Greenbaum, who simply walked toward him with the coffee pot and refilled it. He turned to Mr. Greenbaum and said, "Norman, Levi and I have just experienced a frightening vision from God!"

"What?" Norman asked incredulously. "When?"

Paul placed his coffee mug on the table. "Just now, before we came down to breakfast."

"What was it about?"

"It was about the sun turning black in fulfillment of the Sixth Seal!" Levi blurted out impetuously.

Paul explained, "Apparently the Earth is about to experience the next dreadful judgment that will eclipse all the others." He shook his head. "Despite my faith in the Lord, I'm a little nervous about this one. The Revelation 6 passage describes the Sixth Seal, where the sun turns black and the moon turns blood red and the stars fall from the heavens. In addition, there is what is referred to as a 'great' earthquake. Historically, when we read in the Bible where it uses the word 'great' like in the 'great Tribulation,' God really ratchets up the severity of the punishment, commensurate with man's denial and refusal to repent."

Levi reached for his Bible and laid it on the table. "Remember too," he began, "that in 800 B.C., the prophet Joel predicted this, and Christ reaffirmed it in Matthew 24:29. So we can say conclusively that God will bring it to pass—he confirmed it three times!"

Paul nodded in agreement. "The Revelation passage goes on to say that there will be a major shift in the celestial bodies. Namely, there is a realignment of the stars, the sky above us is rolled up like a scroll, and down here on Earth, the tectonic plates will shift so that mountains and islands will be rearranged. All in preparation for the next set of judgments, the Trumpets."

"The prophecy also states that man—including high-echelon government officials—will be so frightened they will run for cover in any underground cave they can find. Probably to the military underground missile facilities and fallout shelters," Levi added.

Mr. Greenbaum sighed as the information overwhelmed him. He looked up at his wife. "The moon turning red is one thing that would take some getting used to. The stars shifting will present quite a problem to astronomers and those using stars for navigation. But if the sun turns black in the very near future to fulfill your vision, wouldn't all life on the planet die off? I mean, we'd never make it through the rest of the Tribulation period until Christ returns."

"Fair question," Paul replied. "Of course, I don't have any scientific expertise in this area, but if I interpret the vision correctly, it appears to be a gradual process, where the Earth is deprived of sunlight over a period of time."

"We've been experiencing a change in our daylight hours for the past nine months or so. Is that related to it?" Norman asked.

"Perhaps. But I'm inclined to think that the decreasing daylight has more to do with an earlier judgment brought on by Nocham and Qadar," Paul said. "When they proclaimed that it would not rain for three and one-half years—and we can see that the world is still overcast—that in itself could account for the decreased daylight and cooling temperatures. You know, like the winters in the Arctic regions. But this judgment is quite different. This Seal makes it clear that the sun is going to slowly extinguish and grow cold.

"But God, in his mercy, is not going to bring it about all at once. Humans and all living creatures depend on the sun for photosynthesis and a host of other radiant nutrients and benefits. So, no, I believe the judgment will extend over the next six years until Christ returns. In the interim, the Earth's ecology and environment will suffer greatly, forcing mankind to develop alternative sources of artificial light."

"What do I have to do to get right with God?" Paul heard from behind him.

Paul turned and cast his eyes on the Greenbaums' 19-year old son. He'd been listening to the discussion from the doorway. "Why, Hershel," he said with a smile, "all you have to do is pray and confess Christ, the Messiah, and he will come into your heart."

Mrs. Greenbaum looked bewildered. "But I thought—?"

"Mom, until now," Hershel confessed, "I've been faking it. I knew becoming a Christian is something you and Dad wanted for me since the time of the disappearance, so I've been going through the motions. But now, it's different. I'm ready to make the decision on my own."

Mrs. Greenbaum began to cry as she walked to her son and put her arm around his waist. Seconds later they were all holding hands as Paul prayed aloud with Hershel to become a Christian.

The screech of tires followed by slamming car doors broke into their prayer!

Levi darted to the kitchen window and looked out from behind the curtain. Two men were exiting from a car with a government insignia on the door. He turned in reflexive alarm. "Mossad!"

Norman motioned to Paul and Levi to make their way out the rear door. They nodded, grabbed their belongings, and began to rush out when Hershel whispered forcibly, "I'm going with you!"

Norman and his wife exchanged glances and gave him the nod. "Paul, there's a gun in the glove compartment if you need it," Norman said softly.

Paul gave him a wave as they slipped out into the backyard and into their car in the parking lot. Seconds later they were out of sight.

Banging at the door!

Norman took a deep breath and opened the door to find the agents standing in plainclothes, one holding a document. "Are you Norman Greenbaum?" the paunchy one asked.

Greenbaum nodded. "What is it you want, gentlemen?" he asked impatiently.

Mossad agents react poorly to insolence. The paunchy agent looked askance momentarily to see if there were any bystanders, then put his foot in the doorway. He snapped the document from his young partner's hand and said sharply, "We have a warrant for your arrest for sedition against the State. We suggest you come peaceably."

"This is an outrage!" Greenbaum declared. "Neither I, nor my family, have committed any such thing!"

"You are on our list of those who have been shielding fugitives of the State and have made divisive statements against political officers. We have ample documentation," the young Mossad agent declared roughly. "Now will you come peaceably, or will we have to cuff you?"

Mr. Greenbaum looked back at his wife, who stood with her handkerchief over her mouth, then turned to the young Mossad agent and said numbly, "peaceably."

Forty-eight-year-old Doug Bennett, with a Ph.D. in solar astrophysics, keyed in the azimuth coordinates for the sun on the 1.6-meter Solar Vacuum Telescope, then pressed the computer console control button to bring the giant telescope into its proper alignment. Then he engaged the red hydrogen-alpha light filter that would enable him to view and photograph the sun close-up, despite its incredible brightness and harmful rays. Once he entered the settings he walked to the observatory window to finish his coffee as the giant telescope slowly rotated to its assigned location. It would be several moments until the precision instrument would be locked in place.

As he looked out the window, his eyes caught several white puffy clouds drifting by and forming wispy circles around his new car. *Do clouds promote rust?* he wondered. Looking down on clouds was a phenomenon that took some getting used to. Rising 6,800 feet above sea level, the 200-acre Kitt Peak astronomy facility provided an extraordinary site to study the planets, the sun, and the vastness of the universe. Kitt Peak was the home of research facilities for two divisions of the National Optical Astronomy Observatories: Kitt Peak National Observatory and the National Solar Observatory, housing the McMath-Pierce Solar Telescope Facility, which contains the world's three solar telescopes, the 1.6-meter main and two 0.9-meter auxiliaries, along with the Razdow small solar patrol telescope.

Bennett heard a beep from the console and gulped down the rest of his coffee. It was time to get to work. He walked to the telescope, removed his eyeglasses before turning the optical adjustment knob to compensate for his deficient vision, then began to study his subject, the very star that provides our solar system, with its nine planets and numerous moons, with sufficient light, energy, and gravitational counterbalance to sustain their orbits in the Milky Way galaxy.

Today was unusual because a gargantuan prominence extended

over 400,000 miles into space. It had been nearly nine months since the last one, being by comparison a minor event, yet significant enough to account for solar disturbances that could affect Earth's atmosphere.

"Whoa!" he exclaimed. He noted the exceptional prominence in his log, then waited to see if the expected repressed convection or spiral sunspot would appear.

"There we go," he said to himself moments later as the strong magnetic field in the northeast quadrant of the sun began to cool and form the dark sunspot. But then he noticed that the sunspot began to spread in that area of the sun's surface at a slow but measurable rate. He looked away from the telescope eyepiece to his instrument panel, particularly at the Stefan-Boltzmann luminosity and temperature relationship indicators, then quickly reached for his eyeglasses to recheck the figures. "This can't be!"

The brightness and temperature reading of the sun's surface area was diminishing at a rate that was relatively insignificant, but over a period of time could be alarming. While the thermonuclear reactions that sustained the incredible temperatures on the sun's surface at 15,000,000 degrees Kelvin appeared to be normal (the temperature that produces enormous pressure, forcing hydrogen atoms to collapse into one another, fusing together to become helium and thus creating nuclear fission that continues to burn), the temperature was now below 14,850,000 degrees Kelvin. That was a drop of over 150,000 degrees. It was a strange phenomenon he had never witnessed before.

He moved to the Spectroscope console and studied the sun's color spectrum, then quickly made another entry into his log. This log entry noted that his observations revealed the possibility that the sunspots were not the usual temporary kind but apparently a new solar phenomenon to which there was no scientific evidence to indicate they would go away.

Bennett then picked up the phone to call one of his colleagues at SOHO.

With the wireless phone nestled on his shoulder, third-year astrophysics student, Scott Sheldon, walked to the SOHO EIT satellite instrument panel and punched in the numbers Bennett was reading off to him. The Extreme ultraviolet Imaging Telescope satellite (EIT) was located at a point in deep space where the Sun's gravitational pull balanced Earth's gravitational pull, so the satellite orbited the Sun with Earth, allowing SOHO to always face the Sun. This provided scientists with vital information about the sun's radiant energy and luminosity.

Eighteen minutes later the EIT confirmed Bennett's data that the structure and dynamics of the solar interior, the heating mechanisms of the solar corona, and the acceleration of the solar wind had changed since it was last recorded only 22 hours earlier. "Something's wrong here, Doug," Sheldon said into the phone with a tremor in his voice. "These figures don't lie," he added with heightening alarm as he scanned the report. "Unbelievably, it appears that the sun is turning black, and remaining so, in the northeast quadrant."

Bennett replied numbly, "I observed the same thing over here, Scott." There was a brief pause. then Bennett added, "I have to make a few phone calls, starting with NASA in Houston."

Bennett ended the call.

Paul Douglas sat meditatively behind the car's steering wheel, deciding how to respond to the vision followed by the Greenbaum arrest. *Time to call Yair,* he thought as he reminded himself, *in the multitude of counselors there is safety.* He lifted his cell phone, then glanced over the steering wheel through the windshield and noticed a colorful banner with many Hebrew letters on it hanging down from the museum's roof. His curiosity piqued, he turned to Hershel in the back seat and pointed to the banner. "What does that say?"

"*Exhibition: Solomon's 'Swan Song,'* "Hershel explained.

Paul surmised from the title that the museum was sponsoring a showing of the archeological artifacts, extant manuscripts, and scholarly essays relating to the last days of the Solomonic dynasty. He wondered if some day in the future there would be an exhibition in tribute to his generation that read, *Israel's "Swan Song"* or *America's "Swan Song"* in memoriam for the fallen empires. He sighed and looked away before pressing the speed-dial number on his cell phone to reach Yair. Five seconds later the connection was made.

Yair read the encrypted incoming call number on his cell phone caller-ID quickly. "Good to hear from you, Paul. Everything okay?"

"No. We have some serious problems up here," Paul replied nervously. "First, both Levi and I had a vision about the Sixth Seal. Since we both had it, the vision is confirmed. And, Yair, it was very frightening..." It took a minute to regain his composure. "I mean, the darkness and the death from the sun turning black. It was really horrible." He paused to take a deep breath. "I believe it's just a matter of time before the seal is opened—maybe just days.

"Then, adding to the drama, the Mossad came to the Greenbaum house while we were there. We sensed we were in trouble, so we bailed out quickly, taking Hershel with us. After we were safely out of the area, I called Mrs. Greenbaum and she told me that Norman had been arrested for 'sedition,' if you can believe that!"

"I was afraid of this," Yair replied in somber tones. "The sun turning black or darkening is going to be a terrible curse on the Earth. Life is going to become extremely difficult. Many will die. As far as Norman's arrest is concerned, this is the implementation of Kavidas' new phases of *Masterlink*. He's beginning to reel in members of the K-group. This kind of thing is probably happening all over the world."

"This is all the more reason to make sure Petra is ready for us," Paul replied. "It won't be long before every Christian in Israel is heading that way."

"I will explain to our section leaders about your vision and that we need to speed up the process of preparing many of the abandoned buildings with provisions and bedding supplies. Of course, if there are more than ten thousand Christians, we'll have to make special arrangements, like placing them in the outdoor arena in makeshift lean-tos if need be, but at least we'll all be together," Yair explained.

"What will you do with the Bedouins?" Paul asked.

"The Bedouin population has been dwindling over the past year, but they are very good at growing and providing food for us so we'll give them the option of staying here in their tents and helping us, or they'll have to leave and fend for themselves."

A grim thought came to Paul. "Do you think there's any possibility that Kavidas could order the police or the Mossad to get to us at Petra?"

"He doesn't have any jurisdiction over here. We're in Jordan," Yair reminded him.

"Right. Well, then, our families are safe. That's good." Paul smiled. "And speaking of good: while we were at the Greenbaums, God's Spirit got hold of Hershel's heart. He prayed to receive the Lord with us!"

"That's marvelous! Praise the Lord!" Yair exclaimed. Changing the subject he asked, "Two things. First, warn any members of the K-group about increasing persecution and possible arrests. If they want to stay on at their own risk to keep spreading the Word, fine. God will protect them. But otherwise they need to go deep underground or clear out of Jerusalem altogether and head for safety down here at Petra. Second, give me your itinerary for the next three days because I'm leaving here either tomorrow or the next day to meet up with you so we can continue our crusade."

Paul rattled off his schedule for the next three days, subject to any sudden change due to Mossad or IDF surveillance or activity. Then he pressed the *End* button. He started to turn the key in the ignition when he heard from the rear seat, "Paul?" Hershel asked. "Can the Tribulation be reversed?"

Paul turned around to see Hershel in deep thought. "What do you mean, can it be reversed? Many of the prophesied judgments have already come to pass."

Hershel looked perplexed, a condition obviously precipitated by his hearing Paul's vision report. "I mean as far as the future is concerned. Levi said we still have over six years of judgments ahead of us. If the world repents, would the Lord relent and withdraw the punishment he has planned for mankind?"

Would the Lord relent? Paul thought on that question. The term his father often referred to, *anthropomorphism,* flew into his mind. A term used to describe the application of human emotion or physical attribute displayed by God, such as in the metaphor, *the hand of the Lord.* "No, I don't think so."

"Why?"

Paul smiled, recognizing that one of the signs of new Christians is their zeal for God, often expressed in zillions of questions. "Well, for the most part because God's Word and will is immutable...unchangeable. The world events we're experiencing have been written about in the Bible long ago. What we're witnessing is the fulfillment of these prophecies that attest to the truth that they are proceeding on schedule. Nothing is going to change that."

"But what if man had changed his ways before the Tribulation began? Repented before God put the Tribulation in motion?"

"Now that's an interesting question." Paul scratched his beard to help him think. "He may have postponed the judgments like he did to the city of Nineveh when they repented of their sin after Jonah the prophet pronounced his message of impending doom. However, during the Church age, mankind had the testimony of the body of Christ, the written Word of God, and the Holy Spirit to look to as a standard of righteousness, but they flouted their sins in God's face and rejected those truths. So now, I believe the bulk of mankind's heart has already become reprobate like the apostle Paul describes in Romans 1, bringing God to the place where there is no remedying the problem except through judgment."

"Oh," Hershel said, then closed his eyes and shot a prayer of thanksgiving up to God for saving him.

Paul pursed his lips as he gazed momentarily at Hershel. *Wouldn't it be neat if you're one of the 144,000,* he thought happily.

Paul then started the engine and drove away, heading for another K-group safehouse to wait for Yair.

Brandon sat at his desk reviewing the company's revenue log for the current month when the office intercom beeped. "Mr. Lane, an unidentified caller who simply said 'Yeshua 777,' then asked for you is on the line. Do you want to take the call?" his secretary said.

Brandon immediately recognized the password as coming from a *Koinonos* group member who did not want to be identified. "Yes, put the call through on my private line."

"Yes, sir," she replied. Seconds later the private line on his phone console lit up.

"Mr. Lane," the caller said, "this is Stanley with an urgent message."

Brandon squeezed his eyes shut as he tried to put a face on the caller. Remembering him from his church Bible study group the month before, he said, "Yes, Stanley, what is it?"

"There is a small item on page three of the *Miami Star* that is of utmost importance. Obviously the media has played it down, but it is crucial to those who follow Bible prophecy. It's about an interview with an astronomer at Kitt Peak in Arizona who discovered some massive disturbance occurring on the surface of the sun. If it's what I think it is, we're really in for it, and I think the network should be prepared."

"Hmm, yes. That is urgent," Brandon replied with controlled alarm. "I'll look into it, Stanley, and if it is a credible threat, I will alert the network." Brandon hung up and pulled out his Palm Pilot. He scrolled through several pages of telephone numbers until he hit on a Lane Drugs associate in Tucson, then he keyed in the number on his private line.

Half a moment later Clayton Munson's phone rang as he sat on his patio cleaning the lens on his Meade 12-inch LX 200 GPS telescope.

"This is Brandon Lane in Miami. Hopefully you'll remember me from a drug company symposium last month."

"Down here in Tucson, right? The son of the owner of Lane Drugs, right?"

"Yes," Brandon replied. "I seem to distinctly remember that when we were discussing your ongoing AIDS vaccine research, you mentioned that you often need a break from the tedium and turn to your astronomy hobby as an outlet."

"That's right. In fact, I'm the president of our local astronomy club. Our group is affiliated with Kitt Peak, so every month we have a seminar up there. They let us use their big telescopes."

Brandon gave himself a thumbs-up since his recollection paid off. "The reason I'm calling is to check out a report an astronomer at Kitt Peak filed with NASA about an unusual sunspot formation. Have you heard anything about it?"

There was a noticeable silence before Munson began hesitantly, "I guess you could say that our club was very disturbed over the way the media just blew it off. Knowing a little about astrophysics and its relationship to the sun, when I read the article, I made some phone calls myself. The media is being told by state and federal authorities to play this thing way down so as to avoid a public panic. Obviously they are dealing with a number of other calamities like rampant AIDS, the drought, increasing food shortages, and skyrocketing inflation, so they may think we're on overload. But this problem has the potential to be much more serious than the scare we had with that asteroid, Eros 433, a few years ago. Fortunately, we had a near miss from that asteroid, but if we'd sustained a hit, at least we might have had a chance of survival; but with this solar phenomenon, we're talking total extinction if the present rate continues. No life on Earth could survive. This planet would turn into a solid ball of ice in short order!"

"Could you explain that?"

"Well, based on my unprofessional calculations and research with fellow astronomers, the rate in which the sunspots are appearing is slow, and due to the sun's vast surface area, it would take several years before we'd see a total cessation of light. That, in turn, would prohibit all life-sustaining effects from the sun from reaching us. Without the solar heating of the Earth, the oceans will freeze like our polar caps. Then we're done! Of course anything could happen to change that since the sun is a star fed by continuous nuclear fusion reactions, so with that kind of instability, things could change for the better."

Brandon quickly did the math to calculate to the end of the seven-year Tribulation period, when Paul claimed Christ would return. He knew in his heart that, until that time, things were not going to "change for the better."

"How about a little over six years? Could the gradual diminishing of light last that long?" Brandon asked.

"At its present rate, it could stretch that long, yes."

Brandon thanked Munson for his help and promised to do his part to prepare the public for the coming cataclysm, believing in his heart that it could only be accomplished by sharing salvation through Christ with them. Something he had to tend to himself first.

TWENTY-TWO

Bayside Mall, Miami

Brandon came to an abrupt stop in the middle of the Bayside Mall promenade, turned in the direction of his pharmaceutical building, then marveled that he'd walked the two blocks to the mall in a complete daze. The phone call to Munson regarding the sunspots had unnerved him. He had reflexively walked to his office window, gazed over at the international flags waving at Bayside, thought about their Brazilian-style BBQ chicken, then mechanically headed out into the warm balmy air toward Elmo's concession. He scratched his head as a smile came over his face.

Remember, Brandon, he scolded himself, *as the Christians say, "God is still in control." You can't let this stuff get to you when we still have a long road to travel in the Tribulation before Christ returns.* He looked up toward heaven and nodded. *Are you talking to me, God?* Then he navigated his way through the busy mall to Elmo's.

Things will look better after lunch, he mused. But as he looked around the mall, signs of the Tribulation were all around him, becoming all-too-familiar sights. Sights that reminded him of God's judgment on man for their refusal to repent and return to him, while at the same time flouting their sins in His face by not only continuing in them, but approving of those who practice them. *Oh Lord, your Spirit must be terribly grieved,* he prayed, *that man will only seek your face during affliction.*

Suddenly a hand touched his shoulder. He turned and looked around him. Nobody was near him. His heart began to race, and his spirit sensed an awareness he'd never experienced before. He dropped his fork onto his plate and closed his eyes. *God, are you talking to me?*

Conversations with his father and David Douglas about receiving Christ as his Savior flashed into his memory. Internal forces and voices in his mind started fighting with God's Spirit.

You already know about Jesus, the voice said. *Why are you tormented like this? You're fine!*

NO, God's spirit commanded him. *You're not fine. You know about Jesus, but you don't know Him. Make your decision now!*

Brandon unwittingly clutched the tablecloth as the inner struggle in his heart yielded to God. "Yes, Lord, I trust Jesus as my Savior and believe he died for me," he said aloud. A God-given release came over him as if a great weight had been lifted from his heart and soul.

Peace flooded his whole being. It was done. He now belonged to Jesus. When he opened his eyes, the waiter was staring at him.

"Are you all right, sir?"

"I've never felt better!" he exulted. "I just made my peace with God." He smiled. "You need to receive Jesus as your Savior, pal."

The waiter looked at him with mock solemnity and said, "Yeah, right," and simply placed the check on the table and walked away.

Brandon held up the check and shook his head as he read the heading: *Masterlink or Business Accounts Only.* This served as a reminder that cash was no longer accepted, being replaced with either a *Masterlink* or corporate credit account. He added the items up and shook his head again as he whispered to himself, "$18.99 for half a chicken breast? $6.99 for a portion of cole slaw? $9.99 for a small bag of crinkle-cut fries?" He was astonished.

Lord, at this rate, who will be able to stand? In three more years, those surviving the spiraling inflation will be decimated by the famine. How will they be able to feed their families?

He sighed and looked out into Biscayne Bay where three tankers were meandering on their way to the oil depot at Port Everglades. Meandering to avoid the sand bars and shallow water due to the drought. *How much longer before our rivers start drying up?* The tankers served as a sobering reminder of the ongoing oil crisis catapulted to an all-time high by Arab sheiks looking to exact recompense from the world for their humiliating defeat in their attack against Israel. *Imagine, paying $9.25 for a gallon of regular unleaded?*

Brandon shook his head once more as he stared at them in disgust while they sailed out of sight. *I wonder if that report I heard about the Arab-bloc states leveraging the price of oil because they know their reserves are limited to the next 40 years is true? Whatever! It doesn't matter*, he thought as he remembered seeing an impressive photograph in a Christian college alumni magazine several years ago of an oil refinery at night. The petroleum tanks, landing platforms, and network of pipes were eerily lit up by selectively placed security lights, producing a foreboding picture. Underneath the photography was the caption, *The Maker of Oil Knows Where It Is and Why It Is There.*

Yes, Brandon thought, *the Arab states will soon find out that God placed all that oil under the desert sands for a reason.*

"Excuse me, sir," a man's voice from behind said. "Is anybody using this chair?" Brandon turned to see a young, dashing U.S. Navy ensign in dress whites with his hand on the extra chair at his table. He quickly surmised that it was fleet week at Port Everglades, where a naval armada was on display and thousands of sailors came ashore for liberty.

"Help yourself!" Brandon replied as he gave him a salute. The ensign hoisted the chair and placed it at the next table, where four other naval officers were settling in with their respective food trays. As they reveled in their comradery, Brandon studied each face with a penetrating stare, reminding himself of the dreadful times that lay ahead for the American armed services. Prophetic times where the United States would be drawn into the worldwide fray ignited by the turmoil in the Mideast, where the United States would join with allied nations in their fight against the marauding enemies of Israel at the great and terrible battle of Armageddon.

The Russian attack of Israel—the seal judgment of war—where weapons of mass destruction were used will be mere child's play compared to what God has planned for Armageddon, Brandon realized.

Despite the diversions, his thoughts returned to his phone call with Munson. He looked up into the cloud-covered atmosphere and tried to imagine what the sky would look like when the sunspots worsened and the Earth began to feel the effect of a dying sun. *A perpetual arctic winter.* A chill ran through his body when he pondered what conditions on Earth would be like when the gruesome trumpet and bowl judgments are declared.

His cell phone beeped.

His secretary's number appeared on the caller-ID. "Yes, Cynthia, what is it?"

"Mr. Lane, you need to come back to the office right away!" Cynthia said frantically. "Julian Trainor from our research and development department has just been arrested by the Miami-Dade police!"

"I'll be there in ten minutes."

The walk back to his plant seemed like an interminable period. From what he remembered, Trainor was the only one at Lane who had opted out of the corporate account that allowed employees to charge their mortgage payments, rent, food, utilities, clothing, and all of their essentials to the Lane corporation to avoid having to go on the *Masterlink* system. Lane's colossal accounting department then deducted the amounts from their paycheck each week. This was his way of allowing his employees to circumvent the final credit system secretly owned by Kavidas and managed by Stein.

But Trainor, a member of the *Koinonos* group in Miami and somewhat of an isolationist, had wanted to fend for himself. It was now apparent to Lane, however, that nobody could afford to remain isolated during these perilous times, but desperately needed to join together to survive the escalating persecution of Christians.

Cynthia was swimming in tears when Lane arrived back at his office that was still undergoing repairs from the bomb blast. "Mr. Lane," she sobbed, "they just came to the welcome center and handed me this document and demanded that I call Mr. Trainor to the lobby, where they announced that he was under arrest. When he came, they hauled him away in a police car."

Brandon grabbed the document and studied it. It was a warrant for Julian Trainor's arrest, charging him with sedition against the Federal government and citing two Executive Orders. Executive Order 9066 had been invoked, allowing the government to seize and arrest any U.S. citizen and place them into labor groups under government surveillance for national security purposes. Also listed was Executive Order 11921, which empowered the government to take over health, education, welfare mechanisms of production and distribution of energy sources, wages, salaries, credit, and the flow of money.

Brandon contemplated the ramifications. What the government considered a violation of national security was obviously in question here. No doubt, any Christian who didn't buy into the *Masterlink* system was now considered a security risk. *This could get very ugly*, he thought. Trainor was probably one of many recalcitrant shoppers who were refusing to take the *mark* of Kavidas. Now the government was testing the enforcement of the Orders. Reading into the Orders, Brandon realized that under this E.O. 11921 that embraced the flow of money, the government could come in and seize his company since he had developed his own credit system opposing *Masterlink*. He steeled himself against such a possibility.

I'll sell the business and divide the profits among my employees and the Koinonos if it comes to that, he promised himself.

"Mr. Lane," Cynthia asked as she wiped away the tears, "is Julian going to be all right?"

Brandon patted her hand. "Of course. They probably will question him. They'll frighten him, then release him. You'll see."

Cynthia exhaled a deep sigh and rubbed her forehead. "This has taken a heavy toll on me."

Brandon looked at Cynthia with sympathy. He'd been told that she was dealing with serious marital problems, then there was the economical issues since *Masterlink* went global. Together with the other national calamities brought on by the Seal judgments, she had catapulted herself into a state of frenzy that was bringing on an emotional meltdown. A condition that was quickly becoming a national pastime. When he noted several bystanders listening to her story, he told Cynthia softly, "Get your things together and go home for the day. You need your rest. We'll get someone to work your station."

Cynthia nodded as a smile broke out across her face.

Brandon returned the smile before walking to the elevator. Moments later he was lying on his office sofa, taking a power nap.

Within 24 hours Trainor would be released from police custody with a severe warning that he must comply with the government mandate or face criminal charges.

When Brandon awoke, he sat at his office computer terminal and keyed in the commands to get online with Paul somewhere in Israel. Not knowing how they were managing or where they would migrate to often led him into serious bouts of consternation.

[Sending]
Dear Paul and Yair,
We, here in the States, are constantly praying for you. We pray that your battle against Kavidas and Stein is going well and that you are not allowing any discouragement from dissuading you from the cause of Christ.

[Receiving party is off-line. No response]

[Sending]
Well, I'll continue to report on the basis that you can retrieve this letter when your situation permits.
     I thought I would start my letter to you with good news! I know that over the years my father and your father, David, urged me to trust Christ as my Savior and be saved, but I wasn't ready. I guess the Lord had to bring me to the state of fear, where I recognize that he is in control of all things, including the disappearance, the Tribulation, and all of my life. When I was in Israel I was too busy doing my own thing for God to get my attention. But now that I am in charge of my father's business, I cannot afford to be selfish any longer. Because of this, I have been more attentive to the things of God. Today he spoke to me loud and clear. He commanded me to make a decision. I really believe that the corridor for decision-making to receive Christ as Savior is narrowing very quickly in our world. But God was gracious and enabled me to say "Yes" to him. I know you will rejoice with me.
     It's a great relief to know I'm on God's side now.
     Regarding things here, it is my guess that the Lord is dispensing his Seal judgments at a time when mankind is unable to discern his actions and repent of their sinful ways to avoid further disasters. I haven't seen a single incident of a person coming to repentance due to the judgments coming upon the earth. This unfortunate aspect of

man only proves the Scripture you often quoted in Revelation 9:20-21 that man will not change his mind toward sin until God severely punishes him.

It grieves me to say this, but I see that punishment increasing in intensity. In particular, I just learned from a reliable source that the sun is undergoing radical changes that will affect our entire way of life here on Earth. The sun is experiencing enormous sunspot activity that will ultimately result in the diminishing of light to our planet, which in turn will bring catastrophic events to bear on our world. This must be the opening of the Sixth Seal. But as I read Revelation, this Sixth Seal also brings with it a severe earthquake, and the moon turns red, and the stars fall to earth. I profess that I am not able to understand what that all means, but in time we shall find out.

Because God is faithful and promises to protect his people, I have every confidence that we shall persevere until the end. Let me know what you've heard about the sunspots, if anything, since the news broadcasts here in the States is conspicuously devoid of any information.

There is something else you should know. A member of my staff was arrested today for the trumped-up charge of sedition against the government. Although I believe he will be released, this may be the beginning of a practice that will soon become common in all parts of the world. As Kavidas grows in power, he must remove the Christians who represent the enemy to him or he will be exposed.

Finally, I don't know how the economy is over there in Israel, but as for us here in the States, the inflation rate due to the exorbitant water, food, and oil prices is making it extremely difficult for people to live. Many people over here are taking second mortgages on their homes just to meet their living expenses. In addition, the rate of foreclosure on new homes is at an all-time high, and I fear that the unemployment rate is not far behind. The price of gold is now over $1200 per ounce. Things look very dismal for the non-Christian, while the *Koinonos* Christian seems to be experiencing God's panoply of protection where they are eluding the enemy for the time being. Until the next time...

God's richest blessings to you, your families and the *Koinonos*.

As Azib rounded the corner of the Renaissance hotel to meet Stein in the rear patio, surprise came over his face when he saw Stein waving him toward the lobby luncheonette. *To what do I owe this demotion?* he wondered.

Stein took notice of his new suit, then read his facial expression. "Time is too short to be concerned with appearances," he remarked as they walked to the luncheonette and then to a table garnished with a plastic floral piece and a small tray filled with condiments. "Now is the time to get down to business."

Azib shrugged and quipped, "What's wrong with the main dining room?"

"Don't push!" Stein snapped as they sat down. *These Arabs get on my last nerve!*

Azib slowly looked around, giving the room a bemused visual audit before lifting the menu. "Today, I will indulge myself," he said with a smirk.

Stein glared at him, surmising the time had come when this arrogant Bedouin realized he possessed the very commodity that warranted this insolence. *He must have the forces in place that I need.* Stein cracked a smile. "Order what you want."

Once the orders were placed, Stein bent in closer, "There's been a change in plans. We're going to need some of your people to take care of a problem that has developed at Petra—" he paused to choose the appropriate adjectives—"your old place of business."

"Those Christians and converted Jews down in the 'rocks' are becoming a problem, eh!" Azib retorted. "I knew the day would come when those rodents would have to be ferreted out and stepped on."

Stein quickly processed the jab and anti-Semitic remark. Both Jew and Arab were considered Semites, but the Arabs looked at the Jews with a hatred powered by centuries of warring that would not abate. "Yes, the time has come for us to deal with them, putting our master plan on hold for now."

Azib looked puzzled. "Meaning?"

"The last time we met I ordered you to dig up and amalgamate your resources for future deployment," Stein answered.

"Agreed."

"This change involves an immediate partial deployment with a deferred full deployment at a future date. I need you to call up your people, the PLO, Hamas, Hezbollah, and any of the PLO survivors to form an invasion force to go into Petra after the initial wave by IDF."

Azib's lips pursed in a soundless whistle. "To come in behind the IDF? That's crazy. They won't need any mopping up from us."

"It's not crazy, and they will need a mopping up! Listen to me carefully." Stein was not taking any chances on Drori or Weinstein not coming through. "I know the entire plan from a high authority that the IDF is only going to do a 'sweep.' It's not going to be an invasion in the true sense of the word; they're not looking to annihilate them. They're going to bring in a great show of force—helicopter gunships, tactical forces, and probably several hundred soldiers—to scare them into dispersing. That's all they really want to do. The Israelis don't want the civilized world to find out that unarmed Christians, converted Jews, and many of your fellow Bedouins are being singled out for extinction, nor do they want to destroy an archeological monument and cause problems with Jordan. It's bad politics. Just as it was bad politics when the PLO was performing the suicide bombings. No matter what Israel did to combat them, Israel always came away looking like the bad guy who picks a fight with the poor kid on the block. So, for their part, the IDF will only perform a token raid where several of these rebels are killed as representatives for the entire group. That way, everybody goes home happy."

"Sounds like everything is firmly entrenched in mid-air," Azib scoffed as he scratched his head. In his reasoning, it was simple: it will always be the Arabs against the Jews and the Americans. But this so-called "covert operation" sounded more like the government's way of ridding the land of potential terrorists. *Why not just come right out and say it?*

Stein clamped Azib's hand to get his attention. "No, it isn't, Mibsam! This plan has been thoughtfully worked out, but it could be a real tricky operation. It must be handled carefully and decisively to accomplish our goal. You probably haven't done much reading," Stein instructed with a tinge of sarcasm, "but Petra has a long history as being an impregnable fortress that has defied armies much greater than the IDF. In 312 B.C.E, the Nabatean city successfully defended itself against several attacks by the Greeks. In 63 B.C. E., the Roman General Pompey couldn't take the city until Trajan finally defeated the Nabatean army elsewhere and they subsequently forfeited the city to Rome in A.D. 106. So, even though these people are not military, wiping them out is not going to be all that easy. They'll hide out in the nooks and crannies for months. That's why we need a second wave to go into the city to exterminate them." *Besides, if they get any help from the "two performers,"' it will be your people who will die....*

Azib stared at Stein as the remarks got persuasively through to him. *Makes sense*, he thought. A quote from Anwar Sadat flew into Azib's mind, strengthening his resolve. *"The assassination of Arab brethren, like Goliath, by Jewish sheep-herders like David, is the sort of shameful ignominy that we must yet set right in the domain of the occupied Palestinian homeland."* Azib nodded to himself at the logic of Sadat's statement then said aloud, "If this will help our cause of getting back our land from the Jews and the Jewish infidels-turned Christian, we will throw whatever it takes at them in order to win."

"Now that's what I wanted to hear!" Stein said with a wink. "And to cover the cost of such an operation, I will transfer into your *Masterlink* account one-million EU credits." He tapped Azib's *Masterlink* chip imbedded in his right hand. "And for your troubles, I will deposit an additional 200,000 EUs."

The staggering sums startled Azib at first, until he realized that his forces were like mercenaries—hired guns—to do Stein's dirty work. "Make it 300,000."

Stein snickered at the bandit before him, then broke out into a broad smile. "Done."

After the dessert was served, they worked out the details of the time and date of the attack, then agreed to label the operation *Trajan* in honor of the Roman emperor credited with conquering Petra.

Paul smiled at his K-group hostess, Marta Shiller, as the olive-skinned Israeli Sabra handed him a freshly prepared vegetable juice drink. He hoisted the plastic cup, took a long pull, then set the cup down to boot up his laptop computer. Within minutes he was online to retrieve his encrypted E-mail. The audible greeting announced he had two E-mails—a welcome sign. One was from a K-group member in northern Israel, the other from Brandon Lane. He opened Brandon's first.

Marta heard Paul whistle, then exclaim in surprise.

"Bad news, Paul?" Marta asked.

Paul just shook his head as he continued to read Brandon's E-mail. Seconds later Levi and Hershel walked into the room; they too had heard his exclamation.

"Developments?" Levi asked as he sat down next to him.

Paul looked up from the laptop and said with joy, "Brandon received the Lord!"

A tear formed in Levi's eye. "Oh, thank you, Lord!"

Hershel poked Paul. "God is awesome. He's raising up his workers!"

Paul closed his eyes and shot a praise offering up to God. "A welcome piece of news."

Moments later Paul returned to reading the E-mail. "Our vision of the sunspots is coming true," he noted. "Brandon checked with a reliable scientific source and concurs that it's the start of the Sixth Seal."

"The earthquake and the red moon cannot be far behind," Levi lamented.

"What does this all mean, Paul?" Hershel asked anxiously.

"It means God is moving His timetable along. The next item on God's itinerary is the Sixth Seal, which includes the darkening of the sun, the reddening of the moon, a great earthquake where mountains and islands will be reshaped—"

"The sky tears apart; the stars are realigned," Levi interjected. "A time when mankind will be so frightened they will be running to hide in the holes in the ground—underground shelters—seeking protection from the wrath of Almighty God!"

"Where will I be?" Hershel asked with a slight titter.

Paul patted Hershel's arm to calm his nerves. "You'll be safe. All those who have called upon the Lord will be kept in perfect peace."

Hershel smiled.

Paul tapped the laptop screen. "One would think that as these divinely ordained calamities intensified, man would turn to the Lord. But as Brandon noted, there are few signs that man is repenting. This is the most grievous of testimonies to the human race."

Levi leaned over to read the letter and noticed another item of concern. "Oh, no! Someone in his firm was arrested for sedition."

Hershel blinked, then grimaced. "You mean like my father?"

"It appears to be so," Paul replied as he scrolled through the letter. "Yes, one of his research technicians was arrested for the same reason as your dad," he added in confirmation.

"Evidently America's economy is being destabilized by the soaring medical costs and oil prices just like Israel's is," Levi noted.

Marta stood listening to the conversation with great interest. Ten minutes into the discussion she asked, "Do you suppose the Earth has indeed suffered the amount of deaths predicted for the Fourth Seal?"

Paul thought on that question. Marta was referring to the Bible's prediction that one-fourth of the population would be killed by sword, famine, plague, and by wild beasts. This was known as the fourth Horseman of the Apocalypse, the rider on the pale horse.

"No," he said, "not yet. In my view this judgment is an ongoing one where the death toll will gradually rise until that number is reached." He motioned with his hands. "The evidence for this is all around us. The increasing terrorist attacks certainly reflect the 'sword,' and the inflation that fuels the famine, and vice-versa, is obvious, while the plagues of AIDS, birth defects, and the newly forming diseases that are ravaging our planet are most certainly in fulfillment of the Fourth Seal."

"So really," Marta observed, "there are many more deaths to come before this prophecy is complete."

Paul nodded grimly. "Many."

"The Fifth Seal refers to martyrs. Does that mean the Christians, along with the newly converted Jewish believers and the K-group members?" Hershel asked intuitively.

Paul looked at him and simply nodded.

As the discussion ended, Paul responded to the second E-mail, then asked Marta for a cup of coffee before replying to Brandon.

Hours later, Paul sat on a folding chair on the porch of the Shiller home, enjoying a rare nighttime breeze that must have meandered off the Mediterranean through the old city streets, finding its way to his doorstep. *Ah, dusk is such a refreshing time of the day,* he mused. *The time when the Lord walked through the Garden looking to have fellowship with Adam and Eve.* It reminded him of his days back in Florida when he would come home after school and just sit on his patio, meditating on God's creation as nightfall descended.

Marta Shiller handed him a cup of coffee as she pulled up another folding chair next to him. "Trying to get a handle on the moment?"

Paul nodded. "It seems like an eternity ago," he reflected, "but I remember the nights when I'd sit in the backyard of our home in Coral Springs with my dad and mom and study the heavens, looking at the planets and constellations through my binoculars, just reveling in the awesomeness of God. They were good times."

"Your mother told me she remembered that period as being a quiet time from the Lord," she replied, delving into his reminiscence. "A time of rest where God was allowing your family to take inventory on the blessings he had granted; a time of rest where the Lord was fortifying your family for the future, yet giving your family the discernment to know that the 'vacation' would only be temporary, knowing that soon afterward he would orientate all your lives."

"*Orientate* is a good word," he echoed while muffling a laugh. "But at times it seems like a 'tearing down and rebuilding.' "

Marta, a mother-like figure to Paul, put her arm around him. "You wouldn't want to trade it for anything else, would you?"

Paul momentarily looked up into the overcast night sky and thought about that question. *To be idle and unproductive as a Christian was quite inferior to being used of the Lord. When I am being used by the Lord to further his purpose, my life is full.* "No, I would not."

Levi broke into their special time. "Yair's holding. He needs to talk to you." He handed Paul his cell phone.

"Hello, Yair. Are you all safe?" Paul asked with concern.

"We're fine," Yair replied hesitantly. "We're in the home of a K-group member here in Jerusalem as well, but will be leaving sometime tonight to join up with you tomorrow. You're leaving in the morning, right?"

"That's the plan. I'll catch up with you somewhere in the Old City, and from there we'll all go back to Petra together."

"That's good. We'll coordinate by cell phone exactly where to rendezvous. As for now, the reason I called was to inform you that I just spoke to Brandon in Florida via E-mail, and he confirmed our vision of the Sixth Seal. He said he was notified of a small item in the newspaper regarding solar sunspots, then went on to say that he contacted someone in Arizona to collaborate the story and, as if we didn't know the answer, it's happening already. The darkening of the sun appears to be a gradual thing, but of course that means that the rest of the Sixth Seal, what with the moon and the earthquake and all…we had better start preparing. He also mentioned that one of his staff members was arrested."

"Yes, I know. I heard all about it," Paul replied.

"The part about the sedition against the State is alarming."

"Yes, I agree," Paul said, then shook head in disgust as he processed the information. "Any new activity with Kavidas and Stein to report?"

"You know, Paul, now that you mention them," Yair said curiously, "I find it very unusual that they have been conspicuously absent from the public eye. What's more, there have been no field reports from other K-group members regarding them."

"Maybe they're planning something." A chill ran down Paul's spine.

"I hope not."

TWENTY-THREE

Christian Fortress, Petra

P aul stood in front of a K-group member's mobile home talking with Yair when his eye caught Simon waving to him from his favorite perch on the top of the cliffs. "What's with Simon? You'd think he had enough of climbing the rock walls and bluffs of the compound."

"You know how he is, Paul," Yair chimed in as he poked Jonathan in the side. "He's the mountain climber in the group; always wanting to 'stay on top' of things."

Paul shrugged and returned the wave as Simon disappeared over a ridge. Suddenly a great *whoosh* was heard overhead, followed by the roar of a jet aircraft as it flew by at a tremendous speed. Paul looked up and spotted the wing of the aircraft just as it disappeared out of sight. "That was an Israeli fighter jet!" he exclaimed in shock.

Yair grabbed Paul's arm and pointed up. "Paul!" he screamed, "look at Simon!" Simon was frantically waving his arms, trying to signal them.

Paul looked at Simon and cupped his ear with his hand to hear him. "What's going on?" he yelled.

"I see three inbound helicopters and sand trails from eight vehicles coming toward us at high speeds!" Simon screamed. Seconds later he added, "The vehicles look like those Humvees and troop transports!"

Whoosh! Another jet with engines screaming suddenly flew over them, this time from the opposite direction. "They just did a high-speed reconnaissance of our fortress," Yair exclaimed. "We're being attacked!"

Operation *Trajan* had begun.

Yelling to compensate for the loud droning of engines, Simon cried out, "Paul, those helicopters have landed outside the entranceway, and soldiers with guns are pouring out of them!"

Moments later the Humvees and covered transport trucks arrived and positioned themselves strategically to seal the fortress entranceway while maintaining complete surveillance of the cliffs from the south side. Soldiers disgorged from the Humvees and trucks in a rapid fashion and immediately took up their offensive positions alongside those from the helicopters.

"Paul," Simon yelled again, "they have completely blocked the entranceway." He dashed to peek over the cliff toward the entranceway, then ran back to report. "There's hundreds of them!"

"Simon," Yair shouted, "come down off the cliff immediately!"

In extreme control: "But I can keep watch from here!"

"I said—"

"Paul! One of the jets is coming in low! It looks like it's going to—" Simon screamed.

Rocket launching sounds...BOOM!

Everyone heard the explosion. The American-built F-16 Fighting Falcon swooped down out of the sky and fired a Maverick wing missile at the side of the southern cliffs.

Paul looked around and saw the fortress's citizens running for cover into the ancient buildings. Members of the K-group were scrambling out of their mobile homes and running into the rock shelters carved into the interior cliffs.

"Simon!" Yair yelled, "come down right now!" Then he pointed toward the Nabatean temple and yelled, "Let's run for it!"

Simon turned to see the plume of smoke from the missile rapidly rise into the atmosphere, then just before descending down the cliff looked in the opposite direction to the north and noticed what looked like another contingent or backup group racing toward the fortress. He swallowed hard and in a zig-zag pattern, clambered down the cliff. Once he reached the valley floor, he raced into the temple.

"Paul, we have more company coming!" Simon explained. "I saw what looked like a dozen transport trucks working their way toward us from our northern side."

Paul did a quick assessment based on Simon's observation. *There must be a contingent plan in place to eliminate us. These trucks must be somehow involved in the attack.*

"Simon," he instructed, "here's what I want you to do. Go up the cliff on our north side and be our lookout!" He put his hand around Simon's neck and added, "Trust in the Lord and stay out of sight."

Yair cried out for Simon as he ran out of the building up the cliff to man his post. "Be safe!"

Paul, gathering his presence of mind in the frenetic environment, said to Yair, "I've got to call Shaul and tell him we're being attacked." He flipped open his cell phone and pressed the speed-dial number to reach Shaul in Jerusalem.

There was a pause, then, "Paul," the voice asked after reading the caller-ID, "are you safe?"

"No. Listen carefully, Shaul," Paul began anxiously. "Petra is under attack with what appears to be Israeli forces. There are jets flying overhead along with helicopters, personnel carriers, and Humvees on the ground blocking the entranceway. There are hundreds of troops poised to invade us, and that's not all. There is another column coming in from the north side that will probably form some kind of pincer movement that will trap us inside."

Extremely frightened and nervous: "What can we do to help?"

"Have everybody you can reach pray for us. Next, call the American ambassador and advise him that there are scores of Americans in Petra that are being attacked by Israeli forces as we speak. Call me back ASAP! Got to go!" Paul ended the call.

Defense Minister Drori jumped out of the Humvee onto the hot desert sand and walked over to inspect the rock debris from the F-16s Maverick missile at the foot of the cliff. *That's one powerful piece of firepower,* he thought in admiration. It was a rare event when the Defense Minister actually saw the operation of armaments in the field. As he reached down to feel the fused rock, he felt the billions of shekels paid out by Israeli tax-payers for American-made war machines was justified.

He turned toward the entranceway just as a soldier raced up to him and saluted. "Sir," he announced while pointing to the lead Humvee, "Colonel Delman just received word from our fighter aircraft pilots that they spotted a long line of personnel carriers coming in from the north side. He told me to tell you that they are not ours!"

"Well, who are they?" Drori demanded.

"He doesn't know yet. There are no insignias or markings on the trucks."

"Tell the Colonial to have one of the Blackhawk choppers do a fly-by and find out who those jokers are right now! We don't need any interference from some mercenary group or bands of disgruntled Arabs." The soldier saluted again and dashed off to report to Colonel Delman.

Inside the temple Paul turned to Simon, Levi, and Hershel. "You guys stay here." Then he looked at Levi. "You're in charge. Clear?"

Levi nodded, then intoned, "The Lord will protect us."

Paul signaled Yair and Jonathan to prepare to move out into the valley floor. He believed the security of the ancient buildings would shelter the community temporarily. In the back of his mind he knew that some form of rescue operation by divine intervention would be their only chance at survival.

Paul and Yair walked out into the openness of the valley and stopped short as their eyes spotted over twenty men from the K-group assembled and ready to follow orders. Seconds later he was surrounded by the men. "Tell us what to do," several men said in unison.

"We just can't let them come in and slaughter us!" another cried out.

Paul motioned for them to calm down. "Men, remember, we are unarmed. They must know that, so the only thing we can do is to keep watch while our community remain secure deep inside the buildings. We have no choice but to wait on the Lord for deliverance." Then he singled out five men along with Jonathan and instructed, "You men act as watchmen. Climb the cliffs in all directions and shout to each other what movements you observe." A sudden realization came over him. "Men, hear me! No one is to step outside the confines of the fortress if we are to expect God's protection. Agreed?"

The men nodded.

Paul then rubbed his hand on an ancient Nabatean stone altar. "Yair and I will stay down here behind this pile of rock to direct the flow of information at this makeshift command center." He nodded to the men, who in turn quickly climbed to lower rock ledges that led to the cliffs. Within two minutes they were at their posts. The rest of the men scurried off to keep watch at the passageway that led out of the valley.

The soldier running the reconnaissance report bolted to Drori and saluted. "Sir, the pilot of the Blackhawk advised that they are *Arabs!* He said he flew behind the column and he could see truckloads of men in kaffiyehs holding what looked like semi-automatic weapons."

Drori returned the salute. "Parasites, these Arabs! That's what they are!" He rotated in place then paused to meditate on the news. *Who advised them of this operation?* he wondered. *How could they have known unless they were informed and brought in by...*He scratched his head as the roar of the helicopter engines began to wear on him. *Could these Arabs be part of Kavidas or Stein? Hired to do their dirty work?*

"Sir!" the soldier demanded, "Colonel Delman is waiting—"

Drori motioned him to silence. His mind flashed back to the incident in Kavidas' office where he and Weinstein were overpowered by some unknown force. Where he, for the first time in his political career, was made to look like a puppet. *He made me order this operation! This is all his doing! There is no real threat to national security here! These people are nothing more than unarmed dissidents who have every right in our democratic nation to protest against what they dislike.*

He turned to the soldier with a strengthened resolve and gave the order that would lead to the fulfillment of Stein's prophetic utterance. "Tell Colonel Delman to have two Blackhawks lift off immediately and form up over the column. Threaten them to a halt with two Hellfire missiles in front of them and two in the rear. Then have two Humvees race around the mountain and advise them to turn around and vacate or we will blast them out of existence! Clear?"

"Yes, sir!" The soldier saluted, did an about-face, and ran to Delman.

Four minutes later the two Blackhawks were circling the column. On Delman's command, they fired their Hellfire missiles as directed. The Arab troops recognized the immediate danger and rapidly disgorged from the trucks as the caravan came to a sudden halt. They began to scatter as Mibsam Azib jumped out of the cab of the lead truck and smacked the side of the tarpaulin.

Seconds later two men climbed out, each holding a Soviet-made SA-7 Shoulder-fired missile launcher. Azib pointed to the two Blackhawks and yelled, "Blast the Jew-dogs out of the sky!" The experienced gunners locked their eyes on the helicopters, following them carefully, waiting until they were in a vulnerable dive before pulling the triggers. The four-foot, 20-pound missiles came screaming out of the barrel-canisters and quickly reached 994 MPH until they found their targets.

The Israeli Blackhawk pilots never saw Azib's men ready their rocket launchers. They were totally unprepared and unable to take evasive action. As the missiles impacted, one Blackhawk burst into flames, auto-gyrated for several moments, then crashed and burned. The other went into a headlong dive and slammed against the north cliff, where it virtually disintegrated and fell to the desert floor.

Seeing their temporary victory, the Arabs rejoiced in a victory dance while firing their weapons into the air. Azib congratulated his marksmen then waved the troops back into the trucks. They quickly resumed their attack procession as the Israeli Humvees rounded the cliffs in pursuit.

Paul heard the explosions coming from the north side. He waved to Jonathan high atop a ridge and yelled, "What's going on over there?"

"The Arabs took out two Israeli choppers with missiles!" Jonathan yelled back. "They're still advancing!"

Paul's cell phone rang at that very moment. *Shaul!* He opened the cover. "Shaul, what have you got for us?"

"One—the entire network is in prayer. Two—the American ambassador said his hands are tied. He said that if your people are political insurrectionists, there's little he could do. Besides, he has no jurisdiction in Jordan but promised to file a complaint with the Israeli government and the Jordanian foreign minister."

Paul shook his head in contempt. "That's just what I might have expected." He snorted in disgust. "Once again, we're on our own." He looked up and corrected himself. "Alone with God makes us a majority."

A lengthy silence. Then: "Paul, I've made my mind up," Shaul began with fury, "We're going to get Kavidas!" Shaul ended the call.

Paul gazed down at his cell phone then pressed the speed-dial to recall Shaul. After four rings the voice-mail messaging took his call. "Rats!" Paul cried out. He stepped behind the altar to collect his thoughts.

Why is Kavidas doing this? he asked himself. *Why? Because men want power, that's why.* He shook his head and thought on a book his father shared with him by Samuel Chadwick, who maintained that there is probably no instinct of the human heart so strong as the craving for the sovereignty of power. Might is the attribute of God most coveted by men. It's the dominant passion of the human race and the key to its history. The determination to possess it is responsible for more than half the bloodshed of the world, and its urge has been the dynamic of civilization in all ages. The devil's doctrine has always been that might is right. No authority must stand between man and his will. Animal instinct, the gratification of desire, the passion to have and to know, are declared to be the only justification man needs for taking what he wants, provided he has the power.

Paul mentally transported himself to Shaul's place, secretly hoping he would kill Kavidas and put an end to this madness.

Seconds later he was filled with remorse that he allowed himself to be in the place of God.

Drori stood and watched the fireballs from the downed Blackhawks rising into the air. He raced back to Delman, who sat in his Humvee giving orders. "Our aircraft?"

Delman climbed out of the Humvee. He was breathing in ragged gulps. "The Arabs fired two missiles at our Blackhawks. They took both of them out. We have two Humvees closing on them as they are approaching the northern entranceway!"

"Order your F-16s to strafe them in a guarded fashion. No missiles. We don't want to promote an international incident with the Arabs right now, nor are we prepared to fight on two fronts out here in the desert. Killing several of them should deter them."

Delman turned and began climbing back into the Humvee when he stopped and pointed to the troops standing ready at the entranceway. "Sir, we need to move our forces forward, or we will miss our window of opportunity."

Drori exploded angrily. "Am I to understand you are really concerned that hundreds of *unarmed* men and women are going to mount a counter-offensive against us? What are you expecting them to use against our armaments—sticks and stones? Rush us on their camels? Get serious! This mission is for butchers, not military warriors."

Delman glared at Drori for several seconds. He saw a different man than when they'd started out in the mission. *What happened to him?* Delman wondered. *He's suddenly gone soft and is in danger of insubordination against his appointed official.* Yet Delman knew that even if Drori was only the Special Advisor, he was still his superior officer. "Sir, I have a job to do. I am merely trying to—"

"Save it, Delman," Drori snarled back. "Go and give the order for the F-16s and then get back to me!"

Delman saluted and jumped into the Humvee, grabbed the radio transmitter handset, and gave the order.

Azib ordered his truck to a halt at the northern entranceway, then jumped out and waved the rest of the caravan to pull into the clefts of the cliffs for protection from the oncoming Israeli Humvees. Once unloaded, Azib looked back at his forces and smiled. They might look like a bunch of rogue Arab nomads to the Jews and Christians, but to him they looked like a formidable little army, once again called upon to fight for Allah and Mohammed and their right to exist.

Azib saw this mission as a divine appointment to pay back the Jews and Christians for the seething resentment that had simmered for centuries in the Islamic world. He didn't see this as an act of terrorism, although he wholeheartedly subscribed to the collusion between dictatorial states and an international terrorist network to accomplish political goals. More so, he saw this as an opportunity from the sovereign Allah who arranged an appointment where destiny would sort out who was to be the victor: the Jews, the Christians, or the Arabs. In his mind, this battle would then be representative of future warfare that would involve other enemies—America, Great Britain, et al. A war that would be needed to achieve Islam's rightful place in the world.

A bearded Hamas with a Soviet-made Makarov 9-mm pistol in his hand and a SVD Dragunov sniper rifle tightly slung around his back ran to Azib, pointed at the Israeli Humvees, and said, "Mibsam, the Jews are almost on us! What is your order?"

Azib turned to gaze at the smoldering remains of the two Blackhawks, then remembered one of the rudimentary laws of predators: you wait until your prey stumbles, then you pursue and attack. He turned and put his hand on the bearded Hamas brother and breathed, "Destroy them with missiles and then prepare to breach the entrance into the fortress."

The bearded Hamas warrior grinned and darted off to carry out the command. Azib then walked the distance to the Blackhawk and stripped the dead pilot of his weapon.

"What do you see up there?" Paul yelled to Jonathan, who was crouching behind a boulder on the northern cliff. He'd just heard the booming resonance echoing off the valley walls from two missile strikes.

"What looks like a small army of Arabs fired missiles at two Israeli helicopters. They were direct hits! Now the Arabs are forming their troops up to attack through the entranceway!"

"Lord, we need your help," Paul prayed aloud then quoted from Psalm 31: " 'Turn your ear to us, come quickly to our rescue; be our rock of refuge, a strong fortress to save us. Since you are our rock and our fortress, for the sake of your name lead and guide us. Free us from the trap that is set for us, for you are our refuge. Into your hands we commit our spirits; redeem us, O LORD, the God of truth.' "

"Paul!" Jonathan yelled down from the cliffs, "Israeli fighter jets are strafing the Arab caravan! They are scurrying like rats running from a burning house!"

Paul embraced Yair, then raised his hands in thanksgiving and shouted, "Praise the Lord!" Then he yelled up to Jonathan, "Keep your head down!" Jonathan gave him a thumbs-up, then ducked below a rock ledge that overlooked the northern entrance.

Paul wiped his brow as he surveyed the valley floor. There was only strewn rock covering the ground. All personnel and animals were hiding, securely protected behind thirty feet of rock for the time being, but...Paul was still worried. That safety could change quickly where everybody would be defenseless if the enemy either marched through the entranceway or flied a gunship into the compound and started shooting.

Suddenly elements of the scene that appeared in his mind several weeks ago came into view. He remembered seeing a great battle where the Kavidas-directed Israeli forces with their modern war machines would attack Petra, yet be defeated by God's mighty hand.

He sighed in relief as the truth that God was in control swept over him and turned to Yair. "Watch and see what God is going to do for us."

The IDF troops were becoming increasingly more impatient with each passing moment. They were trained for action, not to stand down. To expect them to remain in full battle dress in the hot desert would only lessen their military capabilities and effectiveness. Their platoon officers were aware of this and began to get fidgety. As Drori sat on the hood of a Humvee, he watched two platoon officers walk to Colonel Delman's vehicle and start up a conversation. Seconds later they were pointing to Drori and raising their voices. It was then that Drori made a command decision. He had a personal responsibility to both his position as an elected official as well as a patriot of Israel. Then there also was his humanitarian side that had to be honored. He approached Delman while he was engaged with his officers and said, "Time to move! We will advance through this southern passageway into the fortress— leaving the Arabs alone for the time being. There will be no gunfire unless at my command. We will see if these people will leave peaceably. Understood?"

Delman made a face that smacked of disappointment. "Yes, sir," he said with a snort. As Drori walked away, Delman motioned to his line officers to carry out the order.

With both hands balled into fists, Azib called his lieutenants into a huddle behind a huge boulder emerging from the desert floor about 50 yards from the northern entrance. He pointed upward as the Israeli F-16s circled off in the distance and said, "We have sustained some casualties, but remember who we came to serve. Allah! True?"

The lieutenants replied with a chant, "Allah is god, Allah is good!

We will serve Allah!"

"Good, good!" Azib chortled, eyes gleaming with fanatical power as he postulated the Islamic creed. "Now if Allah calls upon us to sacrifice ourselves so that our people will be vindicated from these Jew-rat and Gentile oppressors, then our lives have not have been in vain," he began fiercely. "Our lives will count for Allah, and we will be rewarded in paradise. Are we ready?" They all fired their weapons into the air to signal their readiness to die for Allah. Azib smiled, then slammed a full cartridge into his Galil ARM machine-gun that he had taken off the dead Israeli pilot and led his men toward the passageway.

"Paul, the Israelis are moving into the southern passageway!" Paul heard from a watchman perched upon a cliff.

"Paul," Jonathan cried out in the next instant, "the Arabs are clinging to the cliff walls as they move toward the northern entrance!"

Paul and Yair traded looks. Paul raised his eyebrows as he registered the look on his companion's face. He sensed that adrenalin was sweeping through his body like a flash flood. "Remember, Yair, God is in control. Right?"

Yair just sighed deeply and squeezed his eyes shut momentarily in a meager attempt to block out his fears.

Independence Park, Jerusalem

Shaul pulled his car into the Independence Park apartment complex and turned off the ignition. Then he examined the K-group network logs for their surveillance reports on Kavidas one more time. Their logs accurately indexed his schedule, from high-level meetings at the Knesset down to his lunch breaks. It was in the providence of God that Shaul choose this time when Kavidas went to the office after lunchtime.

He turned to Shlomo at his right, then Shira in the back seat, and said guardedly as he checked his wristwatch, "We're ready to defend our people, right?"

They nodded, then exchanged looks.

They may not believe on Yeshua as I do, Shaul thought, *but they have the passion for what's right for their nation.*

"Shaul," Shira said, definitely emboldened and agitated, "remember I have my weapon with me."

Shaul stopped short and carefully pondered his next move. *There must be a security agent in the lobby. There has to be surveillance cameras connected to a central station. How can we get past them without a weapon? Use harsh words on them? No! Shaul,* he said to himself, *remember Jesus said, 'For all who draw the sword will die by the sword.'* He looked at Shlomo then to Shira. "Okay, Shira, only if our lives are threatened. Agreed?"

Shira nodded reluctantly.

"We'll have to trust the Lord on this one," Shaul said. He held up his hand, inviting them to join him. "Let's pray." They quickly bowed their heads as Shaul whispered, "Lord, we need you to open up a path for us. It is not for us to use violence such as the nonbelievers do. We are relying upon you to provide us access." Then he opened the driver's side door and said, "Let's roll!"

The Independence Park had two aluminum with gold-trim-framed doors and safety glass incorporating key-card access. There was no valet or doorman present, only a rotating surveillance camera mounted inside the lobby. "We lucked out! No guards, just the video camera and the automatic door," Shlomo said as they rushed to hide behind the shrubs by the front door.

" 'Lucked out?'" Shaul quipped. *Since when did "luck" have anything to do with God?*

Shlomo poked Shira and corrected himself. "Ha, ha. I really meant God is watching over us."

Shaul pointed to the key-card reader. "Shlomo, study it quickly. See if you can run a by-pass when the camera moves out of view."

Shlomo waited for the camera to turn, then looked under the card reader before pulling out a four-conductor multi-colored cable. He reached into his pocket to retrieve a Leatherman Squirt S4 all-purpose knife.

"Nice," Shaul said with a grin.

"Hurry, Shlomo," Shira said as she heard footsteps coming from the parking lot. "We have company coming."

Shlomo shot up a prayer, glanced at the camera, then cut and skinned the black wire. Then he cut and skinned the red wire. *One more pass,* he thought, *and we'll have it.* At the very moment the camera turned away he crossed the black to the red. There was a small spark at the connection, then a relay inside the door jamb clicked and the doors swung open.

"Outstanding!" Shira said, just above a whisper. "I'll see that you get extra shekels in your paycheck this week for that one."

Once they defeated the door mechanism, they dashed to the camera. Shlomo opened up his Squirt all-purpose knife with scissor attachment and cut the cable under the camera. Then they ran to the elevator and quickly pressed the *Close Door* button.

"We want the sixth floor," Shaul instructed.

Shlomo hit the No. 6 button and said, "A fitting number for the Antichrist. Number 6."

"Yeah, really," Shaul said as his smile faded. "The number of the beast, 666!"

When the elevator doors opened, Shlomo stuck his head out into the corridor to find an aged couple standing in the vending machine room doorway. They appeared to be arguing. He turned to Shaul and Shira. "Slight problem. People in hallway. Need to wait one."

Shaul studied his watch.

Thirty seconds went by.

Another thirty seconds passed.

Shaul strummed his fingers against the elevator wall. "We're out of time! We'll have to chance it."

Shlomo motioned to wait then peeked around the elevator door once again. "They're leaving!" Seconds later they heard a door close. Shlomo looked again then announced, "All clear!"

Shira let out a sigh of relief as Shaul said, "He's in 634. Let's hustle!"

They bolted to the door and abruptly came to rest. Shaul pointed to the nameplate on the door that read, *Gregory A. Kavidas.* They exchanged looks, then Shaul nodded to Shlomo to initiate their plan.

Shlomo pulled a folded piece of paper from his pocket, then knocked on the door. "Mr. Kavidas, this is security. We have a message for you from your office."

A long 15 seconds ensued.

Footsteps came toward the door, then: "Slip it under the door."

Shlomo shot a quizzical look at Shaul. Shaul motioned with his hand. "You have to sign for it," Shlomo replied.

They heard the deadbolt unlocking and the door chain being unlatched. The second Kavidas stuck his head out, all three pushed the door in, knocking Kavidas to the floor. "What's going on here!?" he exclaimed.

Shaul motioned to Shlomo and Shira, who grabbed Kavidas' arms and dragged him back into his living room. Shaul quietly closed the door and said with a smirk, "It's time we had a little chat, Mr. Kavidas." Kavidas stiffened then scanned the room. His eyes stopped at his cell phone on top of his television. "Forget it!" Shaul said fiercely.

Kavidas glared at Shaul, then turned in disgust at Shlomo and Shira. "You fools have made the biggest mistake of your life. Do you really think you can hold me against my will?"

Shlomo and Shira simultaneously squeezed his arms and nodded to Shaul. Shaul put his hands around Kavidas' neck and pressed his thumbs against his windpipe. "You will call off the attack on Petra right now, or we will help God out and kill you here and now!"

Kavidas sneered at Shaul and gurgled out, "You have no power over me."

"Oh, yeah," Shlomo said as he jerked Kavidas' arm upward, "that's what you think!"

Shaul raised his fist and held it above Kavidas' face. "Call off the attack and we'll let you live."

Kavidas snickered. "You'll what? You'll let me live?" he gasped. "As if you or anybody else on earth has the power to decide whether or not I live."

Shaul tightened his grip, causing Kavidas' eyes to bulge as he struggled for air. Then Kavidas cracked an evil smile as Shaul fixed his gaze on his eyes until Kavidas closed his eyes. Suddenly Shaul began weeping.

The color drained from Shlomo's face. "Shaul, what's the matter?" Shlomo asked.

Shaul suddenly relaxed his hands, then looked up at an imaginary spot on the wall as if in a trance and said, "I see this man—this lawless one—performing terrible things in the days ahead. He will bring great harm to the earth, causing many to follow him and die in their sin without Christ. He will bring great destruction upon the earth, disasters that have never been unleashed before. As Jesus said, "Time of 'great distress, unequaled from the beginning of the world until now—and never to be equaled again.'"

"Poetic," Kavidas scoffed in a muffled voice. "Now let me go!" He closed his eyes once again as if to concentrate on his next move, then blinked his eyes several times and shouted, "Enough! Be bound!"

Mysteriously, unseen hands grabbed hold of Shlomo and Shira and flung them against a wall. They crumpled in heaps as Shaul's mouth dropped open in surprise.

Shaul looked up in horror as an invisible force latched onto his neck and pulled him up off Kavidas. He found himself standing as Kavidas stood up.

"You see," Kavidas said in triumph, "I told you that you have no power over me."

"Maybe I don't, but Jesus Christ does!" Shaul retorted.

"Sure, sure," Kavidas mocked. "Maybe in the kingdom to come, but right now you three fleas are under my control." He raised his hand, then gave a command in an unknown tongue.

Without warning, Shaul was being dragged to the wall next to Shlomo and Shira.

"Breaking and entering the residence of a Knesset member is considered a threat to national security. Did you know that? You will *all* spend time in jail for this."

Shaul simply glared at him with eyes blazing.

Covertly in one smooth action, Shira reached inside her jacket and released the safety strap off her Barak 9mm service weapon, then pulled it out and pointed it at Kavidas. "Hold it right there!"

Kavidas stood immobilized, shocked at the arrogance of this young woman. Seconds later: "Ha!" he said with a smirk. "Do you really think you can harm me after I rose from the dead?"

Shira blinked in confusion, totally disoriented. "I will shoot if you move one muscle," she ordered haltingly.

Kavidas glowered at her with malevolent eyes, then pointed his hand at her weapon. Without warning Shira turned the weapon on herself, holding it to her temple.

"No!" Shaul screamed.

Entranced, Shira remained motionless with the weapon at her temple, as if waiting for the next command.

Kavidas lowered his hand. "I will show mercy," he said as if mocking one of God's attributes.

Shira fell limp with her weapon at her side.

Kavidas casually walked over and pulled Shaul's cell phone off his belt and crushed it with his heel. "You won't be needing this," he said with lips curved sardonically. Then he walked to Shira to disarm her.

Shaul looked over at his dazed companions then struggled with all his strength to break free, but the invisible bonds enveloping them held them fast.

Paul looked at his watch. *Shaul , where are you? I desperately need to hear from you!* He attempted to hide his escalating fears from Yair but his facial expressions gave a tell-tale message: time was running out. "Remember, Lord, it's the eleventh hour," he prayed aloud. He opened his phone and pressed the speed-dial to reach Shaul. It rang four times before being sent to voice-mail. *Shaul, where are you?* he repeated.

"Paul, the Arabs are all assembled in the north passageway," Jonathan shouted down. "They're going to attack any minute now!"

Paul assumed the Israelis were now in position as well. He took a deep breath then exhaled slowly as he put his hand on Yair's shoulder. "Run and see if the rest of the group are all right. I'm afraid things are going to get a little dicey from here on out."

Yair read the concern on Paul's face and sped off to the temple.

When he arrived, the group was all kneeling in a circle in fervent intercessory prayer. "We have been storming the throne room of God for you and Paul," Levi said, breaking out of the circle.

"What is the situation out there?" Simon asked rising from his knees. "Are Paul and Jonathan okay?"

Yair blinked as the skin on the back of his neck began to crawl. "He wanted me to check on you."

"What is it?" Levi asked instinctively. "You can tell me."

Yair shook his head and said glumly, "Things look bad. The Arabs are ready to attack from the north entrance while the Israelis are poised in the south passageway."

"What does Paul say?" Levi pressed.

"He didn't. I can read his face, though. He's worried."

Levi seized the moment for God. He placed his hands on Yair. then looked heavenward. "You go back to Paul and tell him there are over 15 people in here who are praying for God's deliverance and that he *will not* abandon us!"

Tears filled up in Yair's eyes. That was the kind of thing he could expect from a passionate man of God in a time of crisis. He sniffled several times and replied with heightening resolve, "I will tell him." He composed himself, then ran out of the temple building.

"The Arabs are now just standing in the passageway, waiting, Paul," Jonathan yelled, his voice growing in intensity.

I get it now, Paul realized. *The Arabs will do the cleaning up and take the spoils after the Israeli operation is over.* Images of Arab barbarisms and war atrocities flew into his mind.

Paul signaled the watchmen at the south entrance. "Movement?"

"They're forming two columns and snaking in as we speak," the watchman replied.

Yair ran to his Paul's side. "Levi wanted me to remind you," he began as he gulped in air, "they are all praying for God to intervene! Just hang on!"

Paul sighed and smiled at Yair. "He's right," he affirmed.

Gunfire erupted!

"Paul," a watchman shouted, "several soldiers fired their weapons into the air, then a man who looks like Defense Minister Drori emerged from the troops. He's waving for us to come down off the cliffs. What should we do?"

"This must be a trap! Hold your position!" *Lord, help!* Paul prayed silently then turned to Yair. "You stay here. I'm going to talk to them."

"NO!" Yair screamed as Paul ran toward the entranceway.

TWENTY-FOUR

Christian Fortress, Petra

Slowing to a walk, Paul held his hands high above his head and headed directly for who he thought was in charge. Next to two infantrymen holding Galil ARM machine-guns stood an officer and a man in civilian clothes. It was Drori and Colonel Delman.

"I come in peace!" Paul said aloud as he came to a stop.

Drori reached over and put his hand on one of the soldier's machine-guns and pushed the barrel toward the ground. "Come forward!" he cried out as Colonel Delman fixed a penetrating stare on Douglas.

Paul turned around quickly and caught a glimpse of the watchmen full of anticipation standing on the ledges of the cliffs.

Drori's shoulders rose and fell. "So you're Paul Douglas, I am told. The young brash crusader for some God-forsaken cause," he said as Paul approached. "I am Defense Minister Zeev Drori."

"Why are you doing this?!" Paul asked while giving him a lethal glare, ignoring his caustic salutation. "We have done nothing to warrant this attack. We are all unarmed, peaceful people," he spouted. "Many of which are your own Jewish citizens who have embraced us Gentiles in a loving friendship. Is there something unlawful about this?" He put his hands on his hips. "I demand an explanation!"

"We don't have to explain to you!" Delman fired back as he placed his hand over his sidearm.

"Now, now, Colonel Delman, just relax," Drori soothed as he looked at them both. "We should be able to work this out. We were given orders to rid this fortress of subversives who had barricaded themselves in to form a resistance wing against the Israeli government."

"Who told you that? Kavidas right?!" Paul flared. "Well, both he and his buddy, Stein, are nothing but liars." He turned and waved his hand horizontally. "Now that you're here, you can see we're totally unarmed and harmless. We are only a band of Christians along with some Bedouins who have been awarded custodial care of this archeological site. That's it. Is that subversive? Hardly," he added sarcastically.

"I can see that," Drori conceded. He turned slowly to Colonel Delman and whispered in his ear, "Pull your men back out of here and take care of those Arabs on the other side."

"What would you have me do to them?" Delman replied gruffly. "Throw sand in their face?"

Drori put his hand on Delman's shoulder. *This guy is looking for a fight!* "There will be plenty of battles for Israel's warriors in the future, of that I am sure of. For now, force the Arabs out of the northern passageway and scare them back to Lebanon or wherever they came from."

"Yes, sir," Delman said with a half-hearted salute.

A booming voice roared from above: "YOU HAVE CHOSEN WISELY!"

Every eye turned upward to locate the utterance that reverberated off the cliff walls. Atop the cliff just above the southern entrance stood Nocham with a shepherd's staff in his hand. He raised his other hand and pointed to Drori. "Since you have determined not to fight against God's people, you have been granted freedom," he said solemnly. "Now go, but remember this place is a sanctuary for God's people—"

He stopped short and locked his eyes on Delman as the colonel began to raise his rifle. Nocham pointed his staff at Delman and cried out, "Your heart has been judged and you have been found to be wicked!" He waved his hand and shouted, "Stand back!"

The three men began to scatter when all at once a fireball shot out from Nocham's staff and struck Delman in the chest as his finger pulled the rifle's trigger. His finger fused to the metal and continued to fire aimlessly until he fell in a heap of ashes on the ground. When the firing stopped, two IDF soldiers were holding their wounds in sheer astonishment.

At the northern cliffs Qadar stood with his shepherd's staff on a high ledge, carefully watching the Arab force thread their way through the entryway to the mouth of the valley. He purposefully waited until every last man was confidently assembled and poised to attack, knowing they presumed they were securely protected by the towering rock walls. "TO THE ENEMIES OF ISRAEL AND THEIR GOD, YOUR JUDGMENT HAS COME!" he wailed thunderously. The Arab armies froze in place as the divine decree bellowed forth. Then he jammed his staff into the rock he was standing on.

Zsssst!

A bolt of lightning shot out of the sky and struck the very spot his staff designated. The rock vibrated for several seconds then suddenly cleaved in two. The outer half flew into the air then plummeted down the rock wall, collecting loose mantel along its path. The small avalanche buried ten would-be assassins.

Then without warning the ground in the passageway began to violently shake. The subterranean engines deep within the desert floor began to churn and twist, applying titanic force against the earth's mantle until the tectonic plates shifted, causing the cliffs to move apart. The gap between the cliffs slowly began to widen as the Arab army desperately tried to hold onto any vestige of rock ledge they could. As they looked on in horror, the surface of the earth between the cliffs cracked and opened, exposing a fiery crevasse with bellowing flames that reached out and seized the attackers in groups and pulled them back into the newly opened cavity. Shrieks and screams erupted in a strident dirge from the attackers who were singed and burned as they fell into the bottomless pit, where they would be tormented for all eternity. Once every Arab attacker was consumed, the cliffs ceased their movement and the earth slowly closed and became still.

Qadar suddenly appeared next to Nocham, where they joined hands and cried out collectively, "The time has come to announce the opening of the Sixth Seal! The earth will violently shake and its mountains will move as the Son of Man foretold! The warnings of Joel,

Amos, and Zephaniah will soon come to pass as man's rebellion against God continues unabated." Qadar slowly raised his staff toward the sky as Nocham pointed his staff toward the earth.

Then the unleashing came!

An invisible hand parted the clouds above them, revealing a panoramic view of the blue sky. Then in the next instant, the sky, clear to the horizon, peeled back to uncover the blackness of space. Out of the black backdrop of space appeared a vast telescoping corridor-like opening extending from the lower troposphere, through the stratosphere, the mesosphere, the ionosphere and clear through the outer exosphere suddenly appeared. The moon in its full phase could be seen inside the corridor. "Behold, the symbol of the blood of the Son of Man!" Qadar cried out. As if the observers were viewing this phenomenon through a polar projection, a streak of light that resembled a shooting meteor arced across the celestial dome and slammed into the moon's surface.

"Oh, God of Abraham, Isaac, and Jacob!" Drori gulped as he covered his eyes. Scores of soldiers just fell backward to the ground and clutched the desert sand for some semblance of earth's security.

Paul Douglas just shook his head in utter amazement and exclaimed, "How manifold are your works, O Lord!" Behind him all the citizens of Petra slowly began funneling out of the buildings to observe the supernatural events.

Regolith lying loosely on the moon's surface was instantly pulverized by the meteor's impact. A massive dust cloud erupted and flew out into space, allowing the sun's rays to refract off the particles, creating a rainbow effect. The dust particles suddenly turned scarlet red, then were quickly drawn back to the surface by the moon's gravitational pull. The red dust particles settled upon the entire surface of the moon, casting a red hue clearly visible from the earth.

"You have witnessed the beginning of great disturbances that will occur in the heavens!" Qadar announced. "And still, man does not repent of their unbelief!"

Nocham tapped his staff on the ground to signal the next phase of the Sixth Seal. On the surface there were only seismic tremors that caused the surface sand to vibrate. But under their feet was the Afro-

Arabian Rift Valley fault plane, the longest, deepest and widest fissure in the earth's surface. This fault extended over a distance of 4,000 miles, beginning in the Amanus Mountains of southeastern Turkey and continuing southward through western Syria, Lebanon, Israel, as far as the Red Sea. At its deepest point, near the Dead Sea, the rift descended below sea level to more than 24,000 feet. This fault plan was now undergoing tremendous seismographic registrations. A gigantic cleavage in this sunken block began to occur, splitting and fracturing the underlying geological plate.

Several minutes into the earthquake, the fault plane built up enough velocity at the transform plate to cause a strike-slip that ruptured. The velocity of this thrust fault at the two adjoining plates boundary was enough to bring about a collision that dipped at a very low angle through the lithosphere, forming a fault plane with a huge surface area. This was now a major earthquake.

The dragging sound of gigantic subterranean rock strata being compressed and folded by tremendous forces horrified the onlookers. The desert mosaic that lay before everyone's eyes was suddenly transformed as the earth's crust opened, allowing the desert sands to cascade like ocean torrents emptying into a tidal basin, into the gaping chasms that led to the interior of the earth.

"Everybody on the ground!" Paul yelled as the prompting of God's Spirit warned.

The boundless energy exerted by the internal engines deep in the earth refused to abate. Seconds later the massive rock cliffs, those stone monuments that had stood unassaulted since primordial times, yielded to the all-mighty power of being unchained and suddenly began to sway. Loose stone and gravel began to shower beneath them.

Every man fell to the ground. Drori then screamed as he pointed to the cliffs, "They're going to topple over and crush us!"

Paul shot his hand to his mouth, gasped, then muttered, "Lord, help!" He managed to turn and wave to Yair and the rest of the group as they looked on with horror-stricken faces.

All at once Nocham lifted his staff, pointed to the cliffs, and commanded the stones to rest. "Stand fast!" The stone sentinels forming the boundary of Petra immediately stopped swaying.

As the bystanders to God's wrath rose to their feet they realized the prophets of judgment had disappeared.

Drori dusted himself off as shudder after shudder convulsed his body. After several moments he put his hand on Paul's shoulder. "What is to become of our nation? Our people?"

"First, your nation and you, yourself, Mr. Drori," Paul instructed, "need to embrace Jesus Christ as your Messiah. When that happens, the world will change. Secondly, you need to leave our people here at Petra alone. And finally, go back to Jerusalem and tell Kavidas—the enemy of God, the Antichrist—what happened here and remind him that our God is still in charge."

Drori nodded as he realized his life had been spared. Then he scratched his ear. "Did I hear you right? Did you say, 'The Antichrist?'"

"You heard correctly," Paul replied. "We know Kavidas orchestrated this attack because we know he is trying desperately to silence the only voice that can expose him." He patted his chest several times. "I know in my heart that he is the evil one prophesied by both the Old and New Testament prophets. What's more, his friend, Mortimer Stein, is his false prophet, and their scheme is to dupe and mislead the world, starting with God's covenant people, Israel, into thinking he is their salvation. His colossal lie will be their destruction." Paul's eyes met Drori's eyes. "Do what you can to stop him."

Drori motioned for several soldiers to come and gather Colonel Delman's remains. As he was about to depart, he turned to Paul and said, "Protocol demands that I leave a contingent force here to guard this reservation and the road leading into it." He wiped his brow and added, "But I promise you that as long as I'm alive, I will do everything in my power to protect your people."

Paul smiled. "I believe you. It's Kavidas I do not trust." Paul kicked the sand under his shoe as he contemplated an additional response. "You will honor the God of your fathers if you do everything in your power to extricate Kavidas from office." Paul knew full well that God's plan did not allow for that possibility, but believed that resistance, in any form, would frustrate Kavidas' purpose and was therefore welcome.

"May the God of Israel give me the strength," Drori concluded. He signaled the retreat, then led his men back through the passageway into the desert.

Yair and the rest of the group ran to Douglas and hugged him as the rest of the community surveyed the damage brought on by the earthquake.

Paul then announced, "God has made it clear to us today that he will protect us as long as we stay within the confines of this fortress. No man is to leave here unattended."

The community at Petra would come to find out in the days ahead from God's witnesses, Nocham and Qadar, that God would protect them in other areas as well. He would send them fowl off the desert for meat, and water from the deep wells of the ancient city for drinking.

Many hour later, reveling in the God's victory, Yair lifted his wine glass. "May the enemies of God and Israel be forever vanquished as they were today!"

All but Paul lifted their glasses to the toast. Paul nodded and, with his carrot juice. said, "May it be so."

Paul's cell phone sounded. He looked at the caller-ID.

Yair asked, "Is that Shaul?"

Paul shook his head wryly. "It says *Unknown Caller.*"

"Be careful, Paul," Yair warned. "Kavidas could be tracking your calls." Despite the safeguard of encryption, Kavidas could have technical resources to unscramble the message or to locate Paul via triangulation.

"With Shaul and the others out there somewhere, I'll have to take the chance," Paul said, then pressed the *Talk* button.

"Paul Douglas?" the caller asked.

"Who's calling?" Paul replied cautiously.

"This is Gadi Shamni, a new member of the *Koinonos* group in Jerusalem," the caller answered. "I have an important message for you."

"How did you get this number?" Paul asked suspiciously.

"Your number came to me through a man who went to visit Shaul and his people in jail."

The hair on Paul's neck stood up. "Won't work. Explain that."

"Shaul, Shlomo, and Shira were arrested early today by Mossad for attempting to assassinate Gregory Kavidas," Gadi reported. A slight pause. "They are being held without bail in a military stockade outside Jerusalem."

Paul turned to Yair and the others and quickly explained. Levi simply looked up to heaven and held his hands up on the air, as if praying and praising while the others just shook their heads in shock.

"What else can you tell me?" Paul queried.

"The whole city of Jerusalem is still in chaos from the earthquake. Several hundred lives were lost from collapsing buildings and the ensuing fires. It'll be weeks before the State even looks at Shaul's case. The way things stand now, I guess they'll be in jail for quite a while."

Paul glanced at Yair and the others, but he remained very still, like a statue. Only his eyes moved as he tried to understand in some small way the mind of God. *Lord, what's happening? Suddenly, Kavidas' clutches seem so powerful while we seem so helpless.* He sighed deeply and forced himself to rely upon the promises of God once more.

"Gadi," he said with strengthened resolve, "I'll locate you when I get back to Jerusalem. Then we'll arrange a meeting with the K-group to form a strategy to get our family back. In the meantime, keep me informed. And remember, no one is to get this cell phone number. Clear?"

"Clear." Gadi got off the phone.

Paul raised his eyebrows as the group waited with baited-breath for his report. Instead he began to hum his dad's favorite hymn: "Redeemed." He turned away from the group as he and Yair exchanged glances.

"Paul!" Yair demanded. "Talk to us!"

"It's a long way from being over," Paul replied somberly. "The earthquake from the Sixth Seal has taken its toll in Jerusalem. Many have died, and the city is a mess from the collapse of buildings. This will slow down the process of investigation and trial for them." Paul kept his eyes on Yair and Levi. "Keep your faith and strength up," he encouraged. "You'll see—our God will not leave them defenseless."

TWENTY-FIVE

Jerusalem

There was a heated argument going on behind Kavidas' office door, of that Stein was sure of. He could hear Drori offering his best excuses while Kavidas simply ranted about his disloyalty and failed mission. A fleeting thought about how Gregory would correct the failed mission whizzed past his mind. *There will be another opportunity, of that I will assure him,* Stein thought.

A pounding on a desk!

The sounds of a soft voice speaking filtered through the heavy door. Stein moved his head closer toward the door in order to overhear the conversation. *Must be Drori making a peace offering,* he thought.

"I will not tolerate your defiance against my orders!" Kavidas snarled at Drori, his voice vibrating with intensity. "It sets a precedence and a bad example."

Sitting in the seat before him, the "hot seat" as he called it, Drori raised his hand to voice an objection to his superior's complaint. "In my judgment—" Drori fumbled for words—"it was the only humane thing to do! Those people were not only unarmed, but they were completely harmless. They're nothing but a group of evangelists camping out waiting for their Jesus to return. They were completely harmless."

"Not to me!" Kavidas snapped. "They represent a faction of people that are against the sovereignty of Israel as well as a subversive force working within our borders to undermine my authority."

Drori took a hard look at this Kavidas fellow standing before him. In reflection, Israeli's Special Advisor was quickly taking on the form of the very person Paul Douglas described back at Petra: the Antichrist. *I wonder if Douglas' claim is true? That Kavidas is the Antichrist?*

Kavidas read Drori's thought. "What was that?!" he screamed in his face. "Did I hear you correctly? Did you equate me to the Antichrist?"

Drori reflexively took a quick survey of the room. *Did I unwittingly voice that thought?* he wondered. *How did he know what just went through my mind?* Drori, a seasoned warrior of sorts, refused to compromise in the face of pressure. In his mind's eye he was grappling with the enormity of the possibilities and consequences for his nation if indeed this Kavidas was the Antichrist. He jerked his thumb over his shoulder and said forcefully, "Back in Petra, Douglas made the claim that you're the Antichrist. In fact, he seemed quite convinced of it."

"And you?" Kavidas shot back.

Drori sat in the chair and steepled his fingers as he carefully calculated the consequences of his answer. Finally, being true to the Jewish patriarchs that made Israel great, he said, "My heart tells me that you are very self-serving and dedicated to using Israel toward your own purposes." He looked Kavidas squarely in the eyes. "To answer your question, after carefully observing your actions since you came to Israel, I believe it's possible, yes."

"I see," Kavidas said with a slight nod. With that he stood up from the chair behind his desk and walked to Drori, where he slowly circled him. "It is very unfortunate for you, Zeev Drori, that you have come to this place in your political career where you commit insubordination that borders on treason."

"What are you talking about?!" Drori flared. "I have given my country over 27 years of faithful service, and never once have I been accused of insubordination." He began to rise from the chair as he added boldly, "This is an outrage!"

Kavidas abruptly stopped circling him and touched the side of Drori's head with his index finger. Drori flinched and dropped back into the chair. "I'm sorry you feel the way you do, Mr. Drori," Kavidas said as if it were an eulogy. "Perhaps you should go home and think on some of the things we discussed and get back to me in a few days."

Drori began to rise from the chair once again, then suddenly slumped sideways in his seat. He remained inert for nearly a minute, then stood up and started toward the door. He stopped midway and turned to Kavidas with a blank look on his face, then gabbled, "I think—well, my family is looking forward to my retirement from public service...I should really think about where I want to live when I retire." He gave Kavidas a salute and smiled as he walked out the door.

Three days later Zeev Drori would die in his sleep from a cerebral hemorrhage. Unfortunately, he did not take the time to explore Paul Douglas' claim that Jesus Christ was indeed the Messiah.

Kavidas went to his door and waved Stein into his office, then walked to his window that overlooked Jerusalem. There was a noticeable darkening in the daylight hours taking place, causing the earthquake cleanup crews to utilize portable halogen lamps to supplement the much-needed illumination to locate casualties, repair damaged buildings, and to repair gas and electric lines. Fists clenched, he looked up at the ever-present low cloud cover and gave birth to the blasphemous thought, *Some planning, God! Sure, there is no rain, but nobody but an astronaut can see the astrophysical disturbances— including the red moon, through this dense layer of clouds.*

But it was the earthquakes that really bothered him. The last quake was very severe, and there was the promise of even greater catastrophes to come. *Well, this must come to pass, he reasoned, in order for more souls to jump on board with us. Enough,* he commanded himself, *concentrate on the here and now.* Obediently, he relaxed his hands and turned around to find Stein sitting in the seat Drori formally occupied.

"The world took a heavy hit from that Sixth Seal," Stein began in a subtle attempt to attenuate any blame for his failure. "That was a savage quake. Really made a mess of things here in Jerusalem. Over in the States, they're reeling from an 8.9er. The whole nation is in a state of emergency."

Kavidas was not moved by Stein's assessment of current events, despite the tragic influence it had on humanity. He was all-too-familiar with the timetable that scheduled the destruction of the world. But when failure to crush the opposing committed Christians occurred, a serious setback in their mission would follow. That could not be overlooked. "Mort, I would like to hear your excuse for failure to reach your objective at Petra." A reasonable, controlled voice.

Stein braced himself for the verbal assault to follow. Beyond that, he wasn't prepared. "The mission was going along as planned until the *two performers* appeared. Then everything went into the toilet, so to speak."

A frosty silence, then, "Ah, yes, the 'two performers.' "

Stein threw his hands up in the air. "Certainly you didn't expect those Arabs to stand up against them and defeat them, did you?"

"You could have executed the plan when there was an ongoing diversion so the two witnesses would have been unable to stop you. They would have been too busy elsewhere. For instance, you could have arranged the raid simultaneously with the bombing of several churches here in Jerusalem that would have required their attention. I'm sure they would have showed up for that."

Stein scratched his head while attempting to sort out Kavidas' reasoning that seemed to border on nonsense. *How would it be possible to outwit God's two witnesses who were acting on behalf of God?* It wasn't logical. He had to resolve this. He cleared his throat and explained with a tone of contrition, "I don't believe it was our time. There will be another time portal for us to achieve our objective there at Petra. The forces working against us were far too powerful for the terrorist-army we sent.

"From the moment I learned of the problem in Petra, I have been in contact with other al-Qaeda, Hamas, Hezbollah, and Wahhabisi operatives who vow revenge on both the Jews and the Christians. I am committed to the mission of using the Arab-bloc people to serve our purpose and dispose of those who obstruct our path to victory."

Stein's lucid justification appeased Kavidas. He nodded in affirmation. "I'll take your word to mean that you will regroup and plan an altogether different form of attack. Correct?"

"Correct. One that will not fail."

Kavidas breathed deeply, then walked to his chair and sat down. "It is unfortunate that the IDF met with the same failure out there at Petra. But as you might have imagined—" he pointed to the door—"I have dealt with that failure. He will no longer pose a problem to us."

"Interesting," Stein replied with a victory gesture. He shifted his weight in the chair and asked about the outcome of a problem that he was immediately informed of by Kavidas moments after it happened. "What's the story with Douglas' partner, Shaul, et. al?"

Kavidas smiled mirthlessly. "They're in jail for the time being. Shaul and his friends are out of commission pending a hearing for attempted murder, breaking and entering, malicious mischief, and last but certainly not least, conspiracy against an elected official."

"Sounds like they'll be away for a long time," Stein chortled.

Kavidas expelled a sigh. "By the time they're released, this world will look totally different."

Time, that elusive demon that robs us of life. Stein squeezed his eyes shut as a jolt of fear struck him. His mind fast-forwarded to the time when the next Seal would be opened, a time he was dreading. He resolved to leave the problem with his master. "Have you thought about how you are going to respond to the next Seal?"

"Of course," Kavidas asserted reflexively. "We're going to feed upon man's inner fears when the panic and suicide frenzy sets in. Because man has never experienced the kind of horror that will soon unfold, they will flock to us for spiritual guidance and salvation. The opening of this Seal will bring to bear every imaginable nightmare conceived by man since the introduction of *fear* back in the Garden." He rose from his chair with a gleam in his eye. "This upcoming event is a golden opportunity to make a quantum jump in the advancement of our cause. I would dare to say it will enable us to—" he paused to garner a suitable quote—" 'I will repay you for the years the locusts have eaten,' isn't that what the prophet foretold? Well, it will enable us to make up for the ground we've lost in the past failures when the Seventh Seal is opened, I am sure of it."

Stein squirmed in his chair. He hated it when Gregory cited Bible verses out of context. It made him nervous and uncomfortable.

And rightly so, because Stein should have recognized that he uttered a lie and then connected God's Word to it. Now it was blasphemy.

Home of Gadi Shamni, Jerusalem

Driving his motorcycle through the early morning hours, Paul arrived at Gadi's Shamni's home on Narkiss street at 9 A.M., one hour later than he expected. The earthquake debris in the streets severely impeding his travel.

I don't believe I ever met Gadi, Paul thought as he knocked on the door of his modest condominium. *This is the greatness of the K-group; it provides a network of believers who form the resistance to combat Kavidas.*

Someone peeked through the peephole, then opened the door.

Paul was met by a gregarious man wearing a yarmulke and a prayer shawl. Glimmering out of the folds of the prayer shawl was a gold Magen David, a medal of the shield of David. They exchanged handshakes, then Gadi quickly ushered him into the kitchen where his wife, Dalia, sat having a prayer meeting with their two teenage sons. "This is Paul Douglas," Gadi said with a gush of enthusiasm.

Dalia rose to shake his hand. "Our home is your home," she said graciously, then motioned for their sons to accompany her as she left the room.

"I am indebted to you," Paul replied humbly as he took a seat.

Gadi discerned the anxiety on Douglas' face. "I'm sure you're concerned about Shaul and the others," Gadi began. "Well, since I talked to you on the cell phone, our intelligence network has established that they are being held without bail pending a pre-trial hearing, and that Kavidas is pulling the strings on this one. He has instructed the governing attorney to press for the death penalty for the attempted assassination." He clutched Paul's hand and quoted in sympathetic tones, " 'For the message of the cross is foolishness to those who are perishing, but to us who are being saved it is the power of God.' "

Paul nodded gloomily, then forced himself to admit that he was allowing a doubting spirit to emerge in his heart. "Jesus is still on the throne, right?" he said, smiling.

"That's the spirit, Paul!" Gadi said as tears welled up in his eyes. "Our God is an awesome God, because the weapons we fight with are not the weapons of the world. On the contrary, they have divine power to demolish strongholds.'" He patted Paul on the back several times, then said with a dogged resolve, "We can band together and find a way to 'demolish the stronghold' where Shaul and the other are being held." He said fiercely, "If the Hamas terrorists can do it, we can do it! And since we have the Spirit of the Lord on our side, we cannot fail!"

Paul sighed as a fresh breath of air filled his lungs. "You're right. We cannot accept defeat when we have the Lord on our side. After your family leaves, we will use your place here as a planning center to map out our strategy."

"Now you're talking!"

Paul was suddenly distracted by some strange artifacts and photographs hanging on the walls. His curiosity compelled him to ask, "Where are you from, Gadi?"

"I am a diamond merchant, originally from Morocco. We relocated to Israel ten years ago," he said as he removed his yarmulke.

"Interesting," Paul remarked as he surveyed the walls. "Ancestry?"

"Orthodox Jews. We have family archives and genealogical records dating back to the eighteenth century that prove our lineage originally came from ancient Judaism. Perhaps even the early priesthood."

"Very interesting," Paul replied with heightening concern. "When did you receive Yeshua as your Messiah?"

Gadi grabbed his Masoretic text Bible off the table and turned to the opening leaf. There was a date inscribed in ink. "Six weeks ago. Right after the great disappearance. I started reading my Bible. Since that time, my wife and sons have also received Yeshua as their Messiah. God is faithful."

"That He is," Paul affirmed. *I wonder if his sons could be part of the 144,000?* Stifling the thought he said abruptly, "It will be interesting to see how God uses your family in the days ahead."

"We have heard about the Christian fortress in Petra," Gadi said, almost pleading, "and my spirit is heavy for your *Koinonos* group. Would it be possible for my wife and sons, Chaim and Asher, to go there and be a part of the movement?"

Douglas' face lit up. "It certainly would be possible! In fact, God may be drawing your family there for the purpose of raising up your sons as members of the 144,000 Jewish witnesses."

Gadi clapped his hands then hugged Paul as he exulted, "That would be wonderful!" He gazed off and added, "To think the Almighty Yeshua would want to use my sons to bring in the kingdom is far more than any man could ask."

"We will wait upon the Lord for their anointing as well as the proper time for them to leave," Douglas advised. "God seems to be calling out his witnesses now."

"Once they're gone we will have the freedom to plot our course to 'spring' Shaul without fear of reprisals on my family. Then, after that, we can mount another campaign to fight Kavidas in the public domain."

Paul couldn't help but admire the zeal by which Gadi wanted to go about fighting the enemies of the cross. But the battle was the Lord's and without him, any effort to engage Kavidas would be folly. "We will take it slow as the Lord leads. We really need to hear from God's two witnesses, Nocham and Qadar, before we attempt to tackle Kavidas again."

"This is good counsel," Gadi replied, then poured himself another glass of kosher wine.

Paul's phone rang and he automatically tensed. He opened the cover and read the caller-ID. It was Yair. Four minutes later he ended the call. "My companion at Petra tells me that things are quieting down and that God is right on schedule. Some of our K-group geologists have located an underground spring that is supplying the fortress with fresh water. And if that weren't enough, there are migrating quail flying in every day like they did for the Israelites during the wilderness journeys. The people are rejoicing that they have unlimited 'kosher chicken.' "

Gadi shook his head and smiled. "Unbelievable."

All of a sudden there was a violent shaking of the building!

Paul grabbed hold of the table. "Another quake?"

"Aftershock," Gadi said calmly. "We've been getting them every few hours since the big one."

Paul breathed a sigh of relief. "I guess I should E-mail my friend Lane in Miami and find out what's going on there."

Gadi handed him his Blackberry handheld computer. "Help yourself." As he walked out of the kitchen Paul heard him discussing the family's journey to Petra. A warm feeling came over him as he thanked God for sending such a loyal and supporting family to continue their crusade.

Immediately after he keyed in Lane's E-mail address, the Instant Messaging logo popped up. He welcomed the online conversation.

[Sending]
Brandon, we've had some harrowing times since our last conversation via E-mail. Kavidas authorized a military strike at Petra by the IDF while, I guess you could say it was a regiment of Arabs—mostly Hamas and other renegades—launched a simultaneous attack. It was probably aimed at finishing us off. But praise the Lord, he sent his two witnesses to rescue us so that none of our people were hurt. The IDF backed off when God sent the earthquake that marked the opening of the Sixth Seal. The quake destroyed all the Arabs who came up against us. This is another example of God's retributive laws. At the same time, unfortunately, Shaul, Shlomo, and Shira made an attempt on Kavidas' life and were arrested by Mossad. They are in jail facing serious charges. We're not sure of what the outcome of their arrest is going to be, but for sure, we need all the *Koinonos* family of God to be vigilant in prayer for them.

[Receiving]
Paul, I've been worried about you and your group since the earthquakes. The network news stations here in the States have been televising the worldwide destruction from the quakes, Israel being among them. We, here in the States, have been devastated by two powerful quakes, one under the Sierra Nevada range and the other along the notorious San Andreas fault. Richter scale readings have been in the 8.3 to 8.7 range, causing the seismologists and

402

geologists to wonder how much more the earth's crust can take. And if the quakes weren't bad enough, it seems the connecting bridges from Long Island and Hilton Head Island to the mainland collapsed after the two quakes, indicating that those islands are experiencing major movements. Scores of earth scientists are studying the problem as to whether or not there was some mantle displacement here on the east coast. Residents are being ferried off those islands as we speak.

One would think that these scientists would look at the volatility of the earth's core as evidence of a young Earth, but alas, they are blinded to that. What they don't realize is that God has ordered even more severe quakes for the days ahead. It is not hard to imagine that there is a heightened state of hysteria permeating our society here in America. An outcrying of the people for relief, yet not from God. Obviously the military is privy to classified and secret information that is being shielded from the public because my sources tell me that there are hundreds of military and political leaders that are securing for themselves priority placement in underground shelters in the event that God's wrath intensifies and these national catastrophes worsen.

Cheyenne Mountain Directorate (NORAD) at Cheyenne Mountain in Colorado and their other locations in Nevada and New Mexico are all on DEFCON 3 so they are prepared to take on priority personnel ASAP. Of course they are looking to their own strengths and assets to get them through what they believe is only a temporary crisis. I wouldn't say that panic has set in just yet, but it is not far away. Yet, and I believe you've experienced this spiritual phenomenon over in Israel, there is not one sign that man has reached that place where they are looking up and asking God for a spirit of repentance. There is no inner reflection or self-examination going on over here. It is a pity.

I am ambivalent about your news. On one hand I rejoice that the Lord has seen fit to deliver your K-group from the clutches of Kavidas and the forces he controls, while on the other hand, I am anxious about what lies ahead. Shaul, Shlomo, and Shira being arrested is representative of the kind of persecution we can expect for the Christians in the future.

How have you been bearing up under the darkening of the sun? Here in the States we've experienced serious consequences emerging from the opening of that last Seal. We hear stories every day of supermarkets being cleaned out of all their canned goods by frightened shoppers who fear that the reduced sunlight is going to have a damaging effect on the food chain—the interrupting of growing and harvesting of crops—so that the famine will worsen. Hoarding, price gouging, and grocery store parking lot assaults have become a way of life. To avoid this, most people are shopping online and having their food delivered to their homes. I think they are under the misapprehension that the supplies will last forever since they don't actually see them disappearing from the supermarket shelves.

In other developments, I was just informed that the FBI uncovered a plot by an Islamic militant group to blow up an aircraft carrier at the Naval Amphibious Base in San Diego. It seems this al-Qaeda sleeper cell was infiltrated by an undercover Arab-American who in turn came across detailed ship movement and deployment plans for the Seventh Fleet. How they got those plans is the basis of the ongoing investigation. It seems to me that these terrorist groups are determined to keep the U.S. in their sights as a way of provoking us to sever our relationship with Israel. And from what I see and hear on the street, it won't be long before all nations will do just that. This includes America. The prophecy of the four kings and their nations coming from the four compass points against Israel does not seem so far-fetched any longer. I only pray that America's Christians and members of our K-group are able to stand up to the future conflict that will come upon us. What we need here in America and especially in South Florida is a group of serious Christians that are really sold out to Christ who can lead the campaign against Kavidas' influence and help the church when the next set of judgments come.

[Sending]
I am not surprised to learn that America is in the cross-hairs of the Muslim extremist/terrorist gun once again. We find America's stand on radical Islamic groups to be utterly ridiculous. We have adopted the Israeli perspective, which believes that the U.S. should have deported any disloyal groups long ago. That's the way the Israelis deal with terrorists and anti-Israeli sentiment. To think that after September 11, 2001, America would continue to tolerate any subversive elements on our soil by those who have not denounced

their call of jihad or their allegiance to Hamas, al-Qaeda, or Hezbollah, is analogous to Americans during WW II tolerating Nazi spies working in our munitions plants. It's just outrageous!

Regarding your question about the sun. Yes, we are experiencing the darkening along with the rest of the world. Fortunately for us we are not dependent on the world system for our food; we are receiving our foodstuff from the Lord! He is providing all our needs according to his riches in glory while we are at Petra. But as far as the unbeliever is concerned, it is amazing how they are adapting to the environmental changes and still, they don't ask God, "Why is this happening?" Instead, unbelieving mankind just goes about his business in a constant state of flux and anxiousness, numbing himself with any form of anesthetic he can get his hands on. But, as you mention, the day will come when they will surely notice—when the sun goes completely black. That is going to be scary!

You mention your need for help. We shall make that a matter of serious prayer. We will petition the Lord to send you someone who can bring fresh wind and fresh fire to your crusade.

[Receiving]
God Bless all in your house. Brandon.

Christian Fortress, Petra

Continuing to enjoy God's victory over the IDF and the Arab forces amidst much good-spirited back-slapping bravado, Jonathan turned to Simon and said, "My spirit is restless, and my heart is heavy. Let's go for a walk."

"What's up?" Simon replied with a shrug. The notion that Jonathan had a restless spirit had an edge to it that raised his suspicions. God was about to do something.

"Let's go," Jonathan urged as they waved to Paul and the others and walked out on to the valley floor. Moments later the two brothers were sitting together on an ancient stone bench at the amphitheater.

Once situated, Simon turned and looked at his brother who was gazing off into space. A pair of minutes passed before Jonathan said softly, "Let's pray."

Simon's heart starting racing with the realization that within seconds his life would change once more. "Okay," he gulped.

Instantly they were transported by some divine carrier into the heavenly realm and saw themselves walking on a path toward a celestial city perched on a high and lofty island that appeared to be suspended in space. The city resembled John's description of the Holy City, the new Jerusalem, descending from heaven. By divine transport they found themselves standing before a company of angels who were guarding a throne. Out of the host of angels came forth one that possessed unique features that set him apart from the others. He had towering wings and held a gold sword. "I am Gabriel, who stands at the left hand of God!" he announced in a voice that thundered.

Jonathan hid his face in his hands while Simon's mouth hung open in astonishment as Gabriel approached them. He lifted his sword and lightly placed it on Jonathan's right shoulder, then repeated the act for Simon. Jonathan jerked his head up as Gabriel explained, "You have been chosen to go and proclaim the gospel in these End Times. You are being sent to nations who profess their love for God, but bear little evidence of their beliefs."

Then Gabriel turned to Jonathan. "You will go to America, where you will testify of God's judgment." He turned to Simon. "You will go to Rome, where you will also testify of God's judgment."

"But, sir," Simon begged, "I am afraid."

Gabriel raised his sword, then placed it once again on Simon's shoulder. "You have been given a double portion. The Lord has read your heart and has seen your unbelief. Now doubt no more and live your life as unto the Lord."

Simon nodded in solemn obedience.

Gabriel slowly elevated the sword above his head while pointing back at the earth with his other hand and said to the brothers, "Go, and be faithful."

When the vision ended, Jonathan and Simon cried tears of joy, for God had seen fit to answer every question in their hearts.

TWENTY-SIX

Mount of Olives, Jerusalem

T he Eucalyptus restaurant at the Mount of Olives Hotel featured a taste of Israel from biblical days. Featuring excellent meat, fish, and vegetarian dishes enhanced by masterful use of herbs and spices, under the watchful eyes of the kosher rabbinate, the restaurant had become Kavidas' favorite dining place since the great earthquake. Captivating his interest was not the splendor of the hotel's architecture, although he enjoyed the Mediterranean style building, but the elevated view of the Kidron Valley and the Temple Mount.

His predilection was to frequent the restaurant during periods when the hillside gardens were replete with cypress and olive trees, Narcissus and Pancratium lilies; when the ancient tombs that dotted the hillside cast long shadows from the autumn sun that meandered through the sky. But that was a time long past. Now the landscape had taken on a different demeanor, one of devastation and desolation. *I now see the land of Israel as a cesspool of conflict.*

He preferred a table by the giant windows that offered a magnificent panorama of the Judean hills as far as the Dead Sea to the south and the mountains of Moab in the east. But presently, some thirty days since the massive quake, that view was cluttered with industrial and sacred site debris, trailer trucks carrying refuse, and construction crews determined to rebuild the holy city once more.

Two miles west of his observation point stood the depot building where the armaments from the invasion were being stored. *Time is moving quickly. The invasion was over one and one-half years ago.* Field reports from the Economic Resource Office advised him that there was plenty of fuel from the burnable weapons for another five and one-half years. *I suppose that's good.*

He tasted his wine and gazed out the window once again, this time to take inventory.

Throughout the hillside and surrounding vicinity, scant remnants of green vegetation were slowly being blotted out by brown soil brought on by the lack of moisture and reduced sunlight. It was of little concern to him. Fleeting images of gaunt-looking, homeless children, roaming the streets of the Old City in Jerusalem drifted through his mind...the outworking of the famine. He shrugged. *What is that to me?* Cars already had their headlights on; commercial buildings and homes were illuminated at 3:00 P.M., signifying the reduced daylight hours. *This must be in order to bring about the consummation*, he realized as he took a sip of his wine. Countless dead from the invasion, the earthquakes, the work of the "two performers"—*certainly not our doing*, he rationalized, *but of the other side. No, I shall not take the responsibility for them.*

Ah, my rising from the dead, Masterlink, and the Temple completion, the arrest of those troublesome Christians! Now, there we see fruit from our labors. Yes, even the Stateside destruction of those Christian assemblies, he exulted, *and there are many victories ahead!*

He nodded to the waiter and pointed to the outside veranda. The waiter acknowledged the signal. Kavidas carried his glass of wine outside and walked to the railing, where he stood enjoying the activity below him. He noticed several workmen wearing Arab kaffiyehs. *Yes, the Arabs. They shall be very useful in the days ahead, when the Muslim-Americans join in the future war over here. I know they will always side with their Muslim bothers and choose loyalty to Islam over any American creed they may profess to believe in.*

He paused abruptly in his ruminations then slowly turned his head southeast toward the Kidron Valley. He stopped and listened. Then he turned his head due west toward the Temple Mount. He stopped and listened. A chill ran up and down his spine.

"It has started," he muttered. He carefully placed the wineglass on a nearby table and walked to the waiter, where he canceled his dinner order.

Home of Gadi Shamni, Jerusalem

Dalia pushed a hearty portion of matzo ball soup toward Paul and ordered, "Eat, eat! You're becoming skin and bones."

Paul took a quick survey of his physique and realized he had lost some ten pounds over the past thirty days, often attributing the loss to hyperactivity from K-group business and periodic visits to Petra. He nodded and grabbed a hunk of challah bread left over from the Sabbath and gorged himself to make his newly adopted Yiddish mamma happy.

Gadi walked into his kitchen to join Paul for lunch. He was carrying the *Haaretz*, the leading daily paper used to voice government trial balloons. Opening to page four, he said, "Paul, there's an article in here about Shaul, Shlomo, and Shira. Now that thirty days have passed, they are appointing them an attorney from the public defender's office. Do you think we should solicit the K-group and hire an attorney to represent them?"

Paul reached for the newspaper and read the article while he downed his soup. "No, I don't. Any attorney of ours that does not employ the *Masterlink* system would be cattle fodder for Kavidas. I have every confidence that this trial is going to be nothing more than a mockery of the judicial system. Kavidas will see that Shaul, Shlomo, and Shira never see the outside of a cell again. I hate to say it, but releasing them is going to be a 'God-thing.' This predicament is way beyond our power to use the legal process at this time."

"Are you suggesting we use another 'process' to get them released?"

Paul set his soup spoon down. "We will need to form a team that can perform secret operations in the future. A Christian counterpart to the Israeli General Security Services or Shin Bet, the counterintelligence branch of the Mossad. This will protect our families while we stage operations to defeat and frustrate Kavidas' mission. Freeing Shaul will be our first priority."

"Then we're in agreement!" Gadi exclaimed with clenched fists.

"Of course, our operations will be subject to God's leading. We don't want to act like Peter did in the garden when Christ was arrested and he pulled out his sword and cut off the high priest's servant's ear. We don't want to be religious fanatics that work independently of the Lord. We will work within the parameters set by God."

Gadi, who had grabbed a carving knife out of the kitchen drawer, sighed in disappointment. He lifted the knife in the air and said, "Can't I just take a 'little' piece of Kavidas?"

"Taking care of Kavidas is God's job, Gadi." Paul pushed the soup bowl away and rubbed his stomach to express his contentment. "For you and Dalia, I believe you should petition the Lord to determine your place in our crusade." He pointed outside the kitchen. "I believe the Lord may have a special anointing for your boys."

Gadi relished the thought. He smiled as Dalia walked in and reached for her hand. "What would you say to the Lord if he called our sons out to be part of the 144,000?"

Dalia raised her hands in praise and rejoiced by saying, "*Gam zo le-Tovah*, this too is for the good."

Gadi broke out in a smile from ear to ear.

Paul's spirit testified that their sons would indeed be called into the special group of witnesses, along with many from other sects such as the Sabras, the Hasidim, and the Euro-Jews that had settled in Israel. "We shall see how the Lord directs them," Paul said, smiling.

"Paul," Dalia asked, "how will God make the selection?"

"Good question," Paul answered. "Of course only God knows everybody's DNA all the way back to Adam, so he will confirm their appointment once they are chosen. Then we will know for sure." He lifted up his coffee cup and gestured to Gadi for a refill. "Their confirmation will be different than Jonathan and Simon, who were called to Rome and America. What is clear is that the Lord is calling out his evangelists to carry the Gospel message in these last days."

The front door opened and closed abruptly. One of Gadi's sons, Chaim, bolted into the kitchen. "Dad, I think you should come outside. Something freaky is going on."

Paul and Gadi exchanged glances, then walked out the front door behind Simon. Once outside, Gadi looked around then turned to Chaim and held his hands out, palms up. "So?"

Chaim pointed to his ears, then up at a tree. "There are no sounds coming from the birds! No singing, chirping, cackling, or wailing, no fluttering of the wings. Not one decibel of noise coming from them!" Then he pointed to a shrub. "No sounds of insects. The insects are flying, crawling, and digesting the foliage as usual. The cicada, beetle, fly, mosquito, and every other kind of insect is still busy doing their thing, but there are no sounds!" He started crying. "There is only silence!"

Paul turned his head in every direction to analyze the situation. Chaim was right. While he could hear the wind, the clatter of automobile traffic, dogs barking, people talking, and the rest of the world's cacophony, the bird and insect world could be seen but not heard. *Either nature was rebelling after centuries of human abuse of the environment, or God was up to something.* He took a deep breath, exhaled and said, "This may be the start of the Seventh Seal judgment."

Gadi swallowed hard. "Really?"

"What does that mean?" Chaim asked with a nervous titter.

"The Seventh Seal marks the end of the Seal judgments with an interlude of silence before the next series of judgments begins. It is probably one of the most horrific of the judgments because it is almost as if God abandons man for a period. When God is bringing his physical wrath upon mankind, we know that he is still concerned with us. But when there is no evidence—only silence, a form of psychological torture—like when Noah and his family was shut up in the ark before the flood came, that can be the worst kind of punishment."

"You mean like God is 'reloading,' " Chaim said solemnly.

"I'm not crazy about that expression, but it certainly fits here," Paul replied as he looked up toward the sky. He could only imagine that there was a great silence in heaven taking place at the same time. *It's as if the angels and redeemed saints are holding their breath, anticipating the unfolding of a great mystery—a kind of "great pause" to offset the "great parenthesis" of God dealing with the Church before dealing with Israel. Yes, it's a "great pause,"* he affirmed in his heart.

"Do you think it's progressive, Paul?" Gadi asked intuitively.

His stomach flipped. But Paul kept walking around the yard. He spotted a grasshopper perched on a branch. He picked it up and inspected it. The legs that rubbed together to make the chirping sound looked normal. *No mutations. The bugs and birds are all working fine; it's just that man can't hear them now.* He scratched his head and tried to figure out how the silencer worked. *Talk about a conundrum or a mystery wrapped up in an enigma.*

"Yes, I believe it to be progressive. What's more, I don't think man is equipped to handle the intellectual and emotional ramifications that will be unveiled once this judgment intensifies."

They walked inside and closed the door.

The first phase of the judgment of silence on the earth had begun.

Gershon Agron Street, Jerusalem

Kavidas was deep in thought as his chauffeur drove his black Mercedes out of the Independence Park apartment complex unto Gershon Agron Street. The chauffeur rolled down the privacy window and asked with a tight smile, "Mr. Kavidas, what are your thoughts regarding this bird and insect business that's been going on for the past ten days? To watch a crow in a tree bellow without hearing him caw or a dragonfly whizz by and not hear his wings buzz is very strange. Don't you think it's really weird?"

"What do I think?" Kavidas echoed. "For the last ten days every ornithologist and entomologist on the planet has been wondering that same thing." *As if I would tell you what I really think! Or even know!* "From what I hear and read, the scientists are claiming it has something to do with chemical pollutants in the air. You know, like the impact the oil spills have on marine life, or the effect of chemical wastes that contaminate well water and bring on a massive wildlife kill."

The chauffeur blinked several times as he processed the answer. It seemed logical. "Some say it's another judgment from God. I even heard someone say that God is dealing with his people, Israel, preparing them for his coming, and until we get the message, there'll be no letting up."

"Nonsense!" Kavidas snapped.

412

The chauffeur had heard many reports about Kavidas and his ability to connect with God. He believed he truly knew what he was talking about. He shrugged. "You should know." Seconds later the privacy window went up.

Kavidas returned to his thoughts. The degree and duration of the silence was yet to be revealed, that much he surmised. The silence was only one-half hour in heaven, but that's celestial time, he reasoned. Who knows how long it will be played out here on earth? Then there's the possibility that a greater silence lies ahead. *That's troubling.* He gazed out the window and asked himself, *How do we counter this attack? Do I have the power to combat it? Can we overcome it?*

The car pulled over to the curb. The privacy window dropped down again.

"What's the trouble?" Kavidas asked.

"Sir," the chauffeur said, "something's wrong with the car." He pointed down to the dashboard gauges. "The engine is on, but I can no longer hear it running." He got out of the car and lifted the hood so he could fiddle with some of the wires, then closed the hood. He walked to the driver's side door and stood for several moments with his hand cupped to his ear, then opened the door and sat down. He was slightly numbed from shock. "You're not going to believe this," he said with a start, "but there is no noise, I mean NO noise coming from anywhere now!" He pointed to the cars driving by and said trenchantly, "there's no noise coming from the traffic. You can't hear horns, wheels hitting potholes—nothing!" He turned around and faced Kavidas. "Sir," he said somberly, "this is unreal. A terrible nightmare. How can this be?"

Kavidas pulled a guess from the air to placate his chauffeur. "Some kind of electromagnetic flap from a nearby power plant? Who knows?"

The chauffeur broke out into a sweat and simply sat inert, wagging his head.

Kavidas picked up the car phone and keyed in Stein's number, then placed the handset next to his ear. There was only a loud silence. "Get me to my office, quickly!"

The chauffeur nodded and closed the privacy window once again. There was no sound to the window motor.

The drive to the Knesset was sheer pandemonium. Motorists who suddenly realized that all sounds coming from mechanical devices were silenced either pulled into parking lots or abandoned their cars on the roads. Commercial vehicles along with public conveyances like buses and taxis crept along to avoid collisions in absence of traffic noise. Only the brave continued to travel to their destination.

At the Knesset building, the chauffeur pulled into the parking lot to find hordes of angry diplomats and employees waving their fists at the sky or kicking the tires on their cars as the frustration emerging from the mechanical silence began to set in. Kavidas stepped out of the car to see several of the employees flinging their cell phones up in the air and watching them crash to the ground. One man stood at his car, laughing hysterically as he opened and closed the door. Kavidas assumed he was wondering where the usual noise disappeared to. He dismissed his chauffeur and began walking toward the Knesset building, then stopped short when he noticed an El AL jetliner climbing into the sky in the nearby distance, but he couldn't hear the jet engines roaring. *This is going to get serious. This will have a profound, altering affect on the human state of consciousness.*

Home of Gadi Shamni, Jerusalem

Paul and Gadi sat on a sofa in front of the TV reading the news ticker and narrative words as they scurried across the screen. After two days of silence with no radio wave transmission, only those viewers whose TVs were equipped with subtitling were tuning in; getting used to a world that was experiencing progressive silence was not an easy task. On the TV were a series of montages depicting the effect of the silence on the world. International scenes of people kicking their dogs because they couldn't hear their barking to people waiting on long lines at

414

veterinarian hospitals with their voiceless, soundless pets in their arms.

"Paul, do you think this phase two of the silence is temporary?"

"If we go by phase one of the Seventh Seal that lasted only ten days, I would say yes," he replied. "But if this indeed is progressive, occurring in ten-day intervals, what can we expect of the last ten days?"

Gadi raised his hands in surrender. "I don't want to even think about that." He jumped up from the sofa and walked to the living room window. As he opened the vertical blinds, his eye was drawn to a dog running across his lawn chasing a cat. He could see the dog's mouth opening and closing rapidly as if he were barking vigorously, but no sound came out. He quickly closed the blinds and returned to the sofa.

Paul was still hung up on the Seventh Seal judgment and what may unfold in the future. Unlike Gadi, he did have to think about that. The first phase of this judgment only influenced birds and insects. Although that was strange for the ten-day period, it didn't radically strike out at humankind. But with the second phase now two days old, people were beginning to react in bizarre ways. Most of the physical world, cars, telephones, TVs, radios, all forms of electromagnetic communication, were shut off. Man was once again relegated to writing letters and notes to converse with others. *Thank God for E-mail!* The sounds normally coming from animals, both wild and domestic, was also suspended. Despite this escalation in the plagues, man somehow invented ways to circumvent God's judgment and continued to live as if he didn't exist.

Paul flipped from FOX news to INN and chuckled when some liberal scientist announced that he understood what was happening once the second phase set in. He postulated a theory that a Supreme Being was giving man a taste of silence to show humanity what damage noise pollution has inflicted on the human race. He used graphs on sound intensities that reflected the range from the threshold of audibility to whispering, to wind in leaves, to waves on seashores, to human shouting, to vacuum cleaners, to rock music, to jet engines— until the graph maxed on the threshold of pain. He then proved that the levels of sound pollution in the representative city of New York was at a constant 110 decibels for eight hours of each day, six days a week. This was only 10 decibels away from causing potential hearing loss and tissue damage.

But Paul had his own theory. He believed God was showing his power through silence. The kind of silence Christ displayed as he stood before his accusers—when he answered not a word to those who maligned him, holding in reserve his divine power when he could have easily consumed them with a fiery rebuke. But he stood in the power of silence, letting His heavenly Father provide and deliver the final blow in his own limitless, faithful love. *Now that's the power of silence.*

From a scientific viewpoint, Paul had another theory. He remembered reading about the nuclear strong force, that invisible electromagnetic force holding divergent electrically charged atoms together, and how it contradicts the Coulomb repulsion rule. In physics, positive and negative atoms should fly apart—repel one another—but they do not. While scientists considered this a mystery and applied inept explanations, Paul pointed to Colossians 1:17: *He is before all things, and in him all things hold together.* Clearly Christ was controlling the electromagnetic field on earth, holding it together, and now it was time for a change. So he changed the way sound, made up of electromagnetic waves, travels. For Christ, it was easy.

Renaissance Jerusalem Hotel

Deep meditation was Stein's catharsis for stress. He sat fully dressed on the edge of his bed with his eyes closed, contemplating the ramifications of God's curse on man. A plethora of thoughts about the current Seal judgment saturated his consciousness as the deafening silence continued to grate on him. The thought of altered states of consciousness affecting the unaware or unsuspecting follower, the subscriber to *Masterlink*, was a good thing in his estimation, but a bad thing when it came to himself. He found himself experiencing lethal thought processes, augmented by sleep deprivation brought on by recurrent nightmares. He recognized that in this perilous state of mind he was becoming very irritable during the day, and on several occasions, found himself wondering what suicide would be like. *If I'm encountering this strange phenomenon, knowing what I know about the future, I can't imagine what the man on the street is experiencing,* he thought in a rare moment of compassion.

The public was indeed undergoing severe psychological damage. Despite the Nuclear Regulatory Commission's claim, along with other governmental authorities and political leadership who assured their constituents that this escalation in silence was nothing more than the byproduct of a nuclear weapons test, the public remained unconvinced. Explaining away the graduated degrees of silence by claiming that the electromagnetic pulse (EMP) generated by a nuclear weapon test was responsible for the interruption in radio and sound waves came under severe criticism. It seemed that nuclear non-proliferation protest groups knew better. They believed the governments of the world were hiding something much more sinister. Some groups claimed that various government-funded private contractors were experimenting with Ultra-low Frequency Infrasound weapons that transmit a wave between 16 and 20,000 Hertz, or cycles per second, unheard by the human ear, but felt by the human body in the form of pure vibrations. These vibrations, dependent upon their intensity, can induce a wide range of symptoms from nausea, headaches and vomiting, chest wall vibrations, gag sensations, and respiratory rhythm changes, to the rupturing of internal organs and even death. They believed the experiments went awry like they have in many nuclear power plant accidents, and the strange silence was a direct result of government meddling with uncharted science once again.

Many citizens world-wide were, in direct contradiction to Kavidas' prediction, seeking spiritual counseling and guidance in an attempt to find solace to the ongoing, frightening silence. The public consensus was that something more ominous was about to be unleashed upon the civilization.

They were right.

TWENTY-SEVEN

Office of the Special Advisor, The Knesset Building

G regory Kavidas paced back and forth in his office as uncertainty gripped his mind and indecisiveness assailed his heart. Global reports of widespread panic after 20 days of progressive periods of silence that affected the entire world could not be idly dismissed. Leaders from the American, European, Asian, Australian, and African continents were looking to spiritual and academic brain trusts for answers to public demands for explanations. The Israeli population, believing their Special Advisor to be a divinely appointed instrument of peace, looked to him to allay their fears and satisfy the rest of the world. Members of the Knesset cabinet, in turn, looked to him for answers as well. What troubled him was that he was powerless to halt the judgment or to provide any solution.

Thoughts of counterfeiting God's miracles came to mind. *I can call upon those forces available to me for help to create an illusion that will make people think there is no judgment of silence. That would work,* he reasoned. He recalled the unique way in which pharaoh's magicians and sorcerers duplicated several of Moses' miracles with their enchantments in an attempt to diminish God's power. Then again, he remembered as he checked himself, *God had the final say in those episodes.*

No, it wouldn't work, of that he was convinced. He made a profane gesture toward heaven to display his contempt, then stopped to open the glass-paneled door leading to the veranda. He took a deep breath in an attempt to soothe his anxiety. But instead of fresh air, the smell of lingering death from the earthquake filled his lungs. He walked out onto the porch and scanned the horizon, then his eyes settled on the street traffic below. The silence coming from the mechanical world was still overwhelming.

Several egrets flew by, squawking loudly. He rubbed his neck to relieve the muscle tension. *In a way it is good to hear the sounds of birds and nature once again. No!*, he instantly corrected his human thinking, the return of these sounds of life only served as a reminder that *he* was not in total control. He slammed one fist down on the veranda railing, then shook both fists at heaven.

Without warning, the clamor of the cars moving in traffic was suddenly audible! Horns were honking and beeping! Tires screeching!

He heard his TV!

The mechanical world was making noise once again!

He clapped his hands as his mood changed to one of relief and hope. Things were not so serious after all.

He hurried to the TV to see bulletins announcing that there was a breakthrough. Whatever science had been experimenting with, the gods of technology had seen fit to fix it. The assault on the world's sound sensors was over.

Kavidas stopped his thinking short and took notice of the time sequence. This was the tenth day of the second phase. Reflecting over the past 20 days he realized that the judgments in silence were coming every ten days.

He walked back out onto the veranda. The noise of the city was thundering once again. In fact, it sounded much louder than ever before. *That's because we haven't been hearing any mechanical noise for the past ten days, and our senses need to re-acclimate,* he reasoned. Logical.

He waited. No change.

He sat down and waited for two more hours, then came to the conclusion that this was indeed a cessation in the Seal judgments. It was over for now.

But he was wrong.

He returned to the veranda to assess his surroundings, then casually looked down to the corner of the veranda where the railing met the edge of the building. There was a breath of wind that picked up several dead leaves and scraps of paper and began to swirl them into a tiny eddy. Particles of dust were sucked into the vortex as the air current accelerated, but alas, he realized, there was no sound to the wind. There was no noise coming from the rotating air mass, nor was there sound from the leaves as they rustled together in the whirlwind that hit the building.

It worsened. As he looked into the distance and saw the wind's force bending palm fronds and moving branches on trees, there was no sound. He turned his face toward the sky in fury and hissed, "I hate your guts and everything you stand for!"

His phone rang and he automatically tensed.

He snorted several times, then walked to receive the call.

"We're in trouble!" Stein announced as he labored to catch his breath. "I'm down here at the shoreline of the Mediterranean—just having a quiet lunch—when *bam, bam, bam*, this silence thing gets ratcheted up! Now there is no sound coming from the sea! Waves crash against the sand, but you can't hear it. It's really eerie!" He snatched a breath and continued, "Sure, I'm glad my phone works now, but Gregory—" he paused because his tone conveyed disbelief and he needed to check himself—"what are we to do?"

"You're starting to have a shelf-life problem, Mort," Kavidas said impatiently. "You need to calm down." A frosty silence. Then: "Come up to my office so we can thrash this thing out. I'm of the persuasion that we're in for a bumpy road."

Click.

Home of Gadni Shamni, Jerusalem

Paul Douglas, Gadi, and his two sons sat in folding chairs on their front lawn watching people react to the newest phenomenon orchestrated by God. Chaim and Asher nodded in wonder as they surveyed the street before them. There were several pedestrians walking with their hands upheld in what looked like an attempt to feel the wind they couldn't hear. "I'm anxious to hear how Kavidas explains this phase away," Gadi observed. "They'll be no scientific gobbledegook for this one."

A brilliant flash of light dazzled them. "Lightning!" Gadi gulped. Everyone held their breath.

No thunder.

More lightning bolts!

Still no thunder.

A series of strobe-like lightning strikes lit up the sky with successive bolts hitting high buildings and cell phone towers in the nearby distance. People began running for shelter, but when the thunderclaps never came, they shrugged and resumed their journey, wondering what demon was terrorizing the earth once again.

"This must be an attack on the environment," Gadi suddenly realized.

"A curse on the ecology I would add," Chaim suggested.

"Yes," Paul said, "an execration. It's almost as if the Lord has called down a curse to deprive mankind of his sensory indulgences. A stripping of the aural attributes that we take for granted where any sound resonance coming from the natural sciences has been deafened." He cupped his ear and turned his head into the breeze in mute testimonial of the sounds one normally heard as air brushed past the ear and sent vibrations to the auditory system to register and identify the sound.

"No doubt we'll be hearing reports for the next ten days," Paul postulated, "of silent babbling streams and volcanoes that are silently groaning and rumbling as well as mother earth muting the shifting of her tectonic plates—silent earthquakes if you can believe that—" He stopped his narration abruptly and blinked at Gadi. He was shaking. He reached over to him and asked, "Gadi, are you all right?" His brow was dripping from perspiration and his face was flushed. He looked faint.

"I, eh, don't feel well," he groaned. "This whole thing is getting to me."

Chaim bolted inside to get his mother while Asher fanned his father's face.

Paul fully understood Gadi's plight. The assiduous silence in varying degrees made everybody stop and think about their little cubicle of space in the big world around them. It was tantamount to being placed in solitary confinement or a sound-proofed room used to break down the spirits of PW's to gain military secrets. After a while you begin to lose touch with reality as you slip into an ephemeral euphoric state before descending into the pit of unexpected surrealism. From there one is simply detached.

Dalia popped her head out the front door, took one look at her husband, then slapped her cheek and said, "*Oy Gevalt*, 'Oh dear.' She hurried to his side and assisted him as he struggled to walk in the house. Moments later she was putting him to bed.

As Dalia walked out into the yard, Paul scanned her face. "Is Gadi all right?"

"I'm sure he'll be fine," she began. "He's just overwhelmed as we all are, but probably overexcited as well. He's the type that doesn't like to sit down but would rather get up and fight any enemy of his Lord." She smiled in reflection and added, "Whenever he is able to put in a good word for Jesus, he's right there! He is a powerful testimony for a changed life." So her sons couldn't hear, she turned and whispered in his ear, "He used to be a real womanizer and loved to gamble, but Yeshua changed all that. Now he's on fire for the Lord!"

"Paul," Asher interjected curiously, "when do you think we'll be going to Petra?"

Jerking his thumb over his shoulder, Paul replied, "Assuming your Dad is okay, I would say by next week."

Both Chaim and Asher nodded and exchanged smiles. They were looking forward to the adventure at Petra.

Dalia gave her sons a signal to leave, then dragged her aluminum folding chair closer to Paul and said softly, "Do you see a parallel between what's going on today and God's biblical period of testing?"

Interestingly enough, Paul had thought about it when the first ten-day period ended. "Yes, in a way I do. God has appointed certain numbers to represent definite facets of his divine plan. Several instances come to mind: I see that the number 3 refers to the unity of God; the number 4, the world; number 6, man; number 7, perfection, and the number 40 indicates both testing and preparation. We can look at the 40 days of rain in Noah's time, the numeric relative of 400 used for the Egyptian bondage, the 40 years of wilderness journeying for Israel in preparation for their entrance into the promise land. We can also see Christ's 40 days of testing before his ministry began, and now, it appears that there is another 40-day testing period unfolding before us."

She counted off three fingers. "That would mean we're in the beginning of the third interval, right?"

"It would appear so, yes."

"The next interval should be even more frightening." Her voice was calm, but full of anxiety. "I can't imagine what can be silenced next."

Paul picked an imaginary spot in the air and focused on it. Random thoughts of the next series of judgments, the Trumpets, assaulted his mind. Then thoughts of calling Yair tumbled into his consciousness. *Yes, I need to call him to see if all is well.* Then he returned to Dalia's last statement and realized that he couldn't imagine, along with her, what kind of silence could possibly happen next.

Office of the Special Advisor, The Knesset Building

A wave of trepidation swept over Stein as he knocked on Kavidas' door. He couldn't understand why he experienced such feelings, but in his solitary hours, he attributed it to impulses of faithlessness. A lack of faith in Gregory's purpose and oftentimes, a lack of faith in who he represented. From the time of his calling, he recognized that a foreordained plan had chosen both Gregory and himself, along with the Master, to form a formidable trio, which would bring about a harvest of souls that would follow them to a place in destiny unlike the saints of God, but offered other rewards until that appointed day. Rewards that would allow them to enjoy all the riches and power on earth imaginable. But, at times, he questioned that arrangement, wondering if it were possible to change it as the Day of Reckoning approached.

The door swung open. Stein immediately recognized a disconcerted Kavidas, only adding to his anxiety.

"The next ten days will be tense throughout the world as mass hysteria grips the population, Mort," Kavidas said.

"Why the increased hysteria now?"

Kavidas paced the floor in moderate alarm. "Because the masses will come to realize that this segment of the curse is not connected with humankind. No mad scientist or research lab experiment gone awry could possibly account for this type of environmental disaster. They will easily recognize that there is an operating force at work that is going well beyond human meddling in the business of science. It will be revealed that divine interdiction is taking place." He threw his hands up. "And we won't be able to do anything about it."

"But I thought you said they would flock to us and—?"

Kavidas waved him off. "Yes, yes, I remember I predicted that any escalation would result in there being a great gathering to us for spiritual guidance, but that was before we came to know what the actual judgment would be. Who could have predicted this?"

I thought you would have, Stein thought, but he didn't say that. The red flag of *trust* shot up in Stein's mind. He instantly suppressed it. "Meaning?"

" Meaning we will lose a great deal of the stragglers who have not come on board yet."

Stein knew from *Masterlink's* central bank in Athens that over 90 percent of the earth's population had subscribed to their financial system and in turn were marked as the non-elect. Still, the reluctant 10 percent represented a substantial number. "You think this will drive the stragglers over into the other side?" The other side meaning Christianity.

"Could happen," Kavidas said laconically. "Possible."

"How do we counter it?"

"Simple. We use a notorious tactic that has worked for centuries: we tell a lie frequently enough until people believe it as truth. Since the bouts of silence are coming every ten days, we can—"

Stein quickly connected the dots and finished his sentence. "...we can make a prediction about the next phase."

Kavidas snapped his fingers. "That's it!"

424

Two days later, Stein alerted the media that the nation's Special Advisor had a press release that needed to be broadcast over the airwaves. An announcement of global importance that would have vital impact on the present environmental crisis. The following day, now three days into the third phase of silence, Kavidas sat in the TV station as cameramen and make-up artists prepared him for the eight-to-ten-minute announcement. He did not have to rehearse his lines nor read from a prepared script, much to the station manager's surprise.

The program manager stood in front of the camera and started the cuing countdown. *Five, four, three, two, one...* "People of Israel and the world: the Special Advisor to the nation of Israel."

The cameras focused on Kavidas' face that appeared both resolute and caring. "People of Israel, the time has come for an official government statement regarding the ongoing series of 'sound disturbances' we have been experiencing throughout our world. While at first we may have attributed these disturbances to some mishap in nature, we can no longer view them as such. As of today, I have commissioned a federal think tank to use every resource available to explore the causes for the phenomenon we have been encountering. In the meantime, I have gone before God and asked him for guidance and supernatural insight into what we may expect in the future. I am happy to stand before you and report that God has answered my prayer."

He lied.

"God has told me that he is testing his creation to see if they—" he paused to pull a Bible quote out of the air—"to see if we 'are one, even as he is one.' To see if we are truly united in every facet of life. Therefore it is incumbent upon us to show our collective purpose. As you may have determined by your own calculations, these disturbances have been coming in multiples of tens. This means each phase is lasting ten days. Extrapolating from the past, we can determine that we must endure seven more days of this present ecological silence before, and I know I'm stretching myself here, the final phase is meted out."

Kavidas shifted in his seat and smiled luminously. "I believe that final phase will involve humans in a silence that has never visited our world before—where we will be deprived of our natural ability to communicate. A frightening silence designed by God to bring our world together in unity. A silence fashioned to compel every soul on this planet to draw upon their hidden resources—the id that is within us...the inner strength that has made our nation great. Together as one, we can defeat any adversary that comes up against us. This is God's purpose in bringing this trial."

He nodded to the program manager, who interpreted the signal to mean he was almost finished. "Remember, God has chosen me as a vessel to meet your needs, and he will not leave us defenseless. Thank you, and may God bless you."

The red light on the camera went off. Off in the corner, Stein waved a victory sign to him.

As they walked out of the studio into the parking lot, Stein asked with his voice vibrating with intensity, "How did you know that the next phase will involve humans? Did you really receive a 'revelation'?"

"Some proleptic powers are reserved for me," he replied cryptically. "In the past I have used them in dire emergencies. I simply called upon those latent powers to help me determine what the next component of this curse will be."

"So that when it occurs, we can take the credit for it."

"It's better for our purpose that we control, or have the appearance of control, of as much of the events as possible," Kavidas affirmed.

Stein nodded as his spirit soared. Once again his doubting had led him to a downward spiral that could only lead to disaster. But that was before this announcement. Now he reveled in the hope that Gregory was indeed capable of earning his trust and receiving his admiration.

Home of Gadi Shamni, Jerusalem

Paul sat in front of Gadi's TV with Dalia and her two sons, stunned at the insanity of Kavidas' broadcast. To think Kavidas had the audacity to blaspheme against God by pretending to receive divine revelation could only be labeled "a sign of the times." Another token of his contempt against the Almighty. Another gesture on his part to beguile and delude mankind into thinking he was a heavenly messenger, when in fact he was a colossal liar whom the apostle Paul called, "the Lawless One…who will be in accordance with the work of Satan displaying all kinds of counterfeit miracles, signs and wonders…employing every sort of evil that deceives those who are perishing."

On the other hand, Paul thought it a stroke of genius. End-game tactics called for desperate measures in an all-out effort to win. That's what the game of life was all about, the humanists and secularists claimed: to win. And for Kavidas to link his name with God at a time when the world would only attribute the current silence to a supernatural event arranged by a Supreme Being was indeed a maneuver to win—and take as many souls with him as he could.

"You're quickly becoming a 'news junkie,' " Gadi teased as he walked in the room to see Paul and his family surfing the news stations.

"It's good to see you up and around," Paul said with a smile.

Dalia rose and gave her husband a peck on the cheek. He expelled a sigh as he sat down on the sofa. "Just needed to rest. What's this I hear about Kavidas making a national announcement about the continuing judgment of silence?"

Paul put the TV on *mute*. "That's right. He claimed to have 'talked to God' and that he received 'supernatural insight' into the curse—namely, that it will broaden in the next phase to include humans."

"Is that possible? I mean, could he receive a revelation like that?" Gadi asked hesitantly.

"Probably," Paul replied with a shrug. "Demonic abilities, especially in the End Ttimes, will greatly intensify because the fiendish ones know their demise is near. Remember Jesus predicted that, during the Tribulation period, 'false prophets would appear and perform great signs and miracles to deceive even the elect—it that were possible,' meaning we should expect a great outpouring of supernatural capabilities that include precognition and premonitions—all designed to lure the unsuspecting away from Christ.

"If you remember in the book of Acts, I believe it's the 16th chapter, that the apostle Paul and Silas encountered a slave girl who had an evil spirit that enabled her to predict the future. She, in turn, used it as a money-making scheme of fortune-telling." He paused and pointed toward the TV. "Kavidas is nothing more than a sophisticated fortune-teller."

"Hmm, yes, that makes sense."

A knock at the door!

Everybody froze.

Gadi tiptoed to the door, peered through the peephole, and whispered, "It's our neighbors from across the street, Sol and Ruby."

Dalia jumped to her feet and made a sweeping motion. "Let them in!"

Gadi opened the door and ushered them into his home. He greeted them cordially, then made a visual audit of their faces. "Is everything all right?"

Ruby's face turned red. "Can we sit down for a moment? We would like to ask you some questions." They both appeared nervous.

"Of course," Gadi said graciously. "Our home is your home." He pointed to Paul and introduced him: "This is Paul Douglas, a very close friend of ours."

"I've seen your face on the TV," Ruby noted.

Paul's stomach fluttered. "Oh, really?"

"We want you to know that we agree with your crusade," Sol said as he nodded to Paul, dissipating the rising tension. "And we came here to get some help."

Paul moved over to allow them to join him on the sofa as Gadi fetched some folding chairs. "What kind of help?" Paul asked with caution, probing.

"We see what's going on all around us," Sol began, "and we know that something is radically wrong." Squirming, he shot a look at Ruby, who nodded her approval. "We're afraid of what has become of our nation, and we're not sure of this person, Gregory A. Kavidas. With all the strange events that has occurred over the past year or so, we have been asking God for some answers. With the disappearance, all this silence stuff, and then Kavidas' announcement today..." He trailed off as the realization of events overwhelmed him.

Paul glanced at their hands.

Ruby saw the look. "You're looking to see if we have subscribed to *Masterlink*, right?" She rolled up her shirt sleeves. "See, no mark!" She reached over to Sol's arm and pulled up his jacket to expose his hand. "No mark of *Masterlink* on him, either. We're clean."

Gadi shook his head in wonder at the middle-aged couple before him. "How have you been managing without it? I mean, how do you secure and buy the essentials?"

"We are both self-employed mercantile agents," Sol explained, "independent of any government affiliation, and we have friends who are food wholesalers, others who work in public utilities, and a group of other retailers who swap favors with us."

"Sounds like they have their own 'network' apart from *Masterlink*, much like our Christian K-group, Paul," Gadi noted.

"I believe there are many like us around the world,"Ruby propounded, "who are flocking to churches and spiritual advisors to find out why these plagues have come upon us."

"For countless others—those with *Masterlink*—that option is no longer available. It's too late," Paul lamented. "But for those without it, it appears that the Lord is opening up a door, perhaps for the last time, to bring those seekers of truth to himself to be saved."

"What does that mean?" Sol asked reflexively, "to be saved?"

Gadi spoke up. He believed Sol needed to hear the plan of salvation from a fellow Jewish man. "It means you still have a chance to receive Jesus Christ as your Messiah by believing that he died on the cross, or tree, for your sins at Calvary. Once you've acknowledged that in your heart, you are granted eternal life with him in glory." He pointed to himself and Dalia. "We've experienced God's forgiveness and joy from the moment we called upon Messiah Yeshua to be our Messiah, and we've never regretted making that decision." He patted his chest. "We know in our hearts that when we die, we shall be with him in heaven. He has given us that peace." He held up his Bible and with a big smile summarized his position, "We have God's promise—in writing!"

Sol reached over and grabbed Ruby's hand, then pointed to Gadi and exulted, "We want that! We want that peace in our hearts!"

Everyone exchanged looks as God's Spirit suddenly moved in Sol and Ruby's hearts to receive Christ as their personal Savior.

Paul led the prayer where Sol and Ruby confessed Christ. Ten minutes later, Gadi closed the prayer meeting. Paul smiled as he hugged the new Christians and imagined all the angels in heaven rejoicing over their decision.

For the next seven days, the people of the world held their breath in anticipation of the next round of silence.

But for the Christians, they rejoiced in the great harvest of souls.

TWENTY-EIGHT

The Streets of The Old City, Jerusalem...
And the Rest of the World

Gadi stood outside the Jaffa Diamond Exchange on Shonei Halachot Street in the Old City, one-half mile west of the Temple Mount, keeping watch for Mossad. After 25 minutes, Paul and Sol emerged, signaling their victory with a united thumbs-up.

"Any problem?" Gadi asked as they furtively walked into the crowd of shoppers scurrying and mulling around the stores.

"Sm-o-o-o-th!" Sol remarked with a hand gesture.

"No problems," Paul said. "The owner didn't ask any questions; he just gave us the diamond equivalency. It seems that we're not the only ones trading cash for diamonds." Over the past four years the Douglas family had been systematically purchasing diamonds and to some extent, gold, to use as an alternative commodity to *Masterlink*, believing history had dictated that, even during wartime, diamonds and gold were needed for bargaining power. With each man pooling their resources, they were able to purchase over $25,000 dollars worth of diamonds for future use. *A smart move.*

Gadi looked at his watch and turned to Paul. "It's almost lunchtime. I know a place around the corner where they still take shekels for currency, so let me buy you two guys a bagel and lox."

Paul and Sol smiled with a thumbs-up and said in unison. "Let's do it."

They walked several yards, and then it happened.

"Stand still!" Paul commanded as he held up his hand in a halting manner. He looked at his watch to check the date, then rubbed the back of his neck out of sheer anxiety. "It started! The fourth phase of silence."

Suddenly Gadi and Sol realized the truth. They turned and surveyed the sidewalks, restaurants, and shops. Everywhere they looked, shoppers and pedestrians alike were twitching and making hand motions as they desperately tried to communicate with one another when they learned their voices and hearing were gone. The forecasts were correct. The next round of silence came precisely ten days from the start of the third phase of the Seventh Seal judgment, and it was more terrible than man could have imagined. *The sound of human speech and hearing was suspended!*

Men and women were gyrating around each other as they fumbled for paper and writing instruments to communicate. Others were hitting their ears, while some just looked stunned as they pointed to their voiceless mouths. Once again, the unbelieving citizens were either attempting field repairs on their cell phones or discarding the useless devices altogether.

"They can't speak or hear one another," Gadi observed curiously.

Paul looked mystified. "Apparently we are able to."

"It's just like the plagues on the Egyptians during the time of Moses," Gadi commented. "The Israelites were immune from the plagues of flies, livestock, and darkness—but all the people of Egypt suffered from them."

Paul nodded in agreement as he studied the outworking of God's next judgment on the human race. Animals, birds, and insects appeared to be unaffected, but mankind was suddenly struck with a fierce curse. Not only did God attack man's vocal cords and ears with a supernatural silence, but he sent a spirit of disharmony as well. As Paul stood and watched people react to the judgment, a series of fights broke out before his eyes. Once humankind was unable to communicate with themselves, they became angry. It was as if they were taking out their frustrations on one another.

A loud crash! Two cars collided at the nearby intersection. Shocked at the horror of the accident, the sidewalk crowds stood somewhat paralyzed. Scores of people held their hands to their mouths and attempted to scream as they witnessed the calamity, but nothing came out of their mouths. Man had become a society of mutes.

Surprisingly, no one moved to rescue the accident victims.

"This is going to get ugly," Paul surmised. He frowned. "We need to get out of here."

They walked another half block until they came upon a young mother holding her infant son in her arms. The mother stood with a blank look at the passerby as the child mouthed repeated, inaudible cries. They stopped in their tracks and gaped at the scene before them. Helpless.

"Oh, God," Gadi sighed with a shake of the head. The mother saw his lips move and grabbed his arm to hold unto what she thought was the last vestige of human communication. Her face was pleading for the ability to speak. Pleading for understanding—pleading for mercy for her infant. Pleading for relief from the cataclysm unfolding before her eyes. Hopelessly pleading.

Sol latched onto Gadi and pried him loose from the mother's clutches. "Let's go!" He urged.

Moments later they were in Gadi's car heading for his home.

After three days, the final stage of silence began to have a profound influence on humanity. A peculiar sense of intense isolation was gripping the souls of men as if each individual were undergoing a kind of solitary confinement. The kind of solitary confinement experienced by recalcitrant prisoners who need to be separated from other criminals and their environment in order to bring about corrective measures. Unexpected repercussions followed. Employers of major firms throughout the world were complaining of huge sick-outs by employees who simply could not cope, nor had the confidence that they could perform their duties. Manufacturing plants, factories, and retail stores were opening and closing within two to three hours of operation because of lack of personnel and customers. Small shop owners were suspending their business altogether. Before the end of the second day, all commerce came to a screeching halt. In the social sector, families were wandering around the streets like homeless people in a state of despair, wondering what went wrong.

Because of the sudden deterioration in the population's mental health, the need for counselors soared. Never before in the period of recorded history were there so many E-mails, letters, and personal visits to psychologists, psychiatrists, and ministers for emergency counseling for extremely difficult issues. Thanatologists, doctors, and scientists who study the surroundings and inner experiences of persons near death, were being hired in scores by national governments to treat the masses who were falling prey to catatonia, the behavioral condition in which a person maintains a bizarre, statue-like pose for hours or days. Fears of death, along with serious threats of suicides, were their prevailing concern. The perception that death through suicide—often a symbolic cry for help, or a last effort to receive attention—was the only solution to hopelessness and helplessness was running rampant throughout the world. The entire social structure of the planet was crumbling, leading journalists and newscasters to label the emotionally detached population *schizoid*.

Office of the Special Advisor, The Knesset Building

Stein stood in front of Kavidas' office TV set, reading the news ticker of the global newscasts with a Bible opened to Revelation chapter 8 in his hands. Seconds later he shot a look up toward the sky and began to quote the Scripture when suddenly he put his hand over his mouth when he once again realized he had no voice.

Kavidas gave him a lethal glare. *Use your mind, Mort. You know, telepathy. That's what we do when we can't communicate using sensory perception.*

Right. I need to get used to it. Dripping with concern: *"Then he opened the seventh seal, there was silence in heaven for about half an hour."* He turned to Kavidas as he flicked the side of the Bible in contempt. *Why didn't we anticipate these serious ramifications? The whole world is going crazy!*

434

It has not been given to us to know the whole plan ahead of time. You should know that by now, Kavidas replied with a tinge of impatience.

Stein's hand shook slightly as he held the Bible. *Could it be that the silence in heaven is really an intermission before the next act because...?* he paused to reread the adjoining text, *"And I saw the seven angels who stand before God and to them were given seven trumpets.' It seems the Trumpet judgments are on their way down.*

Kavidas remembered the passage. *But who's to say it's literal? After all, the silence was not in heaven, but on earth, right? And is it for just a half-hour? Hardly.* He waved the complaint off. *So how can we take this so-called prophecy literally?*

Stein vacillated. *Well, I guess you could say that, after all, even the "so-called promises" made to the Christian where all their needs would be met is a great lie. I knew hundred of Christians who depended on their God to take care of them and instead, he dropped them from a great height! Well,* he quipped, *maybe now, the people of the world will learn in the days ahead that they are better off trusting in what they can see and feel rather than what is unseen.*

Kavidas approached Stein, closed the Bible, lifted it out of his hand, and slowly walked to the wall with the built-in bookcases. Slamming the Bible down on a shelf, he turned and mouthed through his teeth, *There's nothing we can do about this curse! So we'll tough it out by keeping a low profile for the next seven days and then we'll see where we stand.* Head down, he walked to a stuffed chair and sat down, then steepled his fingers as he gazed out the window with a frown.

With a deliberate force of his will, he apportioned his mind into those thoughts that brought defeat and those that brought victories. Then he decided to concentrate on his future victories. After a moment of contemplation he slapped his knee and announced, *Once this is behind us, we'll regroup and—*

...start preparing for the Trumpet judgments, Stein interrupted to awaken Kavidas' sense of reality.

You act worried, Mort, Kavidas growled while giving him a sharp look. *There's no place in our work for worry or doubting,* he scolded.

Stein bit his fingernail. *Sorry.*

Christian Fortress, Petra

"Paul, doesn't it feel like the time when the Angel of Death was carrying out the tenth plague on the Egyptians? You know, when he came through and killed the firstborn, but all those Israelites who were at home in Goshen were spared if they had the blood of a lamb over their doorposts?" Levi asked as they sat down for lunch in their mobile home.

It was now the ninth day of the judgment of silence, where only those who were not marked with *Masterlink* were able to orally communicate with each other. Planet Earth was experiencing what the world of the deaf is all about. Inside the fortress there was an aura of divine protection as they rejoiced in the fulfillment of God's promises.

"Yes, in a way," Paul agreed. He turned and smiled at Yair, then grasped his hand to make a tactile connection to let him know that their committed hearts to Christ were not in vain. It strengthened the group's emotional bonds.

"You'll like it here," Simon said to Chaim and Asher. "This place is so interesting that we can explore the ancient buildings together when we're not working."

Yair stood up from the kitchen table and walked outside. Moments later Paul was at his side. He gave him a welcome smile, then gazed off into the distance. With a degree of trepidation Yair asked, "What do you think will happen next?"

Paul patted his shoulder, realizing his concern that had gripped the world and said softly, "Before long we can expect the Trumpet series of judgments to come upon the earth. But remember, 'The Lord has not given us a spirit of fear, but a spirit of power, of love and of a sound mind.' So, we will continue to trust him and take it one day at a time. For now, you, Levi, Hershel, and the Shamni family must continue to lead the rest of the group here at the fortress while I go back and connect up with Gadi, Sol, and Ruby in Jerusalem to wait for any others who have decided to depart from the angry population and join our fight against Kavidas and his gang."

Yair signed deeply as he looked his God-appointed young warrior-leader in the eyes. "Every day I will be praying for you."

"And I, you."

The Third Heaven

The seven angels who stood before God sounded their seven trumpets, then another angel who had a golden censer came and stood at the altar. He was given much incense to offer, with the prayers of all the saints, on the golden altar before the throne. The smoke of the incense, together with the prayers of the saints, went up before God from the angel's hand. Then the angel took the censer, filled it with fire from the altar, and hurled it on the earth; and there came peals of thunder, rumblings, flashes of lightning and an earthquake (Revelation 8:2-5).

After the great silence, the judgments of the Seven Trumpets began....

TO BE CONTINUED IN

THE TRIBULATION SERIES
Book Four

The
Seven Trumpets

COMING SOON!

Bibliography

This novel is a fabrication of the author's interpretation of Bible prophecy. It is completely fictitious, but the support research is real. The following reference works may assist the avid reader of prophetic fiction and eschatology to learn more about the events that may soon come upon the earth.

BOOKS

Archer, Gleason L. *The Rapture: Pre-, Mid-, or Post-Tribulational?* Grand Rapids, MI: Zondervan Publishing House, 1984.

Backhouse, Robert. *The Kregel Pictorial Guide to the Temple.* Grand Rapids, MI: Kregel Publications, 1996.

Baer, Robert. *Sleeping with the Devil.* New York: Crown Publishers, 2003.

Biblical Archaeology Society. *The Origins of Things.* Washington, DC, 2002.

Brickner, David. *Future Hope: A Jewish Christian's Look at the End of the World.* San Francisco: Purple Pomegranate Productions, 1999.

Bullinger, E. W. *Number in Scripture.* Grand Rapids, MI: Kregel Publications, 1996.

Chapman, Colin. *Whose Promised Land?* Grand Rapids, MI: Baker Books, 2002.

Cohen, Gary. *Understanding Revelation.* Chattanooga, TN: AMG Publishers, 1987.

Cooper, David L. *An Exposition of the Book of Revelation.* Los Angeles: Biblical Research Society, 1972.

Crichton, Michael. *State of Fear.* New York: Avon Books, 2004.

Dickason, C. Fred. *Angels, Elect & Evil.* Chicago: Moody Press, 1995.

Edersheim, Alfred. *The Life and Times of Jesus the Messiah.* McLean VA: MacDonald Publishing Co., circa 1979.

Evans, Michael D. *Beyond Iraq, The Next Move.* Lakeland, FL: Whitestone Books, 2003.

Folger, Janet. *The Criminalization of Christianity.* Sisters, OR: Multnomah Publishers, 2005.

Friends of Israel Gospel Ministry. *Eye on the Middle East.* Bellmawr, NJ: The Friends of Israel Gospel Ministry Publication, 2001.

Fruchtenbaum, Arnold. *The Nationality of the Anti-Christ.* New Jersey: American Board of Mission to the Jews, Inc., circa 1978.

Gold, Dore. *Hatred's Kingdom.* Washington, DC: Regnery Publishing, 2003.

Grant, George. *The Blood of the Moon: The Roots of the Middle East Crisis.* Brentwood, TN: Wolgemuth & Hyatt, Publishers, 1991.

Guiley, Rosemary Ellen. *Encyclopedia of Angels.* New York: Checkmark Books, 2004.

Hagee, John. *Jerusalem Countdown.* Lake Mary, FL: Front Line Publishers, 2006.

Hamada, Louis Bahjat. *Understanding the Arab World.* Nashville, TN: Thomas Nelson Publishers, 1990.
Hislop, Alexander. *The Two Babylons or the Papal Worship.* Neptune, NJ: Loizeaux Brothers, 1959.

Ice, Thomas, Randall Price. *Ready to Rebuild.* Eugene, OR: Harvest House Publishers, 1992.

Kennedy, D. James. *The Real Meaning of the Zodiac.* Ft. Lauderdale, FL: TCRM Publishing, 1997.

Kent, Phil. *The Dark Side of Liberalism.* Augusta, GA: Harbor House Publishers, 2003.

Koch, Kurt. *Occult Bondage and Deliverance.* Grand Rapids, MI: Kregel Publications, 1976.

LaHaye, Tim. *No Fear of the Storm.* Sisters, OR: Multnomah Press, 1992.

LaHaye, Tim, Thomas Ice. *Charting the End Times.* Eugene, OR: Harvest House Publishers, 2001.

Lindsey, Hal. *Apocalypse Code.* Palos Verdes, CA: Western Front Ltd., 1997.

Missler, Chuck. *Prophecy 20/20.* Nashville, TN: Nelson Books, 2006.

Netanyahu, Benjamin. *Fighting Terrorism.* New York: Farrar, Straus, and Giroux, 2001.

Patterson, Lt. Col. Robert. *Dereliction of Duty.* Washington, DC: Regnery Publishing, 2003.

Pentecost, J. Dwight. *Things to Come.* Grand Rapids, MI: Zondervan Publishing House, 1975.

Posner, Gerald. *Why America Slept: The Failure to Prevent 9/11.* New York: Random House, 2003.

Price, Randall. *Fast Facts on the Middle East Conflict.* Eugene, OR: Harvest House Publishers, 2003.

Price, Randall. *Jerusalem in Prophecy.* Eugene, OR: Harvest House Publishers, 1998.

Price, Randall. *Unholy War.* Eugene, OR: Harvest House Publishers, 2001.

Ritmeyer, Leen and Kathleen. *Secrets of Jerusalem's Temple Mount.* Washington, DC: Biblical Archaeology Society, 1998.

Sears, Alan and Craig Osten. *The ACLU vs. America.* Nashville, TN: Broadman and Holman Publishers, 2005.

Shoebat, Walid. *Why I Left Jihad.* Top Executive Media, 2005.

Shorrosh, Anis A. *Islam Revealed.* Nashville, TN: Thomas Nelson Publishers, 1988.

Spencer, Robert. *The Politically Incorrect Guide to Islam.* Washington, DC: Regnery Publishing, Inc., 2005.

Steadman, Ray C. *Waiting tor the Second Coming.* Grand Rapids, MI: Discovery House Publishing, 2007.

Walvoord, John F. *Daniel: The Key to Prophetic Revelation.* Chicago: Moody Press, 1989.

Walvoord, John F. *The Revelation of Jesus Christ.* Chicago: Moody Press, 1966.

White, John Wesley. *WW III: Signs of the Impending Battle of Armageddon.* Grand Rapids, MI: Zondervan Publishing House, 1977.

Woodrow, Ralph. *Babylon Mystery Religion.* Self-Published, 1966.

PERIODICALS

Discerning the Times Digest. *The Global Environment Agenda to World Government and Religion.* www.discerningtoday.org. 2001.

Biblical Archaeology Society. *The Origin of Things.* Washington, DC: 2002.

You won't want to miss...

THE TRIBULATION SERIES
Book One

The

Agenda

Ralph D. Curtin

**An AIDS vaccine is being developed in contemporary America,
but the cost is higher than anyone can imagine....**

When pharmaceutical magnate Gregory Kavidas announces that he has
discovered an AIDS vaccine, people laud him as a wonderful
humanitarian. But could he and his partner, entrepreneur financier
Mortimer Stein, have something else in mind?

David Douglas, a Christian college professor, is wary. He's
convinced that Kavidas—an energetic, charismatic man of Greek
descent—is the Antichrist of Bible prophecy. He believes the joining of
forces between Kavidas' Rainbow Pharmaceuticals and Stein's
Redisearch is the first move toward world dominance through a unified
medical and monetary system. But will Douglas be able to expose
Kavidas and Stein before they dupe the world?

THE TRIBULATION SERIES
Book Two

The
Lights
of God

Ralph D. Curtin

**How much would you pay
to know the mind of God?**

In 31 B.C., the Temple high priest, Amariah, flees to the ancient Essene fortification at Qumram, on the shore of the Dead Sea, to avoid Roman persecution. Hidden in his saddle bags is the Urim and Thummim, the revelatory device used to ask and receive answers from God, which hasn't been seen since the Babylonian captivity in 586 B.C. When Amariah is murdered, the Urim and Thummim are buried with his body in a cave-vault, later sealed by an earthquake that strikes Judea in 32 B.C. There they remain until the present day, when they are discovered by Ishmael, a treasure-hunting young Arab Bedouin, then are passed to Rehavam Krasnoff, an unscrupulous chief investigator for the Israeli Antiquities Authority.

When two masterminds in Athens, Gregory Kavidas and Mortimer Stein (who've developed the global financial network *Masterlink*—the precursor to a cashless world economy) become alerted of the stones' discovery, they set out to seize the stones for themselves…before their evil agenda is exposed.

Coming Soon...

THE TRIBULATION SERIES
Book Four

The
Seven Trumpets

Ralph D. Curtin

**Earth is in its final days...
and God is displaying His wrath
against everything unholy.**

Meteor showers blanket the earth. Volcanoes erupt. God's wrath consumes one-third of all trees and grass on the planet. Demonic forces are unleashed to torment unrepentant man. The world is in chaos.

Paul Douglas, son of Bible college professor David Douglas and his wife, Kathy, remains in Jerusalem while Simon and Jonathan Landau, newly acquired members of the Christian resistance group *Koinonos*, join forces with other K-groups in America and Rome to war against the infamous duo, Gregory Kavidas and Mortimer Stein, the masterminds behind the evil plot to take countless souls with them in the Lake of Fire for all eternity.

About the Author

DR. RALPH D. CURTIN is a family man, pastor, and counselor in a large Christian denomination and a college professor at Trinity College, where he teaches Biblical Studies. When he's not preaching or teaching, he's either writing a book or riding his big Harley.

Other interests include a passion for nature photography, of which he has had many of his images published by a stock agent in national magazines. Photographing his grand-children and making DVDs for the family gives him great pleasure as well.

"Through many years of Bible research and being a bit of a news junkie," says Dr. Curtin, "I arrived at the place where I earnestly desired to transform Bible prophecy into reality so that it would be believable. Many people don't read the Bible, but will read biblical fiction. This is my way of educating the public in a non-preaching manner, while giving them a taste of my interpretation of what we may expect in the future. I don't like fluff, so my writing is designed to intrigue the reader, give them facts that interest them, as well as raise their level of understanding on a particular subject. Readers are fascinated with science fiction, so prophetic fiction—which has a great degree of the supernatural—will only excite the reader who craves suspense, yet knows that our Good God will win in the end."

You may write Dr. Curtin at: **drrcurtin@bellsouth.net**